J. Shaw. ⊗ 2 —
(from KC) July 1992.

PENGUIN BO

Celebratio

D0757472

Celebration

An Anthology of New Zealand Writing from
the *Penguin New Writing* Series

EDITED BY
ANTHONY STONES

WITH AN INTRODUCTION BY
JOHN LEHMANN

PENGUIN BOOKS

Penguin Books Ltd, Harmondsworth, Middlesex, England
Viking Penguin Inc., 40 West 23rd Street, New York, New York 10010, U.S.A.
Penguin Books Australia Ltd, Ringwood, Victoria, Australia
Penguin Books Canada Ltd, 2801 John Street, Markham, Ontario, Canada L3R 1B4
Penguin Books (N.Z.) Ltd, 182–190 Wairau Road, Auckland 10, New Zealand

This selection first published in Penguin Books 1984

Introduction copyright © John Lehmann, 1984
This selection and prefatory note copyright © Anthony Stones, 1984
All rights reserved
The Acknowledgements on p. 7 constitute an extension of this copyright page.

Made and printed in Great Britain by
Cox & Wyman Ltd, Reading
Filmset in 9/11½ pt Monophoto Photina by
Northumberland Press Ltd, Gateshead,
Tyne and Wear

Except in the United States of America,
this book is sold subject to the condition
that it shall not, by way of trade or otherwise,
be lent, re-sold, hired out, or otherwise circulated
without the publisher's prior consent in any form of
binding or cover other than that in which it is
published and without a similar condition
including this condition being imposed
on the subsequent purchaser

Contents

Acknowledgements

To Auckland University Press and Roderick Finlayson for 'The Totara Tree' and 'When the Wind Blows' by Frank Sargeson; to Erik de Mauny for 'In Transit' and 'A Night in the Country'; to Rosamund Droescher, the author's daughter, for 'Epilogue' and 'Santa Cristina' by Greville Texidor; to Rupert Glover, the poet's son, and Ray Richards of the Richards Literary Agency for 'Convoy Conversation' and 'It Was D-Day' by Denis Glover; to Alan Roddick, literary executor of Charles Brasch, for 'In These Islands'; to Allen Curnow for 'The Unhistoric Story' and 'Landfall in Unknown Seas'; to Dan Davin for 'Under the Bridge'; to David Higham Ltd for 'The Red Dogs' by Anna Kavan; to Christine Cole-Catley and Longman Paul/Penguin (N.Z.) Ltd for 'A Great Day', 'An Affair of the Heart', 'That Summer', and 'The Making of a New Zealander' by Frank Sargeson.

NOTE. Some of the stories originally appeared in two or more parts: the places where breaks occurred are indicated in the text by three asterisks.

Prefatory Note

There is a certain risk in naming your new publishing venture after a bird which, besides being a non-flier, has inherited the name first given to the ill-fated Great Auk; but Allen Lane's Penguin survived even these hazards and, at fifty years of age, as jaunty as ever, is celebrating a new status as a 'Golden Bird'.

Penguin Books (N.Z.), a mere chick by comparison at ten years old, wished to join in the anniversary celebrations. What better way than to recreate that time when the fortunes of New Zealand literature and those of Penguin Books first intersected, in itself something of a golden age; a flowering, when, in spite of war, with its special difficulties of communication, a newly vital New Zealand writing became accessible to an international audience.

In the well-thumbed pages of *Penguin New Writings* aboard troop ships, on remote airfields or in jungle clearings, a wide and specially attentive audience read work which, in the words of its great editor, John Lehmann, hadn't been written by 'stranded Britishers', but by 'new poets and novelists who thought of themselves as New Zealanders'. There were others, too.

In this anthology I have included all the work by New Zealanders or writers living in New Zealand or with a New Zealand connection which was published in *Penguin New Writing*.

Charles Brasch, in his poem 'In These Islands' writes: 'Always, in these islands, meeting and parting . . .' It is fascinating to note that at the time of publication, to be a New Zealander for him meant to be living in England, waiting to be called up; for Erik de Mauny and Dan Davin to be on active service in the New Zealand Army; for Denis Glover to be variously on Arctic convoys and commanding a landing craft on D-Day. For Allen Curnow, Frank Sargeson and Roderick Finlayson it meant maintaining the difficult balance between living and writing in largely philistine New Zealand. For Greville Texidor and Anna Kavan, blown thither by what James Baxter called 'the winds of a terrible century', exile from England, permanent for the former and temporary for the latter.

War had only accentuated the migrant character of New Zealand life and thus we get stories with a Cretan or an Italian setting written by the

New Zealanders Dan Davin and Erik de Mauny, or one with a New Zealand setting by the Englishwoman Greville Texidor, who also brings news of that earlier war in Spain.

Denis Glover's two pieces from his successive points of view as seaman and then officer are written not as a member of the New Zealand Navy but the Royal Navy and are thus about Englishmen at war. Anna Kavan, from England too, having made her brief 'Landfall in Unknown Seas' (she was in New Zealand for a little less than two years), discovered with Allen Curnow 'that there are no more islands to be found', and in her story 'The Red Dogs' her 'eye scans risky horizons of its own'.

In Roderick Finlayson's 'The Totara Tree', the migrant Irish policeman, Sergeant O'Connor understands the Maori protest because he recognizes correspondences with his own culture:

'A tangi or a wake, sure it's just as sad and holy,' the Sergeant says, and shares with the Maoris a wit that the dour colonial police inspector cannot.

Themes of migration, uprootedness, 'meetings and partings' fill the work of Frank Sargeson. In 'The Making of a New Zealander' he sees the bleak impasse of the struggling Dalmatian orchardist who 'knew he wasn't anything any more'. William Plomer, himself from a colonial background in South Africa, wrote thus about this story in *Penguin New Writing* number 17 in an essay called 'Some Books from New Zealand':

'If Sargeson had written no other story, he would have spoken for all who have seen, sympathized with, or experienced the painful process of adaptation to a new, colonial environment.'

The material has been printed in the form and sequence in which it originally appeared, and the strategies which coped with the problem of obscene language at that time have been retained.

Many people have helped me with advice and information and I would like to thank them, particularly Ian Hamilton for information about Anna Kavan, Dennis McEldowney for advice and encouragement, and not least Graham Beattie of Penguin Books (N.Z.) who took up my idea of an anthology and made it *Celebration*. It is a particular cause for joy that the man who had the editorial insight and courage to publish the material in the first place could be part of the anthology with his delightful Introduction. To John Lehmann New Zealand and New Zealand writing owes a permanent debt.

Allen Curnow, again, in 'Landfall in Unknown Seas', after celebrating the three hundredth anniversary of the European discovery of New Zealand, asks the question, 'Who reaches a future down for us from the high shelf of spiritual daring?' Maybe William Plomer still provides the answer at the end of his essay 'Some Books from New Zealand': 'With the Maoris and these ardent and humorous and critical writers persisting among them, the New Zealanders may yet find their souls.'

Anthony Stones
Oxford, 1984

Introduction

It must have been in the earliest days of *New Writing*, in the far-off middle thirties, when I had scarcely done more than see off the first number to press and had just begun to prepare the contributions for a second number, that a close friend of mine, who had shown himself deeply interested in my venture, lent me one day a little booklet which a fan in New Zealand had sent him. It was called *Conversation With My Uncle*, and consisted of a handful of short sketches and stories by a young New Zealand writer I had not heard of before, Frank Sargeson. I was immediately attracted by the author's wit and style, by his skilful use of the vernacular, and the underlying tension between acceptance and rebellion that gave the pieces their liveliness. Here was a new writer, come to me out of the blue, who seemed exactly to fit the mood and hit the note that I wanted to be characteristic of my new periodical. I was as excited as a boy who on a bird-nesting foray has come upon the eggs, deep in the most unexpected place in the bushes, of a new migrant.

I wrote off to Sargeson at once, and told him of my admiration and what I was planning for *New Writing*. A delightful correspondence started, and went on for many years. I wanted to read his letters again before I wrote this, and then remembered that I had sent them all, long ago, to Texas, to be housed, together with all my other *New Writing* papers, in the Humanities Research Center at Austin. There they are available to all *bona fide* researchers.

Typescripts of new stories of course soon began to arrive with the letters. I published the first of them in the Autumn number of 1938, *White Man's Burden*. By then I had come to know that Sargeson was one of a group of young writers – in fact their leading spirit – who had found a keen and capable patron in Denis Glover, founder and owner of the Caxton Press in Christchurch. I wrote in *The Whispering Gallery*, my first volume of autobiography published two decades later:

> Why was it that out of all the hundreds of towns and universities in the English-speaking lands scattered over the seven seas, only one should at the time act as a focus of creative activity in literature of more than local significance, that it should be in Christchurch, New Zealand, that a group of young writers had appeared, who were eager to

assimilate the pioneer developments in style and technique that were being made in England and America since the beginning of the century, to explore the world of the dispossessed and under-privileged for their material and to give their country a new conscience and spiritual perspective?

The question remained unanswered, and of course it is the fact that mattered, just as it is the fact that Auden, Spender, Isherwood, Day Lewis, Warner, Bell and Empson all appeared as undergraduates at Cambridge or Oxford between 1929 and 1932 that matters, and not the rather mysterious concatenation of circumstances, impulses or what you will, that brought the phenomenon about.

By the time that paragraph had been written, *Penguin New Writing* had come into being, and after forty numbers had come to an end. The New Zealand writers made an important contribution to its history – and to its flavour. I published Sargeson's 'A Great Day' (still one of my favourites, and redolent for me of a country I have never visited but only imagined) in number 5, and Denis Glover's 'Convoy Conversation' in number 16. His 'Something About a Sailor' had appeared in *New Writing and Daylight* (Winter 1943–4) only a few months earlier. I don't give thanks to the war of 1939–46 for much, but I shall always be grateful for the fact that it brought a sturdy, stocky sailor of sanguine complexion wearing a broad grin – looking rather like Mr Punch in naval uniform, I thought at once – to ring at the door of my flat one day in the middle of the war and announce himself as the printer and publisher of the Caxton Press. He had joined up as an Ordinary Seaman in H.M.S. *Onslaught*, and the fortunes of war had brought him on his first leave to British shores. I took to him at once, and enjoyed his salty, humorous company on several occasions when he managed to slip away to London, until he was made Lieutenant in command of a landing craft in the D-Day invasion of Normandy. I particularly remember with admiration and gratitude how, in the middle of a rather nasty air-raid, he calmed a nervous secretary and escorted her home. I am particularly sorry that his death only a few years ago has made it impossible for us to renew our friendship as I had hoped, either in England or in his home country.

As may be seen from the pages of this admirable anthology, many of the New Zealand writers in prose and verse appeared in *Penguin New Writing* during the war years and briefly after: the distinguished fiction writer Roderick Finlayson who only recently reached his hale eightieth birthday, his two younger poet contemporaries Charles Brasch and Allen Curnow, and, among others, two writers who have stayed with us and made a name on this side of the globe – Erik de Mauny and Dan Davin. Looking back on all their contributions to that quite historic series of little booklets we produced, in spite of all bombs and paper rations, I can only say: Thank you, New Zealand!

John Lehmann
April 1984

FRANK SARGESON

A Great Day

It was beginning to get light when Ken knocked on the door of Fred's bach.

'Are you up?' he said.

Fred called out that he was, and in a moment he opened the door.

'Just finishing my breakfast,' he said. 'We'd better get moving.'

It didn't take long. The bach was right on the edge of the beach, and they got the dinghy on to Ken's back and he carried it down the beach, and Fred followed with the gear. Ken was big enough to make light work of the dinghy, but it was all Fred could do to manage the gear. There wasn't much of him and he goddamned the gear every few yards he went.

The tide was well over halfway out, and the sea was absolutely flat without even a ripple breaking on the sand. Except for some seagulls that walked on the sand and made broad-arrow marks where they walked there wasn't a single thing moving. It was so still it wasn't natural. Except for the seagulls you'd have thought the world had died in the night.

Ken eased the dinghy off his shoulders and turned it the right way up, and Fred dropped the anchor and the oars on the sand, and heaved the sugar-bag of fishing gear into the dinghy.

'I wouldn't mind if I was a big, hefty bloke like you,' he said.

Well, Ken didn't say anything to that. He sat on the stern of the dinghy and rolled himself a cigarette, and Fred got busy and fixed the oars and rowlocks and tied on the anchor.

'Come on,' he said, 'we'll shove off.' And with his trousers rolled up he went and tugged at the bow, and with Ken shoving at the stern the dinghy began to float, so Fred hopped in and took the oars, and then Ken hopped in and they were off.

'It's going to be a great day,' Fred said.

It certainly looked like it. The sun was coming up behind the island they were heading for, and there wasn't a cloud in the sky.

'We'll make for the same place as last time,' Fred said. 'You tell me if I don't keep straight.' And for a time he rowed hard without sending the dinghy along very fast. The trouble was his short legs, he couldn't get them properly braced against the stern seat. And Ken, busy rolling a supply of cigarettes, didn't watch out where he was going, so when Fred took a look ahead he was heading for the wrong end of the island.

'Hey,' he said, 'you take a turn and I'll tell you where to head for.'

So they changed places and Ken pulled wonderfully well. For a time it was more a mental shock you got with each jerk of the dinghy. You realized how strong he was. He had only a shirt and a pair of shorts on, and his big body, hard with muscle, must have been over six feet long.

'Gee, I wish I had your body,' Fred said. 'It's no wonder the girls chase you. But look at the sort of joker I am.'

Well, he wasn't much to look at. There was so little of him. And the old clothes he wore had belonged to someone considerably bigger than he was. And he had on an old hat that came down too far, and would have come down farther if it hadn't bent his ears over and sat on them as if they were brackets.

'How about a smoke?' Fred said.

'Sure! Sorry!'

And to save him from leaving off rowing Fred reached over and took the tin out of his shirt pocket.

'That's the curse of this sustenance,' Fred said. 'A man's liable to be out of smokes before pay-day.'

'Yes, I suppose he is,' Ken said.

'It's rotten being out of work,' Fred said. 'Thank the Lord I've got this dinghy. D'you know last year I made over thirty pounds out of fishing?'

'And how've you done this year?'

'Not so good. You're the first bloke I've had go out with me this year that hasn't wanted me to go shares. Gee, you're lucky to be able to go fishing for fun.'

'It's about time I landed a position,' Ken said. 'I've had over a month's holiday.'

'Yes, I know. But you've got money saved up, and it doesn't cost you anything to live when you can live with your auntie. How'd you like to live in that damn bach of mine and pay five bob a week rent? And another thing, you've got education.'

'It doesn't count for much these days. A man has to take any position he can get.'

'Yes, but if a man's been to one of those High Schools it makes him different. Not any better, mind you. I'm all for the working class because I'm a worker myself, but an educated bloke has the advantage over a bloke like me. The girls chase him just to mention one thing, specially if he happens to be a big he-man as well.'

Ken didn't say anything to that. He just went on pulling, and he got Fred to stick a cigarette in his mouth and light it at the same time as he lit his own. And then Fred lolled back in his seat and watched him, and you could tell that about the only thing they had in common was that they both had cigarettes dangling out of their mouths.

'Pull her round a bit with your left,' Fred said. 'And there's no need to bust your boiler.'

'It's O.K.,' Ken said.

'You've got the strength,' Fred said.

'I'm certainly no infant.'

'What good's a man's strength anyway? Say he goes and works in an office?'

'I hadn't thought of that.'

'Another thing, he gets old. Fancy you getting old and losing your strength. Wouldn't it be a shame?'

'Sure,' Ken said. 'Why talk about it?'

'It sort of fascinates me. You'll die some day, and where'll that big frame of yours be then?'

'That's an easy one. Pushing up the daisies.'

'It might as well be now as any time, mightn't it?'

'Good Lord, I don't see that!'

'A man'd forget for good. It'd be just the same as it is out here on a day like this. Only better.'

Ken stopped rowing to throw away his cigarette.

'My God,' he said, 'you're a queer customer. Am I heading right?'

'Pull with your left,' Fred said. 'But I'll give you a spell.'

'It's O.K.,' Ken said.

And he went on rowing and after a bit Fred emptied the lines out of the sugar-bag and began cutting up the bait. And after a bit longer when they were about halfway over to the island he said they'd gone far enough, so Ken shipped his oars and threw the anchor overboard, and they got their lines ready and began to fish.

And by that time it was certainly turning out a great day. The sun was getting hot, but there still wasn't any wind, and as the tide had just about stopped running out down the Gulf the dinghy hardly knew which way to pull on the anchor rope. They'd pulled out less than two miles from the shore, but with the sea as it was it might have been anything from none at all up to an infinite number. You couldn't hear a sound or see anything moving. It was another world. The houses on the shore didn't belong. Nor the people either.

'Wouldn't you like to stay out here for good?' Fred said.

'Ring off,' Ken said. 'I got a bite.'

'So did I, but it was only a nibble. Anyhow, it's not a good day for fish. It wants to be cloudy.'

'So I've heard.'

'I've been thinking,' Fred said, 'it's funny you never learnt to swim.'

'Oh, I don't know. Up to now I've always lived in country towns.'

'Doesn't it make you feel a bit windy?'

'On a day like this! Anyhow, you couldn't swim that distance yourself.'

'Oh, couldn't I? You'd be surprised . . . get a bite?'

'Yes, I did.'

'Same here . . . you'll be settling down here, won't you, Ken?'

'It depends if I can get a position.'

'I suppose you'll go on living with your auntie?'

'That depends, too. If I got a good position I might be thinking of getting married.'

'Gee, that'd be great, wouldn't it?'

'I got another bite,' Ken said.

'Same here. I reckon our lines are crossed.'

So they pulled in their lines and they were crossed sure enough, but Ken had hooked the smallest snapper you ever saw.

'He's no good,' Fred said. And he worked the fish off the hook and held it in his hand. 'They're pretty little chaps, aren't they?' he said. 'Look at his colours.'

'Let him go,' Ken said.

'Poor little beggar,' Fred said. 'I bet he wonders what's struck him. He's trying to get his breath. Funny, isn't it, when there's plenty of air about? It's like Douglas credit.'

'Oh, for God's sake,' Ken said.

'I bet in less than five minutes he forgets about how he was nearly suffocated,' Fred said, and he threw the fish back. And it lay bewildered for a second on the surface, then it flipped its tail and was gone. It was comical in its way and they both laughed.

'They always do that,' Fred said. 'But don't you wish you could swim like him?'

Ken didn't say anything to that, and they put fresh bait on their hooks and tried again, but there were only nibbles. They could bring nothing to the surface.

'I'll tell you what,' Fred said, 'those nibbles might be old men snapper only they won't take a decent bite at bait like this.'

And he explained that off the end of the island there was a reef where they could get plenty of big mussels. It would be just nice with the tide out as it was. The reef wouldn't be uncovered, it never was, but you could stand on it in water up to your knees and pull up the mussels. And if you cut the inside out of a big mussel you only had to hang it on your hook for an old man snapper to go for it with one big bite.

'It's a fair way,' Ken said.

'It doesn't matter,' Fred said. 'We've got oceans of time.' And he climbed past Ken to pull up the anchor, and Ken pulled in the lines, and then Fred insisted on rowing and they started for the end of the island.

And by that time the tide had begun to run in up the Gulf, and there was a light wind blowing up against the tide, so that the sea, almost without your noticing it, was showing signs of coming up a bit rough. And the queer thing was that with the movement the effect of another world was destroyed. You seemed a part of the real world of houses and people once more. Yet with the sea beginning to get choppy the land looked a long way off.

'Going back,' Ken said, 'we'll be pulling against the wind.'

'Yes,' Fred said, 'but the tide'll be a help. Anyhow, what's it matter when a man's out with a big, hefty bloke like you?'

Nor did he seem to be in too much of a hurry to get to his reef. He kept resting on his oars to roll cigarettes, and when Ken said something about it he said they had oceans of time.

'You're in no hurry to get back,' he said, 'Mary'll keep.'

Well, Ken didn't say anything to that.

'Mary's a great kid,' Fred said.

'Sure,' Ken said. 'Mary's one of the best.'

'I've known Mary for years,' Fred said.

'Yes,' Ken said. 'So I've gathered.'

'I suppose you have. Up to a while ago Mary and I used to be great cobbers.'

'I'll give you a spell,' Ken said.

But Fred said it was O.K.

'Mary's got a bit of education, too,' he said. 'Only when her old man died the family was hard up so she had to go into service. It was lucky she got a good place at your auntie's. Gee, I've been round there and had tea sometimes when your auntie's been out, and, oh, boy, is the tucker any good!'

'Look here,' Ken said, 'at this rate we'll never get to that reef.'

'Oh, yes we will,' Fred said, and he pulled a bit harder. 'If only a man hadn't lost his job,' he said.

'I admit it must be tough,' Ken said.

And then Fred stood up and took a look back at the shore.

'I thought there might be somebody else coming out,' he said, 'but there isn't. So thank God for that.' And he said that he couldn't stand anybody hanging around when he was fishing. 'By the way,' he said, 'I forgot to do this before.' And he stuffed pieces of cotton-wool into his ears. 'If the spray gets in my ears it gives me the earache,' he said.

Then he really did settle down to his rowing, and with the sea more or less following them it wasn't long before they were off the end of the island.

Nobody lived on the island. There were a few holiday baches, but they were empty now that it was well on into the autumn. Nor from this end could you see any landing-places, and with the wind blowing up more and more it wasn't too pleasant to watch the sea running up the rocks. And Fred had to spend a bit of time manoeuvring around before he found his reef.

It was several hundred yards out with deep water all round, and it seemed to be quite flat. If the sea had been calm it might have been covered to a depth of about a foot with the tide as it was. But with the sea chopping across it wasn't exactly an easy matter to stand there. At one moment the water was down past your knees, and the next moment you had to steady yourself while it came up round your thighs. And it was uncanny to stand there, because with the deep water all around you seemed to have discovered a way of standing up out in the sea.

Anyhow, Fred took off his coat and rolled up his sleeves and his trousers as far as they'd go, and then he hopped out and got Ken to do the same and keep hold of the dinghy. Then he steadied himself and began dipping his hands down and pulling up mussels and throwing them back into the dinghy, and he worked at a mad pace as though he hadn't a moment to lose. It seemed only a minute or so before he was quite out of breath.

'It's tough work,' he said. 'You can see what a weak joker I am.'

'I'll give you a spell,' Ken said, 'only keep hold of the boat.'

Well, Fred held the dinghy, and by the way he was breathing and the look of his face you'd have thought he was going to die. But Ken had other matters to think about, he was steadying himself and dipping his hands down more than a yard away, and Fred managed to pull himself together and shove off the dinghy and hop in. And if you'd been sitting in the stern as he pulled away you'd have seen that he had his eyes shut. Nor did he open them except when he took a look ahead to see where he was going, and with the cotton-wool in his ears it was difficult for him to hear.

So for a long time he rowed like that against seas that were getting bigger and bigger, but about halfway back to the shore he took a spell. He changed over to the other side of the seat, so he didn't have to sit facing the island, and he just sat there keeping the dinghy straight on. Then when he felt that he had collected all his strength he stood up and capsized the dinghy. It took a bit of doing, but he did it.

And after that, taking it easy, he started on his long swim for the shore.

FRANK SARGESON
An Affair of the Heart

At Christmastime our family always went to the beach. In those days there weren't the roads along the Gulf that there are now, so father would get a carrier to take our luggage down to the launch steps. And as my brother and I would always ride on the cart, that was the real beginning of our holidays.

It was a little bay a good distance out of the harbour that we'd go to, and of course the launch trip would be even more exciting than the ride on the carrier's cart. We'd always scare mother beforehand by telling her it was sure to be rough. Each year we rented the same bach, and we'd stay right until our school holidays were up. All except father, who used to have only a few days' holiday at Christmas. He'd give my brother and me a lecture about behaving ourselves and not giving mother any trouble, then he'd go back home. Of course we'd spend nearly all our time on the beach, and mother'd have no more trouble with us than most mothers are quite used to having.

Well, it's all a long time ago. It's hard now to understand why the things that we occupied our time over should have given us so much happiness. But they did. As I'll tell you, I was back in that bay not long ago, and for all that I'm well on in years I was innocent enough to think that to be there again would be to experience something of that same happiness. Of course I didn't experience anything of the kind. And because I didn't I had some reflections instead that gave me the very reverse of happiness. But this is by the way. I haven't set out to philosophize. I've set out to tell you about a woman who lived in a bach not far beyond that bay of ours, and who, an old woman now, lives there to this day.

As you can understand, we children didn't spend all our time on our own little beach. When the tide was out we'd go for walks round the rocks, and sometimes we'd get mother to go with us. My brother and I would be one on each side of her holding her hands, dragging her this way and that. We'd show her the wonders we'd found, some place where there were sea-eggs underneath a ledge, or a pool where the sea anemones grew thick.

It was one of these times when we had mother with us that we walked further round the rocks than we had ever been before. We came to a place

where there was a fair-sized beach, and there, down near low-tide mark
was the woman I've spoken about. She was digging for pipis and her
children were all round her scratching the sand up too. Every now and
then they'd pick up handfuls of pipis and run over near their mother, and
drop the pipis into a flax kit.

Well, we went over to look. We liked pipis ourselves, but there weren't
many on our beach. The woman hardly took any notice of us, and we
could have laughed at the way she was dressed. She had on a man's old
hat and coat, and the children were sketches too. There were four of them,
three girls and a boy; and the boy, besides being the smallest and skinniest,
looked the worst of all because he was so badly in need of a haircut.

The woman asked mother if she'd like some pipis to take home. She said
she sold pipis and mussels. They made good soup, she said. Mother didn't
buy any but she said she would some other day, so the woman slung the
kit on her shoulder, and off she went towards a tumbledown bach that
stood a little way back from the beach. The children ran about all around
her, and the sight made you think of a hen that was out with her chickens.
Of course going back round the rocks we talked about the woman and her
children. I remember we poked a bit of fun at the way they were dressed,
and we wondered why the woman wanted to sell us pipis and mussels
when we could have easily got some for ourselves.

'Perhaps they are poor,' Mother said.

That made us leave off poking fun. We didn't know what it was to be
poor. Father had only his wages, and sometimes when we complained
about not getting enough money to spend, he asked what we thought
would happen to us if he got the sack. We took it as a joke. But this time
there was something in what mother said that made us feel a little
frightened.

Well, later on my brother and I made lots of excursions as far as that
beach, and gradually we got to know the woman and her children and
saw inside their bach. We'd go home in great excitement to tell mother
the things we'd found out. The woman was Mrs Crawley. She lived there
all the year round, and the children had miles to walk to school. They
didn't have any father, and Mrs Crawley gathered pipis and mussels and
sold them, and as there were lots of pine trees along the cliffs she gathered
pine cones into sugar-bags and sold them too. Another way she had of
getting money was to pick up the kauri gum that you found among the
seaweed at high-tide mark, and sell that. But it was little enough she got
all told. There was a road not very far back from the beach, and about once
a week she'd collect there the things she had to sell, and a man who ran

a cream lorry would give her a lift into town. And the money she got she'd spend on things like flour and sugar, and clothes that she bought in second-hand shops. Mostly though, all there was to eat was the soup from the pipis and mussels, and vegetables out of the garden. There was a sandy bit of garden close to the bach. It was ringed round with tea-tree brush to keep out the wind, and Mrs Crawley grew kumaras and tomatoes, drum-head cabbages and runner beans. But most of the runner beans she'd let go to seed and shell for the winter.

It was all very interesting and romantic to me and my brother. We were always down in the dumps when our holidays were over. We'd have liked to camp at our bach all the year round, so we thought the young Crawleys were luckier than we were. Certainly they were poor and lived in a tumbledown bach with sacking nailed on the walls to keep the wind out, and slept on heaps of fern sewn into sacking. But we couldn't see anything wrong with that. We'd have done it ourselves any day.

But we could see that mother was upset over the things we used to tell her.

'Such things shouldn't be,' she'd say. She'd never come to visit the Crawleys, but she was always giving us something or other that we didn't need in our bach to take round to them. Or she'd give us money to buy pipis. But Mrs Crawley never liked taking the things that mother sent. She'd rather be independent, she said. And she told us there were busy-bodies in the world who'd do people harm if they could.

One thing we noticed right from the start. It was that Mrs Crawley's boy, Joe, was her favourite. One time mother gave us a big piece of Christmas cake to take round, and the children didn't happen to be about when we got there, so Mrs Crawley put the cake away in a tin. Later on my brother let the cat out of the bag. He asked one of the girls how she liked the cake. Well, she didn't know anything about it, but you could tell by the way Joe looked that he did. Mrs Crawley spoilt him sure enough. She'd bring him back little things from town when she never brought anything back for the girls. He didn't have to do as much work as any of the girls either, and his mother was always saying, 'Come here, Joe, and let me nurse you.' It made us feel a bit uncomfortable. In our family we never showed our feelings much.

Well, year after year we took the launch to our bay, and we always looked forward to seeing the Crawleys. The children shot up the same as we did. The food they had kept them growing at any rate. And when Joe was a lanky boy of fifteen his mother was still spoiling him worse than ever. She'd let him off work more and more, even though she never left off working herself for a second. And she was looking old and worn out by that time. Her back was getting bent with so much digging and picking up pine cones, and her face looked old and tired too. Her teeth were gone and her mouth was sucked in. It made her chin stick out until you thought of the toe of a boot. But it was queer the way she never looked old when Joe was there. Her face seemed to go young again, and she never took her eyes off him. He was nothing much to look at we thought, but although my brother and I never spoke about it we both somehow understood how she felt about him. Every day she spent digging in her garden or digging up pipis, pulling up mussels from the reefs or picking up pine cones; and compared to our mother she didn't seem to have much of a life. But it was all for Joe, and as long as she had Joe what did it matter? She never told us that, but we knew all the same. I don't know how much my brother understood about it, because as I've said we never said anything to each other. But I felt a little bit frightened. It was perhaps the first time I understood what deep things there could be in life. It was easy to see how mad over Joe Mrs Crawley was, and evidently when you went mad over a person like that you didn't take much account of their being nothing much to look at. And perhaps I felt frightened because there was a feeling in me that going mad over a person in that way could turn out to be quite a terrible thing.

Anyhow, the next thing was our family left off going to the bay. My brother and I were old enough to go away camping somewhere with our cobbers, and father and mother were sick of the bother of going down to the bay. It certainly made us a bit sorry to think that we wouldn't be seeing the Crawleys that summer, but I don't think we lost much sleep over it. I remember that we talked about sending them a letter. But it never got beyond talk.

What I'm going to tell you about happened last Christmas. It was twenty-odd years since I'd been in the bay and I happened to be passing near.

I may as well tell you that I've not been what people call a success in life. Unlike my brother, who's a successful business man, with a wife and a car and a few other ties that successful business men have, I've never been able to settle down. Perhaps the way I'd seen the Crawleys live had an upsetting influence on me. It's always seemed a bit comic to me to see people stay in one place all their lives and work at one job. I like meeting different people and tackling all sorts of jobs, and if I've saved up a few pounds it's always come natural to me to throw up my job and travel about a bit. It gets you nowhere, as people say, and it's a sore point with my father and mother, who've just about ceased to own me. But there are lots of compensations.

Well, last Christmas Day I was heading up North after a job I'd heard was going on a fruit-farm, and as I was short of money at the time I was hoofing it. I got the idea that I'd run off the road and have a look at the bay. I did, and I had a good look. But it was a mistake. As I've said the kick that I got was the opposite to what I was expecting, and I came away in a hurry. It's my belief that only the very toughest sort of people should ever go back to places where they've been happy.

Then I thought of the Crawleys. I couldn't believe it possible they'd be living on their bach still, but I felt like having a look. (You can see why I've never been a success in life. I never learn from my mistakes, even when I've just made them.)

I found that the place on the road where Mrs Crawley used to wait for a lift into town had been made into a bus terminus, and there was a little shelter-shed and a store. All the way down to the beach baches had been built and lots of young people were about in shorts. And I really got the shock of my life when I saw the Crawleys bach still standing there; but there it was, and except for a fresh coat of Stockholm tar it didn't look any different.

Mrs Crawley was in the garden. I hardly recognized her. She'd shrivelled up to nothing, and she was fixed in such a bend that above the waist she walked parallel to the ground. Her mouth had been sucked right inside her head, so her chin stuck out like the toe of a boot more than ever. Naturally she didn't know me, I had to shout to make her hear, and her eyes were bad too. When I told her I was Freddy Coleman, and she'd remembered who Freddy Coleman was, she ran her hands over my face as though to help her know whether or not I was telling the truth.

'Fancy you coming,' she said, and after I'd admired the garden and asked her how many times she'd put up a fresh ring of tea-tree brush, she asked me inside.

The bach was much the same. The sacking was still nailed up over the place where the wind came in, but only two of the fern-beds were left. One was Mrs Crawley's and the other was Joe's, and both were made up. The table was set too, but covered over with tea-towels. I didn't know what to say. It was all too much for me. Mrs Crawley sat and watched me, her head stuck forward, and I didn't know where to look.

'It's a good job you came early,' she said. 'If you'd come late you'd have given me a turn.'

'Oh,' I said.

'Yes,' she said, 'he always comes late. Not till the last bus.'

'Oh,' I said. 'I suppose you mean Joe.'

'Yes, Joe,' she said. 'He never comes until the last bus.'

I asked her what had become of the girls, but she took no notice. She went on talking about Joe and I couldn't follow her, so I got up to leave. She wanted me to have a cup of tea but I said no thank you. I wanted to get away.

'You've got Joe's Christmas dinner ready for him,' I said, and I touched the table.

'Yes,' she said, 'I've got everything that he likes.' And she took away the tea-towels. It was some spread. Ham, fruit, cake, nuts, everything that you can think of for Christmas. It was a shock after the old days. Joe was evidently making good money, and I felt a bit envious of him.

'He'll enjoy that,' I said. 'What line's he in, by the way?'

'He'll come,' she said. 'I've got everything that he likes. He'll come.'

It was hopeless, so I went.

Then, walking back to the road I didn't feel quite so bad. It all came back to me about how fond of Joe Mrs Crawley had been. She hadn't lost him at any rate. I thought of the bach all tidied up, and the Christmas spread, and it put me in quite a glow. I hadn't made a success of my life, and the world was in a mess, but here was something you could admire and feel thankful for. Mrs Crawley still had her Joe. And I couldn't help wondering what sort of a fellow Joe Crawley had turned out.

Well, when I was back on the road again a bus hadn't long come in, and the driver was eating a sandwich. So I went up to him.

'Good day,' I said. 'Can you tell me what sort of a fellow Joe Crawley is?'

'Joe Crawley,' he said. 'I've never seen him.'

'Oh,' I said. 'Been driving out here long?'

He told me about five years, so I jerked my thumb over towards the beach.

'Do you know Mrs Crawley?' I asked him.

'Do I what?' he said. 'She's sat in that shed waiting for the last bus every night that I can remember.'

He told me all he knew. Long ago, people said, Joe would come several times a year, then he'd come just at Christmas. When he did come it would be always on the last bus, and he'd be off again first thing in the morning. But for years now he hadn't come at all. No one knew for sure what he used to do. There were yarns about him being a bookmaker, some said he'd gone to gaol, others that he'd cleared off to America. As for the girls, they'd married and got scattered, though one was supposed to write now and then. Anyhow, wet or fine, summer or winter, Mrs Crawley never missed a night sitting in that shelter-shed waiting to see if Joe'd turn up on the last bus. She still collected pine cones to sell, and would drag the bags for miles; and several times, pulling up mussels out on the reef she'd been knocked over by the sea and nearly drowned. Of course, she got the pension, but people said she saved every penny of it and lived on the smell of an oil-rag. And whenever she did buy anything she always explained that she was buying it for Joe.

Well, I heard him out. Then I took to the road. I felt small. All the affairs of the heart that I had in my life and all that I had seen in other people, seemed shabby and mean compared to this one of Mrs Crawley's. I looked at the smart young people about in their shorts with a sort of contempt. I thought of Mrs Crawley waiting down there in the bach with her wonderful Christmas spread, the bach swept out and tidied, and Joe's bed with clean sheets on all made up ready and waiting. And I thought of her all those years digging in the garden, digging for pupis, pulling up mussels and picking up cones, bending her body until it couldn't be straightened out again, until she looked like a new sort of human being. All for Joe. For Joe who'd never been anything much to look at, and who, if he was alive now, stayed away while his mother sat night after night waiting for him in a bus shelter-shed. Though, mind you, I didn't feel like blaming Joe. I knew how he'd been spoilt. And I remembered how as a boy I'd sort of understood that the way Mrs Crawley felt towards him might turn out to be quite a terrible thing. And sure enough it had. But I never understood until last Christmas Day, when I was walking northwards to a job on a fruit-farm, how anything in the world that was such a terrible thing could at the same time be so beautiful.

CHARLES BRASCH

In These Islands

Always, in these islands, meeting and parting
Shake us, making tremulous the salt-rimmed air;
Divided and perplexed the sea is waiting,
Birds and fishes visit us and disappear.

The future and the past stand at our doors,
Beggars who for one look of trust will open
Worlds that can answer our unknown desires,
Entering us like rain and sun to ripen.

Remindingly beside the quays, the white
Ships lie smoking; and from their haunted bay
The godwits vanish towards another summer.
Everywhere in light and calm the murmuring
Shadow of departure; distance looks our way;
And none knows where he will lie down at night.

RODERICK FINLAYSON
The Totara Tree

People came running from all directions wanting to know what all the fuss was about. 'Oho! it's crazy old Taranga perching like a crow in her tree because the Pakeha boss wants his men to cut it down,' Panapa explained, enjoying the joke hugely.

'What you say, cut it down? Cut the totara down?' echoed Uncle Tuna, anger and amazement wrinkling yet more his old wrinkled face. 'Cut Taranga down first!' he exclaimed. 'Everyone knows that totara is Taranga's birth tree.'

Uncle Tuna was so old he claimed to remember the day Taranga's father had planted the young tree when the child was born. Nearly one hundred years ago, Uncle Tuna said. But many people doubted that he was quite as old as that. He always boasted so.

'Well, it looked like they'll have to cut down both Taranga *and* her tree,' chuckled Panapa to the disgust of Uncle Tuna, who disapproved of joking about matters of tapu.

'Can't the Pakeha bear the sight of one single tree without reaching for his axe?' Uncle Tuna demanded angrily. 'However, this tree is tapu,' he added with an air of finality, 'so let the Pakeha go cut down his own weeds.' Uncle Tuna hated the Pakeha.

'Ae, why do they want to cut down Taranga's tree?' a puzzled woman asked.

'It's the wires,' Panapa explained loftily. 'The tree's right in the way of the new power wires they're taking up the valley. Ten thousand volts, ehoa! That's power, I tell you! A touch of that to her tail would soon make old Taranga spring out of her tree, ehoa,' Panapa added with impish delight and a sly dig in the ribs for old Uncle Tuna. The old man simply spat his contempt and stumped away.

'Oho!' gurgled Panapa, 'now just look at the big Pakeha boss down below dancing and cursing at mad old Taranga up the tree: and she doesn't know a single word and cares nothing at all!'

And indeed Taranga just sat up there smoking her pipe of evil-smelling torori. Now she turned her head away and spat slowly and deliberately on the ground. Then she fixed her old half-closed eyes on the horizon again. Aue! how those red-faced Pakehas down below there jabbered and shouted! Well, no matter.

Meanwhile a big crowd had collected near the shanty where Taranga lived with her grandson, in front of which grew Taranga's totara tree right on the narrow road that divided the struggling little hillside settlement from the river. Men lounged against old sheds and hung over sagging fences; women squatted in open doorways or strolled along the road with babies in shawls on their backs. The bolder children even came right up and made marks in the dust on the Inspector's big car with their grubby little fingers. The driver had to say to them: 'Hey, there, you! Keep away from the car.' And they hung their heads and pouted their lips and looked shyly at him with great sombre eyes.

But a minute later the kiddies were jigging with delight behind the Inspector's back. How splendid to see such a show – all the big Pakehas from town turned out to fight mad old Taranga perching in a tree! But she was a witch all right – like her father the tohunga. Maybe she'd just flap her black shawl like wings and give a cackle and turn into a bird and fly away. Or maybe she'd curse the Pakehas, and they'd all wither up like dry sticks before their eyes! Uncle Tuna said she could do even worse than that. However, the older children didn't believe that old witch stuff.

Now as long as the old woman sat unconcernedly smoking up the tree, and the Pakehas down below argued and appealed to her as unsuccessfully as appealing to Fate, the crowd thoroughly enjoyed the joke. But when the Inspector at last lost his temper and shouted to his men to pull the old woman down by force, the humour of the gathering changed. The women in the doorways shouted shrilly. One of them said, 'Go away, Pakeha, and bully city folk! We Maoris don't yet insult trees or old women!' The men on the fences began grumbling sullenly, and the younger fellows started to lounge over towards the Pakehas. Taranga's grandson, Taikehu, who had been chopping wood, had a big axe in his hand. Taranga may be mad but after all it was her birth tree. You couldn't just come along and cut down a tree like that. Ae, you could laugh your fill at the old woman perched among the branches like an old black crow, but it wasn't for a Pakeha to come talking about pulling her down and destroying her tree. That smart man had better look out.

The Inspector evidently thought so too. He made a sign to dismiss the linesmen who were waiting with ladders and axes and ropes and saws to cut the tree down. Then he got into his big car, tight-lipped with rage. 'Hey, look out there, you kids!' the driver shouted. And away went the

Pakehas amid a stench of burnt benzine, leaving Taranga so far victorious.

'They'll be back tomorrow with the police all right and drag old Taranga down by a leg,' said Panapa gloatingly. 'She'll have no chance with the police. But by korry! I'll laugh to see the first policeman to sample her claws.'

'Oho, they'll be back with soljers,' chanted the kiddies in great excitement. 'They'll come with machine-guns and go r-r-r-r-r- at old Taranga, but she'll just swallow the bullets!'

'Shut up, you kids,' Panapa commanded.

But somehow the excitement of the besieging of Taranga in her tree had spread like wildfire through the usually sleepy little settlement. The young bloods talked about preparing a hot welcome for the Pakehas tomorrow. Uncle Tuna encouraged them. A pretty state of affairs, he said, if a tapu tree could be desecrated by mere busybodies. The young men of his day knew better how to deal with such affairs. He remembered well how he himself had once tomahawked a Pakeha who broke the tapu of a burial ground. If people had listened to him long ago all the Pakehas would have been put in their place, under the deep sea – shark food! said Uncle Tuna ferociously. But the people were weary of Uncle Tuna's many exploits, and they didn't stop to listen. Even the youngsters nowadays merely remarked: 'Oh yeah,' when the old man harangued them.

Yet already the men were dancing half-humorous hakas around the totara tree. A fat woman with rolling eyes and a long tongue encouraged them. Everyone roared with laughter when she tripped in her long red skirts and fell bouncingly in the road. It was taken for granted now that they would make a night of it. Work was forgotten, and everyone gathered about Taranga's place. Taranga still waited quietly in the tree.

Panapa disappeared as night drew near but he soon returned with a barrel of home-brew on a sledge to enliven the occasion. That soon warmed things up, and the fun became fast and more furious. They gathered dry scrub and made bonfires to light the scene. They told Taranga not to leave her lookout, and they sent up baskets of food and drink to her; but she wouldn't touch bite nor sup. She alone of all the crowd was now calm and dignified. The men were dancing mad hakas armed with axes, knives and old taiahas. Someone kept firing a shotgun till the cartridges gave out. Panapa's barrel of home-brew was getting low too, and Panapa just sat there propped against it and laughed and laughed; men and women alike boasted what they'd do with the Pakehas tomorrow. Old Uncle Tuna was disgusted with the whole business though. That was no way to fight the Pakeha, he said; that was the Pakeha's own ruination. He stood up by the meeting-house and harangued the mob, but no one listened to him.

The children were screeching with delight and racing around the bonfires like brown demons. They were throwing firesticks about here, there, and everywhere. So, it's no wonder the scrub caught fire, and Taikehu's house beside the tree was ablaze before anybody noticed it. Heaven help us, but there was confusion then! Taikehu rushed in to try to save his best clothes. But he only got out with his old overcoat and a broken gramophone before the flames roared up through the roof. Some men started beating out the scrub with their axes and sticks. Others ran to the river for water. Uncle Tuna capered about urging the men to save the totara tree from the flames. Fancy wasting his breath preaching against the Pakeha, he cried. Trust this senseless generation of Maoris to work their own destruction, he sneered.

It seemed poor old Taranga was forgotten for the moment. Till a woman yelled at Taikehu, 'What you doing there with your old rags, you fool? Look alive and get the old woman out of the tree.' Then she ran to the tree and called, 'Eh there, Taranga, don't be mad. Come down quick, old mother!'

But Taranga made no move.

Between the woman and Taikehu and some others, they got Taranga down. She looked to be still lost in meditation. But she was quite dead.

'Aue! she must have been dead a *long* time – she's quite cold and stiff,' Taikehu exclaimed. 'So it couldn't be the fright of the fire that killed her.'

'Fright?' jeered Uncle Tuna. 'I tell you, pothead, a woman who loaded rifles for me under the cannon shells of the Pakeha isn't likely to die in fright at a rubbish fire.' He cast a despising glance at the smoking ruins of Taikehu's shanty. 'No! but I tell you what she died of,' Uncle Tuna exclaimed. 'Taranga was just sick to death of you and your Pakeha ways. Sick to death!' The old man spat on the ground and turned his back on Taikehu and Panapa and their companions.

Meanwhile the wind had changed, and the men had beaten out the scrub fire, and the totara tree was saved. The fire and the old woman's strange death and Uncle Tuna's harsh words had sobered everybody by now, and the mood of the gathering changed from its former frenzy to melancholy and a kind of superstitious awe. Already some women had started to wail at the meeting-house where Taranga had been carried. Arrangements would have to be made for the tangi.

'Come here, Taikehu,' Uncle Tuna commanded. 'I have to show you where you must bury Taranga.'

Well, the Inspector had the grace to keep away while the tangi was on. Or rather Sergeant O'Connor, the chief of the local police and a good friend of Taranga's people, advised the Inspector not to meddle till it was over. 'A tangi or a wake, sure it's just as sad and holy,' he said. 'Now I advise you, don't interfere till they've finished.'

But when the Inspector did go to the settlement afterwards – well! Panapa gloatingly told the story in the pub in town later. 'O boy,' he said: 'you should have heard what plurry Mr Inspector called Sergeant O'Connor when he found out they'd buried the old woman right under the roots of the plurry tree! I think O'Connor like the joke though. When the Inspector finish cursing, O'Connor say to him, "Sure the situation's still unchanged then. Taranga's still in her tree."'

Well, the power lines were delayed more than ever and in time this strange state of affairs was even mentioned in the Houses of Parliament, and the Maori members declared the Maoris' utter refusal to permit the desecration of burial places, and the Pakeha members all applauded these fine orations. So the Power Board was brought to the pass at last of having to build a special concrete foundation for the poles in the river bed so that the wires could be carried clear of Taranga's tree.

'Oho!' Panapa chuckles, telling the story to strangers who stop to look at the tomb beneath the totara on the roadside. 'Taranga dead protects her tree much better than Taranga alive. Py korry she cost the Pakeha thousands *and* thousands of pounds I guess!'

DAN DAVIN

Under the Bridge

Black, opaque and in hundreds they interposed their darkness between us and the smiling Cretan sky, shattered the summer's peace with the death they carried; slew its silence with the roar of their engines and the punctuated thunder of the bombs. Each explosion overtook its predecessor's echo, and merged with it to make a perpetual rumble in the hills.

Sometimes a shadow would pass directly over us, swiftly, with a flitting bat-like quality. The drone increased to a roar and the plane would follow, bullets streaming with the undiscriminating prodigality of rain. Like rain on a gusty day. How long since I had seen and felt rain, refreshing rain not deadly, from grey, unhurrying homely skies, not this lethal metallic rain.

Our hill overlooked the village on its left, on the right front the sea. The sea, smooth and untroubled, its calm a promise of permanence when this tumult should be silent, road home to the lands of rain. Crouched under the lee of the rock, nostalgia gripped me like a cramp, nostalgia for the past or for the future. Anything to be out of this moment where we were held by the slow, maddening pace of time. But not for long this mutiny of the heart. Madness to venture hopes on such a sea, to commit oneself to anything but a prudent despair. Try to save your life certainly, but within the bounds of decency and dignity. And not expect to save it. Fighting was easier, dourer in despair.

Nothing much to do till the air quietened down a bit. There might be more parachutists to follow soon, the concentration was so fierce. But no; it was the town that was getting it this time. Our share was only the overflow. They were solacing themselves for their reverses on the ground in an orgy of undirected destruction, an orgasm of rage and inflicted terror. Clouds of dust and smoke rose, tranquilly, unfolding and expanding with leisure of time itself from crumpled homes and ruined walls. Flames groped up into the afternoon, their red transparent to the day and then as their mounting impetus declined filmy and water-coloured but still bloodshot.

Just outside the village where the last houses straggled like lost children the road bridged a gully. I was watching the bridge. During raids the people sheltered under it. We had warned them to go away, not to wait.

They were obstinate, they would not leave their homes. We told them the bridge would probably be hit, was a military objective, but the mere physical fact of its shelter, its mere bulk blinded them to its danger. They continued to go there.

That would have been bad enough. But now we all had a personal interest there as well. Angela and her grandmother would be there too. And Angela had somehow succeeded in making herself real to us in a way civilians are not usually real. They didn't even belong to the town but had come down from their village in the hills. They used to help us with food sometimes and do the washing. There was something about Angela's smiling freshness, the beauty of her teeth and hands which made everything she did for us seem better than if someone else had done it. Seeing her made you notice how good the weather was and when you looked at the sea you would see how blue it was and the snow on the mountains inland would strike you in all its cold remote whiteness for it seemed the first time. On the old, leisurely standard I would have had time to fancy myself in love with Angela.

From where I was I could see the bridge perfectly. The gully ran out from the foot of our hill and in a straight line away from us till it passed under the road. You could not distinguish individuals. But you could see them praying. They were all kneeling under it, the women and the children and the very old men. You could see them praying, making the sign of the Cross over and over again. Their fear was erect and dignified. For the hundredth time I admired the bravery of these Cretans, their steadfastness. Angela and her grandmother would be there too, like the others afraid, as who would not be, like them calm and accepting with a proviso of reserved revenge.

I felt so close to them that I was with them. I almost blessed myself too when they did. It was like the family rosary of long ago. But the devil 'who wanders through the world to the ruin of souls' sought bodies too. He was real and present. He was death, travelling with every bullet now broadcast from the air and guiding too haphazard chance, now sped from the cool intent of the sniper's eye.

In spite of the intenseness of my presence with them I was aware too of the planes, could see them as one after another detached from the intricately weaving group and swept low with a rising roar over the prostrate village.

They would have been better off spread along the gully. But they might have a chance. The German hadn't yet bombed any bridges to my knowledge. Saving them for himself. But this was a side road. It wouldn't matter much to him. And today he didn't seem to care much where he dropped them: he was out to terrorize. By now the town couldn't be much more than a chaff of mortar and rubble among drunken walls.

From over the centre of the town a bomber came sailing out towards the bridge. Slowly, very slowly. Above the outskirts they began to drop, swift and glistening where the light caught them. I watched them. The first struck the edge of the town. A series of explosions among the scattered houses. I heard them only. I was watching the last. I don't think he particularly meant to hit the bridge. But it disappeared. The whole scene disappeared. It was as if I had become blind with smoke and dust instead of darkness.

I waited for it to clear. For reality to reassemble. The cloud settled into the grey-green olives on either side of the gully. The bridge was still standing. The bomb had fallen in the gully, on the far side. I began to breathe again. And then I saw that the group had changed. They were no longer kneeling. Their small dark knot had opened out like a flower. There were shapes scattered in a semicircle this side of the bridge, still. The bomb blast must have travelled along the gully like an express train through a cutting. Still, I thought at first; but after a while I seemed to discern movement. It was not a movement of whole bodies, a stirring of limbs rather, of extremities, faint and painful like the movements of a crushed insect whose antennae still grope out pitifully with a hopeless, gallant wavering to life.   •

This was the bare slope of the hill. The red clay showed through the thin soil and the olives were few, thickening only at the bottom. And the planes were as active as ever. It was impossible to get down. And anyhow we had a position to hold.

Afternoon became evening since time moved even in that eternity. And day diminished into dusk. The racket slackened. Only an occasional rifle shot or burst of machine-gun reminded the twilight silence of its brief tenure. Silence like us and them was mortal.

I told the others I was going down. They were to cover me across the open patch. I slipped out from cover and holding the tommy gun bolted for the olives. No firing, no vicious swish of bullets. I made my way through the olives, along the lip of the gully. The dusk was deeper in the olives. The hill held its bulk before the sun.

As I approached the bridge I hesitated. I knew what I was going to see. And there had been so much of it in these last days. I stopped and listened. Not a sound. That eternal, suffering grey of the olives, the agony immobilized of their gnarled trunks anticipated and accentuated what must be in the gully. The silence, the patient silence and the dusk, but mostly the silence, were too much. It was silence of mangled bodies, a silence of negation and death. There was no life in the gully. Pain perhaps frozen into immobility, but no life. If I should see it as well, bodies caparisoned in all the bloody trappings of a violent death, blood and grotesque distortions of the body's familiar pattern, it would be too much. Not as if it were new. The very familiarity of the distortion, the blasphemy of it, would prove fatal. I did not want to see any more. I did not want to see Angela, her grandmother, others I had known. Or if I did see them and did not recognize them.

But perhaps there was something one could do. I listened again. Not a groan or sigh. There was much to do, much fighting yet. One must fight for one's sanity as well as one's life. I hesitated. In sudden horror I knew there was something else dragging me to the edge. Appetite to frightfulness as well as revulsion. Death squatted within the hollow like a presence, its emanation came up, grisly, dragging at me. I felt the hair on the back of my head stiffen. I took two steps forward. My eyes saw but my brain would not see. I turned and ran.

At the edge of the olives I halted. My knees were like jelly, with a hot trembling. I waited. Then ran again across up over the bare slope. It was with relief I heard the bullets searing their tunnel through the air. At the rock I turned and dropped into cover, a soldier again. And the bridge and the gully of bodies waited in my memory.

FRANK SARGESON
The Making of a New Zealander

When I called at that farm they promised me a job for two months so I took it on, but it turned out to be rough going. The boss was all right, I didn't mind him at all, and most days he'd just settle down by the fire and get busy with his crochet. It was real nice to see him looking happy and contented as he sat there with his ball of wool.

But this story is not about a cocky who used to sit in front of the fire and do crochet. I'm not saying I haven't got a story about him, but I'll have to be getting round to it another time.

Yes, the boss was all right, it was his missis that was the trouble. Some people say, never work for a woman, women'll never listen to reason. But that's not my experience. Use your block and in no time you'll be unlucky if you don't have them eating out of your hand.

But this time I was unlucky. This Mrs Crump was a real tough one. She and the boss ran a market garden besides the cows. She'd tie a flour-bag over her head, get into gumboots, and not counting the time she put in in the house, she'd do about twelve hours a day, and she had me doing the same. Not that I minded all that much. The best of working on the land is that you're not always wishing it was time to knock off. Nor thinking of pay-day, either, particularly if there isn't a pub handy. I'm not going to explain. If you don't believe me, try it yourself and see.

But a twelve-hour day, every day. I'll admit I used to get tired. Mrs Crump would see I was done in and tell me to stop working, and that was just what I was waiting for her to do. But there'd be a look in her eye. She'd say that I wasn't built for hard work, but she wasn't surprised because she'd never met a man she couldn't work to a standstill. Well, after she'd said that I'd just go on working, and if I was feeling cheeky I'd tell her I didn't mind giving her a run for her money. And before those two months were out I was feeling cheeky pretty often. Once she got going about my wages and everything else she had to pay out. She couldn't keep the wolf from the door, she said. Well, then, I said, if you can't you'll just have to keep the door shut.

Now I'm running on ahead so I'd better break off again, because this isn't just a no-account story about how I began to get cheeky and put wisecracks across Mrs Crump. It's not about Mrs Crump, she only comes into it. I'm not saying I haven't got a story about her, too, but it's another one I'll be getting round to another time.

What I want to tell is about how I sat on a hillside one evening and talked with a man. That's all, just a summer evening and a talk with a man on a hillside. Maybe there's nothing in it and maybe there is.

The man was one of two young Dallies who ran an orchard up at the back of Mrs Crump's place. These two had come out from Dalmatia and put some money down on the land, not much, just enough to give them the chance to start working the land. They were still paying off and would be for a good many years. There was a shed where they could live, and to begin with they took it in turns to go out and work for the money they needed to live and buy trees.

All that was some years before I turned up. The Dallies had worked hard, but it wasn't all plain sailing. They had about twenty-five acres, but it sloped away from the sun. They'd planted pines for shelter, but your shelter has to make a lot of growth before it's any use on land with a good slope to the south. And it was poor land, just an inch or two of dark soil on top of clay. You could tell it was poor from the tea tree, which made no growth after it was a few feet high. Apples do best on land like that, so it was apple trees the Dallies had mainly gone in for.

Of course Mrs Crump gossiped to me about all this. When I was there the Dallies weren't keeping a cow, so she was letting them have milk at half the town price. She didn't mind doing that much for them, she said, they worked so hard. And my last job each day was to take a billy up to the back fence. I'd collect an empty billy that'd be hanging on a hook, and I'd always consider going on and having a yarn with the Dallies. It wasn't far across to their shed but it would be getting dark, I'd be feeling like my tea so I'd tell myself I'd go over another time.

Then one evening the billy wasn't on the hook and I went on over, but the door was shut and there was no one about. The dog went for me but he never had a show. He'd had distemper, he couldn't move his hind legs and just had to pull himself along. I had a look round but there wasn't much to see, just two flannels and a towel hanging on the line, and a few empty barrels splashed with bluestone. Close to the shed there were grape vines growing on wires, then the trees began. They were carrying a lot of fruit and looked fine and healthy, but just a bit too healthy, I thought. You could tell from the growth that the Dallies had put on a lot of fertilizer. For a while I waited about, kidding to the dog until he wagged his tail, then I went back.

The next day one of the Dallies brought the billy over but I didn't see

him. When we were milking, Mrs Crump told me. He was the one called
Nick, and the evening before he'd had to take his mate into hospital. He'd
had a spill off his bike and broken some ribs and his collarbone. Mrs Crump
thought perhaps there'd been some drinking, she said they made wine.
Anyhow, Nick was upset. If his mate died, he said, he would die too. He'd
have nothing left, nothing. And how could he work and live there by
himself when his mate was lying all broken up in the hospital? Every
afternoon he would leave off working and ride into town to see his mate.

'There's a pal for you,' Mrs Crump said.

Well, up at the fence the billy would always be on the hook, but if Nick
was in town seeing his cobber I'd think it would be no use going over. Then
one evening he was just coming across with the billy so I went over to
meet him. We greeted each other, and I think we both felt a bit shy. He
was small and dark, almost black, and his flannel and denims were pretty
far gone the same as mine were. I gave him my tin and told him to roll
a cigarette, and when he lit up he went crosseyed. I noticed that, and I
saw too that there was a kind of sadness on his face.

I asked him how his cobber was, and he said he was good.

'In two days he will be here,' he said. You could see he was excited about
it and his face didn't look so sad. 'In two weeks,' he said, 'it will be just
as if it never happened.'

'That's great,' I said, and we sat down and smoked.

'How's the dog?' I asked.

'He is getting better, too,' Nick said.

He whistled, and the dog pulled himself over to us by his front paws and
put his chin on Nick's legs, and somehow with the dog there it was easier
to talk.

I asked Nick about his trees and he said they were all right, but there
were too many diseases.

'Too much quick manure,' I said.

He said yes, but what could they do? It would take a long time to make
the soil deep and sweet like it was in the part of Dalmatia he came from.
Out here everybody wanted the money quick, so they put on the manure.
It was money, money, all the time. But he and his mate never had any.
Everything they got they had to pay out, and if the blackspot got among
the apples they had to pay out more than they got. Then one of them had
to go out and try for a job.

'It's the manure that gives you the blackspot,' I said.

'Sometimes I think it is God,' Nick said.

'Well, maybe you're right,' I said, 'but what about the grapes?'

'Oh,' Nick said, 'they grow, yes. But they are not sweet. To make wine we must put in sugar. In Dalmatia it is not done. Never.'

'Yes,' I said, 'but you don't go back to Dalmatia.'

'Oh, no,' he said, 'now I am a New Zealander.'

'No,' I said, 'but your children will be.'

'I have no children and I will never marry,' Nick said.

'No?' I said. 'Then your cobber will.'

'He will never marry either,' Nick said.

'Why?' I said, 'there are plenty of Dalmatian girls out here. I bet you could get New Zealand girls too.'

But Nick only said 'no! no! no! no!'

'If you were in Dalmatia I bet you'd be married,' I said.

'But I am not in Dalmatia,' Nick said, 'now I am a New Zealander. In New Zealand everybody says they cannot afford to get married.'

'Yes,' I said, 'that's what they say. But it's all wrong.'

'Yes,' Nick said, 'it is all wrong. Because it is all wrong I am a Communist.'

'Good,' I said. Well, I thought, spoil a good peasant and you might as well go the whole hog.

'I bet you don't tell Mrs Crump you're a Communist,' I said.

'Oh, no,' Nick said, 'she would never be a Communist.'

'No fear,' I said.

'I will tell you about Mrs Crump,' Nick said. 'She should go to Dalmatia. In Dalmatia our women wear bags on their heads just like her, and she would be happy there.'

'Yes,' I said, 'I believe you're right. But Nick,' I said, 'I thought you'd be a Catholic.'

'No,' Nick said. 'It is all lies. In Dalmatia they say that Christ was born when there was snow on the ground in Palestine. But now I have read in a book there is no snow in Palestine. So now I know they tell lies.'

'So you're a Communist instead,' I said.

'Yes, I am a Communist,' Nick said. 'But what is the good of that? I am born too soon, eh? What do you think?'

'Maybe,' I said.

'You, too,' Nick said. 'You think that you and me are born too soon? What do you think?'

He said it over and over, and I couldn't look him in the face. It had too much of that sadness. I mightn't have put it the way Nick had, I mightn't have said I was born too soon, but Nick knew what he was talking about.

Nick and I were sitting on the hillside and Nick was saying he was a New Zealander. And he knew he wasn't a Dalmatian any more.

He knew he wasn't anything any more.

'Listen,' Nick said, 'do you drink wine?'

'Yes,' I said.

'Then tomorrow night you come up here and we will drink wine,' Nick said.

'Yes,' I said, 'that's O.K. with me.'

'There is only tomorrow night,' Nick said, 'then my mate will be there. We will drink a lot of wine, I have plenty, and we will get very, very drunk. Oh, heaps drunk.'

'Yes,' I said. 'Sure thing!'

'Tomorrow night,' he said.

He got up and I got up, he just waved his hand at me and walked off. He picked the dog up under his arm and walked off, and I just stood there and watched him go.

But it turned out I never went to Nick's place. When I was having my tea that evening Mrs Crump told me about how a woman she knew had worked too hard and dropped dead with heart failure. 'But there's nothing wrong with my heart,' she said.

'No,' I said, 'except that maybe it's not in the right place.'

Of course it must have sounded like one of my wisecracks, but I was thinking of Dalmatia.

Anyhow, Mrs Crump said she'd stood enough from me, so when I'd finished my tea I could go.

I wasn't sorry. I stood on the road and wondered if I'd go up to Nick's place, but instead I walked into town, and for a good few days I never left off drinking.

I wanted to get Nick out of my mind. He knew what he was talking about, but maybe it's best for a man to hang on.

DENIS GLOVER

Convoy Conversation

It was cold at the four-inch gun. They had been closed up at action stations since the early Arctic dawn, and they had watched the great convoy change from a black smudge against the darkened sea to the high, clear shape of ships. And it was at dawn they had beaten off the usual submarine attack.

Now they were awaiting the first wave of planes.

The gun crew was dressed, as destroyer crews do dress at sea, in anything that would keep out the cold – balaclavas, bulky oilskins, dufflecoats, leather jerkins. They were unshaven and very dirty. Some were stamping round the gun platform to warm their feet, some were slapping their arms against their coats; some smoked with unconcern, and others with a cat-like nervousness kept glancing at the sea and sky and at the herd of freighters moving slowly, oh, so slowly, towards its dangerous destination.

The ready-use lockers were open, and the beautiful bronze-tipped shells lay stacked near the breech of the gun, where the communication number sat with the telepads over his ears drumming with gloved fingers on a gaudily decorated tin hat, and listening with his eyes to the chatter of his mates.

Geordie was spinning a yarn. 'So I says to this party, I says, "Well, ain't you glad to see me?" And she says, "Why, George, where did you come from?" and she starts to wrap herself round my neck. "Wait a minute," I says, "what's all this here? What about that bloody pongo what's been loafing round since I come ashore last?" By Jeez, I was chocker, I was, from what I hears from a townie up north, which is why I never told her I was goin' up the line. Just walked in, see, like that – thought the bastard might be there, and I was goin' to vittle him up.'

There was noisy appreciation of this sentiment, because Geordie was like that. He used to let his feelings run away with him, and puzzle things out afterwards.

'And she says all sweet like, "Why, Gee-orge, you know I wouldn't go out with nobody while you was away,"' Geordie pantomimed expressively, and those who were listening laughed again, because sailors are always as worried as hell about what the girl friend is getting up to while they're away.

'Not bloody much she wouldn't!' suggested someone.

'"Not suckin' much you wouldn't," I says, "but what's to stop him comin' here? What d'ya fancy I am, bloody wet?"' And Geordie laughed sardonically, the joke being on him in this piece of deduction.

'Plane out there, man,' interrupted Taffy excitedly, pointing to the horizon.

'Only Charlie loafin' round,' commented Big Scouse. Charlie the Barman was Jerry reconnaissance, and there he was, artlessly cruising round the horizon below the cloudbank. 'Better report him, Bill.'

'Where?' said Wacker Pine, the captain of the gun, anxiously peering round the sky. But the communication number was already making his report.

'Four-inch T.S., four-inch T.S. Aircraft bearing green one six oh, angle of sight oh five, goin' right to left. What's that? Lookout reported it five minutes ago? How the hell are we to know that?'

At the news that the plane was somebody else's business, no one took any further notice of it, except that every now and then someone would glance up to see if it was still there, the first evil warning of what was to come.

But no sense of impending danger was going to put Geordie off his narrative. '"Ally," I says, Ally bein' her name like, "Ally, you must fancy I'm bloody wet." And I puts me cap on, and she says "Where you goin', George?" So I says, "I'm goin' to find that bastard pongo and flake him out."'

There was a pause while they turned over this highly satisfying prospect in their minds. 'How d'ja know where he was, Geordie?'

'I never,' said Geordie. 'In fact, I never knew there was no bastard for certain, only what that townie tells me, so how the hell was I goin' to find him?' Big Scouse, who had been idly tossing a fuse key into the air, shook with laughter at this statement. 'Go on,' he said, retrieving the key with a flood of obscenity from under a locker. 'What did she say?'

'Not a bloody thing.' Geordie spoke with disgust. 'Just turned on the tap and snivelled to herself a bit. And after a bit she says, "You better have some supper first if you're goin' out." Of course I never goes much for the big eats when I'm up the line – gimme a couple of pints and a bit of the old doughmaker's and I'm set.' He thumbed with suggestive enjoyment, and grinned. 'But on account of I never et in the train at all, I says,

"What've you got?'' Christ, boys, and in less time than that I was woofin'
down eggs and chips and a big lump of steak, and there was afters, too,
but I forget what it was –'

'Four-inch T.S.!' roared the com number. This contact with the trans-
mitting station, the nerve centre of the ship, always hushed all talk.
'Aircraft reported thirty miles away. What's that? Repeat. Large group,
comin' in.'

There was a startled pause. So this was it, at last?

'Better stand by,' said Wacker with sudden resolution.

'Jesus Christ, man,' said Taffy, and started to unbutton his coat with
nervous haste. He hadn't been in air action before this trip, and he was
jumpy. Not that everyone didn't show some signs of strain, waiting for it
like that. But the convoy and its escort continued to move imperturbably
onward.

'You're for it now,' said Scouse, watching maliciously and hooting with
laughter. Just as if he wasn't in it, too. But Scouse had survived so many
dive-bombings he never seemed to mind another one or two.

'Plenty of time,' put in Geordie with annoyance. He very firmly put
down the shell someone had passed him. 'Let me finish what I'm tellin'
yer, for suck sake.'

'Are you all ready, Pine?' It was the first lieutenant from the after
conning position just for'ard of the gun.

'All ready, sir, yessir.' Pine had been moodily staring out to sea, looking
with dislike at the lumbering and vulnerable freighters huddled together
like a mob of sheep for the butcher. 'Better close up, boys. Come on now,
get cracking!'

The crew moved to their action positions, trainer and layer at their
platforms, the fuse-setters each clasping a shell beside their receiver,
supply numbers near the magazine hoist. Pine, by the breech lever,
examined the interceptor contacts with worried concentration. He
looked up suddenly. 'I wish we was back in harbour.' The candour of this
admission made everyone grin, and Pine felt it necessary to exert his
authority as captain of the gun. 'Now you follow them pointers, Gorman,
see? It'll be barrage at first, and they'll be comin' in faster than that.
Everyone do what I tell you and you'll be all right, see? Hey, you quit
skylarkin' there, Drennan; pay attention to what I'm telling
you –'

'Ah wusna skylarking, Wacker,' protested Drennan in voluble indigna-
tion. 'A'm juist keeping ma honds warrm.'

'You do what I tell you!' roared Wacker. 'I'm the captain of this gun, and if anything goes wrong it's me takes the can back, not you, see? And when I says you was skylarkin' you was skylarkin', see?'

'Ah wusna –' This altercation broke the tension of waiting, and there were suppressed catcalls and a great simulation of choking laughter just to relieve the feelings and show Wacker it was sink or swim this time, and no gunnery school flannel either.

'Orright,' said Wacker ominously. 'Someone might go on the quarter deck over this. I'm the captain of this gun, and I'll do all the funny stuff round here, see?' Then coaxingly, 'We gotta get these prodgies up the spout, orright? and get 'em away quick as Christ'll let us. You do what –'

'Four-inch T.S.' There was strained silence again. 'Forty aircraft approaching right ahead. Follow director. Barrage, barrage, barrage!'

The ship woke to life with a shuddering blast as the for'ard guns opened up, and all the way to the horizon ship after ship took up the tune till the noise of the battle rolled over the empty acres of the sea.

'Four-inch won't bear,' shouted Wacker as the fire buzzer rang for the second salvo.

'Four-inch T.S. Four-inch will not bear.' Standing ready for the moment it would bear, the crew searched for the as yet unseen enemy. 'Bombs!' shouted someone as a great explosion rent the sea a mile away. It was followed by others, and looking up they could see the sinister black eggs sailing down here and there from the low cloud. But the bombers above were not the target for the moment.

'There they are!' Strung out in line the torpedo planes swept in from ahead, skimming the surface of the water, undulating as they poised for attack.

'Gun bearing,' yelled the trainer, and with a roar and a blast the long barrel spat flame, and the after guns followed, and the for'ard guns bore round on the beam, till the whole ship heeled and flamed in the shock. The pompom opened up like the rapid hammerblows of a giant, the deadly Oerlikons joined in, and through the sharp ginger smoke of the burnt cordite they could see the cherry-coloured tracer playing like a host of fire along the bodies of the swooping planes.

The air seemed full of falling bombs, and tinfish like carelessly dropped cigarettes splashed among the crowded ships. Guns of all calibres punched and coughed and boomed. The clouds were pitted with shell-bursts. There were explosions everywhere, and a tremendous roar as an ammunition ship disintegrated into flame. There were planes screaming past in a dive or spinning down to the sea. And in the middle of all this the gun crew toiled and sweated like busy coordinated ants to keep their weapon bearing and firing.

'Got him!' A plane roaring past not three hundred yards away broke into flame as the tracer caught it. The flame streamed in the wind, went out, blazed up again, and wearing a plume of smoke like a shroud the machine plunged into the water.

'Four-inch!' The first lieutenant's voice was urgent. 'Train starboard. Green three oh. Come *on*, get that gun *round*!' A lone Junkers came skimming in to attack from an unexpected quarter. It sang at the ship like an arrow, and two tinfish fell lazily from its belly. The destroyer heeled heavily as she swung bows on to avoid their foaming course.

'Layer on.'

'Trainer on.'

The gun flicked back with a roar.

'Reload. Come *on*!'

Another shell in the breech, a snap as it slid shut. 'Fire!' The gun smashed a great hole of flame in the air. The shell seemed to burst just behind the plane as it fled astern. It rocked, spun over once, and fell like a diving gull.

The gun crew danced and cheered crazily, like drunk men. 'Good work, good work!' shouted the first lieutenant. The barrel, charged again with death, moved sensitively through the arc of the sky, seeking another target.

But there was no more. Down the lanes of the convoy the firing died away. The last of the attackers were astern, heading for home. Several flew crazily, leaving behind them the black stain of a fatal smoke. A last two high-level bombs smashed harmlessly on the sea; and the convoy moved quietly on. But not all of it. There, already falling astern, were drunken ships, some staggering nose in air, some burning, some heeling with slow finality as the ocean reached upward for their decks. The little rescue ships hunted fussily around them among the wreckage and the rafts. There were heads bobbing in that icy water, little figures clinging to a raft, or a battered boat, sometimes a solitary hand waving. The morse lamps winked and flickered busily from one destroyer to another.

'All right, relax,' called down the first lieutenant. 'Tea interval.'

'Jesus,' grumbled Geordie, 'gimme a smoke someone.' The officer was grinning like a schoolboy, and from his position above them executed a couple of jubilant steps to show his satisfaction. They grinned back at him, grateful in some undefinable way, and they looked at one another appreciatively, in a new and surprising fashion, for they had suddenly become real to one another, working together in the noise and smoke of battle.

'What time is stumps drawn, sir?' inquired Pine, translating himself with petty officer's subservience into the first lieutenant's cricket idiom.

The first lieutenant surveyed the sky with critical concern. 'That depends on the light, Pine,' he replied pleasantly.

'We got that bastard middle stump,' announced Scouse, exploding with greasy mirth.

'Yes.' The first lieutenant turned away to show that this familiarity had now gone as far as the circumstances warranted.

A stoker emerged slowly from below, dragging deeply at a cigarette.

'H'are you, Stokes?'

'What was all them big bangs?' asked the stoker. 'Bombs or depth charges?'

'Both bastards, Stokes, both bastards.' And Scouse rocked with malicious mirth to think of the uncertainty and dread of the stokers below.

'I said there was depth charges,' announced the stoker sourly. 'The boys reckoned they was just bombs. Didn't half make the works rattle, not suckin' much they didn't.'

'How did yer make out, Taff?' inquired Geordie affably.

'Fine, man,' exulted Taffy. 'Jesus bloody Christ it was fine.'

'Yus,' stated Drennan, 'but we dunna· want too much o' it, do we, Scouse?'

'What happened about you and the party, Geordie – you know?'

'Aw,' said Geordie carelessly. 'Nothing much.' It was clear he still harboured some sort of grievance for the interruption of his story. 'Matter of fact, she's a good kid, so I takes her down to the boozer after supper a bit and things is all right. But, suck me! I gets that suckin' boozed up I hardly knows what to do with her when I gets her home.'

'Not suckin' much you never,' commented Scouse with profound disbelief. And everyone shouted with rich enjoyment.

'Four-inch T.S. Repeat. No more planes reported. Port watch to tea, starboard watch close up to A.A. defence stations. Stand fast, anti-submarine party.'

Those of the port watch leisurely hung up their tin hats, took off their anti-flash gear and moved off for'ard to the mess. From other stations the starboard watch arrived in ones and twos to replace them, and lounged about, swapping yarns of the attack.

The pale northern night began to fall. Miles astern now, in the wide desert of the ocean, an abandoned ship burned brightly. Nothing else might have happened. The convoy still moved steadily and changelessly on, and the wilderness of air and water imposed for a short time again its oppressive silence.

FRANK SARGESON

That Summer

I

It was a good farm job I had that winter, but I've always suffered from itchy feet, so I never thought I'd stick it for long. All the same, I stayed until the shearing, and I quit after we'd carted the wool out to the station, just a few bales at a time. It was just beginning December, and I had a good lot of chips saved up, so I thought I'd have a spell in town, which I hadn't had for a good long time, and maybe I'd strike a town job before my chips ran out.

The old bloke I was working for tried hard to get me to stay, but there was nothing doing. I liked him all right and the tucker was good, but him and his missis were always rowing, and there was just the three of us stuck away with hardly any company to speak of. I had to sleep on an old sofa in the kitchen because it was only a slab where they lived in with two rooms, and I got a bit sick of hearing them fighting every night when they'd gone to bed. The old bloke told me he'd had money enough to build a decent house long ago, but his missis said if he did she'd be there for keeps. So she wouldn't let him, but they'd gone on living there just the same.

I had to get up early to walk the six miles to catch the train, and I never saw the old bloke, but his missis came out just when I was going. She had a little bag of sovereigns that I'd never seen before and she made me take one, only she said it was to keep and not to spend, so as I'd always remember her. And when I got down the road she came running along and grabbed hold of me for a kiss, and then she stood in the road and waved. She looked a bit of a sketch, I can tell you, with her hair hanging down and her old man's coat on over her nightgown. I felt a bit sorry and wished in a way I wasn't going, because the farm away back there in the valley looked sort of nice and peaceful with the sun just getting up on such a fine morning, and only a sheep calling out now and then, and the dogs barking because I hadn't let them off the chain when I started down the road. And I looked at the hills and thought what a hell of a good worker I was to have cut all the fern and scrub I had in the winter. But I thought, no, I've got to be on the move. Many a time I've wished I didn't have my itchy feet, but it's never much good wishing for things to be any different.

So I caught the train all right, but I had a few minutes to spare and I talked to the porter. He'd been to a dance the night before; he was yawning his head off and looked as if he needed a wash.

'The old bloke giving you a spell?' he said.

'No,' I said, 'I'm going out for good.'

'What,' he said, 'turning it in? You'll never get another job.'

'I'll be O.K.' I said.

So he told me about how he'd got a letter from his sister, and her husband was out of a job and things couldn't be worse in town. But he hadn't finished telling me when the train came in. So I got on board, but it was a slow train that stopped to shunt all the way along the line, and I was pretty fed up by the time I got into town early that afternoon.

I left my bag at the station, and after I'd had a feed I just walked about the streets looking at the shops and the people. I thought to myself, Now I'll have a good time. I thought maybe I'd pick up with a girl, and with the chips in my pocket I could kick around for a good many weeks before I'd need think about getting a job. I thought I'd go to the flicks, but it seemed better just to be in the streets. I'd have plenty of time to do all the things I wanted to do, so there wasn't any need to go rushing things. Because things never turn out as good as you think they will, so it's always just as well to get all the fun you can out of thinking what they're going to be like beforehand. I went and sat in the park, and whenever there was a girl came past that I thought might have me on, I'd watch out to see if she'd look over me. But there was nothing doing. And I said to myself, Well, a knock-back from one of yous isn't going to make me lose any sleep. But I hoped it wouldn't be long before I had a bit of luck, all the same.

After I'd had another feed I thought I'd better look for a place to sleep, so I went and got my bag from the station, and then I found a joint that was kept by a Mrs Clegg, and I thought it would be O.K. It was a two-storeyed place, standing in between a butcher's shop and a brick warehouse. You paid for your bed and had to get your meals out, but there was a gas-ring at the top of the stairs, and Mrs Clegg said I could borrow a spare teapot and make myself a cup of tea if I wanted to. So I thought that would suit me fine, because I could buy myself a couple of buns and have a lie-in some mornings just for a change after the farm.

Mrs Clegg was quite a decent sort, but she had a glass eye that was cracked right down the middle, and it was funny the way she sort of looked out at you through the crack. Her old man was out of a job, and that was why she was running the joint, though seeing she only had three rooms to let she said she wasn't making a fortune.

When she'd fixed my bed up she took me down to the kitchen to give me the teapot, and her old man was reading the paper, and their little girl was saying pretty boy to a budgie that was answering her back. Though sometimes it would ring a little bell instead. Mr Clegg told me he'd been a cook on a boat, but now he couldn't get a keel. It was hard, he said, because he liked being at sea, though I thought by the look of him it must have been only a coastal or even a scow he'd worked on. He was pretty red, too, though he said he hadn't been until he'd had experience of being on relief.

Of course it was the sort of talk I'd heard a good many times knocking around, so I didn't take much notice. Mrs Clegg kept on chipping in, and they'd squabble a bit, though not as bad as the old couple on the farm, and the little girl left off talking to the budgie and started asking her mother if she could have some money to spend. She asked about fifty times before her mother said no, and asked her if she thought money grew on trees. So then she began to ask if money did grow on trees, and when she'd got to about the fiftieth time I chipped in myself and said I'd have to go.

But it was only to go down the street and buy what I wanted so I could lie-in if I felt like it, and then I turned in, because walking about the town in my good shoes had made me feel tireder than if I'd done a day's work on the farm. And I thought I wouldn't need any rocking to get to sleep, but my room was right over the kitchen, and I could hear the pair of them going it hammer and tongs, and then the youngster got spanked and the way she yelled gave me the dingbats. It was too much like what I'd been used to, and for the first time that day I didn't feel so good about throwing up my job and coming to town. Because I thought there wasn't any sense in having itchy feet if they only got you out of a steady job and into a place like Mrs Clegg's. And there wasn't any sense in having them, anyhow, because they never gave you any peace. Yet all the time I was thinking like that I was asking myself whether I'd get up and clear out right away, or whether I'd wait until daylight, and I knew that wherever I went I wouldn't go back to the farm. But while I was trying to decide I must have gone to sleep because I don't remember anything more.

But it turned out I never shifted from Mrs Clegg's, not for a long time, as I'll tell you.

The first morning I stayed in bed, and I thought nobody could be any better off than I was. It was a good bed to lie on after the sofa on the farm,

I had my chips, and there wasn't a job I wouldn't take on if I got the chance. But for a while I was going to have a good time just kicking around. I laughed when I heard Mrs Clegg chase her old man out of the house, and I tried to get an earful when I heard somebody out on the landing-place. There was only two other rooms upstairs, but Mrs Clegg hadn't said if they were let. I didn't see anyone that first morning, anyhow, because every time I told myself I'd better get up, I thought, No, it's too good where I am, though once I sat up to look out the window, and the weather was good, but there was nothing much to see except the butcher's backyard on one side and the wall of the warehouse on the other, and Mrs Clegg's washing hung out in between.

It wasn't until late that I'd had my tea and was all flossied up, and by that time there was no one about the house except the little girl, and she was hanging the budgie's cage on a nail on the front of the house. She was the thinnest kid you ever saw, with legs like sticks and a real old woman's face. She said her name was Fanny and asked me what mine was. So I told her to call me Bill, and she said:

'Does money grow on trees, Bill?'

'It might do,' I said. 'I couldn't say for certain.'

'We've got a tree,' she said, 'so can you mind the house while I go and look.'

'No,' I said, 'but hang on until tomorrow, and we'll both have a look. See you mind the house,' I said, 'because I don't want anyone to break into my room.'

Then just along the street I passed Mr Clegg. He had a waistcoat on over his flannel, and he was leaning up against the wall of a pub talking to the taxi-drivers. I bought a newspaper, and one of the taxi-drivers asked me if I wanted to take a double, so I took a half-dollar one, even though all the good ones were filled up. Because taxi-drivers are good blokes to keep in with, they usually know of a house to take you to if you don't happen to know of one yourself. And I thought I ought to stand Mr Clegg a drink, but what with the taxi-drivers there were too many around, so I put it off until another time. You could tell by the look of him he got a good few anyhow.

There wasn't much I could do before it was time to eat, so I went into the park to read the paper, but instead I watched an old man who was having a wash in the fountain. After he'd finished washing he looked in the water and spent a lot of time combing his hair, then he came past my seat and asked me if I'd done with the paper, so I said I had and gave it to him. But a young joker got up from the next seat and said he wished I hadn't done that, because he was going to ask me for the paper himself.

'Stiff luck,' I said.

He said he'd had a date with a sheila the Sunday before, but she hadn't turned up. It was right there where he'd been sitting, and he'd been waiting at the same time every day ever since. She might have put an ad in the paper, he said. I felt like telling him to forget it, but he was taking it pretty bad, so instead I asked him if he'd come and eat, because by the look of his clothes I'd have said he was up against it.

I shouted him a bob dinner and I could tell by the way he ate he was in need of a binder, but he never said whether he was out of a job or not. He just wanted to tell me what a great sheila she was that had let him down, so to shut him up I said we'd go to the flicks. But it was a mistake, because after the lights went out a girl came and sat in the seat next to me, and when I put my leg over her way she was willing. I pushed and she pushed back, and it wasn't long before I had hold of her hand, and what with holding her hand and wondering how I'd get rid of this fellow Sam if she looked any good when the lights went up, I never had much idea what the first part of the programme was about.

Well, the lights went up and she certainly looked good. She gave me the once over and maybe she thought I didn't look so bad either, but she could tell I was with Sam and Sam didn't look so good. I said if he liked he could take my tin and go out and roll himself one, but he said no, he could wait till after. He just wanted to talk about his sheila, she was a bit like the girl in the big picture he said. It made me properly narked but I hadn't got the heart to tell him off. Me and the girl got to work again while the big picture was on and this Sam was that thick in the head I bet he never guessed a thing, but as soon as the lights went up she went for her life while Sam was saying he'd have a fag if it was O.K. with me. So I gave him my tin, and I thought that's that, but I could have crowned him all the same. He wanted to get going about his sheila again but I said, 'To hell with all that, let's go and have a drink.'

So we got in a pub and we both had a good few in by closing time, and then they said we could carry on upstairs if we liked, so it wasn't long before we were properly canned. Sam talked about his sheila and once I'd got canned I didn't mind. I didn't mind doing all the paying either, though I spent a lot more money than I intended, and when it was about ten o'clock we took a taxi and went to a dance that Sam knew about. It was a pretty flash turnout with a lot of streamers and balloons, but what with Sam looking like a proper bum and the both of us being canned they wouldn't let us in. So we went to another place that was a lot tougher, and nobody said anything, not even when we started butting in on other blokes' sheilas. We got a couple of them to come outside for a spot, but they went crook when we spilt beer over their skirts, and in the end there was nothing doing. And so far as I was concerned it didn't matter because I was that canned I wouldn't have had a hope of doing anything. And I don't remember getting home to Mrs Clegg's but I was there the next morning when I woke up.

It was Sunday and the church bells were ringing, but after the night before I didn't feel so hot until I had a drink out of a bottle I found in my pants' pocket. Then I felt better, and I looked out of the window and the weather was still good, and Mrs Clegg's washing was still hanging on the line. I thought I might go and lie on the beach in the sun, but Fanny came and asked if I'd go and look at the tree to see if there was any money.

There was nobody about upstairs but Mrs Clegg was in the kitchen, and her old man had put his chair on the bricks outside and was reading the paper. Fanny and I went down to the fence where there was a pretty good smell, because a heap of sawdust out of the butcher's shop was over the other side. We couldn't see any money hanging on the tree and Fanny was disappointed, but I said maybe it was the wrong time of the year. Fanny said perhaps it had fallen in the grass, it would if it was ripe, she said. So we looked and I had my fingers on a sixpence in my pocket, and then I thought no, I'll give the kid a real thrill, I'll make it a bob. So I dropped the bob and so help me if it wasn't the sovereign the old lady had given me on the farm. I put my foot out but Fanny was too quick. She didn't know what to make of it but she wouldn't let me have a look, and before I could stop her she'd run up the bricks singing out that it was a money-tree. Her old man looked over the top of his paper and held out his hand, but Mrs Clegg suddenly showed up and got in first. And then there was a proper hullabaloo, the two of them going it hammer and tongs, and Fanny howling and jumping up and down on the bricks.

'Come on, Fanny,' I said, 'those legs of yours will snap off at the knees if you're not careful.'

I got her to come back and we had another look, and I took jolly good care it was only a sixpence this time. Her old man wanted to take it off her but Mrs Clegg wouldn't let him, so there was another hullabaloo. And Fanny wanted to keep on looking but Mr Clegg said if he caught her near the tree again he'd tan her hide.

Well, I felt a bit sore over the sovereign, but I thought if Mrs Clegg put it towards buying a new glass eye I wouldn't mind so much. Fanny had just about decided I was her property and wanted me to play penny catches, but her mother came out and started to weed round a row of tomatoes she had growing up against the fence, and I said if she'd tell me where the spade was I'd make a proper job for her. Fanny went to get the spade but Mr Clegg came out and said he was going to do a bit of digging himself.

'*You're* going to do a bit of digging,' Mrs Clegg said, but he didn't say anything.

It was under the tree that he went to dig, and off and on he'd be down there for a good few weeks after.

I wished I'd gone to the beach because the sun was real hot and there wasn't a cloud. It had been a dry spring and everybody said it was going to be a hot summer. There was the yarn they always say about how the Maoris had said so. It was getting a bit late in the day to go off to the beach so I played penny catches with Fanny, but the ball kept on banging into the washing and in the end Mrs Clegg went crook, though she needn't have done because her clothes weren't as clean as all that. So then I told Fanny I hadn't any more time to go on playing, but it was really because I'd seen a smart-looking piece of goods drying her face and having a bo-peep out of the bedroom window, which was upstairs next to mine. I went up the stairs about six at a time and she was crossing the landing-place with only a sort of kimono-thing on. 'Hello,' I said, but she only said, 'How do you do,' and went inside and slammed the door of her room. She didn't look nearly so good as she'd looked through the window anyhow, she was a little piece that somehow made you think of a kid's doll and not my type at all. So of course I told myself I couldn't be worried.

I began to feel empty so I went down town and had some dinner in a place that was run by a Dalmatian. Being Sunday there wasn't much doing, so he brought out his two little boys to show me, though one was so shy he got behind his father's legs and only put his head out now and then. And when his missis brought the tucker he said how she wouldn't learn to speak English. You could only grin at her, though I talked to the kids and they were great kids, the sort of little blokes I wouldn't mind if I had myself.

'My wife thinks always of our country,' the Dally said. 'She says that if she learns to talk here I will not take her back to our country.'

'And you will?' I said.

'Yes I will,' he said. 'But first I must have a lot of money. My wife she wants us to go now but I say no. It is lonely for her when she will not talk, but she has her little boys and soon they will take her shopping which she will not go now, because she does not talk.'

Anyhow *he* talked, and I liked listening to him, and I'd grin at his wife now and then just to sort of include her in the conversation, and the kid that wasn't shy sat on a chair with his legs stuck out and took it all in. I thought they were a real nice family, I promised I'd go there again, and when I came out I was wishing in a way I was settled down myself, because here I was in a town all on my own, and that afternoon I felt a bit of a loose end. Sunday afternoons on the farm when there was nothing else doing I'd go and shoot pigeons away up in the bush, and I wouldn't feel as much on my own as I did now in a town full of houses and people. But it's no good letting those things get you down, so I went back to Mrs Clegg's to lie on my bed and read a True Story. I read them sometimes though the yarns are all a lot of baloney, nothing like real life at all. But I'd hardly got started when Fanny came in and I didn't shoo her out because I wanted to do a bit of fishing.

'Fanny,' I said, 'who lives here beside me?'

'Terry,' she said.

'Terry?' I said. 'Isn't there a lady?'

'That's Mrs Popeye,' she said.

'That's a funny name,' I said.

'Mr Popeye doesn't live here,' she said, 'because he's a sailor-man. But he comes sometimes.'

'I see,' I said. And I got the idea all right but I didn't have a chance to ask her any more because Mr Clegg came up and asked if I felt like having a drink. He'd had a shave and put on a collar, though without any tie.

'Yes,' I said. 'But can you get one?'

'Come on,' he said. 'And you clear away out of here,' he said to Fanny. 'Look at her legs,' he said.

'I've got nice legs,' Fanny said, and she pulled her dress up to her waist to show me.

'Of course you have,' I said. 'Only you want to be careful they don't snap off.'

Her old man told her off for pulling her dress up, and we left her talking to the budgie which was kidding to itself in a piece of looking-glass. But all the way along to the pub Mr Clegg kept on about her legs.

'You look at them,' he said, 'it just shows you the way a working man gets it put across him every time.'

'Too right,' I said, but I wasn't anxious to start talking politics.

We went along to the pub where I'd seen Mr Clegg the day before and the pub-stiff that was on the door told us to go upstairs where there was quite a few, including all sorts, men and women. And we hadn't been there long when the barman got the tip, and we were all shoved up a little stairway on to the next floor. But that was the only scare, nobody was caught, and by the time it was dark the pair of us had a good few in, and each time I paid because there never was a time when Mr Clegg even looked like paying. And things being what they were I was beginning to feel like calling it a day, only just then a bloke came in that was a cobber of Mr Clegg's.

He was a cook off a boat too, a tremendous big man, but dressed more like a stoker in dungarees that would hardly button across his chest. He didn't have any singlet on underneath and his chest was all hair, and when he'd had a few drinks he started to sweat, and you could see it oozing out and running down under the hair until it soaked into his trousers. I shouted him and Mr Clegg, and he shouted back, and then I got talking to the barman and dropped out while the cook went on shouting Mr Clegg. The both of them talked politics and the cook sounded a good deal more bolshy than Mr Clegg was. And then a tall bloke joined in. He'd been sitting there on his own listening, and he started off by saying he didn't see anything wrong with capitalism. Well, that got the cook going good and proper, he paid for whiskies for the three of them and they went on and had one after another, the cook always paying and calling the big nobs that run the world for all the names he could think of. Me and the barman just listened, and after the cook had spent about a quid him and Mr Clegg went off together, and then the tall bloke came over and asked the barman what the cook's name was. But the barman said he didn't know.

'Come on,' he said, 'you know.'

'I don't know,' the barman said.

'You heard what he was talking about?'

'Sure,' the barman said.

'He's a bolshy.'

'Maybe,' the barman said.

'What do you reckon's wrong with capitalism?' the tall bloke said, but the barman wouldn't answer. 'What's the name of his cobber?' he said.

'I don't know,' the barman said.

Well, instead of saying anything more he went downstairs and the barman winked at me and said he was a demon, and I wasn't surprised because I'd picked there was something wrong with him right from the start. But it wasn't long before he came back with the boss.

'Terry,' the boss said, 'you know the name of that big fellow.'

'I don't know,' the barman said.

'You better tell.'

'No, I don't know,' the barman said, and considering the way they were picking on him I felt like having a go at cleaning up the pair of them.

Anyhow the boss saw it was no good so they went out and I asked the barman to have a drink. You could see it had shaken him up and we both had double gins. And seeing there was nobody else there just then he said we'd have another two on the house. It would be good for his cough, he said. He had an awful cough. And once having got started we kept on for quite a while. He was a lot older than me, with one of those hard faces all covered with wrinkles like Aussies have, but I sort of had a feeling he was a decent bloke.

'You've got a hard dial,' I said, 'but I bet you've got a kind heart.'

'I'll say,' he said.

'I bet you have,' I said. But of course I was stunned. 'Anyhow,' I said, 'isn't your name Mr O'Connor?'

'Sure,' he said.

Well, I wanted to tell him I'd been sort of trying to place his face right from the jump, and now I'd suddenly remembered. One time when I was working on a farm he brought out a racehorse to graze. It was a good while ago but I knew he was the same bloke, though I didn't get the chance to make certain because a crowd came in and he had to get busy. He pushed me over one more double gin which he only pretended to ring up on the peter, but there wasn't a chance to talk. So I thought I'd better shove off or I'd be ending up tight as I was the night before. I said so long to the barman and that I'd be seeing him, and it was only when I was trying to walk straight along the street, just to see how tight I was, that I remembered the boss had called him Terry. Which made me pull up while I tried to figure out whether he might be the same bloke as Fanny's Terry. I thought maybe I'd go back and find out, but instead I kept on along the street to find out how tight I was. I could walk straight all right but it didn't mean anything, because sometimes you get head-drunk, and sometimes you get leg-drunk, and there's a lot of difference between the two.

I thought I'd better cry off the booze for a bit, so all next week I went to the beach. It was too good to miss, specially as it was so baking hot round the streets. The asphalt went soft and there were marks of motor tyres all over the road, and away in front of you the heat made it look as if water was lying on the road, so you'd naturally think of the beach. And it was certainly great to be out there. I'd go on a tram as far as it went, and then I'd walk on to a quiet bit of beach that I knew about.

Most days nobody'd come around, but I had company, because the first morning on a tram I met a bloke named Ted who was doing the same as myself. I'd meet him every day, and I'd always bring a couple of riggers and he'd buy some buns, and it was certainly nice to have his company. He never had much to say so I couldn't make out hardly anything about him, though I thought he looked a bit of a hard-shot. He wasn't a rangy specimen like me, no, he was nuggety, with one of those faces that is flat on the front of your head. And being dark he didn't get sunburnt nearly so bad as I did. To kick off with we'd fool about in the water, and if there was nobody around we wouldn't worry about any togs. Then we'd fool about on the beach and lie in the sand, and when it was time for the buns and the beer they'd go down well, and in the afternoon we'd just about go to sleep. It was a great life I can tell you, though coming home in the tram we'd be properly tired out, which is what lying in the sun always does to you. Ted'd say, so long, see you again tomorrow, and I'd be too tired for anything except a feed and a talkie, and if the talkie wasn't any good I'd just about go to sleep. And one night the joker sitting next to me had to poke me in the ribs because I was snoring.

Well, it was like that for a whole week, and some nights my sunburn was that bad I could hardly sleep. By Sunday I thought I'd better give it a rest, but the weather was still holding out so I thought no, the going's good, I'll give it one more pop.

And that day Ted was there as usual but he had his girl with him. I didn't feel like butting in but he called me over and gave me a knock-down, and she was certainly the goods, a good-looker and a great figure, sort of streamlined all over though you could tell she had a temper. She wasn't like Ted, she was a mag, and all the way along until we got to our beach she talked about how nice the water looked, and she'd make us stop to pick up shells and look in the pools to see things. But it wasn't long before we were undressed and in the water, and nearly all morning we had a great time just fooling about. Mavis was the girl's name and she'd brought a thermos and plenty of sandwiches, and she made me have some. I'd brought my riggers as usual but Mavis wouldn't have any, because she said drink only brought sorrow into people's lives. Ted said he was willing to take the risk so we drank the beer between us, and then Ted lay on his back with his togs rolled down and said this sort of life would do him for keeps. Mavis kept on looking his way and you could tell she was nuts on him, but I knew there was something wrong because she couldn't help picking on him every chance she got.

'Yes,' she said, 'you can be a sand-boy every day while I go and work in that damn shop.'

'Forget it, kid,' Ted said.

'Listen to him, Bill,' she said. 'The first time we made a date he turned up tight in a taxi. He was broke too, and I had to pay five shillings for the fare.'

And instead of saying anything to that Ted just rolled over and curled himself round Mavis.

'Don't make out you're a smoodger,' she said, 'because you're not.'

'If anyone knows anything better than this sun lead me to it,' Ted said.

'He's a baby over the cold, Bill,' Mavis said. 'Last winter I knitted him a woolly and he used it to go to bed in, with his underpants on too. And what's the good of a man when he goes to bed like that?'

Ted rolled away from her then, he lay on his side with his back to the pair of us.

'Look at the sea,' he said.

But Mavis couldn't stop herself from trying to put nasty ones across him, though I bet she knew she was making him feel sore.

'Yes,' she said, 'it's all right for you, but what's a hot day in that damn shop. It only means us girls have to let our stockings down to try and keep cool. If they didn't let you go home at night you might just as well be in gaol.'

'You'll get over it, kid,' Ted said.

'Listen to him, Bill,' Mavis said. 'He works about three months a year, so where would he be if he hadn't got me?'

'You get your money's worth sweetie,' Ted said.

'Listen to him, Bill,' Mavis said. 'That's what he says. When I knitted him a woolly and he used it to go to bed in.'

Well, Ted got up and went away and tried to see how far he could throw stones up the cliff. And Mavis kept on talking, but I pretended to go to sleep and when I gave a few snores she didn't say anything more. But I looked and she was crying, though when I looked again she was reading a True Romance, but it wasn't long before she gave that up and just stretched herself out in the sun. Ted came back and stretched himself out too, with his arm round Mavis, and we must have all gone to sleep because for a long time nobody moved or said anything.

But when we were sitting up and talking again Mavis must have temporarily got all the dirt out of her system, because instead of picking on Ted she made us laugh with yarns about people she served in the shop, and the way they talked and carried on, and what she'd do with the money if she ever won an Art Union. And afterwards we all went in for another swim, and Ted said he'd bet me I wasn't game to swim round a buoy that was anchored a good way out from the shore. So I took him on, but when I was out there hanging on to the buoy for a rest I got a bit of a surprise, because they'd both gone out of the water and were just about dressed. I swam back fast, but by the time I touched bottom they'd climbed nearly to the top of the cliff, and I could hear Ted swearing at Mavis and telling her to come on. And when I sang out for them to wait Ted sang out that they'd wait at the tram.

Well, I didn't hurry myself. If they waited at the tram that would be all right, but if they didn't that would be all right too. Because I thought it wouldn't be long before Mavis was picking on Ted again, and I wasn't anxious to be there when she started. And it was only when I'd finished dressing that I found out my money was gone.

Of course it was a knock and I certainly felt bad. I thought well, I hope poor old Mavis gets her whack, but Ted being the sort of joker I'd gathered he was I didn't suppose she would. She probably wasn't in the joke. What's money anyhow, I thought. I'd been in town just over a week and had a good time, even if I hadn't had any luck so far as a girl was concerned. To hell with Ted and Mavis, I thought.

But it was hard all the same. I thought I could go into every shop in town until I found out where Mavis worked. But I knew I wouldn't do that. Ted might be no good but I could tell she was nuts on him, and it'd be rocking it into her properly to put the police on to him. I'd never be able to prove anything anyhow, and my idea of the johns is that a man wants to keep well away from them no matter what goes wrong.

My sugar's gone, I thought, that's all there is to it. Now I've got to look for a job.

Well, it wasn't the first time I'd been broke, and I knew I'd feel better if I went home and slept on it. The main thing was to stop myself from doing any more thinking. I didn't have the price of a tram fare because Ted had left me a skinner, so I started to walk into town. But I didn't hurry myself, and I kept stopping to look at everything I saw going on in the streets just to keep my mind occupied.

And as it turned out it wasn't long before I got a notion. I went past a house that was hidden behind some trees and just over the fence there was a garden. So I walked up and down and when there was nobody in sight I hopped over the fence and pulled up a plant that looked as if it might be growing into a little tree. I wrapped it in a sheet of newspaper I was keeping because of the acceptances, and I'd only gone a few more streets when I met a lady that looked as if she might do a bit of business.

'Excuse me lady,' I said, 'but maybe you're interested in gardening.'

'Yes,' she said, 'I am.'

'Well,' I said, 'I'm off a boat and I got this in Jamaica.'

'Why,' she said, 'it looks like a something or other.'

'I don't know what you call them,' I said, 'but I've never seen them out here, and you never saw such a pretty flower.'

So she asked me if it had got long red petals.

'No,' I said, 'the flower's blue-coloured and as big as my head. You don't see many of them even in Jamaica,' I said, 'so I reckon it ought to be worth a good five bob out here.'

So then she said she hoped I wasn't telling her a story.

'Oh no, lady,' I said, 'I wouldn't do that.'

We had a bit more barney and finally she took it for three and six, and soon as I'd got the sugar in my pocket I didn't lose any time in shifting along. But I didn't take a tram, no, I kept on walking and slowed down again after a while, and got into town pretty late, so although I was feeling a bit empty I went straight home to bed and was lucky enough to get to sleep before I had a chance to start doing any more thinking.

And next morning I woke early and the weather still looked good, though of course I didn't think it looked quite so good as it had other mornings. I hadn't anything to eat but I made a cup of tea, then I thought I'd better get down town to see about a job. I looked at the paper in the Library but there was nothing doing, and I spent the morning going round the registry offices but there was nothing doing in any of those places either. And in the afternoon it was just the same. I tried all the registry offices again and when it was time for the afternoon papers to come out I waited outside where they always stick up the front page to let people see the ads. But I could hardly get near for the crowd, and when I did get a bo-peep there weren't any jobs that I thought I'd have a chance of getting. So I went inside to look at the file, because I'd missed seeing the results of the double I had on with the taxi-driver, and what with going to the beach all the week before, and having plenty of chips in my pocket, I hadn't worried. Well, I'd picked a first and a second, and the second had only got beat by a head. It was the first time I'd ever got so close and I got a bit excited, because I thought if I could get that close I could pick two winners, so I decided I'd see the taxi-driver and take another instead of breaking into my three and six, which I hadn't done even though I was feeling pretty empty inside.

But first I hung round the streets a bit longer, standing on the corners to roll cigarettes and watch the crowd, though seeing I have my itchy feet

I never can stand still for very long, particularly when everyone else is on the move. Then I went up to see the taxi-driver but he wasn't on the stand. His cobbers said he'd be back soon so I waited but he didn't turn up, and I had to go into the pub because I wanted to pick up a bit of counter-lunch. I saw Mr Clegg there with a half-handle in front of him and he looked as if he was making it last a good long while, but I dodged about in the crowd to keep him from seeing me and asked for a half-handle myself. The eats were late coming out and I had to make my drink last a lot longer than I thought I would, but when the trays did come I was one of the first to be in, and I finished up by putting away quite a good feed. The barman took my half-handle to fill it again but I said, 'Wait a minute, where can I see Terry?'

'Terry?' he said, 'Terry's left here.'

'All right,' I said, 'fill her up. Where's he working now?' I said.

The barman didn't know, so I had my drink and came out. The taxi-driver was there and I took the double, and he said I was lucky because it was a new chart he'd just got out. There were hardly any taken certainly, so I picked a good one, but at the last moment I decided I wouldn't cough up the sugar just then. The taxi-driver didn't look any too pleased but he said 'O.K. boy, I'm a sport.'

Then I didn't know what to do. I didn't know whether to blow in a bob on a talkie or not, so I put off trying to decide. I thought I'd go and have a lie-down on my bed. But Fanny was just taking the budgie inside, and she showed me the way it could swing a ping-pong ball that was tied to the top of its cage. She'd bought it with the money from the money tree, she said.

'The old man isn't home yet, Bill,' she said, 'we can go and look.'

'No,' I said, 'not just now.'

But she pulled me by the hand, so I gave in and we had to walk on the ground that Mr Clegg had dug to get under the tree, but it was only a tray bit that I dropped. Fanny danced up and down and went to show her mother and I went upstairs and when the old man came home I heard them having a row. And later on I looked out of the window and he was down there digging.

But being all on my pat up there that evening somehow gave me the dingbats properly. I couldn't decide what to do to fill in the time, and I couldn't keep my mind off thinking about a job. I tried reading my True Story but it was no good. I'd just lie on my bed but that was no good either, and I'd have to keep getting up to walk up and down. I'd stop in the middle of the floor to roll a cigarette and listen to them downstairs. I'd think, my

God I've got to have someone to talk to, but even after I'd turned out the light and had my mind on the doorknob I'd go back and just flop on the bed. But the last time I flopped I must have dozed off, because I woke up lying in my clothes, and I wondered where the hell I was. I'd been dreaming, and I still seemed to be in the dream, because there wasn't one sound I could hear no matter how hard I listened. Then somebody started coughing and I knew where I was, but next minute I was back in the dream again, and I kept on dreaming and waking up right until it began to get light, though the last time I dropped off I slept a long time and never dreamt a thing.

It doesn't matter what sort of a night you have, things are always different in the morning. I didn't waste any time hopping out of bed because I didn't want to give myself a chance to start doing any more thinking. And I didn't have much of a chance anyhow, because while I was mucking about getting my bed made, I heard Mrs Clegg come upstairs and start giving somebody a tongue-banging. It developed into a real ding-dong row, and so help me if the other voice didn't sound like Terry O'Connor's, and so far as I could tell he was giving just about as good as he got.

'Shut the door,' was the last thing he sang out. And Mrs Clegg sang out, 'Shut it yourself.'

So I went out to get an eyeful and there was Terry sitting up in bed reading the paper.

'Gee,' I said, 'so this is where you hang out.'

'Hello boy,' he said, and I went and sat on his bed and said I'd heard he'd left the pub.

'That's right,' he said.

'You know, Terry,' I said, 'I remember you. You remember Mr Fletcher's farm?'

'Sure,' he said.

'Well,' I said, 'I remember when you brought out a horse.'

'That's right,' he said. 'Well,' he said, 'it looks like another scorcher,' and he threw the paper away and did a big stretch, and we yarned for a bit and I asked him who the dame was that lived next door.

'That's our Maggie,' he said.

'She's not my type,' I said.

'No,' Terry said, 'nor mine either,' and he said he wouldn't have her on if she was hung with diamonds. 'Well,' he said, 'I suppose a man's got to rise and shine.'

'I've got to go and look for a job,' I said. And Terry said he was looking for a job too, and while he was getting dressed I looked in the paper but there didn't seem to be any jobs going. We went down town together anyhow, and I thought it was certainly great to have a bit of company. We passed a coffee and sandwich place and Terry asked if I felt like a bite.

'Not specially,' I said, 'but I'll have one.'

So we had coffee and sandwiches, and I paid because the girl was waiting and Terry just went on eating. And when we came out we ran right into the taxi-driver that had the double chart.

'Hello Terry,' he said, 'how's things?'

'A box of birds,' Terry said, and the taxi-driver brought out his chart. But Terry said he was stiff because the one he would have picked had been taken. 'Too bad,' the taxi-driver said, and I told Terry the double I'd picked, and he said I'd beaten him to it and I'd be in the money there was nothing surer.

So that was all right, Terry made me think my luck was going to be in, and we went round all the registry offices together, but there was nothing doing. So I asked Terry if he couldn't go to his Union, but he said it wouldn't be any good.

'I had something to say about the Union boss last meeting,' he said, 'and that's why I'm on the street. That and not letting that bloody dee bulldoze me.'

'Gee,' I said, 'that's hard.'

But Terry said it was best to forget it, and I asked him to come to the Dalmatian's for a feed. So we went along and the place was pretty full, but the Dally was working the peter and he remembered me.

'You are back again,' he said. 'That is good for me.'

'Good for me, too,' I said, 'because I want to eat.'

'Good,' he said, 'good. It is good to eat.'

'Too right,' I said.

Well, we had three courses and it certainly felt good afterwards, and after we'd rolled cigarettes I told Terry to wait because I wanted to speak to the Dally. Terry said O.K. and I barged into the kitchen and the Dally didn't look any too pleased.

'What do you want?' he said.

'Well,' I said, sort of embarrassed a bit.

'Be quick,' he said.

'Well,' I said, 'I suppose you couldn't give me a job.'

'No,' he said, 'I cannot give you a job. Already I have too many to pay. They are not too many for the work, but they are too many to pay.'

'Yes,' I said, 'but I thought if anybody turned it in.'

'You think somebody will walk out,' he said. 'But nobody will walk out. It is always easy to walk out but today it is hard to walk in, so today nobody will walk out even if it is easy.'

Then his missis put her head in the door and he told me to wait a minute. And soon as he'd gone the cook, who was a fat little joker and walked like a proper queen, came over and asked if it was a job I was after.

'You come back tomorrow,' he said. And when I asked him why tomorrow he said the bloke they had washing dishes out in the pantry would have to go to the quack.

'What's he got?' I said.

'You know,' the cook said. 'He showed me this morning and he's got it pretty bad.'

'Good,' I said, 'and thanks for the tip.'

And then the boss came back. 'You are still here,' he said, 'but I cannot give you any work.'

'Never mind,' I said.

'You can pay now,' he said. 'One dinner, one shilling,' and he held out his hand.

'No,' I said, 'two dinners, two shillings, and I'll pay you tomorrow.'

And he certainly didn't look any too pleased over that, but I walked out the door and picked up Terry, and the Dally came after us right on to the street but he never said anything. Then just to get out of the streets for a bit the pair of us went down on the wharves, and halfway along one wharf we watched while a lot of wharfies worked on a boat that was unloading guano.

'There's your chance,' Terry said. 'You get extra pay for working that stuff.'

'What about you?' I said.

'No,' he said, 'the dust's no good to me.'

I asked a man and he told me to go on board and ask, and I went on board but I couldn't find the man I had to ask for. I looked down the hold and the wharfies were shovelling the stuff into bags but you could hardly see them for dust. They looked as if they hadn't got a stitch on, and they were sweating properly and the dust was sticking to the sweat, and it was certainly a sight because all you could see was a tangle of bodies nearly the same colour as the guano, except that the colour was darker where the sweat was collecting and running down. The stuff smelt like the bird-dung it was too, it got up my nose and all over me just looking down, so I went back to Terry.

'I can't find the man,' I said, 'but the job don't look any catch.'

'I bet it don't,' Terry said, and we walked on to the end of the wharf and sat on the edge with our legs hanging down. And it was great to be sitting there too. For the first time for days a wind had got up and you could sit in the sun without feeling too hot. There were big woolly clouds in the sky, and blowing up against the tide the wind was making the sea choppy, and I thought no man whose belly was full could have said it wasn't good to be alive. I wondered if Terry was thinking the same way, but a man never does ask those sort of questions, so instead I asked him if he'd have a smoke, and he made one but it made him cough. He threw it away and I asked him hadn't he got rid of his cold.

'It's not a proper cold,' he said.

'No?' I said.

'It was the war,' he said.

I didn't say anything but I thought it was rotten. Terry looked hard and tough, but his face was sunk in, and maybe the wrinkles didn't improve it either, and there was only enough of him to cover his bones and nothing over. But when things are rotten like that what can a man say? But it sort of made it not so good to be just sitting there on the end of the wharf, and so help me if I didn't begin to start thinking about how I was broke, which I didn't want to do.

'Come on,' I said. And I wanted to do the registry offices again but Terry said once a day was enough and we had an argument, and in the end I said I was going to do them anyhow, so Terry came along and waited outside. And so help me if there wasn't a job going at the second one I tried. It was a farm job a good way out of town and you had to pay your own fare, but I knew if I took it on I'd get there all right. But I somehow just couldn't say I'd take it on, and it was mainly because I couldn't help thinking of Terry waiting for me in the street outside. So I got the woman to promise she'd keep it open for me if I came back inside a couple of hours. And I never said a word to Terry but when he stopped outside the next registry place I said no, because I'd got to go back to the last place later on. So to pass the time we went and had a lie-down in the park and Terry put his hat over his face and went to sleep.

But I didn't feel like sleeping. I kept looking at Terry and I kept wondering what the hell would become of him, and I couldn't make out why he wasn't racing horses any more. He looked sick anyhow, and I was practically certain he was a skinner. Of course it was none of my business, but I thought he was a decent bloke and it was certainly nice to have his company. I thought damn it all, it's none of my business, but I couldn't make my mind up all the same. Then while I was wondering what the

hell was wrong with me there was a joker came and sat on the grass right
alongside.

'I say mate,' he said, 'could you give me the lend of a bob?'

'No,' I said, 'and you needn't wake my cobber up.'

'Sorry mate,' he said, and he went and sat down further off.

Well, I thought that showed a sort of nice feeling so I went over.

'I'm on the beach myself,' I said, 'but I can make it a deener.'

'Never mind, mate,' he said.

'No,' I said, 'you take the dough.'

'God bless you mate,' he said.

'That's all right,' I said.

Then he got talking and he said he felt like calling me Bill, because I
reminded him of a mate of that name. It was quite a yarn he got telling
me. This Bill was a pretty good mate he said, and when they were up
against it he didn't mind going shares with any money he got. Though
later on it was different, it was the joker telling me the yarn that usually
did the shelling out. He didn't mind, he said, though he reckoned he
shelled out a lot more than Bill ever did. And Bill would admit that. Bill'd
say never mind, because he'd make it up when his ship came home. Well,
it finally turned out that once when he was away in the country looking
for a job he read in the paper how Bill had won a prize in an Art Union.
And it made him think. He'd been thinking he'd like to make the break
with Bill if he could without letting him down, so now was a good
opportunity. He was up against it at the time and Bill had promised to
make it O.K. with him when his ship came home, but he had the feeling
that a man can say those things, but it's different when you actually have
the dough. So he thought of a stunt, he thought he'd do Bill one last good
turn. He sent him a letter and said he'd heard of a job away down south,
so he'd decided to go and so long and good luck, and he never mentioned
a thing about the Art Union. But he'd hardly posted the letter when he
got one from Bill saying so long and good luck because he was getting out
of the country and sailing that night. And Bill never mentioned a thing
about the Art Union either.

'It just shows you,' he said.

'Yes,' I said.

'A man wants a mate that won't let him down,' he said.

'Yes,' I said. But I wasn't paying much attention because Terry had
woke up.

'I've got to go,' I said.

'Wait a minute, mate,' he said.

'No,' I said, 'I've got to go.'

'Listen mate,' he said.

'No, sorry,' I said, and I went back to Terry and we went down town again and Terry waited while I went in and told the woman I wasn't taking the job. When I came out I told Terry there was nothing doing and he said I was stiff.

'It's O.K.,' I said, and when I turned into the first pub we came to Terry said he knew of a better one, and it was certainly a good one for a feed. The counter-lunch had just come out, and for the price of our half-handles we put away just about as much as we could hold. Then we had another two half-handles which meant I hadn't a razor left. Terry said let's go, and to finish up the day there was nothing to do except kick around the streets. We'd stand in shop doorways and Terry'd pipe off everyone that went past, and outside the picture theatres he'd make me wait to watch people getting out of their cars.

'See that old duchess,' he'd say, 'she wants you to look at her now she's got her feathers pruned, but when she wakes up in the morning she won't look so hot, she won't want anybody looking at her then.'

'I bet she won't,' I'd say, and I'd forgot about being broke thinking what a funny joker Terry was. He didn't seem to be worrying about anything, and we carried on joking all the way up to Mrs Clegg's.

But when we got to the top of the stairs it was different, because all Terry's gear was in a heap outside his door and the door was locked. And Terry got excited and said he'd bust in the door. But I said he'd better not, he could doss in with me, I said, and have it out with Mrs Clegg in the morning. So while I made us a cup of tea he put his things in my room, and then we managed to get pretty comfortable in the bed even though it was a pretty tight fit.

Terry didn't waste any time going right off to sleep either, but I couldn't get to sleep. After all, considering the two of us were broke, and what with turning down a job, a man would have been lucky to get to sleep without doing any thinking. It was one of those hot nights too, and I started to roll round and woke Terry up. So I tried to lie still but when I got the cramp I thought no, this is no good. I waited until Terry was snoring again and then I managed to get out without disturbing him. I went and leaned out the window and I could see Fanny's money tree in the moonlight, and maybe that's what gave me the notion how to pick up a little money before morning. I got into my clothes and borrowed a pair of sandshoes that were among Terry's gear, and out in the street it was nice and quiet and a lot cooler. And a clock said it was going on for one o'clock.

I did a long trek out to one of the suburbs and then I didn't waste any time getting round the back of the houses to clean up any money that had been left for the milkman. Some places I couldn't find any billy, or a dog would bark and put the wind up me properly, but I kept on until I got nearly ten bob all told. Then it wasn't so good doing the long trek back again, and I couldn't stop myself from worrying a bit over pinching money. But I thought when a man's in a jam he oughtn't to let himself be worried, and besides, there were the two of us to consider. Then when I got back to Mrs Clegg's I knew as soon as I was inside the room that Terry was awake. So when I got back into bed I said I'd had to do a job for myself, and when I was nearly asleep Terry said that sort of job didn't usually take several hours to do.

'Oh, I don't know,' I said, 'they say a dog will travel five miles.'

'No,' Terry said, 'more than that.'

Well, you mightn't believe it, but I woke up early feeling just like a box of birds. And it was certainly great to have somebody to talk to, though Terry didn't look any too good so I told him to stay in bed, and while the kettle was boiling I went out to buy him a newspaper, and we looked at the jobs but there didn't seem to be any going. So Terry sat up and read the news out while we had our tea. Then I told him I'd be back in a minute, and I went downstairs and barged right into the kitchen when Mrs Clegg was getting the breakfast.

'Mrs Clegg,' I said, 'Terry's shifted his gear into my room.'

'Then he can shift it out again,' she said.

'No, it's stopping there,' I said, 'and I suppose you don't happen to have another bed.'

'Who's paying the rent?' she said, and I said I was.

'All right mister,' Mrs Clegg said, 'only it'll be extra for the room.'

'Good,' I said, 'but what about the bed?'

Well, we fixed it up. Mrs Clegg said we could have Fanny's bed and Fanny could sleep on the floor. And seeing it was just a stretcher we could fold it up for more room during the day if we liked. I said wasn't it a bit tough on Fanny, but Fanny jumped about and said she *wanted* to sleep on the floor.

So that was all right, and when I went back to Terry there was Mrs Popeye sitting on the bed in her kimono-thing.

'Our Maggie's come to see us,' Terry said.

'Good,' I said. 'How are you Maggie?'

'I'm feeling fit,' she said, and the way she sort of slowly blinked her eyes made me think of a kid's doll.

'We know what you're fit for,' Terry said.

'That's right,' Maggie said, and she asked how was her back hair.

'Bitch,' Terry said, and he went on reading the paper.

'That's no way to talk to a lady,' Maggie said. 'Me being a married lady, too.'

Well, Terry said something pretty rude to her then but she didn't seem to mind. What with her fringe she certainly looked like a sort of cheap doll, though she showed real rabbit's teeth when she giggled.

'Fancy you two boys sleeping here together,' she said.

'That's all right Maggie,' I said.

'Yes,' she said, 'two's always better than one if you don't like a crowd.'

'I don't get you, Maggie,' I said, but just then Terry hit her whack over the head with the paper.

'Get out,' he said.

But Maggie didn't seem to mind. She said she'd be seeing us again and cleared off to her room, and I told Terry I wouldn't mind trying her out even though she wasn't my type, though her being married made a bit of difference. And Terry said she was no more married than he was, and anyhow he wouldn't have her on if she were hung with diamonds.

I thought it was about time I was getting along to the Dally's, so I told Terry I wanted to get down town but he needn't worry about getting up until he was ready, and I told him what I'd fixed with Mrs Clegg.

'I'll meet you at the Dally's at twelve o'clock for dinner,' I said, and I gave him half a dollar. And I went off whistling and feeling life was good when a man had a cobber like Terry to kick around with him, and maybe I was feeling good because I was thinking what a hell of a good joker I was. Though if I was I was kidding myself, because when all said and done I was only doing what I was to please myself, though it might have been a roundabout way of doing it.

I went along to the Dally's anyhow, and besides everything else the weather was still staying good, so I didn't leave off whistling, and the Dally was standing in front of the peter with his hands in his pockets. And he looked a bit worried.

'Hello,' I said, 'here I am and I'm after a job.'

He looked a bit more cheerful when he saw me but he looked suspicious.

'How did you know?' he said.

'Know what?' I said, sort of innocent.

'Never mind,' he said, 'but what do you know? Have you ever done the work?' he said.

'Sure,' I said, 'I've helped the cook in camps out in the bush.'

'It's not the same,' he said, but he told me to come with him and he took me out the back and told me to get busy on a bag of potatoes.

'Wait a minute,' I said, 'what are the wages and how long do I work?'

He didn't look too pleased over that, and instead of telling me he said it was no good me starting if I hadn't got an apron. But just then the cook came out of the kitchen and said he'd lend me an apron, so the Dally said what the hours and wages were, and then I got the apron from the cook and got busy on the spuds. And by the time I'd done a few benzine tins full time was getting on, and I had to get the sink all clear to be ready for the twelve o'clock rush. And when the whistles blew I went outside and Terry was waiting, so I gave him the works and told him to meet me when I knocked off. Then I had to go inside again and get busy, and what with being new to the work, and except for time off to get outside the two meals that were thrown in with the pay, I was kept busy without hardly a minute to spare right until the time I knocked off.

It was good having the job though. I came out feeling everything was O.K. and I met Terry and after we'd splashed on a talkie we went home and the two beds were all set, and Terry had cleaned up the room and made everything real tidy. There was hardly any room to move about certainly, but we didn't let that worry us, no, we made us cups of tea before we went to bed and I said it would be beer once I got my pay. And I wasn't long going to sleep, though I remember Terry woke me up several times with his coughing, and each time I could see the red dot of a cigarette in the dark, and I supposed he felt the need of it but it only made him cough all the worse.

Then each morning it was the same. I'd wake up feeling good and I'd put the kettle on and go and buy Terry a paper, and maybe Maggie would come hanging around cadging cigarettes, and sitting on the beds while she talked. And I wouldn't have minded taking it easy but I'd have to get off to the Dally's, and the morning I went after I'd given Terry my last half dollar I was a bit worried because it was still a good few days to pay-day, and Terry hadn't managed to pick up any sort of job. He just kicked about the town all day and came into the Dally's for his meals, and I didn't blame him if he wasn't trying much for a job because every day he looked more sick, and at night the way he coughed was something awful. I thought if I could get Maggie on her own I might ask her for the lend of a few bob, but I changed my mind because I thought of another stunt.

I got up before it was light and Terry never woke up, and this time I picked on a different locality. It was just getting daylight when I got there, and I picked on a street that ran off the main road from near a bus-stop, and sure enough the papers had been delivered. So I collected the lot and parked them in a heap in a shop doorway, then when the buses began to run I stood at the bus-stop with the papers under my arm, and it wasn't long before I'd nearly sold out. Of course I thought the stunt was a good deal more risky than the last one especially as a good few jokers came out of the street I'd been down and went very crook about their papers not being delivered. So between buses I put what was left back in the shop doorway, all except one which I kept for Terry, and then I had to do the long trek back because I didn't like the idea of being seen on a bus. And it took longer to do because I kept off the main road as much as I could. So it was late when I got back to Mrs Clegg's, and I only had time to look in and give Terry the paper and half a dollar and then get along to the Dally's. And I felt a bit windy all the rest of the day, and off and on for a few days after. But nothing happened, so I was lucky, and what with a half-dollar I borrowed from Maggie Terry didn't go short of any meals before pay-day.

But by the time my second pay-day came round I was well sick of working for the Dally. He was certainly tough to work for. He was tight with the hot water, and it was hard to make a job of the dishes when there was grease floating thick on the top of a sink full of dirty water. And there were things I saw that put me right off the tucker. If the pumpkin wouldn't cook the cook'd put it out on a big dish and work it through his fingers until he'd squeezed all the lumps out. And a man hardly had time to wipe off his own sweat, let alone roll a cigarette, so for a spell I used to go out the back and pretend to do a job for myself. But I couldn't do that too often, because if there wasn't any cleaning up to do there was always the spuds to keep ahead with. You had to put them in a machine and turn the handle to knock the worst of the skin off, and with the weather like it was it certainly made a man sweat doing the turning.

I never got much chance to talk to any of the girls either, and it was a disappointment because there were several good-lookers among them, and I wouldn't have minded trying to fix a date. But with all of us going for lick of our lives there'd only be time for a wisecrack now and then, though one of them began pinching me on the backside every chance she got. I didn't mind, though I'd rather have done the pinching myself, but the cook got my goat when he started trying to do the same thing. He was a tonk all right, just a real old auntie, and I'd met the sort a few times before. Right from the jump he'd come hanging round me if the boss wasn't about. He'd want me to let him do things for me, so just to keep him quiet I brought along a big bundle of washing which included Terry's as well, and so help me if instead of turning it down he didn't do the best job I've ever seen done. And it was then he started doing the pinching, which made it mighty awkward for me seeing I'd let him do the washing. And what with working alongside him every day he had me a bit worried, and what with the tough work I knew my feet would get itchy and I wouldn't be able to stick it out at the Dally's for long.

And I haven't mentioned it before but it was coming on to Christmas, and it worked out that pay-day came just the day before. So after I'd knocked off me and Terry had a spree up in our room. We got Maggie to come and be in as well, and so help me if she didn't know how to drink beer. And when the party was going properly we got Mr Clegg to come and be in too, and even his missis came and had a few. So that night we were all happy.

Then when I knocked off Boxing Day Terry was waiting to tell me I'd landed the double I had on with the taxi-driver. So that was a bit of real All Right. We decided to have another spree, which we did with the same crowd, and we were all happy a second time. Then the next morning I decided to turn in the job at the Dally's. What with my wages and winning the double, I had a fair bit of sugar in my pocket even though the two sprees had knocked me back considerably. And Terry said why not try my luck at the races. Well, the weather was still staying good as gold, and I thought it would be great to have a day out at the races with Terry. So I told the Dally a yarn about how I had to go home and see my mother because she was sick, and he let me finish up that evening. And when the cook found out I could hardly stop him from sort of getting all over me, and you can believe it or not but he went out and bought me a bunch of flowers. I thought he must have heard the yarn about my mother, but when I said something so help me if he didn't begin to cry. He hadn't bought the flowers for anyone except me, he said.

*   *   *

II

It turned out a bosker day the day I went out to the races with Terry.
Though it hadn't rained for so long, each day was just about as good as
the one before if you didn't mind the heat. I paid Mrs Clegg some rent in
advance just in case, then we went out in the tram, and there was a
tremendous crowd going, all flossied up for a day out and looking a lot
different from what they looked like coming home. Though, of course, I
wasn't thinking of that at the time. No, like everybody else, Terry and me
were out for the day, and you know the feeling. Terry looked good and
didn't cough much; he was funny the way he piped off people he saw in
the crowd, and I could have grabbed him round the waist and chucked
him up in the air, I was that full of beans I was sort of feeling that way.

But once we were on the course, which had all the grass burnt off by
the sun and looked hard going for the horses, it was easy to see that going
to the races wasn't exactly a holiday for Terry. He took it all very serious.
And if I said anything when he was standing in front of the Tote trying
to figure out what he'd back, he'd go crook and tell me not to be a nark.

Well, I said, put on ten bob and we'll go down and see them at the
barrier.

No, he said, you go.

No, I said, you come, too.

No, he said.

So I said O.K. and gave him a couple of smackers. And after he'd been
up to a window we went and got a good possie, and it wasn't long before
the balloon came down and then they were off. And it was certainly great
to watch; you could see the colours on the jockeys coming round the rail,
smooth as if they were birds flying, and I wished Terry had said what we
were on, but I felt that way I didn't care. It was only ten bob, anyhow,
and I got all worked up just out of the fun of the thing, though Terry didn't
look any different, not even when they were coming down the straight.
Of course, I thought he'd say if we were in the money once they'd passed
the post, but he never said anything, so I thought we must be stiff. He just
waited until the judge's placings went up, then we went down to the
birdcage to watch the horses coming in for the next race, and I forgot all
about being stiff because I was thinking what real good horses they looked.
There were a couple I thought I wouldn't have minded backing if I'd been
there on my own, but I thought no, Terry knows his stuff, so I'll just leave
it to him. But when the prelims were over and we were going back to the
Tote, Christ, if Terry didn't pull out four tickets that were duds.

Gee, four! I said. But I knew I'd torn it soon as I spoke, because Terry pretended he was too busy with his card to take any notice. So I just said too bad, and I gave him a couple more smackers.

And so help me if this time it didn't turn out that Terry was on a good thing. But, gee, I felt sore I'd opened my trap, because it turned out he'd gone easy with only ten bob and it was a pretty good divvy. All the same, we went and had a few beers on the strength of it, and I was feeling that sore I had to make Terry let me shout. Then next race he went in solid, but he had no luck, and after that it didn't matter what he did, he couldn't do anything right. And I was trying all the time to laugh it off, but there were times when I'd be feeling that bad at the sight of people coming away from the pay-out windows. Because they'd be sticking money in their pockets and looking that pleased with themselves. I knew I'd have looked the same way myself, but I couldn't help thinking it just showed what money does to you.

Then it came on to the last race and Terry hadn't had any luck, so I told him to take my last quid, though I didn't tell him it was the last. He didn't want to take it, but I had to make him, because I was still feeling sore over not keeping my mouth shut.

We better quit, he said.

No, I said, give it one last pop.

No, Terry said, better not.

Go on, I said, you take the sugar.

Well, Terry put the quid on, but we didn't go down to our usual possie. Terry said he was getting done in, and you could go round the side of the Tote where the pay-out windows were and see the finish of the race pretty good from there. So we stood on a seat under the trees and joked about how we'd be first to the pay-out windows, anyhow.

But I never took much interest in the race because I was busy getting an eyeful of a joker that was already waiting over by the pay-out windows. He looked a weak sort of joker, just a little runt, though all turned out in his Sunday best. And to begin with I thought he was canned, because fast as he was eating a sandwich it came out his mouth again. I told Terry to look, but just then they were coming down the straight, then when I turned round again the joker was coming over our way.

What won? he said, and he stood there with lumps of chewed bread coming out of his mouth.

Teatime won, Terry said, and I believe the joker would have fallen down if he hadn't grabbed us round the legs. So we got off the seat and sat him down, and for a while he looked real sick.

I knew he'd be tough, he said. I saw the way he lifted his feet in the prelim, he said, and he had me and Terry staring at a handful of tickets.

I put a tenner on, he said, and he'll pay that.

Maybe, Terry said, and then the figures went up and Teatime had paid a tenner sure enough.

Twenty tickets, the joker said; it was all the money I had. I lost my job, he said, and I've got my mother to keep, but I did like the way he lifted his feet up.

Well, we got introduced all round and the joker said his name was Reg, and Terry began to get sort of friendly with him, and maybe I began to get an uneasy sort of feeling. But I'd had enough experience of opening my mouth for one day, so I didn't say anything.

Terry said we'd take Reg over to collect his dough, so we went over and got first at a window, and we all stood in the queue, this Reg in between the pair of us, and Terry talking nineteen to the dozen about racehorses. I'd never heard him say so much before, though I noticed he never said a word about how Reg was going to collect a hundred quid.

Then after a bit the windows went up and Reg got his money and Terry took us out a gate where he said we'd get a taxi, and sure enough we were lucky enough to get one. And the first pub we came to Reg wanted to stop for a drink, but Terry said leave things to him, and we finally pulled up at the biggest pub in town. Reg paid for the taxi, and inside there was a crowd, but Terry pushed up to the counter and Reg stood us drinks just as fast as we could get the barman to serve us, and although it wasn't far off closing time we all had a good few in by then.

But right until we were turned out I hadn't sparked up much, because Terry was still doing all the talking, and he was getting that friendly with this Reg. He certainly had me thinking things, though I admit I couldn't properly get a line on what it was all about. But I didn't want to interfere, so when we were all standing outside in the street I said I was going home.

No, Terry said, you come in and eat.

No, I said, I want to have a lie down.

What you want is a bellyful of tucker, Terry said.

No, I said, and I said so long and shoved off, and I thought Terry would go crook, but he just let me go.

I wasn't happy about shoving off, but I was in one of those moods you get in sometimes. Before I turned the corner I took a look round, and Terry and Reg were still standing outside the pub, and it looked as if Terry was still doing all the talking. It made me feel sore, though I couldn't get things at all straight in my mind. Terry's after that boy's dough I told myself, but

I didn't believe it all the same. No, I thought, Terry's a decent bloke, and I don't reckon he'd do a thing like that. On the other hand, what did I know about Terry? He wasn't the sort that ever lets you know much about himself, though you could tell he always had a lot going on in his mind, even if you had to guess what it was about. Terry wouldn't do a thing like that, I kept telling myself, but I sort of felt it was no good telling yourself that about anybody. Anybody is liable to do anything, I told myself, particularly where there's money concerned. And I remembered how out at the races I'd been thinking what money does to you.

But what was I worrying about, anyhow? Because, Terry could do what he liked so far as I was concerned. He was up against it the same as I was, and when things are tough a man can't be worried. That's what I'd thought when I pinched the money out of the milk billies, so where was the difference? And then I thought maybe I was only feeling sore because I was jealous of this Reg. Because I'd thought Terry was the sort of joker who'd go solid with a cobber, and quite apart from the money business I didn't like the way he cottoned on to Reg.

But it was no good letting myself be worried, and I wasn't doing myself a bit of good standing there watching the pair of them. So I turned the corner, thinking I'd go to the flicks, but then I remembered I only had a few odd bits of chicken feed left in my pocket, and that made me start thinking all over again. Oh, hell! I said to myself, I'll go and have a feed.

So up towards Mrs Clegg's place I turned into a quick-lunch eating joint, and so help me if I didn't run into Maggie.

Hello, Maggie, I said. All on your pat, I said, and seeing she was eating a pie I asked for one myself.

Fancy meeting you without your boy friend, Maggie said.

That's all right, Maggie, I said. And who's my boy friend, anyhow?

As if you didn't know, she said, and she started doing the blinking doll stunt.

No, Maggie, I said, I don't know.

Go on, she said.

So I told her not to talk like a blinking idiot and that sort of shut her up, though it was a blinking doll I should have said. And I started to kid to her a bit, and you could see she was in the mood for a bit of kidding, too. I put my hand on her leg underneath the table, and instead of carrying on and acting silly she just let it stay there, so when we'd finished eating I asked her what she was doing to put in the evening.

I got nothing on, she said.

Then let's go somewhere, I said.

No, she said, I better not. My husband's ship comes home any day now, so I better be a good girl.

Sort of save up, I said.

That's right, she said. Matelots have got to save up, so I ought to, too.

Do they save up? I said.

Well, she said, you're asking me.

And what about you? I said.

Well, she said, sometimes. It all depends. Anyhow, she said, what about yourself?

You can save up too damn long Maggie, I said.

I know, she said. My God! she said.

Come on, Maggie, I said.

So I paid for the pair of us, which left me practically a skinner, but what with the way things were I was too far gone to care about almost anything, except maybe whether I could do a line with Maggie.

Do you want to go to the pictures? she said.

No, I said, let's walk, and we just walked, and Maggie was sort of serious; I'd never struck her in the same mood before. She didn't seem to be taking notice of anything I said, and we just kept on walking and turning corners. But she was the one who sort of decided which corners to turn, and seeing I hadn't taken much notice where we were going, I got a surprise when I discovered we'd parked nearly outside Mrs Clegg's. But I hadn't time to say anything before Maggie said no, let's keep on walking. So we kept walking, but now I was a wake-up to what was in Maggie's mind. I was sitting up and taking notice, so to speak, while we went on turning the corners, and I wasn't surprised when we pulled up outside Mrs Clegg's a second time.

And this time Maggie said come on up, and she went up the stairs pretty fast, with me following. And upstairs I followed her straight into her room, and she shut the door. Then when I looked at her and saw the way she was breathing I knew she wouldn't be able to stop herself, so I naturally felt my heart begin to beat a bit.

Take it easy, Maggie, I said, and we sat on the edge of the bed, and she was shivering, but I told her to take it easy, and I put my arm round her and she cuddled up until I got my hand on her bubs. But so help me if she wasn't that flat-chested I couldn't even feel anything. And seeing I didn't know what to say, I said something about that. But it made her go crook as anything.

You needn't be personal, she said, and she jumped up and stood there looking at me, and she looked properly hot and bothered.

Don't be silly, Maggie, I said. Come over here, I said.

But she went on standing there, and I was wondering what I did next, though, as it turned out, she didn't waste much time deciding things for me.

Take it easy, Maggie, I said. Struth, I said, but she was too keen. So I just lay back; I thought I'd let her work off steam a bit. And it was just as well I did back-pedal, because the pair of us were wake-ups when we heard somebody coming up the stairs, and when the door opened we were just sitting on the edge of the bed, though I suppose a man has to admit we must have both looked considerably hot and bothered.

Anyhow, it was Maggie's bloke Bert. And he was a big matelot, though not a Pom, it was easy to tell he was a Pig Islander.

Hello, he said; but he didn't look at all pleased to see me there, though, of course, Maggie jumped up and began to make a fuss of him.

You're looking good, Bert, she said, and Bill said he was a box of birds, and until Maggie chipped in he began telling her how his ship had got in late that afternoon and he'd got leave.

Bert, Maggie said, this is Bill.

How are you, Bill? he said, and I got off the bed, but he didn't shake hands or anything; he just went on talking to Maggie, and I could tell she was worried over the way he was taking it.

Things didn't look any too good to me, so I thought I'd best clear out. I said I was going and Maggie said hooray, Bill, and I went over to my room. And there wasn't any sign of Terry, so I sat down for a bit. I felt I needed to pull myself together, because what with running into Reg at the races, and now this Maggie business coming afterwards, everything seemed to have gone wrong. And the last few weeks things had been that good.

It wasn't a bit of good just sitting there, though; I knew I'd have to get out in the streets. But I hardly made up my mind to go when I heard an argument start over in Maggie's room, and I opened the door a bit so I could listen. And, to begin with, I couldn't hear much, and later on, when they'd got to arguing loud enough for me to hear, I didn't want to hear. In a way I didn't, anyhow, because my name was being brought in, and the way things were developing it sounded as though there was going to be a serious row. Things didn't ease off any either; they got a lot worse. It was you did and I didn't more and more and louder and louder, and when it developed into let me go and you're hurting me, I knew things were getting serious. He's going to beat her up, I thought, and I thought it was about time I got off down the street. Because what could I do? Terry's always reckoned Maggie wasn't married, but who could say? No, I told myself, I'm not going in there. I felt sorry for Maggie, naturally, but I thought it was no good trying to do anything if I was the cause of the trouble. So I went out, and in the street you could still hear the pair of them tearing into each other, and it only took a minute or two before Maggie began to yell. Christ, I thought. But I knew it was best to keep out of it, and I began walking the streets just the same as I'd done with Maggie.

And I didn't go home for a long time that night. I thought I'd wait until Terry was sure to be home, so I kicked around the streets until it was well after midnight, and it did me good, because there's always plenty to see going on round the streets, and it takes your mind off things when they go wrong. There's lots of other people in the world, you tell yourself, and you start wondering what they're like. And maybe you decide everybody must be pretty much the same in most ways if you could only find out. That's my idea, anyhow, though I admit it may be wrong.

I walked about for quite a while, then I decided I'd go and sit on a seat on the waterfront. And down there I watched some white patches that you could just see rocking on the water, and I decided they must be seagulls. I wondered why you never see them sitting on wires like you do other birds, and I decided it must be because of their feet. And thinking of birds made me remember about the pigeons I used to shoot in the bush, and next minute I'd started calling myself a fool for wanting to come into town. Town's no good, I told myself. A man doesn't have any say; he just gets pushed about. And when I started to go the length of the main street just once more, I was thinking I'd go and try for a farm job first thing next morning. But next minute I was remembering how I'd nearly come a thud over Maggie, and then I forgot everything else because I was thinking about Terry again.

But I got a knock, because up at Mrs Clegg's there still wasn't any sign of Terry, and all the stuffing sort of went out of me, so to speak. I certainly felt blue. But I thought, chin up, a man can't be worried. I listened, but there wasn't any sound from Maggie's room, and it sort of cheered me up. I bet it all ended up in a good old kafuffle, I thought. Good luck to them, anyhow, I thought. Then I turned in, and never thought I would, but I went right off to sleep without doing any more thinking.

But when I woke up late next morning Terry still wasn't there. It made me feel bad, but I thought never mind, he'll turn up. Yet I felt sort of jumpy. All sorts of things that might have happened kept coming into my head, and just because there wasn't any sign of life from Maggie's room I worried over that as well. Though I told myself I needn't, because they'd naturally be sleeping in, that was if Bert hadn't had to go back to his ship.

Then when I had a cup of tea I didn't know what to do. I didn't want to go out and miss Terry, yet I knew it would give me the dingbats if I just stayed on there waiting. So I decided I'd leave a note and then go out. Which is what I did, and along the street I caught up to Mrs Clegg, who'd gone out ahead of me and was pushing an old pram. And walking along I looked in the pram, and it was filled with things out of the kitchen, including a good few tools that must have belonged to her old man.

Gee, I said, selling up the home.

Not yet, she said. It's this weather, she said; it makes that man think he can take things easy.

It makes me lazy, I said. I wouldn't mind if it rained.

You know, she said, he never done that to her before.

Mr Popeye? I said.

If it wasn't for the money I'd turn her out, she said.

Yes? I said.

Then next minute she pulled up outside a pawnshop I'd noticed there before.

I go in here, she said, and she wheeled the pram inside. Things must be tough, I thought. And then I turned the corner and ran right into Terry.

Hello, boy, he said, and I couldn't help it, I had to tell him I was that pleased to see him.

How are you feeling? I said.

Good, he said, but I thought he looked pretty crook on it.

Have you had your breakfast? I asked him.

No, he said, I haven't had anything.

Come on, I said, and when we passed the pawnshop I could see Mrs Clegg still inside. Let's step on it, I said, and soon as we got in I let Terry go upstairs while I went into the kitchen. I couldn't find anything to eat, though; there was nothing that would have fed even the budgie. But Terry said never mind, he couldn't eat anyhow. So I made him a cup of tea and he drank that, then he took off his coat for a lie down, and I was all the time wanting to ask him if he had any money, but I didn't like to.

It was good having him back, though, but while I was wondering whether I couldn't think up another of my stunts for picking up a little ready cash he went off to sleep. So I thought I'd walk about in the streets for a bit and maybe I'd get an idea. But when I got downstairs there were two jokers knocking at the door. I picked them for what they were right away, and so help me if it wasn't me they were looking for, and when they said they wanted to ask me a few questions I told them to go ahead, but I admit I had the wind up considerably.

You'd better come along to the police station, they said.

All right, I said, but what's it all about? And they said I'd soon find out about that.

O.K., I said, but first I want to speak to my cobber upstairs.

Then I thought no, why worry Terry when he needed to get some sleep. And I wouldn't be away long, I thought. So I told them it didn't matter about my cobber.

Well, they walked one on each side of me, and I tried to talk to them now and then, but they took no notice. Though sometimes they'd have some joke on of their own, they'd talk across me much as if I wasn't there, and it made me feel as if I was some sort of wild animal they were taking through the streets. And occasionally I'd see people we passed who'd pick them for dees, and I knew they'd be turning round for an eyeful. So, all things considered, I wasn't feeling so good by the time we got to the police station.

I didn't feel any better there either, because it was a big place, not at all the sort of place you feel you can make yourself at home in. We went up a lot of stairs and finally they took me in a room and we all sat down round a table.

You've been interfering with a woman, one of them said.

Go on, I said. Have I?

But you'd never have guessed the way I was feeling from what I said.

It won't do you any good telling lies, the same one said, and he looked at some papers and said it was a serious something or other. Anyhow, he said, all we want you to do is answer a few questions.

All right, I said, first you give me the works, then I'll tell you my story.

And it was Maggie who'd been putting it across me, which is what I'd guessed, though how it had all come about I didn't know. You'd have thought they'd have told me that, but they never did. Instead they just sort of threw out hints, and the way they made out they knew everything that had happened just about had me thinking they must have had somebody there watching.

There's no question about what happened, one of them kept on saying, and they kept on at me until I said, all right, I'll tell you my story. Which is what I did, though I didn't say anything about Bert beating her up afterwards.

So then they sort of went over it all again.

You admit you put your hand on her, the one who did nearly all the talking said.

Yes, I said, but she didn't object.

She objected all right, he said.

Well, I said, maybe she did, but afterwards she didn't.

No? he said. Then why did her husband come in and find her fighting to save herself? And that was a new one on me, because they certainly hadn't told me that part of Maggie's story.

That's just baloney, I said.

Well, he said, she can show the bruises.

So then I said how Bert had beaten her up. But they said I'd only just made that up; if I hadn't, why hadn't I told them before? And they said it would make things a lot worse for me if I told lies.

Well, I tried to explain, but it did no good; they just went on saying I'd admitted I put my hand on her and she'd objected. And I got that fed up of arguing I felt that way I didn't care much if they believed me or not, though I sort of woke up when they said they were sorry, but they'd have to bring a case against me.

And it was certainly a knock because up till then I'd never realized I was properly in the cart; I certainly had no idea it was going to end up in a court case. And it naturally made me begin to worry about Terry. I didn't know what to say, and they said I was lucky it wasn't a more serious charge, and seeing I'd admitted what I'd done and hadn't told any serious lies I'd probably get probation.

I still sort of had too much stuffing knocked out of me to say anything, but probation didn't sound so bad, and maybe I wouldn't have minded so much if I hadn't been thinking of Terry. All the same, I didn't see how they could prove anything against me, but when I told them they said there wasn't any question about it because of what I'd admitted. And finally they said it would be best for me if they put it all in writing. And after we'd argued a bit more I got fed up that I thought writing it down wouldn't make any difference, so I went over it all again while one of them did the writing. And I admitted I put my hand on her, and I admitted she objected, and I admitted I let her go when I heard Bert coming, but I never admitted anything more, and besides other things I wanted them to put in about Bert beating her up, but they said it had nothing to do with it, and I couldn't say I'd actually seen him do it, anyhow. Then when it was all finished they got me to sign, and I could sort of tell they were thinking they'd done quite a good stroke of work. But I was so fed up I was past caring about anything much.

They wouldn't let me go away then, no, they said they'd try to have the case brought up in the police court that afternoon, but it mightn't be until the next morning. So I asked them if I could send a message to my cobber. I wanted him to come and see me, I said, and they said that would be O.K., they'd see Terry got the message. Then I asked them what the time was, and I'd no idea it had all taken hours and hours. The twelve o'clock whistles must have blown and I'd never even heard them.

I'll admit another thing, I said; I'm feeling empty.

We'll soon fix you up, one of them said, and they took me downstairs and turned me over to a john who wrote my name down in a book and told me to hand in all my money, but there was nothing doing, because I didn't have any. Then when he'd taken my belt off me (it was so as I couldn't hang myself, I suppose), he took me along a passage and locked me up. I sat down to save myself from holding my pants up, and I was sitting there thinking how it was the first time I'd ever been in one of those places, when the john came back with a tray that was loaded up with a big dinner. It was a real good dinner, too, two courses and plenty to eat, and I could have eaten the lot and more, but I thought gee, so far as tucker goes I'm better off than poor old Terry is. I might be, anyhow, I thought, because I remembered I didn't know whether he'd got any money out of Reg. All the same, I didn't like to think of Terry going hungry, so I tore some pages out of a Western that was in the cell and wrapped up half of both courses and put the parcel in my pocket. All in together, it certainly looked an awful mess, but I thought Terry wouldn't mind if he was feeling empty.

Then when I'd got outside the tucker I felt a lot better. I stretched myself out on a sort of long seat that was the only bit of furniture in the cell, and I thought if only a man never had any cobbers or anything, getting picked up by the police would take away some of your worries, anyhow.

I must have gone to sleep, because it seemed no time before the john was unlocking the door and telling me to come along. And along at the end of the passage Terry was waiting for me. And if I wasn't pleased to see his wrinkled old Aussie's face! I certainly was. He grinned back at me, too, and the john let us sit together on a seat there, and I asked him how he was feeling now. And he said he was feeling good.

You don't look any too good, I said, but he said not to worry about him.

I'm in a jam, I said, and I gave him the works, and, Christ, if he didn't begin to laugh when I told him how I'd nearly had Maggie on.

How far did you get? he asked me.

This far, I said, and I showed him. But I never even felt anything, I said.

I bet you didn't, he said. But go ahead, he said, and I told him the rest, and when I'd finished he said some pretty rude things about Maggie.

But don't you worry, he said, because there won't be any case.

They going to bring one, I said.

Don't you worry, he said.

I'll need to get a lawyer, I said.

You won't need any lawyer, he said. Listen, boy, he said, you don't need to worry, because I'm promising you there won't be any case.

All right, Terry, I said, but are you sure?

Shake, he said.

All right, I said. And I certainly felt bucked, though I had no idea what he was going to do, yet I felt dead sure I could depend on him all the same, which was a peculiar feeling to have after the way I'd been feeling only the day before.

When does the case come on? Terry asked me. And he said there was just one thing. I've got to get hold of Maggie, he said, and he told me if he couldn't get hold of her by next morning the case might go as far as the Supreme Court, which meant they'd keep me in clink until the sittings came on unless somebody would go bail.

Do you know anyone? I said, and he said yes, may be he might be able to fix things.

All right, I said, I'm leaving it to you. But, Terry, I said, how are you off for sugar?

I'll be O.K., he said.

Have you got any? I said.

I've got a few bob, he said.

What about Reg? I said, and I couldn't help asking him but I bet I went red in the face.

I won't be seeing Reg, he said. He sounded a bit annoyed, and I didn't know whether I felt glad or sorry, because Reg might have been good for a loan.

I'll be worried about you, Terry, I said.

You got no need to worry, he said, and I knew I'd better lay off, because I was getting him narked.

So I said O.K. and I told him not to move, and it was easy to put the parcel in his pocket without the john seeing. Then I couldn't think of anything more to say, so we just sat there, and I wouldn't have minded if it had lasted like that for hours. But the john said if we'd finished talking I'd better come along, so we shook again and Terry said he'd tell Mrs Clegg some yarn if she asked. Then we said cheers and I went along and was locked up, thinking everything was going to be O.K.

Nothing happened that afternoon. I had a lie down on the seat again, and I must have gone to sleep, because I don't remember anything until the john brought me another feed. And it was just as good as the one before, and I thought it was no wonder there were such a lot of cases when they stood you good tucker inside.

Then when the john came for the tray he brought me the blankets to sleep in, so after I'd had a read of the Western I decided to turn in, and I'd have had quite a good night if I hadn't been waked up by somebody who started kicking up a row somewhere along the passage. And by the sound of the voice I thought it must be some old girl who'd been picked up for being tight. It kept me awake for hours, anyhow, but when I woke up at daylight everything was quiet.

And I woke up still feeling that everything was going to be O.K., so I was sort of impatient for them to take me into court and get it over. I had bacon and eggs for breakfast, then the doors all along the passage were unlocked and we all came out and they collected us along at the end where Terry and me had done our talking. There was a fair collection, too, I'd had no idea, though only one woman, and if she was the one who'd kicked up the row you could hardly believe it, because she looked quite all right. I thought she might have been any man's own mother, but of course it's a fact that nobody's the same person once they've sobered up.

We had all to stand there with a crowd of jacks in plain clothes standing round, and one in uniform called out our names and said what we'd been picked up for. And I didn't know what it was all about, but I suppose it was so as they could get us taped and pick out anybody they had anything else on. It made me go red, though, when I heard what it was I was charged with. It didn't sound too nice, I can tell you, and I thought damn it all, why give it that sort of name? Anyhow, I thought, I bet all those jacks have done plenty they wouldn't like anybody to know about, particularly when you can give it such a rotten name.

Still, there was nothing I could do about it; I just stood there with the rest, and when it was all over they put us back in our cells again. Then when I was beginning to get the dingbats through being there so long on my own I was taken out by the two demons who'd picked me up. It was time to go over to the court, they said, and they asked me if I'd got a lawyer.

No, I said, I don't want any lawyer.

All right, one of them said, but don't say we didn't ask you.

Then they told me to come along, and it wasn't far to the police court, but I wished it could have been further. Because it was a fine summer's day (though no different to what it had been for weeks), and we cut across an open place where there were flowers and trees. The grass was all dried up by the sun, yet it looked nice and cool there, just seeing a hose going made you feel cool. And it was nice to see some kids that were cutting across on their way to school, but I thought if a pair of dees hadn't been taking me to court I might never have noticed these things.

But, as I say, the walk was over too soon, and when we got inside the court we had to wait quite a time before my case came on. First there were traffic cases, then after a few drunks had been hauled up an old man that nobody could have much liked the look of was told off by his nibs for trying to do himself in. The bandage round his neck didn't improve his looks either; he looked sick, I can tell you, and you'd have thought no man would have treated him as rough as the magistrate did. But I bet he thought he was treating him good by letting him off.

Then after the old man it was my turn, and I'd been sitting down with one of the dees while I kept my eyes open for Terry. And there wasn't much of a crowd that'd come to watch, so it was easy to tell he hadn't turned up. I had to stand there while they told the magistrate the case, and then Maggie was brought in to say her piece. And she only took one look at me and never looked my way again. And you'd hardly believe anyone could tell a story that was all baloney as well as she did, and it certainly knocked me plenty. She was all flossied up, and to begin with, you sort of felt she was enjoying herself properly. But when she'd got nearly to the end something went wrong, because instead of answering a question she suddenly went white and hung on to the rail in front of her. And his nibs said to let her take her time, and he looked at me as if he thought I needed to be watched or I'd be trying to swing another one across her. But it never worried me much because it was just then I spotted Terry. He was standing in front of the crowd with a grin a mile wide, and when he saw me looking at him he winked and jerked his head over towards Maggie. And it certainly gave me a nice feeling to know he was there, but things were sort of going round in my head so much I couldn't even wink back.

Maggie got going again and I fixed my attention on her, and when she'd finished one of the dees went into the box and read out what they'd written down. Then there was some talk about Bert, his ship was away, they said, but the magistrate said it didn't matter about Bert because of what I'd admitted in my statement. And then he went on and said a whole rigmarole about what he was going to do, and what would happen if I said

I was guilty or not guilty. But I never had much idea of what he was saying, because I was suddenly a wake-up to what I'd let myself in for when I signed that statement. I understood things then, I can tell you, and it made me feel hopping mad. Instead of listening to his nibs, I just couldn't take my eyes off the two demons. And, Christ, I thought. And I couldn't think of anything except Christ!

But I knew it was no good letting my feelings get the better of me. So I told myself to hang on. I said not guilty all right, and when he asked me something about bail I said I didn't want any bail, because I'd looked at Terry and he'd shaken his head. I remembered how he'd said the case might go as far as the Supreme Court, anyhow, and way at the back of my mind I was still feeling dead sure of Terry even if things had got in a worse tangle than I'd expected.

All the same, it was a hard job trying to stop my feelings from getting the better of me when I was walking back to the police station with the two dees. Because I thought they'd played me a rotten trick. But I didn't say anything except ask them what happened next.

You wait, one of them said, we'll look after you.

Yes, I said, I'm reckoning on that.

But I needn't have tried to be sarcastic, because a man needs a lot sharper tongue than I've got to get under any dees' skin.

It was all right being back, though, because of the tucker. I asked the john who fetched the tray what happened next, and being quite a decent bloke as I'd thought he was right from the beginning, he stayed and talked and told me a lot.

They'll take you out there, he said, and he said it might be in a taxi or it might be in the Black Maria. And when I asked him what it was like out there he said he didn't know much about it, but he reckoned they'd treat me all right until I got convicted.

I'm not getting convicted, I said, but he only said, good luck, boy, and shook hands.

Well, it wasn't until late in the afternoon that the Black Maria came for me. It had blokes on it dressed more like soldiers than cops, and another joker was taken out and put inside as well as me, and there wasn't much room inside because it was chock full of stuff they were taking out to the gaol, and I had to sit right up behind the driver's seat, where I could look out a little window and see what streets we were going through. And instead of going straight out to the gaol we went down the main street and pulled up outside a butcher's shop while they put some boxes of meat on board, and it looked more like dogs' meat to me. But while we were waiting I looked out the window, and so help me if Maggie didn't go past. She stopped to cross the road, too, and watching out for the traffic it seemed as if she looked right at the window. I don't suppose she did really, and it was only for a second, but it made me feel very funny inside.

There were no more stops, though. After that we kept right on to the gaol, which was a long way out of town, and soon as we were out there we had to help unload the stuff. Then they took us inside and put our names down, and after they'd put black stuff on our fingers and got our fingerprints, they took us into a big sort of hall with iron doors along both sides, and locked the pair of us up on our own.

So there I was. And I'd only had time to look out through the bars and see there was nothing to see except a concrete wall and some sky above, when they brought me a hunk of bread and a pannikin of tea, which was certainly not so good after that I'd been getting. Then after a bit the light went on, and to stop myself from doing any thinking I had a read of a detective mag that was lying there. But the yarns were all about crooks, and I reckoned they were a lot of baloney, nothing like the real thing at all. So I chucked the mag away and walked round a bit, and I may as well tell you that when you're in clink there's always a spy-hole in your door. You can't see out, but if you keep your eyes skinned you can always tell when anybody has come along for an eyeful. And that first night I just happened to be watching when somebody came along and moved the slide, so I asked could I have a dab of vaseline to put on my piles. And mister peeping Tom said he'd have to see about that.

Of course, it was mainly a gag just to have somebody to speak to, though as a matter of fact my piles were hurting pretty bad. And while I was waiting I thought I'd have a read of what was left of a Bible, and I'm blowed if I didn't strike the yarn about Joseph and his coat of all colours. It was a real good yarn, too; I liked reading it a hell of a lot, but before I'd got through the light went out, and there I was in the dark, and it didn't look as if the vaseline was going to turn up. So I thought I'd better turn in, and it sounded as if the jokers locked up alongside were doing the same thing because I could hear their beds creaking.

And maybe it was because of the way those beds creaked that I couldn't get to sleep. They didn't stop creaking, and I thought maybe they were jokers like me who'd been locked up for the first time. It made me start thinking about what makes a man get tough and land himself in clink. Because all those jokers must have been the same as I was once, too, just kids. And I started to remember the times when I'd get a kick on the behind for pinching out of the bin where they threw the rotten fruit along at the auction mart in the town where I lived. And the times when the old man would come home tight, and us kids'd go out in the morning and find him lying in the onion bed without hardly a stitch on. And I remembered other times, too, and I never thought about Terry or Maggie much. I just couldn't take my mind off the jokers that were locked up alongside me, because their beds never left off creaking all night.

I was glad when it was morning, because, as I say, it doesn't matter what sort of a night you have, things are always different in the morning. When I heard a noise of doors being unlocked I got up and put my pants on, and when the doors were all unlocked you had to stand outside while a sort of procession came round. First you had to empty your jerry into a can, then you got your tins of porridge and stew off a tray, and last you got your pannikin full of tea out of another can. Then you had to be locked in again while you ate your breakfast. But that first morning I couldn't eat much of it, because they might have called it porridge, but you couldn't tell by the taste. You could hardly tell the tea by the taste either, but I'm not going to tell all about what it's like in clink. Most things you soon get used to; if you don't eat you feel empty, so it's best to eat and after a while you never leave any. And maybe the main reason why I couldn't eat my breakfast the first morning was because I was wondering whether they'd leave me locked up on my pat all day. Also I was beginning to worry about Terry again. I wondered how the hell he'd get on for chips, and I was hoping to God they'd give me his letter if he wrote one, though it turned out I needn't have worried about that.

It wasn't long before the doors were unlocked again and they took us out in a yard with concrete walls all round, and I thought it was all right because of the company, though a screw shouted out we were not to tell each other about our cases. Everybody had plenty to talk about without talking about their cases, anyhow, and when it got too hot in the sun all went under a little roofed-in part, and with everybody squatting down and taking it easy while they talked the usual sort of talk, it might have been any crowd of jokers that were cutting scrub or working on the roads on relief. Because they all had ordinary clothes on, and up till then I hadn't found out they were all jokers that were waiting to come up in court, though a few were dinkum lags who were all togged up to go into town in the van because they needed to go into hospital.

But, as I say, I'm not going to tell all about what it's like inside just because I was in for a few weeks. There'd be too much to tell, anyhow.

I never got any letter from Terry the first day or the day after, and I felt if one didn't come soon I'd have the dingbats worse than I'd ever had them before. What with hardly getting any sleep and listening to the beds creaking all night, I thought I'd go silly, and then maybe they'd have to take me away to the rat-house. But a letter came all right. And was it a relief! Terry said chin up and cheers and I needn't worry because he'd fixed things, though he couldn't get anybody to go bail, he said, but he was still trying and maybe he'd have some luck. And he wound up that I was not to worry if he didn't write again because things were fixed for sure (with a line under the word sure), and I needn't be worrying about him either because he'd be O.K.

So while I was feeling the relief I wrote back saying what a great cobber he was, and how he certainly had my thanks. And I put a letter inside for Fanny. I told her I'd gone away for a few weeks, so I was leaving her to look after Terry. Get your mother to give him something to eat sometimes, Fanny, I said. And I put in a bit about the money tree, and how I knew for certain it liked little girls that were kind to people. I didn't think it would do much good, but maybe it was worth trying. And I asked her in a P.S. if she'd taught the budgie to do any new tricks.

And it wasn't until several days after I'd written the letters that I began to get the jitters again. Because Terry didn't write any more, and even though he'd told me he mightn't I couldn't make it out. And lying in bed at night when I couldn't sleep I'd start thinking he might only have pretended to help me, while all the time he hadn't done anything at all. I hadn't said anything about my case to anybody inside, but quite a number had told me about theirs, and they all said you were a goner once you'd signed a statement admitting anything you'd done. There was no way of getting out of it then, they said, and they'd be that certain they knew the whole works I'd get the wind up considerably. So lying awake at night I'd start thinking rotten things about Terry. He wants me put away, I'd tell myself. Yes, I'd think, that's what he wants, because I'm the only bloke that knows he was with Reg after he collected the hundred quid. And once I'd got as far as thinking that way I'd sort of let myself go, and work out all the different ways he might have used to get the money out of Reg. And I'd tell myself I could bet he'd left Mrs Clegg's and I'd never see him again. Because say they put me away for five years? I'd think. And I couldn't help it, I'd break out in a sweat.

But of course it was mainly during the night-time that I'd be thinking these things. When it was daylight I'd sort of feel maybe I'd gone off to sleep without knowing, and only dreamed all I'd been thinking. I'd go out into the yard thinking everything was going to be O.K. and I'd be all right unless any joker said something that was liable to start me worrying again. Some days they'd talk about their lawyers, and they'd all reckon they'd got good ones. If they didn't get off, they reckoned, they'd get only a light stretch. And I hadn't got a lawyer. I had the law dead against me, and instead of trying to do anything about it I was just relying on Terry. And I'd ask myself what could Terry do against the law all on his own any more than I could? But then I'd think if I tried to do anything I might only spoil what it was that Terry had said he'd fixed. So there I was, sort of feeling I was liable to be caught whichever way I went, and some days I'd feel if things didn't stop going round in my head I'd end up in the rat-house for sure.

I've never known time drag like it did during those weeks. Some days were that long I thought they'd never finish, and the nights were worse. Yet it seemed no time when they started taking away a few jokers each morning to have their cases tried. And when I sort of woke up I found I'd got easy about things. I felt I didn't care what happened. When they asked me didn't I want a lawyer to defend me, because the country would pay if I couldn't, I still said I didn't want any lawyer. Because I'd worked myself into a state. Things couldn't be any worse than they were, I thought, and if Terry was going to let me down it was just too bad. Yet even though I'd got to the stage of thinking I didn't care what happened to me, I'd be liable to break out in a sweat at the thought of what might be happening to Terry. He might be no good, I thought, but he was sick, anyhow; I'd liked having him for a cobber and we'd had some good times together. And the thought of him having nothing to eat was the one thing I could never make myself feel easy about.

You could feel the difference in the place once the van started going in each day with a few jokers to be tried. All the rest were wondering which day it was going to be their turn, and that's the sort of thing that would give any man the jitters. We'd always be keen to find out how things had gone, yet we never got much chance. Because several got off and never came back, and those who'd got convicted would be wondering how long a stretch they'd get, and that's the sort of time when you don't feel like asking a man too many questions. Or if their cases hadn't finished they'd be in just as rotten a state, so it wasn't easy to find out anything much.

Then the morning came when it was my turn, and I was told to get myself shaved and make myself look respectable. And I was just a bundle of nerves waiting to be taken out of the yard, but once we were in the bus, three of us, each with our pannikin and a hunk of bread to eat at midday,

I didn't feel so bad. I was lucky enough to be sitting up by the window again, and it was good to look out and see the places we went past.

We didn't see much of the outside world, though, because the bus backed right in at a door, and we were taken out and locked in a cell right away, all of us in together. And it was easy to tell the courtroom was somewhere upstairs because of the sound of feet moving. My two mates were going up for sentence and it wasn't long before they were taken out. I was left there on my pat, so just to calm myself down I walked about the cell, and it was a terribly dirty place, nothing like what I'd been used to. All over the walls there were drawings that must have been done by jokers who'd had to wait there, and they were nearly all drawings of jokers being hanged or lying on their backs with knives stuck through them. And underneath it would say: NEVER MAKE A STATEMENT TO A DEE. Or: THIS IS A BLOODY DEE AND THIS IS WHAT HE'S GOING TO GET. And calling the dees for all the names you can think of.

But it wasn't long before one of my mates was put back in again, and I didn't know what he'd got, but he took it pretty hard. He just sat there with his head in his hands and didn't say anything, and I would have liked him to talk because it was hard to bear the sight of him sitting there. I'd been told he had a missis and several kids, too. But I didn't have to put up with it for long, because my other mate came back, and then it was my turn. I said O.K., but before I got out the door the first joker jumped up and gave me his fist to shake. Good luck, boy, he said, and I thought it mighty nice of him. It made me feel as if I was nearly going to cry.

Well, the screw took me along a passage to the bottom of a little stairway, and I had to sit there and wait, and another joker was waiting there as well, and when he looked at me so help me if it wasn't Ted, the bloke who'd pinched my money that day on the beach.

Well, I'm blowed, I said, and just for a second I thought he was going to pretend he didn't know me.

No talking about your cases, the screw said.

O.K., brother, I said, and I asked Ted how things were, though it was a stupid question to ask.

Not so good, he said.

I'm telling you in your own interests, the screw said.

That's O.K., brother, I said, and I told Ted I was pleased to see him, anyhow. Though that was a stupid thing to say, too, because before I could say any more another screw came down the stairway to fetch Ted, and I thought he might be going up thinking I was trying to rub it in over pinching my money. Which I hadn't intended to do at all; no, it was just that seeing somebody I knew I was only trying to be friendly.

And waiting there on my own I began wondering what had happened to his girl Mavis, but it seemed hardly more than just a few minutes before he came down again, and this time I didn't say anything because he looked well shaken up. He certainly looked white. The screw took him straight off down the passage, and he said something as he passed me, but he seemed to be only talking to himself. And I was wondering why I'd never struck him out there; he'd been out on bail, I supposed, when it was my turn to go up the stairway.

And it was a surprise to find I'd come out right inside the dock where I had to stand while my case was on. It wasn't so good standing up there with the court full of people that had come to watch, all sorts, besides men for the jury and all the officials and lawyers. But after a time I had a look round to see if Terry was there, though I soon turned round again, because there were too many that were looking me straight in the face and taking me in as if they'd never seen anyone like me before.

There was nobody on the jury I could have said I'd ever seen before, and I had to wait a fair time while it was being called. I thought things would never get started, but they did at last when the charge was read out and I was asked if I pleaded guilty or not guilty. Then a lawyer got up and said what my case was about, and after the judge had said something, sort of saying it so nobody could get the guts of it at all, Maggie's name was called out and she came in looking all flossied up. She had to swear on the Bible and the lawyer asked her her name and other things about how we'd been living at Mrs Clegg's. Then he asked her to tell about the night of such and such a day, and he gave the date, and how anybody had remembered I don't know, because I hadn't. And Maggie said how I'd come into the quick-lunch place and started talking to her, and afterwards we'd gone up to her room.

Did you invite him to go with you to your room? the lawyer said, and Maggie said she didn't remember.

I didn't mind him coming, she said, and the lawyer said oh. Then he blew his nose and looked at his papers before he said anything more.

Well, he said, what happened?

There wasn't anything happened, Maggie said.

You must tell the court what he did to you, he said.

He never did anything, Maggie said, and the lawyer said oh again.

Come along now, he said, we can all understand your feelings, and he sort of looked round at everybody. But you must tell the court, he said.

And Maggie began to go red, but she still said I never did anything. And you could tell it was a surprise to everybody. They stayed that quiet listening you couldn't hear any sound except the sound of breathing, and when the lawyer blew his nose it sounded that loud everybody jumped, and after that it wasn't quiet any more. You could hear people talking, and they had to be told to pipe down.

Maggie didn't go any redder than the lawyer did, anyhow; he started to get in a temper, I can tell you, but the judge chipped in and started to talk to Maggie, but she went on saying no and no. Then the judge said something to the lawyer, and he went on asking Maggie questions. Hadn't I done this to her? he said, and hadn't I done that? And Maggie got a bit rattled, but she still went on saying no.

So in the end the judge chipped in again, and I couldn't hear all he was saying, nobody could, but he said something about wasting time, and when the lawyer said something about what I'd admitted in my statement he said he wasn't going to let the case go to the jury just on that. And he went on and said a lot more that I couldn't get the guts of at all, but in the end he did say I'd have to be discharged.

And he hardly got finished before the screw that had been sitting on the stairs, where he was just out of sight of everybody, told me to come down, and while I was going down he grabbed me by the hand and said I was the luckiest bloke he'd ever known in his experience.

You mind your step in future, my boy, he said, and going along the passage I was in a sort of daze. All the screws came round to shake me by the hand, and I had to sit down because my legs felt as if they wouldn't hold me up.

When I was outside I was still shaking, but I felt a lot better after I'd taken a few big lungfuls of air. And I reckon that's what anybody would feel the need of if they'd just walked out of court without getting a stretch.

But of course I was thinking of Terry, so I didn't waste any time getting round to the front of the court. There were people standing about talking and a few recognized me, and I noticed that now I wasn't standing in the dock they looked at me in quite a different way, but I couldn't be bothered because I had Terry on my mind. I looked inside, but there was no sign of him, the place was empty, so just as fast as I could travel I made tracks for Mrs Clegg's place.

*   *   *

III

The budgie was out on the front of the house, but inside it was all quiet down below. I went up the stairs a good many at a time and Terry's and my room was empty, the bed was made up, but the stretcher was gone and there was no sign of anybody's things, and I couldn't help noticing a smell of disinfectant. So, without hardly knowing what I was doing, I went over and opened Maggie's door, and there was an old man lying on the bed with only his shirt on.

'Sorry,' I said, and I said, 'Where's Terry?' But instead of saying anything he just heaved a half-eaten apple at me. So I slammed the door and called out 'Sorry' again: then when I looked out the window of the other room I saw Mrs Clegg along at the end of the clothes-line, and I didn't waste any time in getting down to her.

'Hello,' I said, and straight off I said, 'Where's Terry?'

But she bent down and put a clothes-peg in her mouth, and I had to wait until she'd pegged it on the line before she answered.

'He's in hospital,' she said.

'Where've you been?' she said, and I looked her straight in the eye, even if I did pick on the glass one.

'I've just been away,' I said.

'Look at that,' she said, 'that's where he coughed up his blood,' and she pointed to a sheet on the line.

'How long ago?' I said, and she said 'Two days,' and I turned round to go without saying anything more. But Mrs Clegg called out:

'There's rent owing, mister,' she said.

'O.K.,' I said. 'I'll come back.'

And making fresh tracks for the hospital I felt in as bad a daze as I'd felt in only a short time before.

Up at the hospital they wanted to make a fuss about me seeing Terry.

'Are you a relative?' they said.

'No,' I said, 'just a cobber.'

And the bloke on the other side of the counter looked at me as if he was down on anybody that was just a cobber.

'Well,' he said, 'don't you come here again out of visiting hours.' And he told me the number of the ward and said to ask for the sister.

The sister wasn't a bad sort, she gave me a smile and took me out on the veranda, and there was old Aussie sitting up and leaning on a heap of pillows. He grinned when he saw me too, but, Christ, if he didn't look crook.

'Hello, Terry,' I said, and he said 'Hello, boy,' and for a while we didn't seem to have anything else to say. I just sat there holding on to his hand, and after giving us a few looks the jokers in the other beds looked away, and I thought it was mighty nice of them.

'You're not feeling too good,' I said, but just as usual Terry said there was nothing wrong with him.

'I want to be out of here,' he said.

'You'd better stay if you're crook,' I said.

'I'm not crook,' he said. 'Listen, boy,' he said, 'tomorrow they're going to put me down in a shelter,' and he sat up further to look over the veranda rail, and I could see the little shanties he was talking about. 'It'll be easy to walk out from there,' he said.

'But can you walk, Terry?' I said.

'I can walk,' he said; 'You come up tomorrow afternoon. They can't keep me,' he said.

'All right, Terry,' I said; but I knew I'd have to think it over.

'You fix things,' he said.

'I'll have a try,' I said. 'But have you got any chips?'

'No,' he said.

'Never mind,' I said, 'I'll fix things.'

'So you got off all right,' he said.

'How did you work it, Terry?' I said.

'I worked it,' he said, and he wouldn't say anything more.

'Forget it,' he said.

Then the sister came back and said my time was up. So I said 'So long' to Terry, and caught up to the sister and asked her a few questions. Terry was pretty bad, she said.

'How bad?' I said, but she said I'd better ask the doctor if I could find him.

And my luck was in, because going down the stairs I stopped a young joker in a white coat, and he just happened to be Terry's doctor.

'That man's in a bad way,' he said.

'That's no good,' I said. 'But will he get better?'

'No hope,' he said.

'Well,' I said, 'how long will he last?'

'Too hard to say,' he said. 'It's just like that,' he said, and he ran on up the stairs.

And it's too hard to say just how I was feeling when I came out of the hospital. I got the feeling again that my legs wouldn't hold me up, so I went and sat on a seat in a bus-stop shelter-shed, and I remember I was in such a daze I didn't seem to be thinking of anything at all, not even Terry. Nor noticing anything, either. Because people would go past, or they'd come in and sit on the seat and talk, but I never moved or took the slightest bit of notice.

I sort of began to take notice when a dog came up and started sniffing me. 'Hello, dog,' I said, and he stood there in front of me with his tail going. And after a bit his mouth started dribbling. 'You're thinking of tucker, are you?' I said, and I remembered the piece of bread I had in my pocket, and when I took it out the dog's tail wagged faster. I didn't know the time, it must have been well on in the afternoon, but I hadn't felt hungry. The bread tasted good, though, and I broke off small pieces and gave them to the dog, and when I had no more to give him he went down on his belly with paws stretched out in front, and his tail swept a clean place on the floor of the shed.

But when I'd eaten I decided I'd have to do something, so after I'd kidded to the dog a bit, I went down town and waited until I got the chance to use the phone in a pub. Then I looked in the book and rang up a parson that came visiting once while I was out there. I got him all right, and he said he remembered me, and after he'd talked a lot of palaver, I said I'd got no money and was in need of a job.

'Well,' he said, 'I know a gentleman who helps young fellows in your position. He's a very fine gentleman, indeed,' he said and he told me the name and I waited while he looked up the phone number.

'You ring that number,' he said. 'And remember,' he said, 'anyone of us may stumble if we depend on our own strength alone.'

'That's right,' I said.

'Goodbye,' he said. 'May you receive grace and strength,' he said.

'Yes, good-oh,' I said, 'and thanks very much.'

Then I rang the other number, but a girl said the joker wasn't there. She told me to ring his house number, which I did, and got on to his missis. And she said he wasn't home, but he would be in that evening, and instead of ringing again I'd better call and see him.

So I promised I would, and then I went into the bar, but the counter-lunch hadn't come out. I went outside and waited and then I went back and picked up a pretty classy joker that was there on his own. I just went straight up to him and asked him if he'd stand me a half-handle.

'Sure,' he said. 'Have a large one,' he said, and he called the barman and got the drink.

'Things a bit tough?' he said.

'I'll say,' I said, and he talked about the depression and I made the drink last until the tucker arrived. Then we both went over and I put away quite a lot in quite a short time, and when the joker saw the way I was eating, he sort of turned the plates round so as the biggest pieces were next to me.

'Eat up,' he said.

But next minute some of his cobbers came in. They were all classy jokers, too, and the first one didn't take much notice of me because he was too busy talking. I stood there finishing the drink, and so help me if I didn't hear them start talking about the court cases. And by the way they talked I thought they must be lawyers. It made me feel a bit nervous, because I thought they might say something about my case, so when they had more drinks all round, and my joker turned and asked if I'd have another, I said 'No, thanks,' and shoved off.

I thought I'd need somewhere to sleep that night, though I wouldn't have minded flopping in the park with the weather so good, but, of course, there was Terry to consider, so I thought it wouldn't do any good to put off trying to fix things with Mrs Clegg.

But soon as I got up there I ran right into Fanny, and it was a hard job getting her to put off paying a visit to the money tree.

'You promised, Bill,' she said.

'Yes, I know,' I said. 'But did you look after Terry?'

'Yes,' she said, 'because he was sick.'

'You're a good girl, Fanny,' I said. And seeing I was feeling glad that Terry had been looked after, I said that later on I might buy her another budgie, though, I told myself, I oughtn't to be making any rash promises.

Then I went in and Mrs Clegg and her old man had finished dinner and were having a cup of tea. So I sat down and had a cup and we had quite a long talk, though Mr Clegg was all the time going on about politics and rocking it into the government. Off and on he was reading the paper, too, and I had the jitters wondering if he might come across my name.

'If things don't improve, there's going to be hell to pay,' he said.

'You may be right,' I said.

'Yes,' he said, 'when the winter comes there'll be trouble.' And it was a fair dinkum prophecy, though I had no idea at the time.

But later on when he went off down the street, I had Mrs Clegg on her own, and it was a hard job putting it up to her.

'I have to think of the money,' she said.

'I know,' I said. 'But, listen,' I said, 'you've got two rooms empty now, because when people can live in wash-houses and sheds for a few bob, they won't rent rooms. So why not take Terry and me?'

'You mightn't pay,' she said.

'I'll pay,' I said. 'Look,' I said, 'I've got hands, I can work. If I don't pay today, I'll pay tomorrow.'

And in the end I got her to say yes when I promised I'd let her have ten bob just to show her, first thing in the morning.

Well, that was something off my mind, and when I looked at the clock I thought it was about time to go and see the joker the parson had put me on to.

I had to walk a long way to get there, and it was a posh house, one standing in a big garden. But I thought, 'Well, he can't eat me,' and I rang the front doorbell. It was his missis that opened the door though, and she took me inside into a big room that was fitted up like a sort of gymnasium. Over in the corner there were parallel bars and all that sort of gear, and a heap of things like soccer balls, crash helmets, and golf sticks. And all round the walls were pictures out of the Bible with texts underneath.

She made me sit down, and then she said she was sorry but her husband had gone out.

'He's so busy,' she said, and she asked me if I'd ever been there before.

'No,' I said.

'Well,' she said, 'my husband is such a busy man. I'm sure you wouldn't want to come and take up any more of his time,' she said.

So I asked her how did she mean?

'My husband is so good to all his boys,' she said, 'but if he doesn't give it all up, I think he'll have a breakdown. I do, really,' she said.

I said I was sorry to hear that, but I was only being polite because it was her I felt a bit sorry for. She looked pretty sick on it. I've never seen anyone look as black round the eyes, and, besides everything else, she looked a bit batty because her hair was all over the place.

'I only wanted to know if he could get me a job,' I said, and I told her how the parson had put me on to him.

'Yes, I know,' she said, 'he sends so many,' but she smiled and said of course it wasn't my fault.

'Couldn't you go away and do farm work?' she said.

'Yes,' I said, 'I'd like to, but just now I haven't got a penny to my name.'

'Then if I give you a pound,' she said, 'will you promise you won't waste it or spend it on drink?'

'Yes,' I said, 'I'll promise that.'

'And you'll try very hard to find a place on a farm?' she said.

'Yes,' I said, 'I'll do that.'

'Very well,' she said, 'here's more than a pound,' and she got up and took thirty bob off the mantelpiece. Though she held on to it until we were out on the veranda, and before she handed it over she said there was just one more thing.

'I want you to promise you won't ring my husband up any more,' she said.

'All right,' I said, 'I'll promise that.'

'The poor man,' she said, 'he's just wearing himself out.'

'You want him to get to take a holiday,' I said.

She said it was nice of me to say that, and I went down the path thinking she must be a bit crazy. But I had the thirty bob in my hand.

Well, it was late by the time I got to bed, and when I woke up in the morning I felt done. Another day, I thought, and I sort of didn't want to face it, so I kept my eyes shut and turned over and tried to go off to sleep again. It wasn't any good, though, I was only kidding myself, and I knew I'd better get moving. I hopped out of bed, and while I was stretching I looked out the window at Mrs Clegg's washing, which was hanging on the line just like it was on the first morning I stayed there. The weather didn't look any different, either, it was just as hot, and I wasn't sure, but I thought I could get the whiff from the heap of sawdust in the butcher's back yard; and just for a second it all gave me a sort of peculiar feeling, because it seemed to be that first morning all over again, and as though I'd gone back and started again, and nothing had happened in between.

If only it hadn't all happened, I thought; but then I thought if one thing doesn't happen another one does, so what's the difference? But I couldn't help feeling there's always a difference, all the same.

I went downstairs and collected my things and Terry's from Mrs Clegg and borrowed the teapot again, and she lent me a few teaspoonfuls of tea. And she looked bucked when I gave her half a quid. I fixed up with her about the stretcher, and told her I'd be bringing my mate home later on. Though I didn't say anything about how I was going to manage about his tucker if he had to stay in bed. I thought it best to leave that over in the meantime.

Then, when I'd had my tea and was out in the streets, I felt life wasn't so bad, though I had a longing to go up and see Terry right away. But I'd looked in the phone book and found out the visiting hours, so I was putting it off until the afternoon.

I went and looked at the paper in the library, but there didn't seem to be anything doing, so instead of trying the registry offices I decided I'd go and have a shot at getting on relief. And after a long wait in a queue down at the place I got to a window, and the joker there said right away that as a single man they wouldn't consider me unless I'd go to a camp in the country.

'Yes,' I said, 'but I've got a sick cobber.'

'That's nothing to do with us,' he said.

'No,' I said, 'but I've been sick myself.'

'What's wrong with you?' he said.

And I didn't know what to say, so I said I'd strained my heart.

'Who's your doctor?' he said.

'Well,' I said, 'I haven't been to one here,' and I told him I'd had a job in the country, which I'd had to give up because of my heart.

'All right,' he said, 'we'll see if you're fit.' And after he'd written on a form, he gave me a slip of paper and told me where to go.

'If you go now,' he said, 'he might put you through this morning.'

So what was I to do? I'd told the yarn about my heart, but I didn't think there was anything wrong with me. Yet I thought I might as well go and give it a pop, so I went round to the place, and it was a broken-down building in a back street, and when I looked inside there was a big dark room with rows of jokers sitting on wooden seats. They didn't look any too cheerful either, no, most of them were old jokers, and they all looked as if they were properly up against it.

And while I was standing there a door opened up the far end, and an old joker came out buttoning up his pants. Then a young fellow came out and called a number, and another one of the crowd got up and went in, after which I was called up and had my slip changed for a piece of cardboard with my number.

'Sit down and wait your turn,' he said.

So I went back and sat with the last row of jokers, and the one next me started talking.

'Wait your turn's right,' he said. 'That's what I've been doing all my life.'

'It's no good,' I said.

'Yes, wait,' he said. 'You can wait here or you can go home and wait, it don't make no difference. It might as well be your funeral you're waiting for,' he said.

'It's certainly no good,' I said.

'Wait,' he said; 'yes, wait till the guns go off. You wait, boy,' he said; 'you'll find out you were born just at the right time.'

But, knocking around, I'd heard all that sort of talk, so I asked him how long you had to wait.

'It depends,' he said, 'you never can tell. We might have to come back tomorrow if the quack's not through by the time he feels like having a bite. I bet he has a good bite, too,' he said.

'I bet he does,' I said. 'Anyhow,' I said, 'I'm going out for a breath of air,' and he said I'd better be careful if I didn't want to miss. 'You never can tell,' he said.

I went outside, anyhow, and just across the road there was a parking place for cars, and up against the wall of a building I noticed a lot of bikes were parked. And so help me if I didn't get one of my notions.

I picked one of the bikes and rode off, and not far along there was a street that cut right up through the park. And I pedalled up that hill just as fast as I could make the bike go. When I got to the top I was done, and I turned round and let her run down again. I parked the bike outside the place and looked inside, but there was still nearly the same number of jokers, not counting a few more that had turned up. So I came out and repeated what I'd done, and kept on several times over. Then I reckoned I'd have time for just one more, and when I got back I was that done I could hardly stagger over and put the bike back where I'd got it from.

Well, I timed it pretty nicely. I just had time to cool off and get my breath under control when it was my turn, and once inside the room the quack asked me straight off what my trouble was.

'I've got a bad heart,' I said. And without saying anything he put the things in his ears and had a listen. He listened for quite a time, too, then he stood back and looked at me.

'Who's your family doctor?' he said.

'You are,' I said.

'You look all right,' he said.

'I don't feel too good,' I said.

So then he had another listen.

'Breathe naturally,' he said.

'I'm trying to,' I said.

And after a bit he sat down and wrote, and before he'd finished writing he told me to go back to the office next morning.

'Next,' he said, and the young fellow shoved me out, and I came away without having any idea how things had gone.

It was over, anyway, and next minute the whistles blew and I decided I'd go a bob dinner. It seemed a mean thing to do, considering the hole Terry and me might be going to be in, but I thought it might be as well if I kept my strength up. I risked going to the Dally's, and as usual at that time he was standing behind the peter, and he seemed as if he was quite pleased to see me.

'Is your mother better?' he said.

And I had to think, because I'd forgotten that yarn.

'She's fine,' I said.

'Good,' he said. 'That is good for you. And it is good for me now you are back to eat here.'

'Yes,' I said. And I sort of realized for the first time he must talk about it being good for somebody to just about all his customers. And I thought that, seeing he hadn't said anything, it was no good asking him about a job just then.

After I'd eaten, I just slowly worked my way over to the hospital. Visiting time hadn't started when I got there, but I risked going round the building, and I found Terry all right after I'd looked in a good few shelters. He had one all to himself, though there was another bed, and he said he'd have a mate by tomorrow. But he started on right away about wasn't going to be there tomorrow.

'There's nothing wrong with me,' he said.

'Did you walk down here?' I said.

'I can walk,' he said.

'Have you tried?' I said.

'Listen, boy,' he said, 'there's nothing wrong with me except I feel a bit done-in.'

'O.K.,' I said, because it wouldn't have done any good telling him he looked awful, and I knew if I kept on I'd only get him narked.

'I never could stand being kept in at school when I was a kid,' he said.

'No,' I said, 'no more could I.'

'How did Mrs Clegg take it?' he said.

'She took it good,' I said. 'She's a real nice woman,' I said.

'She's all right,' Terry said.

'Listen,' I said, 'I've got enough chips for a taxi, so why not come now?'

'No,' he said, 'because I don't want any fuss. And you hang on to your chips,' he said.

So I said 'O.K.,' again, and he started talking horses, and all the time I was hearing about which ones would be certain to win the autumn meetings, I was wishing he'd give me the works about Maggie instead, because I still couldn't get that business out of my mind. But Terry was still talking about the horses when a bell rang and a nurse came past and said visiting time was over. And Terry told me to come up again after nine o'clock, when lights were out.

'Nobody will see you if you come up from the bottom of the hill,' he said.

And I thought that was a good idea, so I said so long and went straight over the grass and down the hill from where I was, just so as I'd have an idea of the way in the dark. And I knew it would be easy, because I could turn round and wave to Terry almost until I was down on the road.

It was lucky I went that way, too, because some relief jokers that were working on the road had just finished up for the day. They were locking their shovels in a box and putting their barrows all together, and as I went past I couldn't help thinking that one of those barrows might come in handy.

Well, I kicked about the streets until it was time to pick up the usual bit of counter-lunch, then I went up to Mrs Clegg's and got her to lend me a piece of dripping, which I thought I might need just in case the barrow wheel started squeaking. And I took the blanket off my stretcher and carried it folded up over my arm, though I thought Terry wouldn't need it on such a warm night.

Then time began to drag pretty badly while I was waiting to bring off the stunt, but I went and had a cup of coffee in a coffee and sandwich place, and a hard-case old sheila in sand-shoes came and sat next to me. She was the sort you see going into pubs carrying shopping bags with good wide mouths. She kept putting her hand on my arm, so I bought her a cup of coffee, and she said wouldn't it be nice to go for a run in a taxi.

'Sorry,' I said, 'nothing doing.' But with things as they were, I thought, maybe, I wouldn't have minded if I could have got her to pay *me*.

By nine o'clock, though, I was up on the road below the hospital, where it was pretty quiet at that time of night. I tried the barrows until I got the one that ran easiest, and after I'd greased her up and left her by the fence, I climbed over, and Terry saw me coming up the hill and struck a match so as I wouldn't mistake his shelter.

And everything went O.K., though all the time we were a bit windy in case some joker in one of the other shelters might ring the bell and give the show away. Terry had managed to hang on to his clothes and they were folded in his locker. He could hardly stand, but I got him dressed, and before we shoved off he left a note he had written all ready. Then I got him on my back, and it was easy taking him downhill, because he didn't seem to be any weight at all.

'We've got our taxi waiting,' I said, and he said, 'Oh, yeah!' but he thought it was a great stunt when he saw the barrow.

He didn't need the blanket, but he sat on it folded up, and to begin with it was easy because it was still downhill. But then there was a long hill to go up, and I had to keep stopping for rests, and Terry joked about how I needed more benzine, and said, 'Horsey, keep your tail up.' And a few people passed us, though no cops, and if we saw them coming I'd have a rest, and Terry'd get out and sit on the edge of the barrow, just so as not to attract too much attention.

We had to get across the main street, though, and that was worrying me considerably. But we took the barrow down pretty close and parked it on the edge of the footpath, then Terry got out, and with me hanging on to him he could walk, though only slowly, but I got him across, and propped him up against a railing, where he could sort of half sit down while I went back for the barrow. And wheeling the empty barrow across didn't attract much attention, and we were lucky, because there weren't any cops.

And we got up to Mrs Clegg's all right, and I got Terry on my back again and carried him up the stairs, though when I'd put him on his bed I just had to flop myself, because I was nearly busted.

Maybe it was the joke of my weak heart that helped me to get my strength back, and I certainly needed it because Terry was lying there helpless just like I'd dumped him. And I thought I could bet he looked a long sight worse than I did, even though I'd been doing all the work. So I doubled his pillow up and used my own as well, then I got him undressed, and I'd never noticed it before, but there was a string round his neck with a medal thing at the end of the loop. I had a look and it said: I AM A CATHOLIC. IN CASE OF ACCIDENT, SEND FOR A PRIEST.

It was a new one on me, but I asked him if he wanted me to.

'If you like,' he said, and he closed his eyes again and I had to pull him about until I finished off trying to get him comfy.

'Are you all right?' I said.

'I'm O.K., boy,' he said, and I turned off the light and left him, because I knew I'd better go and put the barrow back, even though I was feeling more like leaving it until the morning.

Gee! but I was tired the next morning. My head felt as if it was stuck to the bed, and my eyes felt as if they'd had some glue used on them as well. But there was Terry with his wide open. And that was always one thing about him, no matter how crook he was, his eyes always looked bright and lively as a bird's.

I just lay there trying to get over the tired feeling, and after a bit I started joking with Terry about how we only needed to ring a bell and we'd get our breakfast brought in; and in the end I hopped up feeling quite lively.

'You won't be getting up today,' I said.

'Not today, tomorrow,' he said.

So I mucked about and got two cups of tea, and then Terry said how about the paper? I went out and got him one, and bought a loaf of bread and a quarter of a pound of butter as well, and he said he didn't want any breakfast, but he ate some. And while he was eating I got him to look at the jobs, but he said there didn't seem to be any going.

Then, when I'd got myself looking tidy, I told him I was going out but I'd be back to see him at midday, and I gave him the tobacco I had left, and he was sitting up reading the paper and looking as if he never had a worry in the world when I went out. Except that he looked so crook.

I went straight down to the unemployment office and waited in the queue, and when I got to the window the joker looked up my papers, and then I had to go round to a counter and wait to see another joker. And he said they wouldn't send me to camp, instead they'd give me about a day-and-a-half's relief work a week, and I'd draw fourteen shillings. I thought that would be all right because it would pay the rent with quite a few bob over, but when I'd filled in the papers he said I'd have to wait a fortnight before I began. And I tried to argue it out with him, but it did no good; he said I could take it or leave it. So there wasn't anything I could do, but I came away feeling sore over having to wait a fortnight.

Except for a ten-bob note and some chicken feed, I had hardly anything left in my pocket, so I went down on the waterfront for a sit-down while I tried to decide what I'd do next. Though what with the ships and the wharves there was so much going on down there, my mind would sort of shy away from trying to decide anything for me. And I was just beginning to think I'd better get off up the street again when a young joker came and sat next to me. We got talking, and he said he was out of a job, but he'd soon be going back on a farm again. He'd been working there before, he said, and the farmer bloke had sent him a letter to say he could come back if he liked to break in twenty-five acres of rough land, and take it over on easy payments. He told me all about it, and if there wasn't any catch it sounded as if there might be something in it. So I told him the jobs I'd had on farms.

'Well,' he said, 'how about being mates and going together?'

And I liked the look of him, so I said 'O.K.', right off, and the thought of being back working on the land again made me feel suddenly all worked up. But next minute I remembered, so I said wait on a bit, because I'd need longer time to decide.

'Where can I see you tonight?' I said.

'Well,' he said, 'it will have to be early,' and he said how he was sleeping in a railway carriage, but you needed to be early if you wanted to get a decent possie. So we fixed a date for the afternoon.

'Where do you eat?' I asked, and he said he went on the ships; there were some of them that stood you quite a good feed, he said.

'I'm going on now,' he said, 'so you come along.'

'Sure,' I said, and we'd got a fair way along the wharf before I remembered again. I stopped, and said I'd changed my mind, and I suppose he thought I was batty, because he went on without stopping. And I suppose he knew I'd never turn up at the place where we'd fixed the date.

But I put it all out of my mind, and went up the street and spent my chicken feed on a couple of pies, and got the girl to put on tomato sauce just to give them a taste. Then, coming out, I ran right into Maggie, and she went red, but she stopped and said she'd been wanting to see me.

'How are you, anyway?' I said.

'I'm feeling good,' she said.

'You didn't look as if you were feeling any too good in that witness box,' I said.

And she looked away and said wasn't it a pity, and she'd been wanting to apologize.

'He beat me up that bad,' she said.

'He certainly did,' I said.

'He was a brute,' she said. 'I ran away right into a cop, and he stopped me, and I said a man had tried to put one across me.'

'Too bad,' I said.

'I didn't know what I was saying, Bill,' she said. 'He wouldn't let me go, he made me go to the police station so he could give me to those awful men.'

'The two demons,' I said.

'Yes,' she said. 'They kept on that long I had to say it was you.'

'You didn't have to, Maggie,' I said.

'Yes, I did,' she said, and she went red again. 'I didn't want to get Bert into trouble. Bert's all right,' she said. 'I like Bert, he's been good to me.'

So I said I suppose that was why he beat her up?

'I can't help liking him, Bill,' she said.

'All right, Maggie,' I said, 'let's forget it. You put things right again, anyhow.'

'But I had to,' she said. 'Terry said he'd put me away if I didn't. I'd forgot about Terry,' she said.

'I don't get you, Maggie,' I said.

'Yes, you do,' she said. 'You can't tell me you don't know.'

'Skip it, Maggie,' I said.

'Of course you know,' she said.

'Cut it out, Maggie,' I said, and was feeling pretty annoyed.

'All right,' she said, 'but you can't kid me.'

Well, I didn't know what she was driving at, and I thought the pies would be getting cold. I said I'd have to go, and Maggie asked me how Terry was keeping, and I told her the way things were.

'Poor old Terry,' she said. 'I might come up and see him sometime. I might bring Bert and some beer,' she said.

'Beer mightn't be good for him, Maggie,' I said.

'Aw, heck, Bill,' she said. 'Beer's always good for everybody.'

'All right, Maggie,' I said. 'I might be seeing you.'

I said 'So long,' and I hurried up to Mrs Clegg's and found Terry half asleep, though he was lying on the top of the bed. It was too hot under the blanket, he said. He certainly looked hot, and I was worried, because I didn't think eating a pie would do him any good. But he didn't complain, and he ate bread and butter as well, and drank two cups of tea afterwards.

I was worried about leaving him again, and he didn't want me to go, either. He got me to get a pack of cards out of his suitcase and I played him whisky poker for matches. But after a few games he said he felt like having another sleep, so he settled down and I got him to let me put his overcoat on top of him, just in case he caught cold.

I didn't stay long down town, anyhow, because kicking round the streets I couldn't think of a single thing to do. And in the end I began to feel reckless and decided to blow in nearly the whole of my last ten bob. I went to cheap places in back streets and bought mutton fat and things from the grocer's, besides a few nice things for Terry. And when I got up to Mrs Clegg's with an armful she hummed and hahed, but I said everything was for her as well as Terry and me, and in the end she said she didn't mind putting on a bit extra, though she said she hoped Terry wasn't going to be in bed for long.

I thought I'd done a great stroke. I did the vegetables, then I went upstairs to lie on my stretcher and yarn to Terry. And while we were waiting for Mrs Clegg to call out we joked about how it was just as good as staying in a flash hotel.

But later on we'd hardly finished eating when there was a noise on the stairs, and a second later it sounded as if somebody had fallen down. I went out, and it was Bert and Maggie, and Bert had slipped on the stairs and was trying to get up, while at the same time he was hanging on to an armful of riggers. I went down and took the beer off him, and with Maggie shoving behind we got him to the top. Then he was O.K.; he had a good few in certainly, and so had Maggie, but they weren't all that tight. They'd brought a lot of riggers and I was worried, because I thought beer wouldn't do Terry any good; but I couldn't do anything, because he looked that bucked when he saw the pair of them. And he said straight off he was feeling dry.

It gave me a rotten feeling watching Terry put away the first few drinks, but once I had a few in myself, I felt different. Way at the back of my mind I was remembering what the young hospital quack had said. And I asked myself who was I to be interfering with anyone's pleasure in a world like this? Though it wasn't too nice remembering what the quack had said, and I told myself the sooner I got lit up the better for my own peace of mind. And it wasn't long before I was telling myself it was nice to see a bit of colour in Terry's cheeks, anyhow.

It turned out quite an evening, though the pair of them stayed on far too long for my liking. Among four of us the beer didn't last any too long, and when there wasn't any more Bert turned sort of sour, and the way he started picking on Maggie reminded me of Ted and Mavis, though with them it had been the other way about. Maggie was silly, the way she took it, too; she tried to throw everything back, and that only made Bert worse.

'I'll make a proper job of you if I start this time,' he said.

'You'd better not start,' Maggie said, and Bert said wouldn't he start?

'You do,' said Maggie. 'I'll put you away.'

And maybe Bert would have started on her right then if Terry hadn't managed to grab hold of his two arms.

'No rough house,' he said.

'No,' I said, 'because we don't want any more court cases.'

But Maggie was too far gone to hold her tongue.

'Anyhow,' she said, 'I'm sick of wearing these glad rags round my legs.'

'You shut up, Maggie,' Terry said, and he spoke mighty sharp.

'I won't shut up,' she said. 'What do I care?' she said. 'I'll put the both of us away.'

And Bert tried to go for her then, but with Terry and me holding on, Maggie got quite a good start down the stairs before he could tear himself away.

Terry and me just lay back on our beds, and it was mighty nice to lie there listening to the quiet after all the row. And I didn't feel like saying anything, because all of a sudden I was a wake-up as far as Maggie was concerned. I lay there thinking back and trying to put two and two together. And I dozed off to sleep thinking unless you do it on paper, it's not always so easy to make two and two add up right.

I could go on and tell a lot more, but I don't see the use. Terry never picked up after the night of the party; no, he just sort of went steadily downhill. And there was hardly a thing I could say or do, though he never went short of tucker if he felt like eating.

I'd look at him lying there.

'Terry,' I'd say.

'What is it, boy?' he'd say.

'Nothing,' I'd say.

And then I'd say, 'Terry.'

And instead of answering he'd just have a sort of faint grin on his face.

'Terry,' I'd say.

But I never could get any further than just saying Terry.

I wanted to say something, but I didn't know what it was, and I couldn't say it.

'Terry,' I'd say.

And he'd sort of grin. And sometimes I'd take his hand and hold it tight, and he'd let it stay in my hand, and there'd be the faint grin on his face.

'Terry,' I'd say.

'I'm all right, boy,' he'd say.

And sometimes I couldn't stand it, I'd have to just rush off and leave him there.

And one night when I came back again I looked at him and knew it was the finish.

'Terry,' I said, and he didn't answer.

'Terry,' I said, and I said I was going to get the priest.

'Cheers, boy,' is what I think he said, and I rushed off without even saying goodbye.

I found the place, and the priest said he'd come. So I waited and took him along and showed him Mrs Clegg's, and told him where to find the room upstairs. Then I went along the street and the taxi-driver I'd won the double with was on the stand.

'Do you want to take one?' he said.

'No,' I said, and I'd only got a few bob, but I asked him if he knew of any decent sheilas.

He grinned and put away the paper he was reading and told me to hop in.

'You surprise me,' he said.

And it was a fine night for a drive. Maybe if only it had rained, I remember I thought.

GREVILLE TEXIDOR

Epilogue

The small sharp hills over-lapping like green waves converged on the train. The sun flashed out and the dead trees littering the hillside shone like white bones. Then it was raining again. The train stopped at a station and the carriages were suddenly empty. The passengers surged into the café, then hurried back with moist white sandwiches and tea. The station where Rex got down was only a long shed with an iron roof, standing alone in the middle of the green.

It was raining again, and there was no one about to tell him the way to Isaiah Chapman's place. He hailed a car that was passing along the road, and the man driving said he would take him to Chapman's.

'Old Chap, as we call him, is a cousin of mine,' he told Rex. 'We're pretty near all related around here.'

Rex asked about the farm.

'Well, it's a pretty place,' said the man. 'The park we call it. He has this hobby of growing fruit and other trees. It was clear the other dairy farmers thought it a crazy hobby. It's behind the hills over there,' he said. 'There's a shorter way through the paddocks.'

The mountains in the distance that looked wild and grand under the rain were only hills when they got up to them. Little green calvaries topped with tall dead trees.

'I suppose it doesn't pay,' said Rex.

'It doesn't. But Isaiah's an old man. You can't tell him anything. He's really more of an idealist than a farmer.'

Then, remembering he was talking to Rex he looked a bit awkward and said, 'You'll be the new man, I suppose? Oh well, I hope you'll like it here. Old Chap's a great Bible reader and all that, but a real good sort when you get to know him.'

Rex was put down at the gate and waded through mud the half mile to the house. Mrs Chapman welcomed him at the back door and made him take off his shoes in the kitchen. She asked him if he had had a pleasant journey from Auckland and he said, 'Yes, very pleasant.'

'I expect you will find it very wet and muddy,' she said, 'it's our normal winter state. But the spring flowers are coming on apace. Are you a flower lover, too?'

Mr Chapman would be in soon, she said, and Rex would like a wash in the bathroom after his journey. That means they don't wash there themselves, thought Rex. It was cold in the bathroom. The solitary towel hanging beside the coffin-shaped bath was hard and thin. Round the walls stood bottles of petrified plums and jam, all neatly labelled with the name of the fruit and the date. There were several years of fruit and jam on the shelves.

Mrs Chapman was waiting outside in the passage to show him the way to his room. The room held the cold of a whole winter. The lino was shiny as ice. A framed printed card, hung near the dressing-table, looked like the rules they have up in hotel bedrooms. Rex read, TO A POUND OF LOVE ADD A LIBERAL MEASURE OF UNDERSTANDING AND MIX. On the dressing-table was a doyley, and a shell with a ship painted on it that no one could ever mistake for an ashtray.

Facing the walnut double bed with its blue-white cover, two dreadfully enlarged Chapman ancestors in thick dark oval frames possessed the room. They had dark flaws in their faces like craters on the moon. Behind the glass a cheekbone, a button on the man's coat, and the highlight on his hair stared blankly.

Rex began to unpack, looking for dry shoes. His brush and comb looked so uncomfortable beside the shell with the painted ship that he began to feel, not homesick for any particular place, but lonely and stranded. He reminded himself of other rooms he had slept in. This one would be no worse when it had been lived in. Someone must have slept in the bed once, and sat at the dressing-table doing their hair, and looked through the window over the fields when it wasn't raining like this.

Rex opened a door which he thought was a cupboard, but it opened into a small sitting-room which had the same clean but stale smell. This end of the house was a blind alley. There was a fluted fire-place and a firescreen with birds on it, an upright piano, upholstered chairs and a round walnut table. Rex smiled over the things laid out on the table. The velvet album, the stereoscope, the Family Bible. These objects looked familiar, he had met them so often in books. They were always amusing. He tried to think of a funny formula for the room, but nothing crossed his mind but the Spanish slang-word, *fatal*.

Thinking of Spain Rex saw the sun on the white wall of a house. Big black ants were busy about the cracks in the plaster. Pots of carnations basked by the wall. A fat red flower burst its sheath with a silent explosion.

The shadow under the fig tree is round like a pool. Dipping your hand in the shadow you feel its edge like water. Jim is sitting waiting under the fig tree where the plates and salads are set in the shade. The midday silence is full of life, and an exuberant smell of flowers and frying.

An old peasant sits down at the table, and cocking his head at Jim hands him a wine skin. Jim takes off his shirt, is standing up and throwing his head right back to catch the crimson trickle that floods his teeth. He raises the wine skin higher and higher. The wine falls in a thin bright arc.

Rex was lucky. He had had two years of living up to the hilt, then slipped out when the game was up. He hadn't said goodbye to his Spanish friends. Jim had been killed at Huesca.

Perhaps, Rex thought, his excitement over committees, his travels, his political work which had led him in the end to Spain, were only forms of escape from what he was feeling now in the Sunday smell of the sitting-room.

He was young when it first got him. It was after dinner. The rain seemed to have set in and he had settled down with a book, when suddenly the sun came out in a watery way and he was told to go and play in the garden.

There was nothing in the garden but the long watery afternoon with Monday on its horizon. He walked down the path till he came to a jungle of trees and a high brick wall at the end. This was called 'down the garden'. Under the dripping wall was the puppy's grave, and an overturned flower-pot which Rex sat on when he cried about something. He didn't cry now. This wasn't something that had happened. It was there.

'You're just a lump of misery, Master Rex,' his nurse would say when he had the Sunday feeling. He grew out of it. It only came back in waiting-rooms, and long dull dreams. But when it did he knew it was there all the time, and his interesting life was only painted over it.

The door of the sitting-room creaked and a child came in. A plain little thing in a gym tunic.

'Dinner is nearly ready, Mr Rex.'

'So you are Lila,' said Rex, and the child came over to him.

'Were you looking at the pictures? That's St Peter's at Rome on top.'

'I've seen that one,' said Rex. 'It has a great wide space in front dotted with frozen fountains.'

'Oh, Mr Rex, could you play the piano then? Can you play a hymn? "Our Lord Is Ever Present" has a pretty tune.'

'I might have a try sometime.'

'Oh, do have a pop at it, Mr Rex.'

'But not now. I think they're calling you to lay the table.'

Mr Chapman was small and bald, and wore a neat white beard. He shook hands with Rex and they all sat down to the meal. After piling the plates with pumpkin and potato, the old lady abruptly laid her hand on her forehead as a signal. They bent their heads in an attitude of prayer. During the next few minutes' silence Rex looked through his fingers at Lila, searching her dull face for a clue that would lead back to Jim.

Rex sat facing the clear blue eyes of the old man. He talked in a slow, high, gentle voice about the government and the weather. He seemed to be looking at Rex from a long way off. He said something about Spain. That it was through lack of faith that the Republicans had perished. But when Rex began to argue the point he was not listening. Rex thought at first that he was deaf, but he was not deaf. He was only out of focus.

Mrs Chapman kept urging Rex to have some more.

'I hope our simple fare agrees with your taste,' she said. 'Our neighbours don't bother to grow veges, but Isaiah has been on a sort of diet for years. You forget to eat while you're talking,' she said to her husband.

'I have sufficient for my needs,' said Mr Chapman. Then turning to Rex, he began to denounce the forces of evil which he said were undermining the churches. Rex didn't know what the forces were. Whether it was the brewers or the Catholics or the Anglicans who were doing all the harm. When he appeared to have finished Rex tried to say a word about Jim. But the old chap had withdrawn again, and was absorbed in scraping the burnt edge off the pudding dish.

In the afternoon they went round the farm. The mud was so deep it oozed over the tops of the good boots Rex had been given in Spain. Rex had to see everything, Mr Chapman pointing out the places where he should have sown lupins to keep down the weeds, and telling him where things were, and where they used to be, and what might have to be done sometime.

Half his words were lost in the sudden gusts of wind that passed with a rattle of rain on the iron roofs like the sound of machine-guns, leaving a dead stillness behind, and the rain quietly falling. Then the sun burst out with a startling feverish glare between the black clouds and the shivering green of the pastures.

Rex spoke of a plan that Jim had made for the farm. The old man stood very close to him while he was talking, as though he was waiting for something. Like a child who has run up with a treasure in his hand, and well-trained, waits quiet and expectant, until the people have finished their talk and will look at it. The old man waited, then with a meek insistent smile, he brought out what he had hoarded up to say.

They walked and walked through wet grass. Mr Chapman was

amazingly active, and rosy as a child, but from time to time a wave of milky pallor flooded his face, like the first waves of death lapping over him, and receding so gently that he was unaware.

'You see yon trees,' he said happily. 'I have seen them all grow.'

He had started little gardens all over the place. Stopping at one of these forgotten gardens he said, 'That was Jim's garden. It's Lila's now, but she doesn't take care of it much.'

The afternoon seemed endless. When they got back Mrs Chapman and Lila had changed into different dresses and they had tea, stewed apples and scones and home-baked bread. Mr Chapman was quiet now, he had talked himself out. Mrs Chapman was worried because she had made too much tea, and Rex had to have a third cup. The child would go to bed soon, and they would want to hear about Jim's death.

But when supper was over Mr Chapman began to turn the knob of the radio. 'There are several services on the air,' he said. Managing the radio the old man was pathetic. He got first a waltz, then someone talking fast in a frightening voice, but at last the organ burst bitterly through. 'The Presbyterians, I believe,' he said. He smiled like a conjurer. 'I hope that will be agreeable to you.'

Rex longed to smoke to take the edge off it, but it was no good upsetting these left-behind old things the first night.

After the service ended Mr Chapman drew his chair to the table and began to write very slowly in a large book. Rex, passing behind him to get nearer the fire, read, 'August 28. Burnt bullock in three days.'

Mr Chapman read over what he had written and shut the book. Mrs Chapman counted stitches.

'Shall I bring in a log or two?' asked Mr Chapman.

'I hardly think it's worth it,' said Mrs Chapman, looking at Rex for assent.

'I suppose you heard that Jim died very bravely. I sent back the few things he always carried with him. You got them all right?'

Mrs Chapman nodded. 'Yes, thank you, we got the parcel. And then we got your letter saying you would be coming out to New Zealand just the same.'

'I didn't give you the details of his death in my letter.' Rex seemed to be saying a lesson to the old things who happened to be Jim's parents. What was left of Jim seemed now to be lost between the three of them.

'He had only been ten days up at the front. The front was changing all the time and we never knew where we were, but Jim and I were always together. On this day they asked for volunteers to go to some comrades with a machine-gun a bit further up the road that went to Huesca. The road was impassable, but there was some cover beside it. We thought someone could get round with a mule load of stuff. They were out of munitions, you see. Jim passed an open vineyard, but when he was under the trees a stray bullet got him.'

Rex got through the story he had told again and again. It was stale even before he had begun to tell it, because so many people had been killed that way.

The old man frowned, seemed to be groping for something. Mrs Chapman flushed and swallowed. Rex thought, They still don't really believe it.

'Do I understand you to say that my son met his death as a soldier, a combatant?'

'Why certainly,' said Rex. 'He was a good soldier. He died like a hero.'

They sat in silence while a death ripple passed over the face of the old man.

'It must have been a terrible shock to you,' Rex said.

'It is a terrible shock,' said Mr Chapman.

'You see we didn't know,' said his wife. 'He went over to do relief work for the Quakers.'

Of course. Anyone could have known it. Jim had even told him once about some sect his father belonged to. Why couldn't he have remembered? How easy it would have been to say that their son was killed bringing in a wounded comrade. He might have been killed any day bringing children away from Madrid. The idiocy of implying that Jim was a fighter. Even his death of a hero had been an accident. Other people had been over there to the machine-gun post and nothing had happened, till in the end it seemed pretty safe to go.

Done now. Couldn't be helped. He would leave in a day or two and find a job in Auckland, perhaps get back to Europe before the next war started. Thank God he'd hedged when he'd replied to the old man's letter offering him a job on the farm.

'Well, I suppose it's time to turn in,' he said.

'You know the way to your room,' said Mrs Chapman. 'There's an extra blanket under the mattress if you should need it.'

She said good night and went out to the kitchen, where Rex could hear her fussing about preparing for breakfast.

Now that Rex had said good night and was standing up he wanted Mr Chapman to understand. It was easy now. The same as when you leave a house and have a last word over the fence, or when you go to bed and come back for something and stay for hours talking to the person you're supposed to have left.

'If you had been there yourself I know you would understand,' he said. 'At the front it was spiritually safe, but when you went on leave you'd find you couldn't sit in certain cafés because "the others" were there. Jim thought it was mostly the fault of the foreigners who were coming and going, raising money and sympathy for Spain, and raising hell too. Political parties couldn't agree about what their adherents were dying for. Jim couldn't have stood any more without losing his faith.

'I thought Jim stuck to the Quakers because they did the least harm. They were too busy saving children's lives. But as the war went on there was too much advice and relief. Jim said he wouldn't consider the children saved if the war was lost. One day he'd been to the centre with posters they'd asked him to get. Pictures of children playing and studying, with underneath, Revolution in Education. They blacked out the R before they would use them. So Jim walked out and joined the Brigade.'

If only Mr Chapman would sit still. He was busy again searching methodically among some papers on top of the bookshelf. He brought down a brown paper parcel, and coming quietly round the table while Rex talked laid it in front of him.

Some of Jim's books.

Perhaps some weeks before he had thought about the books, and placed the parcel there where he could easily find it, to show Jim's friend. Though he seemed so vague the little plan, independent of anything that might intervene, had firmly stuck in his mind. So now Rex had to sit down at the table again and open the parcel, and turn the leaves of the books. The first page of an exercise book had written on it in curly writing:

September 4th, 1915.   *Padded*
               Purr
               whisker curley
               claws paws
               hungry rosy

Poetry
This is the weather the cuckoo loves
And so do I
Be careful always look first to right and then to left
People generally travel on camels when crossing
Dead said the frost
Buried and lost

The leaf buds are covered with tough leather flaps called scales
We must not bring razor blades to school because they are dangerous.
Do unto others (I know the rest) This is called the Golden Rule ...

'Well, I think I'll turn in now,' Rex said. 'I'll take the books if you don't mind.'

'Certainly,' said Mr Chapman. 'We rise at six-thirty in the winter. I hope you will find your room comfortable. We call it the guest room now. I thought you might find it more convenient later on to sleep in a smaller room that opens on to the back veranda. It's very handy for the sheds and you wouldn't bring dirt into the house. That's a great consideration with Mrs Chapman you know. But there is time enough to make the change after you have started work and become familiar with our way of life. Mrs Chapman was insistent that you should have Jim's room at first. I suppose you saw his picture over the bed?'

ERIK DE MAUNY

In Transit

He dropped off the bus near the big concrete barracks, but having hunched his shoulders to get the heavy pack into a new position he turned his back on the dim, forbidding building and glimpsing through the dusk a pair of concrete gateposts and a stretch of barbed-wire fence, trudged towards them.

Beneath the last luminous glow of the sunset lay a slope of waste land dotted with tents. A shadowy sentry told him when he approached that this was the transit camp.

'I suppose I can get a doss-down here?' he asked.

'Go to that first tent and speak to the sergeant,' the sentry said, motioning.

The pack felt lighter already as he thanked the sentry and stumbled over the rubble to the square tent. The last light was a sickly yellow, reminiscent of a northern winter, but the evening air was mild, faintly perfumed with damp grass and petrol fumes.

Inside the tent, which was partitioned by a blanket, he waited, tentatively striking a match to dispel the gloom. In a moment the sergeant emerged.

'Good evening,' the soldier said with a grin, 'I wondered, could I have a bed here for the night?'

'Going far?' the sergeant said, lonely for conversation.

'Want to get to Egypt tomorrow,' the soldier said, 'last lap. I've been hiking down from Syria. Been on leave.'

'Funny way to spend leave,' the sergeant said. He had lit a pocket torch and was fumbling among some papers. Then he grunted: 'Name?'

'Bennett, George.'

'Just George?' the sergeant asked, and they both laughed.

Bennett slid his pack from his back and a slight muzziness of liquor came over him. 'I suppose I can easily get a lift if I go to the petrol point early in the morning?'

'Depends,' the sergeant said. 'Do you have to go all the way tomorrow?'

'Yes. I was delayed a day in Jerusalem.'

Delayed, by God. Oh Julie, he almost said aloud. She was still so near. It was only an hour since he had said goodbye to her. He felt half-elated, half-sad to be out and alone again. Still, the thought kept running in his head, we had a good time, a bloody good time. Oh Julie, do you miss me now?

The sergeant gave him blankets and pointed out a tent in the gloom, at the end of a row of six standing beside what appeared to be a cow track.

As he stumbled over the deeply rutted field, Bennett was slightly oppressed by the deserted air of the place. It had the lost air of an abandoned picnic-ground. Dim rows of lorries stood behind the tents. He did not see a soul. Pausing for a moment, he faced in the direction of the city he had just quitted. From the deep canyons of Jerusalem, far away, came a hum of activity. He sighed, belched joylessly, and turned about. In the other direction, Bethlehem was already nightbound under sentinel stars.

If only there was a bit of life about the place. He resented the deathly silence. His tired mind craved distraction. God, what a war! he said aloud.

When he pulled back the flap and stepped into the tent, a soft foreign voice said out of the solid darkness:

'Good evening.'

From his accent, the man sounded like a Greek.

Bennett fumbled awkwardly to light a match, the blankets and pack clutched under one arm. In the pale flicker of light he saw a canvas bag on the first board bed and flung his armful down on the second.

'Isn't there a lantern in the bloody place? No, I suppose there wouldn't be in such a god-forsaken hole,' Bennett said irritably, still remembering Julie and the warm little flat.

'You haven't any blankets,' he observed in a second match flare, 'just arrived too?'

'Yes ... I didn't know where to go.'

He looked up sharply at the plaintive note in the man's voice.

'You just ask them over there and they'll give you some.' He made a vague gesture.

After a long pause, the other said, 'I am ill.'

He didn't look very well, gripping the tentpole and breathing hard. He said softly, pleadingly, in that curious, half-Greek accent, 'What should I do?'

'There should be an M.O., you know, a medical officer, about,' Bennett suggested, not very hopefully, remembering the deserted air of the place.

'Oh, no,' the man said, terrified.

'It's too bad. I don't know what the hell you can do.' He glanced with distaste at the dim outline of the man, the rumpled khaki, the pasty-white

face with strained eyes peering at him. Suddenly finding the tent
unbearable he muttered, 'It's so hot in here . . .' and fumbled his way out.

The purplish bloom of night which seems to emanate from rather than
settle upon the sparse, pale green hills of Palestine, had come to the camp.
A wireless, faintly crackling, attracted him. Hearing a faint sound of a jazz
band, he was haunted by a sudden melancholy. A hundred yards away,
after weaving his path carefully between the guy-ropes of deserted tents,
he found a small canteen.

In a pool of light half a dozen drivers were silently consuming congealed
fried eggs off tin plates. They made way for Bennett and he bought a
candle, cigarettes and a cup of tea.

He was standing, sobered, reflectively sipping the strong hot stuff a
moment later when the man from the tent came over, like a dog that is
frightened of being beaten, into the circle. He approached Bennett as a
friend.

'I got blankets. It was so dark there.'

There was such a plangent pathos in his voice and his square face was
so set with humility Bennett wanted to shake him. Instead he said:

'Are you Greek?'

'No. I am an Arab,' the man said. After a moment he said wistfully,
looking at the candle:

'Are you coming back to the tent?'

Bennett put the thick mug down and nodded.

Halfway back, leaning towards him, the man said softly, in an
extraordinarily confidential tone: 'I am a Christian Arab.'

Bennett felt he could say nothing to this. His melancholy, temporarily
vanquished by the hot tea, returned. He hated this sensation of emptiness,
of cessation of activity. It reminded him of seeing people off at a wharf.
He momentarily cursed his own importunity at leaving the city so early.
It was barely eight o'clock and all tiredness had vanished from him. He
was puzzled by his companion, wondering gloomily whether he might not
be a little mad.

In the tent they smoked a cigarette almost in silence. The Arab groaned
once or twice, when he bent down to lay out the greasy blankets. Only
when they were both lying down in the fantastic light of the guttering
candle, he suddenly launched a remark.

'God is very good,' he said. 'You are a good man. May the Christian God
bless you.' This was said with great gravity.

'Thanks,' Bennett said, stiffening. He stifled a wild desire to laugh, which soon turned to pity at the laboured breathing of his companion. The Arab was obviously suffering.

'Where have you got the pain?'

'Here, how do you say?' the Arab demonstrated, tapping his chest, 'and here.' He stroked his stomach over the blanket. 'But I say all the time, God is good.'

Bennett snuffed the candle with spittle on thumb and forefinger. In the darkness the sick Arab began a rambling story.

'I have this pain all the time, ever since I was in Iraq. I was with my brother, a good man. He was not a Christian.' He muttered in Arabic.

'What's that?' Bennett asked, half interested.

'I say, God rest his soul.' He paused. 'We are in a convoy. Many Englisi. Then the rebels chase us. They catch my brother. They say, "You a Christian. You must die." Then he say, "No. I good Mohammedan." All the same, they shoot him. I am hiding under the road.' (Under the road, Bennett wondered, and then realized he meant in a culvert.) 'They come to shoot me. I say, I am good Mohammedan (God have mercy on me) and they are going to shoot me, going to shoot me . . .' his voice was hoarse with fear. 'Then Iraq officer come and say "I won't shoot you. But something more bad." Then I am taken in very bad sand storm to Baghdad and they put me in prison.'

During this recital he frequently stopped, panting for breath and as if on the verge of tears: or paused to mutter some supplication in his own tongue. Bennett made sounds of sympathy, privately disbelieving. The Arab went on.

'For twenty-four days I am in prison in Baghdad. I am in a little room. There is water on the floor. Only one piece of bread to eat every day. There are big rats that come every night and try to eat me. Then I get sick here.' He stroked his stomach and became silent.

'What happened then?' Bennett said at last.

'In twenty-four days the Englisi come. I am free again. God is good. Inshallah. But I am ill.'

'Why the hell don't you see a doctor?' Bennett exploded at last, annoyed against his will at the man's fatalism.

'No. It is no good. They give me medicine. But it is all the same. I get the pain all the time.' His gaunt jaws cracked in the darkness. At length he said, astonishingly, as if it were plain statement of fact.

'You are a Christian.'

'Well, yes,' Bennett said reluctantly. He hadn't thought ever about it.

Through a chink in the tent flap made by a rising night wind, he stared at the wanly lit stony ground and pondered the matter. Stars above Bethlehem. He felt something like gratitude for the stranger beside him.

The man was breathing stertorously. Then he raised his voice.

'You are good,' he said. 'I will pray for you to our God.'

'Thank you,' Bennett said. It was an inadequate, an inane response, but he fell asleep on it, almost lulled by the jerky breathing of the sick Arab.

Footsteps scrunching on the stones awoke him at 6 o'clock next morning. Somewhere a cold truck engine was roaring, dying out and then picking up again. Two or three men went by, shouting, running, and buttoning shirts up as they went. The sun was pallid as an invalid, with its first, feeble yellow light, but the day was already vigorously awake.

'How are you this morning?' Bennett asked.

'Better, God be praised. No pain.' The Arab lay still on his back. His face had a look of both exhaustion and contentment.

So Bennett thought to leave him. Ignoring the smell of breakfast cooking which floated across the line of tents, he was starting without a meal. The Arab suddenly leapt up, dressing with surprising swiftness.

When Bennett had shouldered his pack, the man shook him by the hand. It made Bennett embarrassed; he felt even more so, a moment later when, as he passed the sentry by the concrete gateposts, the Arab called loudly after him:

'Thank you for hearing me. God be with you.'

Bennett winked at the sentry, who winked confidentially back and queried:

'He's a bit barmy?'

Bennett nodded, grinning. But an instant later on the open road, with the day of sun and blinding blue whelming down from the barren hills, his face became set and he was not so sure. The episode might avail him nothing, but it suddenly seemed like an oasis in a lonely, barren plain.

ALLEN CURNOW

The Unhistoric Story

Whaling for continents suspected deep in the south
The Dutchman envied the unknown, drew bold
Images of market-place, populous river-mouth,
The Land of Beach ignorant of the value of gold:
    Morning in Murderers' Bay,
    Blood drifted away.
    It was something different, something
    Nobody counted on.

Clinging like a fly to cape and clouded snow
Cook prisoned them in islands, turning from planets
His measuring mission, showed what the musket could do,
Made his Christmas goose of the wild gannets.
    Still as the collier steered
    No continent appeared;
    It was something different, something
    Nobody counted on.

The roving tentacles rested, touched, clutched
Substantial earth, that is, accustomed haven
For the hungry whaler. Some inland, some hutched
Rudely in bays, the shaggy foreshore shaven,
    Lusted, preached as they knew
    But as the children grew
    It was something different, something
    Nobody counted on.

Green slashed with flags, pipeclay and boots in the bush,
Christ in canoes and the musketed Maori boast;
All a rubble-rattle at Time's glacial push:
Vogel and Seddon howling empire from an empty coast
    A vast ocean laughter
    Echoed unheard, and after
    All it was different, something
    Nobody counted on.

The pilgrim dream pricked by a cold dawn died
Among the chemical farmers, the fresh towns; among
Miners, not husbandmen, who piercing the side
Let the land's life, found like all who had so long
   Bloodily or tenderly striven
   To rearrange the given,
   It was something different, something
   Nobody counted on.

After all re-ordering of old elements
Time trips up all but the humblest of heart
Stumbling after the fire, not in the smoke of events;
For many are called, but many are left at the start,
   And whatever islands may be
   Under or over the sea,
   It is something different, something
   Nobody counted on.

GREVILLE TEXIDOR

Santa Cristina

Each day sheds its skin like a snake,
But not the days of Fiesta.

Yet the first of the summer, when the lilies of Santa Cristina flowered out of bare sand, though still marked on calendars at Lloret, passed unnoticed. No one had come but the old tramp who lived on the hill. It was later in May that the fishermen set up their heather shelter. The visitors came in June for the bathing season.

The fishermen sat at their table of two planks, eating bread and fish under a lantern. 'Sit down with us, Auntie,' they said, and they gave her some warm red wine. 'Drink up,' they said; 'old age comes to all of us. Tell us that salty story about the priest.'

But old Cristina, who liked to exchange words with strangers, to tell them she had never been a gypsy, but as a child had slept on white sheets, now that the chance had come, remembered nothing. The thick curtain of night hung too close round the lighted circle of sand. There was nothing but the night and the taste of death in each suck of a hollow tooth.

'You must have had many, many sweethearts,' they said.

'I was pure as the nuns of Lloret' (at this they were ready to laugh). 'I was, you might say, like the Virgin up on the hill.'

Their faces grew larger under the swinging light, their mouths ready to laugh. 'We can't believe you in that,' one of them said, 'but now you won't be afraid to go home in the dark.'

Their laughter threatened to bring down the rocks and the night. With laughter after her, she fled to the hill.

The vine-house where Juan kept his sprays and sacks was her home for the summer. Juan left his hoes outside, and she took them in and put them out in the morning. No one entered the whitewashed stone hut that smelt inside of stale sunlight and earth. Here after dark, behind the broken door, she kept watch with the frogs that tolled deep, the coastguards whistling from far and near cliffs, and the owls that called and answered from nests of darkness.

But on nights when the moon and the tide of nightingales rose the watchers were silenced, for now the valley was boiling with light and life. Then if a cloud crossed the white life of the valley Cristina would step outside to curse it away, and sit in the doorway keeping an eye on things, till a grey breeze lifted the night and a bird called with a soft human voice.

At sunrise Cristina sat at the door of her hut. Already the black procession of ants was moving along the ditch between dry drifts of snail shells. The ants, dull black of burnt paper like a funeral procession, were strange in daylight. Often Cristina walked with the procession all down the steep road between vines, then under the level shadows of cypresses. But after crossing a corner of the courtyard it disappeared behind the church, where she did not care to follow.

Cristina looked over the valley. On the silent slopes the many vine houses were white and secret in the early sun. The saint's shrine had the more homely air of a brick villa. It stood near the hut, where a turn in the road gave the first sight of the headland lying against the blue, looking small and sheltered between brown slopes of vineyards, and resting there in a nest of pines, like a white egg, the cupola of the church.

Smoke and clear voices rose from the trees. The day beginning. The summer, the season beginning. Plenty of company, Auntie Cristina.

The Alsatian bitch, dusty and decrepit as Auntie, came silently shuffling in the soft dust. She was looking for her puppies, born yesterday, that someone had taken away. She stopped, sniffed sadly, then padded on up the hill.

A stone struck the wall of the hut, chipping the plaster. The son from the hotel was coming up the road, a boy of six with cheeks like purple grapes.

'Don't you remember your old Auntie?'

'You stink,' he said; 'you have lice in your dress.'

'Don't you remember, dearest, we played in the church where the sacred light strung beads of yellow and blue?'

'I must go,' he said. 'I am going to trap birds in the woods.'

On the sun-white dust of the road the priest's black was outside nature. The black drank his sweat. Even his beaver hat was matted and dull.

He had come to make arrangements for the fiesta. The house where priests once lived was now the hotel, and few Masses were said in the church, but the bones would have to be rowed over as usual. He himself had come by boat from Lloret, but the boatman was going fishing, so now he must return on foot in the heat unless he could get a lift along the highroad. People with cars weren't very considerate.

He stopped in the shade of the hut to wipe his face and bless Auntie Cristina. 'You must step into the convent when you are passing. The sisters will welcome you and give you a meal. There is always bread in abundance – good white bread. For a few hours' work you'd be suitably rewarded. The church cares for the poor and lowly,' he said. 'The poorest and lowliest are not forgotten. I could envy you, with nothing on earth to do, sitting here all day in the shade,' he said. And he blessed her and walked away.

Nothing moved. Only the sparrows were keeping it up in the heat, chipping and chipping, like a shower of little pieces of broken china.

Rabbit, rice, spices. A procession of smells took shape and passed the door of the hut on the quivering air. Dinner 'Your dinner, Auntie Cristina.'

Through air of watered silk she moved down the hillside grey in the midday, a gliding dot in the eye, grey on the grey.

Carlotta looked at the heap of rice in the pan. Then, 'You may as well have it all,' she said; 'it would only go to the rabbits.'

'The señores don't eat well?'

'There is only the one señor from Barcelona. Or rather a mechanic, I should say, who comes down on Saturdays. His friend, a foreigner, is here. I suppose he likes to keep her out of the way. She hardly eats anything. She might be an *artista* from one of the vaudeville theatres, but no, she's not pretty enough. She might be a nursemaid. There are plenty of foreign nurses and maïds in town that have been thrown out of their own country, they say. But why should we mind as long as they pay their board? Our regular señores are coming next week. I had such a silly dream the other night – something about a snail I put in the rice.'

'That's all right,' Auntie said; 'it only means the rice has stuck to the pan.'

'Well, that's true, certainly; three months gone now, but why should the dream mean that?'

'Sometimes they mean one thing, sometimes another. It just depends on what's coming, you see.'

Auntie carried her dinner across the sunny sandy space of the courtyard. She set her dinner down on the church steps and went to the tap over a basin of tiles where travellers washed their hands. The Santa Cristina water was cold and good.

One of the maïds came out and stood in the shadow of the balcony. 'Ola Auntie, you're back again,' she said. 'After such a hard spring. March takes the old and takes the young when he can. I'll be glad when the season begins. Nothing much goes on at Santa Cristina, but then, of course, something will happen when you least expect it. The foreign blonde is there behind the church if you care to see her.'

A narrow path led round the side of the church, past the dry scrape of sparrows in the dusty geranium hedge, and the sick smell from the pit where the rabbits waited, twitching and nibbling under a cloud of flies.

But Auntie Cristina did not care to go there because the back of the church was round and blank with no window to open its smooth whiteness. Here on hot afternoons the children played, playing at moving statues. How quiet they were. When you turned they had not moved at all. But at last a shadow fell on the white wall. How quiet it was on the hot afternoons, the trees and the rocks standing so still in their shadows.

It was not yet time for the afternoon wind that lived behind the hills and panted down the valley and fluttered the shutters with hot, heavy breaths. Nothing was moving except the ant procession, making a detour to its dark crack in the plaster where the foreigner sat on the wall that rounded the rock.

Under her eyes the sea spread solid to the horizon, as if it had hardened for ever, the rocks embedded in blue. To the south the still surface was smudged with smoke. There Barcelona, clanging trams and factories and manifestoes. But what does it matter? she thought. I have suffered enough.

To the north, along the slowly curving coast, pale fingers lying stretched on the blue. On a clear day you could count them up to ten, the last one fading into the Gulf of Rosas. Rosas, the frontier and the other countries that he was always asking her about. 'Europe ends with the Pyrenees,' he said, 'and if it weren't for the news-sheet we get through the union we'd have little idea of what's going on in the world.' But nothing can happen, she thought. I have suffered enough.

'She sits there all day doing nothing,' the maid said.

Towards evening she stood near the barred front of the shrine. She carried a straggling spray of the clematis that tangled the bushes and hedges in white webs. She looked down the road, crushed the trailers of flowers, and pushed them inside the bars. She started when Auntie Cristina came through the hedge, rags and bones walking, and a desolate monkey grin. She was angry, too. Nobody should have seen.

'It's all right,' Cristina said, 'he will come for sure.'

From the back of the shrine, just out of the sun, but remote, the little image, in shiny painted robes and a filigree crown, stared straight ahead over a litter of brown flower hay. An engine throbbed like a heart on the distant hills. It stopped. The two stood still in the stillness that was coming out of the shrine. Then they caught it again. He had turned off the main road.

He came rushing round the corner and stopped in front of the shrine.

'Anyone would think you were saying your prayers,' he said. He unwound the silk scarf from his throat and brushed the dust from his light town suit.

'And why not? Dearest, you're looking so well today. The spring here is curative. Apart from all the superstition there is, a doctor in town told me, it's wonderful water.'

He propped his motor-bike against the shrine. 'See what I've brought you,' he said. '*Film Fun* and peanut candy, American cigarettes and a manifesto.' Then he found a silver *peseta* for Auntie. 'Now tell the pretty young lady her fortune.'

'Give me your hand, little one. Don't be afraid. My hands are black, but my heart is white as snow. I see a tall, handsome man – and a priest –'

'A marriage, no doubt. And don't you see a baby? A baby or two? That's the best fortune she can do. If she were only a little cleverer she'd be a saint like my aunt in Badalona. She may be alive still for all I know, bedridden, and lying on the bare bedsprings. One day she bought an old Virgin they were throwing out from the church. Took pity on it perhaps. The carrier delivered it in the afternoon, and the next day it broke out with a miracle. So it went on. Miracles every day. The priests were wild. Of course they tried to buy it back from my aunt, but no. She had come to an understanding with the thing.'

But the girl, though she laughed lovingly, was not listening. The vine-houses, in slanting sun, seemed white shrines, inhabited by a white and simple secret, almost transparent. Finding the church so empty they have tried to cage it here in this pretty villa. The clematis is dying behind the bars. This is the priest's province. The black, busy priest should know. If I thought so I'd go to church, buy candles and other junk. But no, he doesn't know.

'Still, they don't care to move,' Cristina was saying, 'our Virgin now. Her head is down there in the glass box –'

'Well, hurry up and finish the lady's fortune.'

'I think I'll last longer than she will,' Cristina said.

They are angry, Cristina, they are going away.

Dusk comes up from the sea. The saint fades and retreats to the end of a tunnel of silence. An old woman sits alone on the hill.

The days between fiestas are all alike, but the day of Santa Cristina is blue and gold. Christina's procession of golden boats crosses the blue sea. The delicate skeleton, pure as a white flower, wrapped in white shawls, is being carried to Rome.

The wind rises, waves crash on the rocks. The ship is lost, but the skull, frail as an eggshell, finds its way to the beach under the pines. Here she wishes to rest and the church is built. Later her ribs appear on the beach at Lloret and are joyfully installed in the church of Our Lady. Though people think more of the head, there is never ill-feeling, and on her name day there is a sea procession bringing the bones for a visit.

From the edge of the cliff Cristina watched a black fishing-boat beached. Then she hurried down to join the procession. The ribs, resting on velvet, were carried by a priest up the rocky path. A boy walked behind, swinging a censer.

'There won't be much doing today,' she grumbled to the procession; 'the priest, two serving boys and two fishermen and a stranger from town with a cigar in his mouth.'

The church was swept, there was clematis on the altar. Light poured like wine over the rough stones, wax arms and hearts materialized in corners, a model schooner waited a breeze from heaven.

They made good time with the Mass and in half an hour the skull, a desolate monkey grin under its wreath of paper orange blossoms, was reverently hurried back to the glass case. Then they all sat down to lunch in the shade. Carlotta, who had not appeared at the Mass, now came out to ask if the rice was good.

The mechanic walked by with his arm round the foreign blonde. He was saying in Spanish, and loud enough for everyone to hear, 'What a charade! Education is needed in this country. We shall soon see what the Popular Front can do. And if the politicians won't act – then we shall see –'

One of the maids came out and sat down on the church steps beside Cristina. 'Listen to this. A dream ripped through my head. I only caught the tail end of it. You know how the buses whizz down the hill in August? Well, I dreamt the Blue Line bus drove right through the church, shattering it like an eggshell, and then right on over the cliff, with all the holiday-makers still in their seats. I looked in the book. There's brooms and blood and brambles, but nothing whatever about a bus there. What do you make of it?'

But Cristina was out of sorts. All day she'd been whining and worrying the Father for candle ends, though she knew there were only the few Carlotta gave.

'What do you need candles for, old lady? You can say your prayers in the dark.'

The stranger from town wandered out of the church, lighted the cigar that was in his mouth, and seeing Carlotta, gave her ten *pesetas*. 'When do you think they'll be returning the cutlets?' he asked. 'You see, I have to get back to the city tonight.'

He sat down again and gave the priest a cigar. One fisherman was smoking, one was asleep. The acolytes were making obscene shapes with bread. 'Yes, we might as well be starting,' the priest said.

There was no ceremony for the walk back to the beach. A fisherman handed in the bones and shoved the boat off the shingle. Then they rowed away and Carlotta released the rabbits tied by the legs, ready to kill if more people had come to the fête.

The days between fiestas are all alike, but Our Lady of Mercies is a rich day. People leave things behind under the pines. Small and large copper coins fall into outstretched hand. A letter, a visit, some trouble, a dark stranger. Ten centimos for Santa Cristina's sake.

'These are bad times, old gypsy, terrible times.'

'Yes, sir, I know. I know. He played with his son on the sand at the mouth of a cave. How did the story continue? With spinning and suffering. Always the man said Death. There were journeys to make. We lived on the edge of the sea, a phosphorescent thread drawn between us. The end did not kill me. Only a pricking when the King died. It was on the next day that I saw my son. "How do you feel?" I asked him. "I feel all right, thank you, mother," he said. And all the time a grey snail was peeping through a hole in his head.'

'She's like Rosita that runs about on the Ramblas. Coming home from a night out you'll see her all dolled up, on her way to meet the Majorca boat. Her son or lover it was that never came back.'

'No, no, not like that shameless one with bows and paper fans stuck in her hair. As a child I knew the feel of white cambric and the feel of velvet, too.'

The days between fiestas are all alike, but at night the sky is red. To the south the sky is red, and the moon is weak in the dark half of the sky. The old dog whines and circles about the hut. Cristina screams her away and stays at the door, keeping watch with the weak moon.

At the hotel they were just sitting down to supper. 'Something is passing along the road,' they said.

He stood in the doorway, darkening the night. He stood above the hut like a dark tree. 'Let me come in,' he said in a voice that was hardly heard.

Cristina said, in a voice that was hardly heard, 'You can't come in. You have come to the wrong house.'

'Let me come in,' he said. 'I have to lie down here for a while, old mother.'

'I haven't a bed to offer you,' she said.

'I was thinking of white sheets, but never mind. I was on my way when I got this little wound. A little one, you can fix it up for me. Don't be afraid now, give me your hand.' And he pushed her fingers under the folds of his scarf and inside the folds of his scarf it was warm and wet.

She gathered her voice to shake off the weight of his presence. She screamed. 'Take your death out of here.'

'Quiet. This is between ourselves. You know me,' he said. 'I gave you a *peseta* only last week.'

'Take it again!' she cried. And fumbling in her bundle she scattered *pesetas* and pennies over the floor, screaming to drown the voice that was saying, 'You know me.' She screamed and cursed till the doorway was light again. He had gone and she was alone, keeping watch on the empty vineyards.

Down at the hotel they were all awake, listening for late news. 'Oh, hear old Auntie! She's bad tonight with the moon.'

A big black ant was crawling on the white slope of the vineyards. Cristina ran to the hut and hurriedly closed the door on the priest's blessing. 'What do you want this time?' (But the latch of the door had gone.) 'Surely you haven't come so far and so late to take me away to the convent. I know what you have come for, you green old man.'

'You've nothing to fear,' he said, 'now that the devils are loosed. But I'm on my way to the north. Give me a shawl and some rags to cover me, else it's all up with Father Josep.'

He strangled her screams and held her against the wall, dragging at the rags of her petticoats. The skirts gave way without a sound, like cobwebs, and she lay quiet, a heap of pale bones on the ground until a finger of moonlight entered the hut. Then she gathered her bones together and covered herself with a sack.

Down at the hotel they were all awake, listening for shots in the trees. 'How quiet it is,' they said. 'Well, everyone has to sleep sometime.'

Three cicadas were keeping the day going. Aunt Cristina was resting under a fig tree. The midday meal was over, the shutters closed, and the house and the fields were silent. The sea was only a whisper far away. The sky was soft as bloom on grapes, hundreds of soft blue shawls and always another behind. Juan moved along the rows of vines that waited like good children. And when he came up to where Cristina lay and called, 'How goes it, old lady?' because she loved the sound of a human voice, she threw off the blue and answered, 'All is well.'

At least one can say there's nothing wrong with the vines. We know the days of miracles are past, but what luck, all the same. For I don't think the season will open for us this year. No one will come with this unhappy war. When the foreigner heard her young man was dead she lay down on her bed without a cry, and still she's lying there. What could we do? The doctor has gone, they say. No one could do any more.

Let her lie. No one could do any more. The sky sank and covered Cristina with soft blue shawls. Slowly as the afternoon, Juan stooping and stopping, moved on between the vines, over the hill.

Like a ladder the white road stood on end in the heat. The Virgin's villa quivered in the sky. Cicadas screamed. The wind came suddenly up and tapped the shutter of the sick girl's room. The fig tree stretched in its shadow and advanced with all its branches. A wave crashed on the shore.

Cristina slept. She was so tired of keeping an eye on things.

DENIS GLOVER

*It Was D-Day**

The flotilla made a grand sight, steaming down to the open sea, threading its way in line ahead through the massed transports, crowded with men and vehicles that lay at anchor in the land-locked roadstead. In the grey evening could be smelt and felt the fresh tang of the Channel in one of its boisterous, threatening moods. The Commandos on deck looked round at the unfamiliar familiar scene, at the waters they had exercised in so often. They were cheerful but restrained. There was the island, there the spit. The mainland lay on the quarter, misty, indistinct, in the smoky setting sun. For many it would be their last sight of England.

I must close up a little. On this of all occasions our station-keeping must be perfect. *Steady on the stern of the next ahead, Cox'n.* What's that hoist? Good, the Flotilla Officer wants more revs. Let's do the thing in style; might be our last gesture. The unknown morrow lies over our bows. They're cheering us from the transports. 'Give 'em hell!' I expect we all feel how few we are, how small and very much alone. Being cheered makes one feel heroic in a grand and desperate way. We assault early, but the transports will be there soon enough. We're all in this.

Now's the time for our signature tune over the loudhailer. *Switch on, signalman.* Impudent and cheerful. But what's that? The pipes. Damn it, that's the Brigadier's own piper on the fo'c'sle of the flotilla leader. The pipes are best. Mine sounds strident, flauntingly casual about the prospect of death, too flamboyant a gesture – but the pipes, the pipes are striking, fittest music for the fight. *Number One, why isn't that man wearing a lifebelt? Does he think this is a bloody picnic?*

Pray now for luck. The Colonel and all these Commandos, battle-skilled and tough, putting themselves irrevocably into the hands of an amateur sailor. Well, I'll land these troops if it's the last thing I ever do – probably will be – I'll fight this ship till the guns fall off. Land them, if the whole crew lies dead on the deck. Oh, don't indulge in such silly private dramatics with yourself! *I say, Number One, ask the Middy to organize some cocoa.*

*

* Lieut. Denis Glover, R.N.Z.N.V.R., was awarded a D.S.C. for his work on D-Day.

'Look here, you chaps,' said the Flotilla Officer at that last briefing, 'we won't let the Commandos down. We know these troops, we've trained with them, and we think a hell of a lot of them. We can't and won't let them down. We've only got two things to do. First, find the right place over there, then put them ashore at all costs. What if we don't find exactly the right place? Don't start looking for it; land the troops at all costs.'

Port lookout! Keep your eyes open for a light on the port bow. By my reckoning it should have showed up by now. *Cox'n, how's your head?* South twenty east. And I estimate it should be south eleven east. But we can't steer to within ten degrees in this sea. All the same, don't want to end up in Le Havre – we'd look damn' silly making an invasion by ourselves. Where in hell are all those buoys? I haven't seen one yet, and by dead reckoning we've passed at least four. But how can you find buoys, or even lay them, in a sea like this? What a night – dark and wet, with just the sort of sea that makes the old tub wallow like a lovesick hippopotamus. All right for sailors, but I'm thinking about the troops. A lot sick already and half the rest in a stupor. They'll need their strength tomorrow, every ounce of it. I wish to hell I felt certain, absolutely certain, of our exact position. We're too much to the east. They said to avoid easting, emphatically. Wonder if I ought to signal up the line. No, Rupert knows what he's doing, though I wouldn't allow so much for wind myself. Funny, I thought there'd be lots of traffic about, and we haven't seen a single thing. Of course we land pretty early, and are faster than most.

My God! Just these twelve small ships, and all these precious lives, alone in mid-Channel. Query, are lives precious in wartime? Yes, until they can be thrown away for their planned objective. *Hello, Colonel, come up on the bridge.* I wonder how he feels. *How are we getting on? Oh, fine, sir. Right up to time. We'll hit the run-in position in approximately three hours twenty minutes.* Either that or Le Havre Harbour boom. Wacko, Rupert's spotted a dan buoy and altered course. That's better, south five east. *You see, sir, everything weighed off! Buoys laid to mark every channel – can't go wrong! No, the R.N.V.R. hasn't done badly in this war. Do you know, sir, there isn't a single R.N. officer with us. Navigation? That's no worry – it's your seasick troops I'm worried about.* Yes, south five east, that allows for too much easting, and brings us back to my mean course of south eleven east. Navigating all of us to death, that's what I may be doing. To hell, I'm getting my head down for a while now Number One's been called. *Hello, Fitz. Good sleep? Course south five east, position about thirty miles from the run-in. Don't close up too*

*much in this sea. Call me in two hours' time – till then for nothing less than
an enemy destroyer!*

Reluctant dawn drew up the curtain on a grey and heaving sea,
turning fantasies to spray-drenched reality. Far ahead gunfire rumbled
and rolled, and the flashes were echoed faintly on the low cloud.
Overhead through it swift squadrons raced southward. Dan buoys
appeared, floating soddenly, their marker flags drowned and
bedraggled. The deck of the next ahead plunged wetly through the seas;
the next astern, who cheerily signalled Good bloody morning, yawed
and rolled on its course. The flotilla drove steadily on. One or two
Commandos who had elected to sleep on deck all night, damply unrolled
themselves, sat up, and shivered with the cold. This was the awaited
dawn, fatal or glorious, heralded by guns.

Those flashes come from battle-wagons. Too deliberate a fire, too deep
a roar, for anything smaller. *Bearing red one five? Very good, lookout.* Yes,
there she is, and another beyond her. We're not a mile to the east, if they're
in their bombardment positions. There they go again, now wait for the
sound to reach us. Something mighty reassuring about battle-wagons.
War elephants of the fleet, unhurried and packing a wallop. Destroyers
rush about, guns barking like frenzied sheep-dogs. And cruisers slide
swiftly, specialists in pretty shooting, the accurate placing of sweet salvoes.
But the battle-wagon – her great guns swing up in a silent arc. Then woof!
with a sheet of flame that hides the ship she's hurled a packet of one-ton
bricks at something out of sight. Then she stops to think for a while, and
the ginger smoke rolls lazily away. Woof! again. The first for your concrete
wall; now for your bathroom window. *Colonel, I once saw a sixteen-inch gun
blow a perfect and gigantic smoke ring. I half expected the gun to waggle with
pleasure, but it took absolutely no notice.* Now what's Rupert altering away
westward for? Ah, yes, run-in position. *Yes, lookout, I see them.* There they
are, huddled together on the skyline, a lot of ships, too. Lowering position
for the assault craft, just like putting perambulators off a bus. *What's that,
Colonel? Call you when we sight the beach – you know just what it looks like?
Yes, sir, I'll do that. It'll be at least an hour yet.* This is where the old heart
goes thump, thump in that heavy way. One more hour of uncertainty in
which the chill finger of foreboding lays itself across my brow. Hm, line for
a tragedy king. *How d'you feel, Middy? Myself, I wouldn't be elsewhere for
a thousand quid. Well, not for a hundred, anyway.* It's a comforting show of
ships. We're not alone any more. Eight miles from them to the enemy, and

just listen to the gunfire. All the mad dogs of hell barking over a bone on the beach, the invisible beach; and the shattering roll of the bombs. These ships are all too close together, if they're under fire themselves. *There's a wreck, port lookout, only her bows showing. Why the hell didn't you report it?*

Those assault carrier ships look like wolves meditating the attack. Some of their craft will have gone in by now. Small targets, but desperate business in this running surf. Some, maybe many, will be lost, but the rest will swarm on like sea-lice. We ignore this friendly company of ships, and go straight on. Perhaps the admiral there will note with approval that we are dead on time. Our job is by ourselves, a vital job, a kingpin job in the involved machinery of this invasion. *Well, Cox'n, you're a lucky man. Not everyone gets paid for taking a trip to the Continent! What? You'd sooner go to Blackpool?* Visibility is poor. At what distance will we sight that flat and fatal coast? In good time, I hope, to make any necessary alteration of course. Past the lowering position now, and off into the unknown. Nobody takes any notice. We'll show them. *Number One old boy, we are altering to south seventeen west. Eight miles to go, and the revs up to fourteen hundred.* Good old ship, she runs her sweetest at fourteen hundred, and still six hundred in reserve. *No, Middy, the gunners may not, repeat not, open fire if they see a submarine. Nor at anything else unless they're told. It is considered bad form to shoot down Spitfires.* This is exhilarating, this is exultantly fine. Never felt more aware, more full of life – if it weren't for that unpleasant tight feeling round the heart.

What did I say to Frank when we toasted ourselves the other day after those few drinks? Steer for the sound of the guns! Very dramatic, but the guns happen to be all round us, and all ours as far as I can make out. Hello, splashes. Not all ours then. That destroyer is firing as if it's had a fit, yes, and someone's been badly knocked about over there. Can't worry, it's a good gamble. We get a hit or we don't get hit. Shellfire you can't do anything about, but damned if I can feel happy about machine-guns on the beach. Here I am, conning a shipload of one hundred and four hefty Commandos, fifteen seamen and two officers of my own, running on a timetable towards terror. And there are four thousand gallons of high octane petrol under my deck. Wonder how they feel in the engine-room where they can't even see what's going on, just trust in me and hope like hell. I shall light another pipe.

The silhouettes and scale models in the intelligence room looked like toys out of an expensive nursery. It was all there – the canal entrance, the scattered town along the shore, the church spire, the château by the wood, and pill-box, trench, strong-point, emplacement, emplacement, emplacement. Stretching seaward over the flat tidal beach the rows of posts, stakes, spikes and mines bristling like a hedgehog. 'Your particular beach,' said the naval intelligence officer, 'is eight hundred yards long. Its limit on the east is this modern villa by the road, on the west these two distinctive steep-roofed houses. To the west it doesn't matter much – you may get in the way of others, but land anywhere if you must. But to the east, not one yard beyond your limit.' He smiled cheerfully. 'Not that any of these buildings are likely to be standing by the time the Navy and the Raf have got going. All you can expect is smoke and fire and haze and maybe a helpful pile of rubble.' He spoke perfect English for a Frenchman, and knew so much he might have been on that beach for the past few months. He probably had.

There it is, the flat, sleeping coast, charged with peril. Ships, warships, lie all round us. Their guns are going all the time. I like the way they've comfortably dropped their hooks as if they'd come to settle down. *Disappointing from a tourist's point of view, Number One* – why must I give way to this affectation of flippancy? – *but call the Colonel: he wants to view the promised land.* How good our ships look. Small, but purposeful. They were built for this hour. There's a signal hoist – how many have I watched from that same yardarm? – Division, church, order zero: assume arrowhead formation when executed. There's Jack astern looking at me through his glasses just as I look at him through mine. I'll be very funny indeed and raise my cap with extravagant politeness!

That's surely the château, Colonel, through the smoke. A cable to starboard of it is our limit. Can you see the modern villa? Not there. That should be it, sir, that white ruin, what do you think? Good, bang on the right beach. We've been steering a lot more west than seventeen, too. Good old Rupert, good old all of us! Not far to go, and anywhere in the eight hundred yards to the west of the ruin. Any minute, every ship for itself.

Now eyes for everything, eyes for nothing. The beach looms close, maybe a mile. There are people running up and down it. There are fires, and the bursting of shells. Yes, and wrecked landing craft everywhere, a flurry of propellers in the savage surf and among those wicked obstructions. Beach clearance parties, I expect, bloody heroes, every one. Special craft stooging quietly in, some of them on fire, though. Diesel fuel burns black. That vicious destroyer to port is irritating me, but the Colonel doesn't seem to mind. He's cool, but I'll bet he's worried. Curious how all these soldiers dislike an assault by water. I'd hate to dash out of foxholes at machine-guns. Damn him, I can pretend I'm cool, too. *It's the noisiest gun – Starboard ten! – it's the noisiest gun in the Navy, that four point seven – Midships, Cox'n!* What a cool, disinterested reply he makes. Colonel, you make me grin. I like your nerve.

We are on those bristling stakes. They stretch before us in rows. The mines on them look as big as planets. And those graze-nose shells pointing towards us on some of them look like beer bottles. Oh, God, I WOULD be blown up on a mine like a beer bottle! Now for speed and skill and concentration. Whang, here it comes – those whizzing ones will be mortars – and the stuff is falling all round us. Can't avoid them, but the mines and collisions I can avoid. Speed, more speed. Put them off by speed, weave in and out of these bloody spikes, avoid the mines, avoid our friends, avoid the wrecked craft and vehicles in the rising water, and GET THESE TROOPS ASHORE. Good, the Commando officers have their men ready and waiting, crouched along the decks. Number One is for'ard with his ramp parties ready. Everything is working as we've exercised it for so long. Oh, hell, this new tin hat is far too big for me – I'll shake it off my head out of fright if I'm not careful. *Port twenty, Midships. Starboard ten.* That was a near one. Nearly hit it. But we won't, we can't, slow down. *Midships. Port ten, port fifteen, port twenty.* We're going to hit it, we're going to hit it! A beer bottle, I knew it. *Ease to ten. Midships!* Not bows on, though. We'll strike to starboard on the beam. One, two, three, four, five ... Huh, nothing's happened. Must be luck for me in beer bottles after all. Now for the next lot of obstructions.

Don't jump, you fool. It was near, but you're not hit. Straddled. All right, keep on. And here's where I go in, that little bit of clear beach. *Port ten. Midships. Starboard five.* Wish the swell weren't throwing us about so much. Let's be in first, as a glorious gesture, then no one will know how frightened we really were. Tommy always said when coaching us, If you hang round on the outside of the scrum you'll get hurt – go in! *Sorry to give you so much work, Cox'n.* That'll rock him, and I'll light up my pipe, too. What does he say? Nae bother at all, sir, and I'm still sticking to my pipe, am I? Can't even the enemy take the bounce out of this cox'n? *You're not being familiar, I hope, Cox'n?* I mustn't grin. What? Not bloody likely? Anyhow, he's a cocky bastard and cheerful. A shell may kill us both any minute.

Slow ahead together. Slow down to steady the ship, point her as you want her, then half ahead together and on to the beach with a gathering rush. Put her ashore and be damned! She's touched down. One more good shove ahead to wedge her firm. *Out ramps!*

Smooth work, Fitz, oh, smooth as clockwork. *Now off you go! Good luck, Commandos, go like hell! Next meeting – Brighton!* How efficiently, how quickly they run down the accustomed ramps, not a man hit that I can see, and there they go splashing through a hundred yards of water, up over more of the flat beach than that, and out of sight among the deadly dunes. The Colonel turns to wave, and is gone with them. They ignore beach fire. They have their objective, and they are going for it, the best troops we can produce. God go with them.

Rupert's decks were clear before ours after all, there he is to port. And now here's Woodie beside me to starboard. And Chris and Jack grounded on my port quarter. Good work, oh, good for us! *Number One, in ramps! Come on, get those bloody ramps IN!* None of the crew hit yet that I can see. Let's get out quick. Any of our craft hit? Yes, there's Les – seems to be on fire aft, but quite unperturbed. And Chris has a lot of confusion on his fo'c'sle. Casualties. How can I get out with him across my stern? *Middy, take the depth aft.*

Christ, that's too near! Don't want to be killed now. Mortar, fifteen yards. Little bits rattling against the bridge. And a nasty concentration on the beach. How slowly men spin before they fall. Some look surprised as they die. Oh, come on, Chris! Who's that damn' fool opening up with a machine-gun past my bridge? Minor craft astern, I suppose. As if there isn't enough to put up with. No! It's coming from ashore! *Port gunner! Tall building bearing red one five, red one five. Fire!* Hah, quick-triggered, that boy, oh, and lovely shooting: a stream of tracer from both guns hosepiping on every window. Don't you take us on with a machine-gun, Jerry. You'll get hot porridge back. No return fire, anyway. Hope we got the bastard.

Right. *Half astern together.* We're off. Must avoid incoming craft as well as dodge those stakes. Damn, she never would steer coming astern. We hit that one. Never mind, the mines are all set on the seaward side. Turn short round. *That's that, Fitz. Now we'll take a look round. I say! Those aren't chance shots. They're stalking us out to sea!* Splash to starboard, splash to port, ahead, astern. Now I'm in a rage, full of exultation, fear, contempt, intoxication with the hour and the day. Does that damned Jerry think he can hit us going out when he couldn't hit us coming in? Wasting time on an empty ship when the beach is full of targets! Of course, he just might ... Good shooting, oh, very nice. But now I've landed my troops it's ME you're taking on. *Cox'n, steer for that last burst.* Bet he can't put one on the same spot twice.

Hell! What an explosion! And, my God, it's one of ours! *Fitz, who is it, who is it?* Must have been hit in the tanks. God, oh, God, poor bastards! *No, we're too far away. Others are going in.* There won't be a man alive when the smoke clears. But they landed their troops at all costs. At all costs. And blown up coming off. Who's that over there, bows up and sinking? Stan. I can read his number. Abandoned, I think. *Signalman, call her up. Take a look, Number One. I think she's abandoned. Yes?* This area is warming up. Surely the fire is faster and better than it was? Jerry is a stubborn bastard. The landing has been made, and the others are coming in wave upon wave. Now, why the hell must he keep on firing at me?

On the beaches the opposition intensified in many places some hours after the initial assault. The Germans went to earth to fight, using cunning where force had failed. Guns and mortars ranged the landing areas with precision, the sniping was deadly and persistent. But still the assault went on, till the shallow water was crammed with twisted metal wreckage, blazing vehicles and disabled craft. Still the assault went on, and the troops were put ashore with the inevitability of the rising tide that covered the beach obstructions and made navigation more perilous than before.

Who's that hailing us? Yes, that infantry landing craft, full of troops. She's been hit. Listing badly. Sinking. I should say. *LCI(L), LCI(L), I am coming alongside. That's right, Number One, all the fenders you've got. We'll get a bashing in this swell. Give the lines plenty of scope.* Holed on the waterline, she is. I think she'll last, though. Don't like these shells falling round, but it's worse for the pongos, and them still seasick. *Bad luck, chum! But we'll run the ferry service. All aboard for Margate!* Damn silly to shout such rubbish, but it may sound confident. Hell, I don't want to go into that bloody beach again.

Come on, lads, help them aboard, and ALL their equipment. Now, wait for it, there, wait till she rolls towards you, THEN jump. This is going to take time. Horrible being hove-to under fire. Honest, I'm in a worse funk than the first time. Because of that gun that seems told off to get us. Surely it will be easier on the beaches by now. *Casualties? Sure, we'll take them for you. Number One, Cox'n, get them aboard and do what you can. Hello, Major, now where can I take you? Oh, I know where it is; nothing's a trouble.* Bad luck being smashed up before they've landed, but what a load – twice as many as we should take. One hit and this crowded deck will look like a butcher's shop. Troops don't know the craft either. Slow getting on means slower getting off. And all that equipment! Commandos move fast because they're light. Well, in we go again. *Cox'n, steady on the gap between those two buildings ashore. See them? Right.*

This is being under fire in real earnest. Or am I more nervous than I was? We'll pick our way between the bursts, swerving nicely, duck when we hear a mortar, and keep our fingers crossed. *Starboard ten. Midships.* Nearly didn't see that sunk tank or whatever it was. Too many new fires on that beach, and small-arms shooting, too. Hope it's us cleaning up. *Yes, Major, that's it ahead. We've been surf-riding round here all morning. The beach is ours all right. It's just like home to half the army now.*

Good old Fitz. He's standing by to beach as if we were running a London bus. And the crew were lounging as if they'd been under fire for weeks. Showing off in front of these pongos – good. Don't expect they've been through it before, and they're seasick as well. Ah, another row of obstructions. There should be more like these, totally submerged. Horrible to be wrecked now. But take a chance – I'm going in here, and going in fast.

Out ramps! And there goes one right overboard. Preventer stay gone. *All right, you troops, now get off on the other one. Take it easy, but get off, and DON'T leave your equipment behind you.* Nothing to do but wait. And there are more explosions, beach mines, bodies, going up. Men and machines tossed in the air. And that mortar is killing people. Too damned near, and the tank beyond our bows blazing like hell.

Oh, for Pete's sake, why must this big landing craft come in so close to me? His kedge-wire will be hard to miss, and if I go to port I may crash on the wreck there. *Come on, troops, get OFF! Throw that equipment down to them, you, for'ard. No, NOT in the water.* The men are coming off this next craft. And right on to a mine, not twenty yards from our bows. Here's another mortar. *Duck!* Hell, right on her fo'c'sle. If she hadn't come so close we would have stopped that one. Oh, I don't like this at all. *Number One, are those troops getting off?*

Off at last! And still not hit, by some good luck, except for the rattle of fragments on the deck. Some of our troops hit, though. Silly bastards, they should have got up that beach and away, instead of milling around. Now out to sea, Harry Flatters. *See any more of our craft, signalman?* Thank God. I've had enough of this for a while. After how many mathematical probabilities does one run into a shell while trying to dodge them? *Two thousand revs, Cox'n, steer north fifteen east.* We must rendezvous. Heaven knows what's happened to the flotilla. *I say, Number One, we're two miles out and still being shelled. Persistent sods, aren't they?*

So it is. That's Joe's craft. What's he doing as far out as this and sinking too? He can't last long – screws out of the water, and blowing down on the uncleared mines. *Starboard ten. We'd better close him.* Now what earthly good do those stupid Jerries think they're doing by trying to shell a sinking ship? *Flash him, signalman, Will take you off.* O.K., Joe, we're coming. *No, Fitz, he's past towing. Too far gone. We won't be any too soon.*

Hiyah, Joe! I'm coming alongside. Got all your crew there? Underwater damage, I guess. Yes, there's a bloody great hole midships. Silly those propellers look sticking uselessly out of the water. *What's that Joe? Told you to beach yourself in shallow water? Eh? You said you would if you were a bloody Spitfire?* Good old Joe. Perhaps I'm jumpy, but I'm not putting out lines. She looks as if she'll nose-dive any minute. Crash alongside, and get them over. We may still stop a packet. *All aboard?* Yes, she's lurching now. Poor Joe. Nobody wants to see a ship go down, let alone his own. *Well, Joe, if that's Jerry's Atlantic Wall I don't think much of it. What? Just shows you can't trust no bastard, does it?* Good old Joe, that's right in character.

Number One, we will now get to seaward out of here, and find the rest. Issue rum to everybody. And, my God, I'll have a tot myself!

ERIK DE MAUNY

A Night in the Country

In the late afternoon they saw the Divisional sign sticking up jauntily out of the mud, and pulled laboriously away from the weary serpent of complaining three-tonners into a deeply rutted side lane. The lane led past dusty bushes into a large, untidy farmyard, and they were able to take up positions for the night in the shadow of the hayricks without the usual conference between the officers.

The people of the farmhouse were watching them half curiously, half apathetically, from the cobbled inner yard, under the high slope of the greenish tiled roof that ran out from halfway up the building. Judging by the number of shrill children chasing each other through the puddles, and the way the older people had unconsciously drifted into separate groups, there were several families there. Apart from the family groups was a woman of about thirty, in a stained navy-blue dress open deep down her sunburnt throat, bending over a wooden washtub. She had a smooth, rather haggard face, her black hair was coiled neatly back on the nape of the neck, and she took in the arrival of the four trucks with a slow, unflurried stare, holding her lathered hands out over the tub.

The officers had jumped down from their seats and were standing in a bunch, talking in low voices and stamping the circulation back into cramped legs and feet. Towards them an old woman was pushed gently forward by the others. She explained that there were three families from the neighbouring village, and so many children to be fed and fussed over, the farm had been hit only two nights ago, and they had nothing (her voice trembled a little): no meat, no salt, no wine ...

'All right, mother,' one of the officers said, grinning to show they came with friendly intentions, and in halting Italian, 'we want to see the house. Are the rooms upstairs big? Will you show us, please?'

The farm had indeed been hit. One corner had been neatly sliced off the top story, disclosing the intimate anatomy of a bedroom, in almost indecent fashion. A chest of drawers leaned drunkenly over into space, and where the head of the bed had been there was a small shrine with a sombre-coloured Madonna and Infant surrounded by once frivolous red crêpe paper and faded artificial flowers.

While the officers, led by the colonel, were upstairs requisitioning rooms, the sergeant superintended the assembly of the cookhouse in front of the biggest haystack. The hot-boxes were lined up in front of the tent, the big pressure burner was soon roaring with its blue and green dragon's mouth of flame, and cook prosaically began to stir the already prepared meal.

In the dusk, shutters flew open upstairs. The adjutant leaned out of one window.

'Just send Corporal Black up, sergeant,' he called into the yard.

The sergeant found the corporal digging a slit trench. 'Old Ned wants you upstairs,' he said laconically. He glanced at the big house, blurring into the gathering evening. 'Hope we can all crowd in. She doesn't look a bad *casa*.'

The local people were already rearranging their sleeping quarters. The corporal met two pretty girls on the stairs, with arms full of musty-smelling mattresses. *'Sera!'* they said pleasantly, smiling. 'As if we were permanent guests in a ruddy seaside boarding-house,' the corporal thought.

'Hallo, Jimmy,' the adjutant said. 'I want you to bring a fatigue up and sweep this place out. We've got four rooms, including this big centre one. We should be able to get twenty or thirty in here.'

The corporal glanced round. All the furniture had been taken out, and the room was not unlike a barrack hall, except for the several shrines fitted in niches in the wall, each one fastened with faded crêpe paper, which had the desolate air of Christmas decorations left up too long. The old woman who had been pushed forward first was now kneeling on the open hearth in front of the immense stone fireplace, patiently blowing a few embers into a new flame.

'The old girl seems to have taken it very philosophically.' They were used to wringing of hands, lamentations, which usually changed facilely within the first half hour to wonder and protestations of friendship.

'They're all going to sleep down below in the stable,' the adjutant explained. 'I've had a look, and they should be all right – in fact they settled in quite quickly. There are two or three oxen, but that doesn't seem to worry them.'

The old woman stopped blowing the embers as a flame spiralled up, and looked round with a folded smile of her old mouth, as if seeking approval.

'They use the animals for warmth, I suppose,' the adjutant said vaguely. 'Anyway, they're damn glad we're not sending them back to the rear, which is what we ought to do really.'

'Mr MacMahon,' came the colonel's dry, restrained voice from the next room, 'Send some men along to clean this place up a bit, will you? The floor's half covered with corn cobs.'

'Hurry up, Jimmy,' the adjutant said, and made a grimace.

The corporal went clattering down the narrow stone stairway to find his fatigue. At the bottom he paused to glance through the door leading into the stable. They had already made the place as habitable as they could. There was a sweet, warm smell of cow-dung. A cobwebby storm lantern hung from the rafters, lighting the underside of mildewed harnesses. The farm people had put their mattresses in the stalls where the beasts had been, and were hanging up old brightly coloured pieces of cloth to serve as partitions, which made the place look like a series of circus booths hastily rigged.

When he was outside the corporal remembered he would have to borrow a broom – the two on the truck were broken. Apart from the children, who were hopping round the soldiers; all timidity gone, asking for chocolate or biscuits, there was only the woman in navy-blue left in the yard. She was piling the whorls of wrung clothing in the empty tub.

Without stopping her work of twisting dry the thick, doughy bundles, she gave him a slow, candid smile, which spread voluptuously over her cheeks from the little wrinkles at the corners of the eyes, and asked his name. When he failed momentarily to understand, she clucked her tongue with amusement and repeated the question.

'Jimmy,' he said.

She nodded her head sagely from side to side, then put down the last piece of clothing and pointed to his arm.

'*Sergente?*'

'No, *caporale*.' She looked puzzled, and he plunged into the old, laborious explanation, as infallible a conversational gambit as the weather in peacetime. 'In the Italian army two, sergeant,' he said. 'English army, corporal.' Then he remembered. 'Is it possible to borrow a ... O God, what do you call it?' he finished in English. Inspired, he made a series of vigorous gestures over the cobbles.

She understood at once, her eyes lighting up. '*Una vanga,*' she said, laughing. 'Perhaps my son can find one ...'

At her call a sallow youth with glossy black hair of great length, meticulously combed back in sweeping waves, came out of the gloom by the stable door. She said something incomprehensible to him in dialect. The corporal watched him clump unwillingly indoors in his thick boots of untanned leather, with a curious sensation of mingled disgust and disappointment. A useless species, the young Italian male. Besides, he had been vaguely, uneasily stirred by the woman's obvious interest in him. She had really fine dark eyes, and there was something disconcerting in the warm, frank way they appraised him. His own gaze kept falling to the fold of the blue dress over her breast, which half fell open when she bent down for a moment to rearrange the clothes. When the youth had disappeared, he felt himself redden and shifted awkwardly on his feet, not finding anything to say.

'Were there many Germans here?' he asked finally. Apparently she had not noticed his lack of ease. As if his question released a spring, she suddenly began to talk quite freely and grammatically, not making concessions by using only the infinitive of the verbs: almost as if they had known each other a long time.

'Here? No, only a few. But in C—, where we live, there were many. It is a pretty town, really. There are chestnut trees down each side of the street. It is elegant – not like this.' She surveyed the muddy yard, the outcrops of manure with evident distaste. 'Perhaps my son will go tomorrow on his bicycle to see if our house is all right. It is not far, only three kilos.' She paused, then asked: 'Do you think the Germans have left C— now?'

'I'm not sure,' he said; 'we don't know.' How very true that was, he reflected immediately afterwards; one never knew where the enemy was, and this particular enemy, with a shrewd, despairing tenacity, clung to ground like certain burrs cling to your clothing in a walk over the moors. Still, from the road that afternoon they had admired the still standing spire of the cathedral poking into the clear autumn air, and there had been little sound from the direction of the town. He was just going to say 'I'll try and find out,' when the son reappeared, carrying a spade.

The corporal glanced at his swarthy, indolent young face, gave rather a fierce laugh, and embarked on fresh explanations.

The sergeant suddenly came and joined them for a moment, going from one job to another. After an admiring stare at the woman, he said, 'Did she think you wanted to dig a — house, Jimmy?'

But the corporal had to forgo the somewhat savage reply he was formulating. At that moment the adjutant's voice floated sepulchrally out from the region of the stairway.

'For Christ's sake send Corporal Black up; the old man's going mad about these corn cobs.'

Half an hour later, when the rooms had been swept, the corn stacked in a corner, blanket rolls undone and ranged against the walls and the shutters once more fastened securely for the blackout, the men trooped down with a great rattling of dixies to the evening meal. They sat on the running boards of trucks, or on piles of cut wood, and the night began to fold about them innumerable dense blue veils.

The colonel delivered a brief homily to the adjutant as they stood spooning up peas and potatoes and fragments of meat.

'Curious how easily one can see, MacMahon, those chaps who are used to country life and those who belong to the towns. A real countryman takes to this sort of thing like a duck to water,' he said, sniffing the keen tang of the air with relish. The colonel owned several thousand acres of rich sheep country. 'In every campaign I've been in . . .' he began again.

The adjutant gave a mental groan and followed his own line of thought. I expect you think I'm just a bloody cow-cocky too, he reflected. His experience in the army had taught him you could never put people into pigeon-holes in quite the easy, masterful fashion the colonel had a habit of doing. Nevertheless, you had to respect the old boy; he knew how to handle the men in most rough-and-ready situations, particularly when things were hot.

The men stood or sat in groups, too occupied with eating to talk much, but shaken occasionally by a gust of laughter when somebody broke new ground in the realm of obscene repartee.

The children had stopped playing now it was growing dark, and stood under the overhanging roof, suddenly quiet, twisting from foot to foot and staring with huge, wistful eyes at the eating soldiers.

'There's a three-day-old baby in there,' someone told the cook. 'It's that big sheila in green's kid, and now she's up and walking round as if nothing had happened.' The girl in a dingy green jumper was coming from the woodpile with a bundle of twigs, and they watched her curiously. She was stout and clumsy, tottering on high wooden soles as she picked her way between the puddles. Above black ankle socks her legs were thick and marbled with cold, and there was a large sore on one calf. 'It was a Jerry, too, they reckon. Anyway' (with a gossip's note of triumph), 'she's not married.'

'Those bloody Jerries'll go anything,' the cook said, even he repelled by the unintelligent, suety face and graceless form.

The corporal, sitting on a petrol tin almost out of range of this conversation, found his eyes wandering frequently towards the farmhouse. He watched the old woman who had met them first, how, bent and half crippled though she was, she dominated the others so that the sleek-haired dark youths reacted almost timorously to her gestures, and reflected on the matriarchal state of Italian society. He watched the children wolfing down the big chunks of stale bread the cook had given them, while one or two edged up to the parked trucks, fascinated by the mechanical presences, but not yet sure enough of themselves to explore them. He did not entirely admit to himself that he was waiting with a sort of longing to catch a further glimpse of the woman in blue.

The thought of her kept recurring, obsessing and unsatisfying as a fragment of music. He tried to sweep his mind clear with a cold stroke of logic: this is only one more casual roadside encounter. Yet even in the disgust at himself engendered by his own lack of willpower he surrendered again to this voiceless longing, consenting to be duped by it, and dimly aware of the formless, boundless nostalgia that had been mounting like a wave within him for months. Wilfully he continued to evocate the first picture of her as they had come into the yard on the lurching truck. In the face of their habitual activity, which seemed now gross and almost without meaning, she had been cool and detached, going quietly on with the real work of washing the clothes. Mostly he remembered the dark, unhurried way she looked him in the eyes when he had spoken to her about the broom, and savoured the growing sensation of being regarded as a man, as an individual again. Nevertheless, all these sensations were inarticulate, and seemed to lead to no definite end.

It was while he was cleaning up after the meal that the idea came to him quite spontaneously, and was as quickly hardened into decision. It seemed to him that he must act on it at once.

Therefore, with a studied nonchalance, as he went upstairs again, he peered in at the stable door. Through the haze of smoking lamps he could see her, kneeling in the opposite stall, arranging a pile of bedding. With cold detachment he calculated swiftly how many steps it was from the door to the stall. Already he imagined himself stealing in on stockinged feet among the sound of other people's breathing ... a momentary repugnance overcame him, and he thought, 'How cheap, how despicable, all these manoeuvres seem ...' But that did not last long, and his mind was once again occupied coldly with details. 'I must find some place outside where we could go,' he thought. It did not occur to him that she would be surprised at his arrival in the middle of the night.

But it was far too early to make any move. Upstairs, he invented one or two petty tasks to fill in the time and lull his questioning nerves: repacking a bag, cleaning his revolver, engaging in forced conversation in which he tried to prove by purposeless remarks and a forced tone of cheerfulness to the others and to himself that nothing was afoot.

The last of the evening closed down, but there was an early moon, and a faint, greenish-white sheen over the yard and the more distant fields, the broken vines and ragged bushes resolving into cold and formal patterns.

There were four large haystacks. Under the furthest off he found, as he had hoped, the small straw-lined shelter which in normal times housed scythes and pruning-hooks and pressing tubs, and which was now quite empty.

Just as he regained the house the guns opened up. The barrage was so intense that the others came crowding down to look.

There was an attack on in the northern sector, the colonel explained. The fire was going overhead at an oblique angle. There were murmurs, the usual banal comments. 'We're giving him some English *cioccolata* tonight.' That was what the Italians called the shells.

But it was truly a magnificent 'show'. At minute intervals, behind each haystack, flared a raving cockscomb of red light, and each fresh illumination revealed the piled coils of smoke, blue and thick, waving like tresses of hair in the dusky night.

They counted the seconds between flash and explosion. A 7.2 behind the hedge, only about a hundred yards away, brought miniature landslides of debris down from the shattered angle of the house.

'We won't get a hell of a lot of sleep tonight.'

The remark brought the corporal back from the region of stupor and puny impotence into which the sight and sound of a major barrage always plunged him, and took on another shade of meaning. Possessed now by a demon of restlessness, he attempted to amuse himself upstairs in the big room for a further hour. Four or five of the others had made up a game of cards and invited him to join them, but he could not keep his mind on it and soon gave up.

Ten o'clock came at last. Only the card-players were left: the others were already curled up in their bedrolls. But when the corporal arrived at the foot of the stairs he was suddenly intimidated by the thought of the dark stable.

I need some air, he thought, and made his way out on to the cobbles. The guns had ceased, and the quiet on the air was doubly significant for the absence of their angry tumult, like the peace of a sick man released from a bout of pain. The cold air striking his temples had a sobering effect, and he was content to stand quietly gazing up into the star-filled sky, with the pinch of night air at his nostrils, filling his lungs with the clean cold, and unaware that he was not alone.

When a shadow detached itself from a pillar nearby he gave a violent start. But the shadow had already reached him, and he recognized the sergeant, who gave an admonitory hiss with fingers to lips. At once it struck him that the sergeant was behaving in rather extravagant fashion, whispering something incomprehensible and continuing to hold aloft a finger as a warning to silence. In fact, in the shadow of the sloping roof, he acted like some elaborate villain of melodrama. It was a ridiculous situation, and the corporal gave a short, dry laugh. The laugh broke the tension, and the sergeant raised his voice a little, taking out a cigarette and lighting it. In the flicker of the match he closed his left eye slowly at the corporal, then swore when the flame burned his thumb and forefinger. He emanated a gentle odour of wine.

'Shhh ... don't want anyone upstairs to hear,' he said, 'but she's coming out in a minute.'

'Who?' the corporal asked.

'You know the one,' the sergeant said; 'the one you were talking to this afternoon, the one who was doing the washing. Her name's Irina.'

The corporal realized that he had not until then known her name. It had not occurred to him to ask.

'She's a good thing.' In profile this time the sergeant's eye could be seen to lower with sinister jollity. 'I had her on a bit after tea, and I could see she was a player right away. She said she'd come out after ten, when the others were asleep.'

'She's a good thing all right,' the corporal said. He loathed the bright falsity in his own voice. He considered bitterly the reptilian character of the sergeant. Yet, in an inexpressible way, he was as relieved as if he had been walking along some treacherous jungle and the person in front had suddenly fallen into the pit of bamboo spikes. Faith, hope and charity ...

The sergeant, probably under the impulse of the wine he had somehow found, wanted now to confess his entire plan.

'But shhh,' he kept saying, each time a little louder. 'Mustn't let the old chap hear; don't want the boys to know. Found a good little place. Over there, under the haystack. Plenty of nice dry straw.' He made a clicking noise with the corner of his mouth, then pulled back his greatcoat sleeve to look at his watch in the glow of the cigarette end. The fact that the hands showed ten sobered him a little, and as if regretting already his confidences, he became silent. Obviously he wanted the other to go.

But the corporal was inspired by a perverse desire to stay. He lounged against a pillar and surveyed the night. How strange the silence was, and how remote the glitter of stars. Only a little time ago battery after battery of guns had sent the shells trundling overhead with a sound of giant wooden rollers. Now there was this crisp, cool peace. Breathing in the sodden smell of wet leaves, the acrid stench of the poultry yard, the subtler, sour scent of damp, pressed hay, it occurred to him how alien he was in a country setting, how strange and unsettling this country night was to him. By contrast he had almost accepted the routine of war, the incessant, panic utterance of the guns. But these vast spaces of the starry night suddenly impressed on him his own loneliness more painfully than he had ever before felt it. It was a night of huge, inscrutable presences, which seemed to brood timelessly over the scarred earth.

A strange landscape that he now discovered, and suddenly matched in strangeness, suddenly as full of doubts and terrors, as the inner landscape of his mind. No more neat, ordered symmetry of thought and feeling. His motives were utterly confused, for now he felt no vestige of desire left, no remaining trace of the acrid, dry-eyed lust he had chafed under all evening. And yet, at the very moment when relief seemed uppermost in his mind, there entered a feeling of chagrin, of ineffable sadness, as if he had shown himself wanting in some subtle respect, as if he had ceased long ago to be a complete being.

For the sergeant, after a brief spasm of annoyance, he felt no particular emotion: neither dislike nor envy nor compassion. He was simply outside, entirely uninterested, having no part in this internal drama in which the corporal, breathing deeply the scented country air, found himself suddenly a stranger to himself.

He might have remained there almost indefinitely, wrapped in this trance-like reflection, if the sergeant had not consulted his watch a third time and said, now with unconcealed impatience and hostility, 'She should be here any minute now.'

It was ten past, the corporal discovered, and felt suddenly that he had grown very cold in these ten minutes. There was gooseflesh on his bare arms. He muttered a brusque good night and went up to bed, dismissing the affair as best he could from his mind.

But in the morning, even before breakfast (and he got up as late as he could generally), he could not resist going over to the haystack and peering down into the shelter. The straw lay undisturbed. He was almost certain no one had been down there.

The sergeant did not come down to breakfast.

As they were cleaning up a Don R. arrived with an order to move in half an hour.

So he did not see the sergeant until they were both climbing on to the back of the truck; and then, at his glance, the sergeant merely shook his head cynically, and he could not repress the thought, 'Poor bugger, after all that trouble!'

As the heavy truck manoeuvred into position in the yard, they all looked across to the house. The woman in navy-blue was standing once more behind the washing-tub, smiling her candid, placid smile. She gave a special wave to the corporal when she saw him gazing at her, remembering the amusing incident of the spade. She thought: they're good-looking boys, really, so young and so fresh. She had forgotten all about the sergeant . . .

An old man came in from the fields, carrying a box full of grapes stiffly on his head.

From the truck they bent down to take a bunch or two, but he crooked his neck and said, 'No, no, they're no good. The grenades have spoilt them all.' And in fact their lustre was gone; they were shrivelled up and cracked, the juice congealed where they had split, with a pallor of dust over the once glossy skins.

The truck lurched and jolted forward over the ruts, and someone fell amid a clatter of wash-basins, mess-tins and rifles, and began to swear and grumble quietly to himself, '. . . — the bloody thing! Always on the move. Can't we ever stop in one place more than twenty-four hours?'

They rejoined the weary serpent of complaining three-tonners.

FRANK SARGESON

When the Wind Blows

I

Who loves you?
Mummy and daddy.
Who else?
Auntie Clara.
And who else?
Gentle Jesus.
And who else?
Our Father which art in heaven . . .
And when that was over mother said:

> *Good night, sweet repose,*
> *All the bed, and all the clothes,*

and she kissed you and took away the candle, and you were left in the dark, warm in the hollow of the bed, *snug as a bug in a rug*.

And if you woke up in the night and cried father came and carried you, and you slept in the big bed between mother and father. And in the morning there was only mother, and the smell that was always her, father's place empty. But there were the sounds of father lighting the fire in the kitchen, and mother got up, too, and alone in the big bed, all eyes, you lay there and watched, all of mother inside her nightgown, all except her head, the sleeves hanging empty, and bit by bit mother's clothes went inside the nightgown until she took it off and she was standing there with all her clothes on.

On mornings when you woke up in your own bed it was father who came and dressed you, standing you on the bed, lifting your arms to put them through the armholes of your stays, turning you round to do up the buttons at the back. Then you could go with father, help him feed the chooks, if you were lucky see the rooster get on top of one of the chooks and give it a hiding. The rooster was big enough to give you a hiding as well, but of course it couldn't with father there. Nothing could hurt you when you were with father or mother, and if you did hurt yourself sometimes, playing by yourself, then you could always run to father or mother and they'd kiss it better.

And feeding the chooks with father was the beginning of all the things you did and saw every day, and that was how you lived. It had always been so, and it would never be any different – because it had always been so as long as you could remember, a long, long time, and it would never be any different because you had never noticed any change. There was just mother and father, and Auntie Clara and Arnold your brother, who was older than you and went to school, but he had always gone to school, and they said you would go to school too, some day. Some day. That would be a long, long time, because just one day was a long, long time, and when mother said, It's your bedtime now, you never wanted to go, because it was such a long, long time until the next day. Mother always said, There's another day tomorrow, and there always was, but it wasn't any good saying there was when you had such a long, long time to wait for it to come.

The morning he went to school for the first time he made an awful fuss. They were all there in the kitchen, mother and Auntie Clara with their aprons on, and father putting his bicycle clips on his trousers, and Arnold his brother waiting to take him. And mother said, Now Henry, and father said Buck up, and Auntie Clara called him a great crybaby, and Arnold said wasn't he a silly boy? And he had on his new boots and stockings, and his pants that had been his Sunday best, and the new shirt he had watched mother make on the sewing machine, and the cap that had got too small for Arnold but was still all right, and the new schoolbag made of real leather he had gone with mother to buy. He looked a real bobby-dazzler, was what father said – but there he was with his face dug in between mother's legs, and his arms around them. And he wouldn't let go and he wouldn't leave off crying.

It was no good though, he had to go. Mother dried his eyes, and told him all over again all the nice things she was going to do for him, if he was a good boy. And she told Arnold to take his hand, and father wheeled his bicycle out of the woodshed and told him to be a Briton, and Auntie Clara stood on the veranda and laughed, and after he'd had a drink of water to stop his hiccups he took Arnold's hand and held tight, and they went over to the fence and out into the side street. Mother waved and Arnold pulled him, and then mother was out of sight, and they went past the sawmill and over the railway line, and then you could hear the sound of the children playing around the school on top of the hill.

And just when you could hear the children wasn't a good time for Arnold to let go his hand, he said there were frogs in the ditch across the road, he said he saw one, and went over to look. And it was too much for Henry his young brother, he stood there and bawled, awful to see yet funny, standing pigeon-toed, his mouth open, the rest of his face screwed up, and all of him without a sound or a movement for one long second before the awful sound came. And Arnold was frightened and came running back to take his hand, but, angry as well, he squeezed it to hurt him. But the yells made him sorry he had, and he said, Don't cry and I'll show you something. And Henry his young brother stopped crying; but Arnold said he'd show him after, he promised, though a lot of things he wouldn't say – whether it was a big thing or a little, and whether he had it on him then (he might have, he said), and whether it was anything you could eat (it might be, he said). And thinking what it could be, and because he'd been promised, he took Arnold's hand again and didn't cry any more.

And up in the playground the children were running about and shouting, girls playing 'The Farmer Wants a Wife', boys 'Foxes and Hounds', some big rough boys throwing stones and hitting each other with schoolbags. But he held tight to Arnold's hand and they found the teacher, and then he was all right because she was his Sunday-school teacher as well. And right up until it was playtime that first morning he liked going to school, you did pothooks on a slate, and drew a pussy cat on a blackboard, then you all had to go out in the playground. He didn't want to go, he would rather have stayed in, he hung back, but his teacher told him to run along outside and play. So he went out and the little boys and girls like himself were playing Here We Come Gathering Nuts And May but he didn't go near them, he looked for Arnold instead and couldn't find him, so he went right to the end of the playground and through the fence and down the road he had come up with Arnold. The further he went the faster he went, until when he crossed the railway lines he was running. Then as he ran he began to cry, softly at first, then louder until he was running and sobbing and choking, a terrible hullabaloo, and a man looked out of the sawmill and stared at him. And his sobs turned into screams, and he ran faster, and mother heard him coming and was halfway down to the fence when he flung himself on to her.

For a little while until he quietened down mother might let him stay there with his face dug in between her legs, but it was no good, she was changing her dress and putting on her hat to take him back to school when Arnold came home. He'd been sent to find him and fetch him, so mother took off her hat again, and Auntie Clara said if you asked her what he wanted most was a good thrashing, and mother said, Clara! She got him a clean hanky and held his nose with it and told him to blow; she said she knew he'd be a good boy this time, and Arnold took his hand again and he pulled it away. And he wanted to run back to school again, but Arnold wanted to walk and stop to look in the ditch to see if there were any frogs. And Arnold took him to his teacher, and she said he had to promise to be a brave boy and not run away from school any more. So he promised and it was easy, because he'd only run away home to see if mother was all right without him there to look after her, and now he was all right because he'd found out that she was.

So now he was a big boy going to school, not a little boy who stayed home all day, that had all been a long, long time ago. But of course you remembered, and sometimes remembering all of a sudden you stopped in the middle of a game, and said you didn't want to play any more. And sometimes you remembered early in the morning when you were getting ready for school, and you felt sick and told mother, and she felt your forehead and asked how long it was since you did number two. And sometimes instead of feeling better you felt worse, and cried and said you wanted to be sick, and mother held your forehead while you bent over and threw up. And afterwards she nursed you for a little while until you felt better, then you had to go to bed and the doctor came and said you had to stay in bed, and you had to take medicine and sometimes it was weeks before you went back to school again. But you didn't care if you never went back to school, because even if you were a sick boy and had to stay in bed, mother would always come and hold your forehead every time you threw up. And when you were getting better you could have all sorts of things to eat, just about anything you asked for, and if you did things you weren't supposed to do (I'm a sick boy, I can do what I like, was what you would have liked to have gone round saying), instead of father saying he'd have to give you a hiding, all he'd say was it was time you went back to school again. And that was nearly as bad as if you'd been promised a hiding, it made you feel sick again. So you'd do things round the house to help mother and try to be a good boy, and times when mother would let you hem handkerchiefs for her on the sewing machine, and call you to eat up what was left in the basin when she'd finished making a cake, you thought you could easily have promised to be a good boy for the whole of your life.

Sooner or later though, you'd have to go back to school again. And before you'd finished breakfast you began to make a fuss, though nothing like the one you'd made that first day. I don't want to go to school, you said, and mother said, Why don't you want to go to school? She said that when she was little she liked going to school, she'd even cry if she wasn't allowed to go. And instead of listening you went on saying you didn't want to go to school because. And father said, Now look here, Henry, and Auntie Clara and Arnold tried to chip in, but father went on and gave you a good talking to, telling you all the things you wouldn't get or be allowed to do if you didn't buck up. So you thought perhaps it would be best if you didn't make any more fuss just then, not with father there. Because with mother it was different, but with father there you had to do what you were told.

* * *

II

It started before school went in. And soon everybody knew. Everybody told everybody else, and everybody else knew already. After school, in the old gravel pit down by the river.

Knocky was going to fight the both of them together.

The afternoon before they'd had paints, and Knocky said he'd taken it out and painted it red, white and blue, then he'd kicked the girl in front and told her to look under the desk. And Phil called him a liar. So Knocky said he'd fight him for that. And Lanky said liar as well, and Knocky turned round and said he'd fight him for that. He said he'd fight the both of them together. And the both of them said they'd take him on.

And some were on Knocky's side, and some were on Lanky's and Phil's. About half and half. At playtime they didn't play games. No, they all got round Knocky and Lanky and Phil, the one lot on one side of the playground, and the other on the other. And at lunchtime Knocky's lot went right down into the far corner of the playground, underneath the trees. So two out of Lanky's and Phil's lot went down there to see what they were doing. But they got stones thrown at them and were chased off, and they came back and said Knocky still had it on, and was showing them. Just to try and prove he wasn't a liar.

But Lanky and Phil said it didn't prove anything.

But one or two said they'd like to see if it was painted red, white and blue.

But Lanky and Phil said it didn't prove anything.

Then after school the two lots were there all together, all mixed up in the playground. Every boy in the class was there, everyone. And everyone went down to the gravel pit. There wasn't one that stayed in the playground to play, and not one that went home without going to the gravel pit.

And going down to the gravel pit they took a short cut through the saleyards. And that even though you copped it if you were caught in the saleyards. Any boy caught in the saleyards would get the cuts for sure, but all together, all talking and shouting together, all at once, they climbed the fence and went right through the saleyards, treading with boots and bare feet the muck from the sale that day. The muck that stuck to their boots and got squeezed up between the toes of the barefooted ones, and was all over the cow that lay on her side in a pen right in the middle of the saleyards. She was lying on her side in the muck, all the time making a soft mooing sound, her eyes big and staring, her four legs stretched out and moving, and another leg that didn't move, just one more, sticking out from the back of her. And the muck red with blood all around her.

And some of them knew and some didn't. They climbed up all round the pen and stared down, all eyes, looking, not shouting, not talking much, asking each other and looking. And asking each other. And looking. Lanky and Knocky and Phil all in a row together, looking with the rest. Until a man in the distance shouted out, Hey there you kids!

And they got down in a hang of a hurry and ran, ran until they were across the railway line and out of sight of the saleyards.

And just where they turned off down to the gravel pit there were girls going home out of the same class.

Oh my finger, oh my thumb, oh my belly, oh . . .

Somebody started it, and they all shouted.

Oh my finger, oh my THUMB!

And one of the girls shouted back to let them just wait, because they were going to tell.

So they ran again, ran down to the river, and down into the gravel pit. Everybody shouting. And in the gravel pit they never stopped shouting and running, around and across, this way and that, all except Knocky and Lanky and Phil, and one or two that helped them off with their schoolbags and held them.

And then Knocky and Lanky and Phil were all together, there in the middle of the gravel pit, with the rest all round. Most of them had stopped running, though just a few hadn't. And Knocky got ready, and Lanky and Phil got ready, and Knocky tried to hit Lanky and missed, and then Lanky hit him, and then Phil came from behind and hit him too.

So Knocky said that wasn't fair. He made for the side of the gravel pit and stood with his back to it. And Lanky and Phil followed him over, and Lanky rushed in to hit him and missed, he hit Lanky instead, but Phil was there and hit him a beauty right on the chin. And he had his tongue out. He opened his mouth and the blood came, and he backed up against the side of the gravel pit and stood there, his mouth open and his tongue hanging out, and the blood running down, and if you went near you saw a cut wide open nearly right across his tongue.

And everybody looked. And shouted louder than before, and ran around and across, faster and faster, coming up to look and see the blood dripping and shout, and running again. Lanky and Phil looking too, not hitting him any more, and then talking together and starting to run. But instead of running around and across they ran up out of the gravel pit. And the rest followed them, just one or two running up to Knocky for one last look, and then running up out of the gravel pit. And looking back from the top and seeing Knocky still standing there up against the side of the gravel pit, all by himself, his mouth open and his tongue hanging out, and the blood running down.

And all of them ran and kept running, not shouting any more, leaving others behind, turning off up streets and running. Nearly all running alone, but each one running.

Running for home.

* * *

III

The three of them were together after school that afternoon. Their names were Charlie and George and Henry.

They all went home the same way, so unless one of them got kept in they all went home together. Any one of them might be liable to get kept in, because George wasn't much good at anything except sums, and Henry wasn't much good at anything except drawing, and Charlie was no good at anything at all. But if it was George that got kept in, it was no good him thinking the other two would wait for him. And if it was Henry it was the same way. But if it was Charlie, the other two would be waiting for him. If Charlie and George got kept in together, then Henry would wait. Or if Charlie and Henry got kept in together, then George would wait. But if George and Henry got kept in together, then Charlie wouldn't wait. Though just occasionally he would.

And all this was because Charlie was hang of a funny to be with. He could make you laugh, Charlie could. He was hang of a funny. He could say things to make you laugh, and do things too. So everybody in the class liked being with Charlie, and George and Henry were lucky because they both went home the same way as he did. Though Henry wasn't nearly so lucky as George was, because you came to Henry's place first on the way home. And George could go all the way home with Charlie because they lived nearly next door to each other. And Henry wasn't allowed to go down there and play with Charlie, because mother always said, Those Browns aren't quite our sort of people. So all Henry could do was get ready for school in plenty of time, and then hang about by the fence waiting for Charlie to come past. And hope George wouldn't be with him. And hope that George would get kept in after school. And save up lollies and pennies and pieces of cake to give to Charlie, and say he didn't want them himself.

Anyhow, that afternoon the three of them were going home together. And before they crossed the railway line Charlie asked them if they knew what was the height of impudence. They didn't know so he told them, and asked if they knew the height of impossibility. They didn't know the answer to that either, so he told them and asked if they knew what was the coolest thing on earth. They didn't know, so he told them.

Well, he was hang of a funny, Charlie was. And he was going to ask them another one, but they'd come to the railway line, and away in the distance you could hear a train whistling. So George said to Charlie, why didn't he lie down under the cattle-stop while the train went over, like he'd always said he was going to? And Henry said, No, don't you, Charlie. Because Charlie might have got killed, yet at the same time he was wanting to say, Yes, go on Charlie. But Charlie wasn't having any. Not today, but let them wait and they'd see. And George said gee, he hoped he wouldn't get kept in that afternoon. And Henry said Charlie ought to promise to let them both see. But Charlie said he wasn't making any promises. Instead he asked them if they knew what was the most slippery thing on earth. And the driest thing. And what was the height of anticipation. And then, when they were passing the sawmill, he asked did they know why a lady's leg was the funniest thing on earth. And then George said he knew one about a lady's leg. Why was a lady's leg like the Wanganui river? But Charlie knew the answer and he yelled it out. And by that time they'd passed the sawmill, and passed the fence at the back of Henry's place, and were alongside the hedge at the front. And all of a sudden Henry remembered. Sometimes in the afternoon his mother would be sitting out in the garden on the rustic seat up against the hedge –

oh no no please no

– So he said, Shut up, don't talk so loud. And George said, What's the matter, are you frightened your old woman will hear? –

no please no God please

– And George said a kid that was tied to his old woman's apron strings oughtn't to be allowed to go to school. Because he might wet his pants.

Well, Henry couldn't say anything. In case his mother might be able to hear. But, anyhow, *he* hadn't said anything. Though if she'd heard *that* wouldn't make it any better.

Charlie and George left him by the gate at the corner, and he was frightened to go in but he had to. And going in he looked along the hedge and she wasn't on the seat. It was all right then, and he felt happy. And good. He'd prayed and God had answered his prayer and taken care of him. He'd been let off this time and it wouldn't ever happen again. If there was ever any chance of mother being on the seat he'd have to give up going that extra little bit along the hedge with Charlie. And he'd have to tell Charlie and George they'd better look out. Because if mother heard she might write a letter and get them expelled, though it wouldn't have mattered if it had only been George.

There didn't seem to be anybody home at all, though the back door wasn't locked and he called out, Anybody home? And he heard Auntie Clara say, Well? Where are you? he said. And she was in the bathroom having a bath. So he took off his schoolbag and looked underneath the clean tea-towel that was spread out and covering something on the kitchen table. Mother had made some date rolls so he took one, he was allowed to, then he went into the dining-room to get his book, and going past the bathroom door he could hear Auntie Clara in the bath. He went back into the kitchen because he wanted another date roll, and he sat on a kitchen chair to eat date rolls and read his story book, but before he found his place he looked at the picture on the cover. It showed a little girl sitting on the big green leaf of a water lily. She was a pink colour, without any clothes on, and she had green wings growing out of her back. She was one of the water babies. Then he found his place, but he'd only just started to read when Arnold came home. And Arnold just looked at him, threw his schoolbag in a corner, and took a date roll. What are you reading, son? Arnold said. Henry showed him. Kid's book, Arnold said, but Henry wanted to read. Is mum home? Arnold said. And Henry said Auntie Clara was having a bath. Arnold took another date roll, and Henry got up to take one too, and by the sound of the water in the bathroom Auntie Clara had pulled the plug out. Say we go and have a look through the keyhole?

Arnold said. And Henry looked up at him and said, No. Come on, Arnold said. And Henry looked up from looking at the picture on the front of the book and said, All right. ·

So they went into the passage, walking softly. And Arnold looked first, then Henry, but all he could see was a towel moving about. Then Arnold looked again, then Henry again, but he couldn't see a thing. So they went back into the kitchen and Arnold said, I never saw anything. So Henry said, Say we go and look through the window? And Arnold tried to stop him. She'll see you, you fool, he said, and then you'll cop it. He got frightened and tried to hold on to his brother but he got away. He wanted to look, he had to look, and hanging on to the windowsill, getting his eye up against a scratched place in the frosted windowpane, he did look. But at the moment of looking everything was changed, because at the same time that he saw, Auntie Clara had nearly all her clothes on, he also saw that she was looking at the window, and could see him looking there.

He dropped down from the window and ran. He heard Auntie Clara call out something, but he ran. Out behind the woodshed, across the paddock and into the fowl-run. Then he climbed the macrocarpa tree and hid up there in the branches. But Arnold found him. Arnold climbed the tree and sat on a branch near him. Arnold said, You won't tell, will you, son? And Henry his young brother started to cry. Arnold said, Do you want a lend of my magnifying glass? But Henry went on crying. Arnold said, Listen, you can have it for keeps if you like. But Henry couldn't answer. And it wasn't long before they heard mother calling out from the kitchen door. And Arnold said, It'll be all the worse for you if you don't go, but you won't tell, will you, son? And Henry his brother didn't say anything, but he tried to leave off crying. He slid down the branches on to the ground and left Arnold up there. And mother was in the kitchen bending over the stove. She came straight for him, holding on to him while she hit him on the head with her knuckles. Her face was white and she was nearly crying too. To think I've reared such a boy, she said. And she hit him. After all the years I've tried to do my best for you, she said, to think I couldn't bring you up *clean*. And she hit him again, and he got hit with her wedding ring as well as her knuckles. If you were a few years older, she said, you'd deserve to be locked up for the rest of your life. Go into your room, she said, and wait there until your father comes home. And then he couldn't help it. He said, Arnold looked too.

And face down on his bed, crying, he heard mother calling out, Arnold! Heard her push him into the bedroom, heard him start to cry when she gave him the first hit with the hairbrush.

IV

It was the first time he'd ever been away for a holiday by himself. He'd been looking forward to going and staying with Cherry and Auntie Flo, mother had said it would be ever so nice for him, and he thought so too, but now that he was at the station, sitting in the train and waiting for it to go, he wished he was staying at home. Because say he got sick? And mother wouldn't be there to hold his forehead –

no please no

– Mother was standing on the platform looking in at the window, and she was reminding him to remember and change his singlet, and remember to give her love to Cherry and Auntie Flo. And to have a good time, but promise to behave himself. And he promised and said he'd remember. And then the guard blew his whistle, and mother put her head in the window to give him a kiss. And then the engine blew its whistle, and the train jerked and bumped, and banged and rattled, and mother was being left behind on the platform. He waved and mother waved, and then he put his head out the window and waved. And kept on waving. Until the train went round the bend and he couldn't see mother any more.

And sitting in his seat he had to keep looking out the window, because he didn't want anyone to see that he was crying. Because he could still see mother standing there on the platform. And going home all by herself, crossing the streets she would have to cross –

the motor car was coming no please no time to cross in front no mother had to wear her glasses the motor car was oh please and mother and the wheels going up and down bump! bang! oh! and blood no please no

– And if he'd been there to look after her it wouldn't have happened. It wouldn't have. Father would send a telegram to Auntie Flo, and he'd have to catch the first train back again. So he'd be in time for the –

no please God please NO

– And then the old lady sitting next to him said didn't he think it a little too draughty with the window open? So he got up and shut the window, and the old lady said it was nice to meet a boy with such good manners. She said the boys you met nowadays were so rude, and that wasn't the way she'd brought her boys up when they were little chaps. No indeed, it was not. But she said she supposed you had to blame the mothers and fathers for letting the little ones have their own way, and not correcting them when they needed it. Now, she said, I'm sure you've got a good mother, so you are a very lucky boy.

And looking up into her face, with tears coming into his eyes, he said, My mother is dead.

Oh dear oh dear, oh dearie me. The old lady was quite upset. She took out her handkerchief and wiped her eyes, and said, You poor little boy. And she made him tell her all about it. She said she thought that lady had been his mother who kissed him goodbye at the station, but he said no, that was his auntie. And he told her all about how his mother had got run over. And the old lady blew her nose and patted him on the hand, and opened her handbag and made him take an orange and a cake of chocolate. She said these motor cars were a pest and you were always reading about accidents in the newspapers, and if you asked her she'd rather go for a ride in a buggy any day. She told him about some accidents she had heard of, and it took such a long time that before she had finished the train was beginning to get in at the station. And then, all of a sudden, he was standing on the seat and getting his luggage down out of the rack, but leaving the old lady's up there and forgetting all about his good manners. Because Cherry and Auntie Flo would be on the platform to meet him, and say the old lady started talking to Auntie Flo? Father –

what are people going to think, a boy going about telling strange people lies about his mother no no, now listen to me no money to buy any lollies and a good thrashing is no please no

– But he was lucky, because there was a crowd on the platform and he couldn't see Cherry and Auntie Flo out the window. The old lady was speaking to him but he said goodbye and shoved past people, treading on their toes. Then he jumped off the step before the train had finished moving and ran along the platform. And Cherry came running, leaving Auntie Flo away behind, and then she was just about squeezing him to death. And her kisses! – gee, he started to feel hot all over. And then Auntie Flo was there, laughing, and giving him a kiss, but a different sort of one. And once they'd hurried and caught the tramcar he was safe, because there wasn't any sign of the old lady, and he was even beginning to feel glad that he'd come for his holiday with Cherry and Auntie Flo.

And each day, more and more, it turned out quite a different sort of life from what it was in his own home, something he hadn't known about before. It was such a small house for one thing, and he slept in Cherry's room, and Cherry went and slept in the big double bed with Auntie Flo. But first thing in the morning, on her way to the kitchen to put the kettle on for a cup of tea, she'd pop her head in and blow him a kiss. Cherry was older than he was too, she'd left school and was old enough to go out and work in a shop or an office, but Auntie Flo wouldn't let her. When Uncle Jo had died he hadn't left her very well off, she said, but all the same Cherry was all she had, so she wasn't going to have her running the risks girls had to run when they worked in shops and offices. But Henry, her young nephew, didn't know what she meant.

Though it wasn't long before he found out that Cherry was properly mad over boys. Her mother wouldn't let her go round much on her own, but it was different with Henry there, and she'd let the two of them go together. So Cherry would cut some lunch and they'd get ready and go off to some place like the zoo. At any rate that was where Cherry would tell her mother they were going, or some other show place, but usually they'd go somewhere quite different. And sometimes he would get in a temper, and Cherry would get scared in case he'd tell, because naturally he wanted to see places like the zoo, and didn't like being dragged off to see one of Cherry's girl friends, just so that Cherry could see the girl friend's brother while he was home having his lunch. And of course Auntie Flo would ask questions about what sort of animals he'd seen at the zoo, and he'd have a hard job pretending that he'd seen them.

There were times though when Cherry would get one of her girl friends to go out with them, so then he'd get his visit to some show place after all. And on those days Cherry was always good fun. She'd sort of half-dance along the street, and she'd make eyes at men like tram conductors and postmen. She'd sing too. Her hair was frizzy black, and showed under a little red hat she wore. And she was pretty with her bright dark eyes, her red dark cheeks, and her hair showing from under the little red hat. She'd have a bag of peppermints, and if she saw a boy hanging over a gate it was ten chances to one she'd ask him to have one. Then she'd begin to talk to the boy, and after a bit she'd tell Henry and the girl friend to go on and wait for her at the next corner.

Well, that was Cherry. And going round with her, listening to her talk and the talk of her girl friends, seeing all she did, he'd think he was a lot more grown-up than people might think from his bare knees and his school rig-out. And living all this different sort of life he found the days going quicker and quicker, until in no time it began to get to the end of his holiday, and Auntie Flo let Cherry have a party.

And the night of the party was a great time for Cherry, because all her girl friends came and brought a good number of their brothers. And with the house full of them Cherry was sort of dancing about the whole time, and couldn't keep still a moment. She looked prettier than ever, her cheeks bright red with all the excitement, as well as from all the cooking that she'd been doing all day, and that she'd got her cousin Henry to help her with. And besides all the wonderful cakes and jellies, the trifle and the whipped cream, there were songs and games and all sorts of competitions. And it was clever of Cherry the way she worked things so that it was nearly always her that had to go out into the passage in the dark with some boy. And not come in until they were called. Even then they'd be quite a time coming in, but the boy would beg everybody's pardon and say it was his fault. And that would be sure to make somebody start giggling.

Then the day after the party it was Sunday, and even though she was tired after the party Cherry said she was going to church as usual. And she begged so hard that Auntie Flo let Henry go as well. Because Auntie Flo had turned Catholic when she married Uncle Jo, and Henry had heard his mother say often enough that you could hardly call Catholics Christians at all. And Auntie Flo must have had strict instructions, because she said she knew she was doing wrong, but Henry could go if he promised he wouldn't ever tell his mother. So he promised, and Cherry danced about and clapped her hands. Until all of a sudden she started scolding Auntie Flo for not going too. She was committing a mortal sin, she said, and right until they left for church she was stamping her foot and telling her mother she ought to be ashamed of herself.

It was something new for Henry anyhow, he had never knelt in church before, you only did that beside your bed at night when you were saying your prayers. But he knelt there beside Cherry while she was saying the rosary, and afterwards, with her there beside him, he did everything that she did, until at last everybody was kneeling and it was so quiet you almost held your breath, and the bell rang, and rang again, and rang a third time.

And going home with Cherry after it was all over he didn't listen much to what she was saying, because he was thinking how many long days must pass before he could go to church with her again next Sunday. Until all of a sudden he remembered. He'd forgotten all about mother and father, yet tomorrow he would be going home. And he wanted to stay and live with Cherry and Auntie Flo always, and go to church every Sunday with Cherry always. And instead he had to go home and live with his father and mother.

And that night, the last night of his holiday with Cherry and Auntie Flo, he couldn't get to sleep for a long time. And when he did go to sleep he had a dream. The house was full of old ladies who were standing all round him, and they kept on saying, You poor little boy. And he could look out the window and see the cemetery, and they were ringing a bell and burying a smashed-up old motor car that had Cherry sitting in it, with her

little red hat on too, and she was laughing and bouncing up and down
on the back seat as it went down into the hole.

And then, even though he was still in the dream he was at the same
time awake, and Cherry had come into his room and was getting into bed
with him. It seemed part of the dream, yet it wasn't. Because Cherry was
saying that her mother would think she was out in the kitchen waiting
for the kettle to boil, and that he mustn't ever tell, he'd got to promise her
he wouldn't ever tell. Well, it must still be the dream, yet at the same time
it wasn't. And Cherry hugged him and kissed him as he lay there,
trembling all over, his teeth chattering, yet the sweat pouring off him, and
all the time praying and praying for the kettle to hurry up and boil.

And even when they'd all finished breakfast he was still praying.
Praying for the time to come when they'd have to leave for the station,
and praying that the train would take him home to mother and father,
faster and faster. It was hours and days and years and ages, yet it all
happened at last. Auntie Flo said to be sure and give his mother her love,
and she kissed him. And he didn't want to let Cherry kiss him but he had
to. And when the train began to move they waved, and Cherry blew him
another kiss, and the last thing he remembered was Cherry's face, with
her hair that was frizzy black, and the little red hat on top. And after the
train, with the sandwiches that Auntie Flo had cut, and the bottle of
lemonade he'd bought out of his pocket money, father was at the station
to meet him. And mother was waiting to put the dinner on the table, and
told him to go to the bathroom to wash his hands and brush his hair.

So he was back in the family, safe again now, and the next day school
started, and it seemed just as if he'd never been away for a holiday. Except
not quite.

* * *

V

For weeks on end that winter there were days without a cloud. Nobody
could remember anything like it. Every morning the frost lay heavy and
white, and in places where the sun never got it wouldn't melt all day.
Where it covered the bricks on the shady side of the woodshed Henry trod
it down, and it turned into ice. Each day the ice got thicker, and boys came
in to see it on their way home from school. They ran and jumped on it
and slid, and talked of getting more bricks and making a proper skating
rink.

You shivered getting up in the morning and going to school, walking with your fingers tucked into the top of your trousers, and maybe you shivered in school as well, but it was nice out in the sun for the morning interval, and sitting in the sun while you ate your lunch. You felt the cold coming on again in the afternoon before they let you out of school, but there'd be drill or football practice to warm you up, and at home the kitchen would be warm with mother getting the dinner, the pots boiling, and the meat sizzling and popping in the oven. And when it was time to light the fire in the dining-room you could go and lie on the hearthrug. Though Henry was getting a big boy now. His mother would come in and say, Get up off that hearthrug, a big boy like you. And father, just home from work, would say, Your mother shouldn't have to tell you. And Auntie Clara might put her spoke in and call you a great lout. It made you feel all sorts of things, things you couldn't say what. You wanted to answer back and sulked instead. But you were hungry and there was the good dinner, mother heaping your plate, and the family talk – Arnold's talk about his boss, and father's and mother's grown-up talk, and Auntie Clara making everybody laugh with the things she said because she was an old maid. And of course you had plenty to say yourself, and sometimes you couldn't wait until other people had finished, and got asked if you'd ever learn not to interrupt.

After he'd helped Auntie Clara with the dishes Henry had to do his homework. It was a worry, a bad spot on something that was perfect, though you never thought of it as perfect – or never did until you remembered about your homework. Wanting to be nearer to the fire you squirmed about on the piano stool drawn up to the table. Your backside (though *derrière* was what you called it now) had had enough of sitting on hard seats for the day, but you had to sit there and squirm, and try to work out your algebra, and learn your French verbs off by heart. Time dragged, but it was done in a sort of fashion at last, and then what had been so wished for and looked forward to came true. That something perfect took the shape of a ball, or so it would seem now and then. You lived inside the ball, and it was lovely to have it all round you, you living contented right inside at the centre. There was room for you by the fire, there was only father and mother, Auntie Clara went to bed early, and Arnold went out always and never said where he went. Anyhow, there was room for you there by the fire, room for your easy chair and father's and mother's, mother with her ball of wool doing her darning, and father reading the newspaper. With your soft slippers on you could even put your feet up near the mantelpiece without having anything said. And with the feel of the fire on your legs you could read your book, not trash, you weren't allowed to read that, but Edward S. Ellis was all right. *The Hunters of the Ozarks*, *The Lost Trail*, *The Last Warpath*, Deerfoot was in every one of them, and from inside that ball where you lived contented, you looked out and saw Deerfoot close his eyes to pray as he ran through the forest (you had tried that once going to school and bumped into a telegraph pole), saw him rescue the paleface boys when they were hard-pressed by the Indians and half-frozen by the snow. It was wonderful. At the same time as you were there by the fire with father and mother, you lived it all with Deerfoot and the paleface boys, away over in America in the frozen forest. You *were* Deerfoot and the paleface boys, though mainly Deerfoot. Yet you weren't either, because the time you were Deerfoot praying with his eyes closed you had bumped into the telegraph pole.

But there was the clock on the mantelpiece. How goes the enemy? you heard people say. And mother looked at the clock and said, It's your bedtime, Henry. And you didn't move or say anything. Mother was going to stop you from being Deerfoot, to make you get out from the inside of that ball. You'd stop her from doing it too quickly if you could, but you couldn't slow her down much with father there. So after mother had told you once more you got up and tidied up your homework, asked if you could have an orange, and said this and that just to put off going to bed for a few minutes longer. But you had to go, and it was cold in the bathroom cleaning your teeth, and you shivered getting undressed and saying your prayers, and afterwards in bed, but everything was all right once you got warm, then you could be Deerfoot again, warm in bed, yet at the same time running through the snow that covered the ground beneath the trees of the forest. And bed was a good place to be Deerfoot in, there weren't any telegraph poles there.

So that was the end of the day, another day gone and one day nearer the grave, you'd once heard a man say. He was only a borough labourer working on the road, and he said it to another like himself, they were knocking off, finished for the day and putting their tools in a box, and Henry heard and remembered – the two men, the man who spoke, and the one who heard and said, Ay. You were liable to remember any time, you didn't know why, but of course if you did remember when you were in bed being Deerfoot, well, it was only for a second and it didn't worry you. You went on being Deerfoot, went on so long you should have heard father and mother going to bed, yet didn't because there wasn't enough difference between sleeping and waking.

The lovely days kept on for weeks on end that winter, the nights and mornings freezing cold, but in between the sun burning in an empty sky. And it was after just such a day that one night there came a knock at the kitchen door. There was only Henry to hear because father and mother had gone to bed early, gone only just a few minutes ago, and Henry could stay up and read while the fire lasted, but he mustn't put any more wood on, and he had to see the fire was safe, and remember to turn out the light. Well, perhaps he might put a piece of wood on, it depended; father might notice in the morning, meantime he was still warm and he was reading – and then came the knock. You never got a knock on the kitchen door at that time of night, and there on your own it made you feel a little frightened. But you were a big boy now, they were always telling you, big boys weren't crybabies and didn't tell lies or do things that you did when you were only a little kid. So Henry, a big boy, went and put the light on in the kitchen and opened the door. But as soon as it was open he wasn't a big boy any longer, because a swagger was standing there on the veranda, though a different sort of swagger from most, they were usually old men, but this one looked hardly anything much more than a boy. He hadn't any money, he said, and he wanted a place to sleep for the night, and Henry said he would have to ask his father.

He left the man at the door and went down the passage, and outside the bedroom he said, Father, there's a man at the door. His father said, What? and his mother said, You can come in. And he went in and his father was kneeling down in his pyjamas saying his prayers, his mother sitting up in bed plaiting her hair. Well, his father listened to Henry, still kneeling and looking out of his hands that were over his face, and he said the man couldn't stay there. Tell him he must go right away, he said. And Henry said, Where will he sleep, father? If necessary he can go to the police station, his father said. Run and tell him, his mother said.

So Henry went and told the swagger, and the swagger stood there and said it was a cold night, then he said he could do with a bite of something to eat. So Henry went back along the passage, and mother was lying down in bed, but father hadn't finished saying his prayers. Mother said to take the man into the kitchen, and told Henry what to get out of the safe to give him to eat, and she said to father, It's no good giving them money, they only spend it on drink. And father looked out of his hands again and said, If you don't get rid of him in twenty minutes come back and tell me. And mother talked about locking the door, but what about Arnold? So when he'd got rid of the swagger, Henry was to leave a note for Arnold to be sure and lock the door after he came in.

Well, there you were in the kitchen with the swagger who looked hardly more than a boy, perhaps not much older than your brother Arnold. He was thin-faced, thin as a match, his clothes were dirty and torn, and he was shivering with cold and no wonder, because the kitchen was cold enough to make Henry shiver as well. And you thought, feeling the cold, and getting out bread and butter and cold meat, and heating some milk on the gas, Where do you sleep when you've nowhere to sleep? The swag was on the floor, only a little swag wrapped in a blanket, if it was all blankets it mightn't be so bad if you had to sleep out, under a tree perhaps or in some shed. But gee, it would be freezing cold on a night like this. And Henry didn't know what to say, and the swagger was too busy eating to talk, but when Henry had nothing more to do he said, Are you out of a job? Then the swagger talked and ate at the same time, telling about the hundreds of miles that he'd walked, and how he couldn't get a job. And when Henry asked him he said he hadn't got a home or any people. But of course mother always said you couldn't believe the things swaggers said, everybody could get work if they wanted it, hard graft never did anybody any harm, but some people weren't fond of it, that was the trouble, and drink.

Then when the swagger had had enough to eat Henry started to put the things away, looking at the clock, and remembering what his father had said. And the swagger asked him if he had a cigarette, but it was no good asking you that. So the swagger got up, and said there were sheds out the back and couldn't he doss there? And you felt yourself go red, but you said it was no good, your father had said he must go right away. And you managed to get rid of him in the end, and mother called out, but softly so as not to wake Auntie Clara, and you went to the bedroom door and said he had gone, and she reminded you about the note for Arnold and told you to go straight to bed. So you fixed the note and remembered about everything, and it was so cold that by the time you'd said your prayers and were in bed your teeth were chattering. But you cuddled yourself up in the bed and soon got warm, *snug as a bug in a rug*, and you thought about the swagger and wondered where he would sleep, but mother and father knew best, you were only a boy, sometimes not even a big boy, it depended, and had no say. And you never remembered anything more, except that you'd been dreaming, until you woke up when it was just getting daylight. And there was a funny smell in the room, not a nice smell, and Arnold was standing by his bed in his pyjamas, and the swagger was standing there too, all dressed but with his boots in his hand, and a cigarette in his mouth but not yet lighted. And before you could speak Arnold bent over you and said, but so as you could hardly hear, that if you opened your mouth and breathed a word you'd never get a lend of his camera again, and you wouldn't ride on the back of his motor bike when he bought it at Christmastime.

*   *   *

VI

When Uncle Bob came out on to the veranda with two bottles of beer, he asked Henry if he'd go and get something to drink it out of.

It was Sunday morning, mother and father and Auntie Clara had gone to church, and Henry would have had to go too, but somebody had to stay at home and keep an eye on the dinner. Henry was quite good at that, though as mother always said, it was never any good depending on Arnold. Besides, there was Bible class in the afternoon, and Henry hadn't quite finished writing the paper that it was his turn to read. It was about the saying, Ye are my friends if ye do whatsoever I command you, and he was trying to answer the question: Was it possible for a young man to be so filled with the spirit of the Master, that his life would resemble His in every possible way? With his pencil and pad, and his books by Fosdick, he sat at the little table in the shady corner of the veranda, getting up now and then to go inside and see if there was enough fire on. And it wasn't such a difficult question to answer, but there was the distraction of the dinner, and the beautiful morning. It was summer, nearly Christmas. The church bells were still ringing, giving a last touch to the Sunday morning feeling, though the popping and banging that came from the backyard, where Arnold was fixing his motor bike hardly fitted in. The sun was getting hot in a sky without a cloud. The tennis lawn was dried up by the sun, the ground baked hard, and with every breath of wind the rambler roses, that covered the wire-netting across the other side, dropped a fresh sprinkling of petals. So it wasn't exactly an easy matter to fix your mind on such a question, even though you *did* know the answer.

And then Uncle Bob came out with the two bottles of beer. He was in his shirtsleeves and stockinged feet, only just out of bed, yet still looking sleepy.

Uncle Bob was mother's and Auntie Clara's bachelor brother. But he lived away down south, and nobody had seen him for years. He'd turned up only the day before in his Ford car, with his tale to tell. Times had been pretty good lately, so he said. He'd bought the Ford second-hand, a regular bargain, and he'd decided to spend his Christmas holidays driving about to see a bit of the country. On the way up he'd come through the town where Uncle Ted lived, so he'd picked him up and brought him along as well. But Henry knew that Uncle Ted wasn't like Uncle Bob. As mother and Auntie Clara always said, Uncle Ted had been sensible and settled down and become a respectable married man while he was still quite young. And it was a thousand pities that Uncle Bob had never had the sense to do the same thing. Anyhow, the two uncles were staying a few days before they went on and drove about the country. And they could make themselves quite useful while they stayed, because Uncle Bob was a carpenter, and Uncle Ted painted houses, and mother told them she had quite a few jobs about the house that were simply crying out to be done.

Anyhow, there was Uncle Bob standing in the doorway, with a bottle of beer hanging from each hand. Henry could see the labels with their four big X's, and Uncle Bob had asked him to go and get something to drink it out of. But just then Arnold came round from the backyard with Uncle Ted, and straight off Uncle Ted said:

Hello, he's fetched out his Indian clubs.

And seeing that Henry hadn't moved or said anything, had only stared, Uncle Bob said:

Come on Arnold my lad, I get wind round my heart if I drink it out of the bottle.

So Arnold went and got the glasses, and they came along the veranda to Henry's table, and Uncle Bob opened up the beer.

Cheers, he said, but where's one for Henry?

Him! Arnold said, he's too young.

Haven't you never had a spot? Uncle Bob wanted to know.

And Henry, colouring, said, No, Uncle Bob –

no no please no

– Well, Uncle Bob said, you look big enough to me. And he said, turning to Arnold and Uncle Ted, If they're big enough they're old enough – it don't make any difference if it's a bit of skirt or new potatoes.

And Uncle Ted, laughing, but looking at Henry and seeing his colour, said, Now come off it Bob, go easy.

Well, Uncle Bob said, pouring out more beer, he's a big boy now. Aren't you, Henry? And his hard-case old face, badly in need of a shave, but good-tempered looking, and always on the point of breaking into a grin, grinned now; his mouth widening, and the corners, always just slightly turned up, turning right up and running away in the direction of his ears.

And Henry managed to grin back and say, Yes Uncle Bob.

Then he went inside to see if the fire was all right, and back on the veranda again he found that Uncle Bob had taken a seat in his chair, and was pouring out the last of the beer.

Ay, Uncle Bob was saying, mother's ruin – straight from the bottle.

And Henry made a joke. Uncle's ruin you mean he said.

That's it my boy, Uncle Bob said. Uncle's ruin. And he held out the glass of beer until it was in the sunlight, with the bubbles rising, and sending up a little spray as they broke on the surface.

Lovely stuff, Uncle Bob said. Grows hair on your chest, makes your eyebrows curl, stops you from getting old – yes. And fills your heart with love for brother man – beg pardon, he ended up.

And then he leaned forward and looked at the pad Henry had been writing on.

What's this? he said. What's this Henry, have you left school and still have to do your study?

And Henry said, it takes a lot of swot before you can be a lawyer –
no

– I bet it does, Uncle Bob said. And what's more you need to have the brains. That was always my trouble – I never had no brains.

No need to tell anybody, Uncle Ted said.

And Uncle Bob grinned.

I don't know, he said. I knew I never had none, but when I wanted to leave school they said no, keep on and be a schoolteacher. It was my teacher-bloke said that. He said I ought to make a good teacher. What do you reckon Henry? D'you reckon I'd have made a good teacher?

You would now, Uncle Ted said.

And Uncle Bob couldn't drink the last of his beer for laughing.

But I know why he said it, Uncle Bob went on. It was because he didn't want to lose me out of the football team. And he was a good coach. But I don't remember nothing about when school was in except him playing pocket billiards – he was certainly the bloke to make the big breaks.

And lying back in the chair he did a big stretch, and a big yawn as well.

So you're going to be a lawyer, he said, and his hand, stretching out, picked up one of Henry's books.

What's this? he said. What's this Henry, do you believe in religion?

And Henry, facing up to it, said, I'm writing a paper for the Bible class.

The boy's got the religious bug, Arnold said. He ought to have lace sewn round the bottom of his pants.

And Henry, hot under the collar, said, You shut up and mind your own business.

Now leave the boy alone Arnold my lad, Uncle Bob said. I don't hold with religion myself, but I don't say nothing against it. Not having the brains, like.

What's all this about having no brains? Uncle Ted said. Don't you reckon you're a good carpenter? And don't you need a few brains for that? And anyhow, wasn't Jesus Christ a carpenter?

That's right, Uncle Bob said, and grinned. I've seen pictures of him getting round with a hammer tucked in his belt. Is that right Henry? he asked.

Well, Henry said, well – yes.

I had a mate once, Uncle Bob said. We had to drive out to a job in the country, and he said (but mind you Henry, just as a joke, like), he said we were two simple carpenters following in the Master's footsteps – only in a motor car.

But Henry didn't laugh.

Why make a joke out of it uncle? he said. Because isn't that what we all ought to be doing? – following Him. Look! he said, that's what I've written here.

And tingling with excitement, his ears burning, looking down on the table so they wouldn't see his face, he turned over the pages of his pad.

Listen, he said (though nobody was interrupting). Listen – And he dared to look up at their faces. Uncle Ted's without any expression at all; Uncle Bob's good-tempered, expecting, a little puzzled; Arnold's impatient and scowling. Listen now, he said –

I'm damned if I'll listen, Arnold said, and he went round to the backyard again.

But the two uncles stayed there and Henry read. And when he'd finished Uncle Bob clapped his hands.

Cheers, he said. You write beautiful Henry. I reckon it shows you've got the brains for a lawyer all right. And he turned to his brother. What do you say Ted?

The same as you, Uncle Ted said. Only I reckon he might find it a bit tough when he's a lawyer.

And Henry said well, it might be a bit tough passing his exams.

No, Uncle Ted said, that's not what I mean.

But Uncle Bob chipped in and said to leave the boy alone. He said you could make pots of money out of being a lawyer, only you needed to have the brains. So let Henry just go right ahead and show them.

And Henry tried to explain, because Uncle Bob didn't understand, but he never had a chance with Uncle Bob going on and telling a yarn he knew about a lawyer that was made a judge, but when he was still a lawyer he said to a witness in court that her name was Molly something or other, but she said, Now Charlie the other night you were telling me it was Molly darling. And he'd just finished the yarn when Arnold came round from the backyard again. He was bouncing a ball on his tennis racket, and he wanted to know if anyone felt like having a game –

no

– And Uncle Bob said he couldn't play for little apples but he'd like to have a go, and Uncle Ted said yes, why not have a game?

Henry said he had to finish his paper, so Arnold played the two uncles. And you could hardly call it a game at all, because Uncle Bob held his racket as though he had hold of a shovel, and tried to scoop up every ball that came over the net, even those he should have left for Uncle Ted. And then he took off his shirt and played in just his trousers and stockinged feet, and with his face split nearly in two by his grin he started jumping over the net, and playing on Arnold's side instead. And the ball would bounce on the roof of the house, or land in the rambler roses and bring down a shower of petals, and getting it again Uncle Bob would shake down more petals all over himself, so they'd be in his hair, or sticking to the hair on his chest.

So what with all the laughing Henry was watching all the time, and wishing he was in the fun instead of out of it. And wishing he was showing the two uncles how he could play tennis. Until at last when the ball came over on to the veranda, and Henry got up to throw it back again, and Uncle Bob said, Come on Henry, don't you reckon you and me could give them a go, he said wait a minute, and went inside for his racket.

Then they played and Henry tried to play his very best to make up for Uncle Bob, all the time trying to do his forehand drives, with the top-spin that made them come up fast and high. But Uncle Bob acted the goat so much they began to get behind. So Henry had to try harder than ever, not laughing at all but looking worried and serious and hot, shouting to Uncle Bob to leave it to him and stay on his own side of the court, yet all the time going off his own side himself. And they drew up even, and Uncle Bob said, Now we've got 'em wet Henry my lad. You only need to take your shirt off like me, and we'll be home and dried.

And Henry took it seriously and pulled his shirt off, looking all white skin and bone beside Uncle Bob with his big muscles and his dark sunburn. But he hardly had time to notice, he needed everything he had to beat Arnold and Uncle Ted, when he was playing with such a passenger as Uncle Bob. Though having such a partner would make it all the better if only they could win. And it was touch and go but he managed it. When both sides

were just one point off game and set he shouted out, Mine! and ran in front of Uncle Bob. And from the hit that Uncle Ted made at the fast one he sent over, the ball went away up over the house, the furthest one yet. So they –
   no he no
– had won! And seeing the look on Arnold's face, hearing Uncle Bob say what a champion he was, he said, Never mind Uncle Ted, I'll go and find it.

But it took him quite a time to find the ball, and then, running back with it at last, expecting to find the three of them having a knock-up while they waited for him, he found nothing of the kind. No! They were sitting on the veranda steps, and looking as though they'd been sitting there having a talk for quite a long time, Uncle Bob with his shirt on now, the rackets put away somewhere out of sight, and that other ball as well, and the bottles and glasses of course; and standing there, all dressed up in his good Sunday suit and his hard-knocker hat, home from church, his hymn-book under his arm, talking to them before he went inside – father!

And Henry turned back but it was too late. He heard his father speak to him, saw his look of rage at the sight of him without his shirt on, with the ball and tennis racket. Then everything was confused, with Uncle Bob standing up and saying it was all his fault, and father stamping his foot and saying he didn't want to hear any excuses; and all of a sudden mother standing in the doorway, her hat still on and her veil pushed up, her face white and angry, holding a pot in her hands, saying that the fire was out and the meat was spoilt, and to just look at the vegetables, they'd never even been put on the stove.

*   *   *

VII

It was only very seldom that the boss turned up before about four o'clock in the afternoon. Which meant that the pair of them were left on their own all day, and most days there was hardly a single thing for either of them to do.

The office was the upstairs part of an old building near the centre of the town. It was quite a small place, and up above there was room for only the office, so only people who wanted to see the boss ever came up the stairs. Some would go away and come back, over and over again; others would say they'd wait, and sometimes the little landing-place at the top of the stairs would be crowded with them, sitting there waiting, hour after hour.

But mainly the pair of them would be up there on their own all day, with nothing to do.

The girl had begun to work in the office at the beginning of the year, at the same time as Henry. She'd only just turned fifteen, so she said, which made her a good two years younger than he was. And while he'd been in his last year at school she'd been going to a class to learn shorthand and typing.

For the first few days the boss had always turned up at the office only about half an hour or so behind the pair of them. And he'd be round and about all day, dictating letters to the girl, getting her to type out this and that, and explaining to Henry about little matters that he could attend to, until he was able to get the hang of the more difficult ones. So Henry thought those first few days were all right, even though it did seem as though, after all the things you'd learned at school, you were still only a kid and had to start school all over again.

And then the boss began turning up at the office only at about four o'clock in the afternoon. Some days he wouldn't turn up at all. And it went on for weeks and weeks, and months and months. Henry tried to do what he could for the clients who were always calling, but it was too much to expect. He undid the tapes round the files and looked inside, but most times he couldn't make head or tail out of what they were all about. So the clients would either go away or say they would wait, and after a time it wasn't so much clients who called as other lawyers. They came with letters to say that Mr S. was to hand over all so and so's business and papers, and the first time it happened Henry got some papers out of the strongroom and handed them over, and told the boss the next time he turned up. But the boss was very annoyed about that. He told Henry he was to do no such thing, because in most cases there were costs to be paid before anything could be handed over, and in any case Henry was to hand nothing over. So then Henry would tell the lawyers they'd have to wait to see Mr S. And they'd ask him when he'd be in, and where he was, and why he was never at the office, and some of them would get in a temper and mutter things when Henry said he didn't know.

And for quite a time he really didn't know. Until one morning when he was late getting to work (because what did it matter?), he got a shock to see his boss walking along just ahead of him. But while he still had the sensation of his heart being in his mouth, the boss turned in at the pub door, just ten yards or so before he would have turned in to go up to the office. So then Henry knew the position. There were the two of them, Henry and the girl, left on their own up there all day with nothing to do, while the boss spent his time drinking in the pub only a stone's throw away.

And with nothing to do Henry thought at any rate it would be a good opportunity to get on with his swot. Yet it didn't turn out that way. Because he and the girl shared the big room (with the strongroom taking up one corner), in the front part of the office, and the girl could never do her knitting or read one of her books for very long, without wanting to talk. So Henry would go across the landing-place into the boss's room and swot in there. But that room looked out the back of the building down on to the river. Summer was hardly over yet, and the days were very hot, and it was distracting to think how nice and cool it looked down underneath the trees on the river bank. And soon the girl would get tired of being on her own, or tired of hanging out of the window of the front room, looking into the main street to see what was going on down there, so she'd come across to the boss's room and start talking, or else she'd hang out that window for a change. So Henry would go back to the front room and try to fix his attention on his swot, but most times it wouldn't be very long before the girl had followed him.

And so Henry found he had to give up trying to do his swot. For days on end he'd be talking to the girl instead. Or for a change he'd go and lean out the window himself. And after a time, whenever he did, the girl would be liable to come over and lean out alongside him, but there wasn't such a lot of room at the window, and for the pair of them to lean out, they'd have to be close enough together to be touching –

no no the book he found on his bed that afternoon after school, mother must have left it there and it was a hard job trying to look her in the face for days, birds flowers and the 'shining creature' a girl who said I have kept myself pure for you, and he said and I for you, and you could get diseases worse than leprosy, yes and secret vice please NO

– At first it used to seem to Henry that each day would never end. Coming along the main street in the morning he'd have to call for the mail. Then, after he'd opened up the office and put the mail on the boss's table there was nothing more to do. After the scare he'd got the morning he'd been late, and seen the boss just ahead of him, he'd always been on time. But with the girl it was quite different. She'd soon got into the way of turning up later and later, and to begin with Henry had thought well, what did it matter? But after he'd given up trying to do his swot it started to worry him. He'd have all day to talk to the girl when she did turn up, yet he was impatient for her to be there. And while he was waiting, he soon discovered, he couldn't even be contented enough to open one of his text books and settle down to do a bit of swot. And then when she did come he'd feel that pleased. It would please him to think of the whole day stretching ahead with the girl there to talk to, and no interruptions to speak of. Yet soon it seemed that the time they had together each day wasn't half long enough. He began telling the girl she was taking a risk by turning up so late in the morning. He'd try to scare her into being punctual – until the girl would say pooh! he needn't think he was her boss. So let him not go and start trying to boss her. And that could be the beginning of an argument that lasted for hours, though it was such good fun the time ran into hours in just no time at all. Until it seemed that these days that he was spending up there, alone with the girl, were the most wonderful he had ever known in his life.

He grew to hate the thought of the late afternoon. It was always there, waiting round the corner so to speak, and it was a corner that you got to before you knew where you were. Round about four o'clock they'd be liable to hear the boss coming up the stairs, and they always knew who it was. Sometimes the clatter he made went on for quite a time, as over and over again his foot slipped down from the step above to the one below. The girl would rattle the typewriter, pretending to be busy, and Henry would have the petty cash book open in front of him, and a pen in his hand. And sometimes the boss would come to their door, swaying only just very slightly as he looked in at them. He'd say, Miss Grigg I want you, his words only the very slightest bit blurred. And other times he would go straight on into his room and close the door, and they'd be all on edge, the minutes dragging themselves out until the five o'clock whistles blew, and they could tidy up and go home. Though it didn't always happen that way. No, sometimes the boss's bell would ring, and it was usually for the girl, and she'd have to take some letters that were always urgent, so the boss said, and had to go by the mail that evening. And Henry would have to wait to press them in the copying book, and sometimes it meant that the pair of them wouldn't get away until long after their usual time. Yet there were times when it didn't happen that way either – times when the boss's bell would ring, and it didn't matter whether it was Henry or the girl who answered. It didn't matter because the boss would be sitting sideways on in his chair, looking out the window, with as likely as not the morning's mail still unopened where Henry had left it. And he'd go on sitting there without moving or saying anything. And Henry would stand there waiting, or the girl would sit down with her pencil and pad all ready – until the boss would say, No, I've got nothing for you to do. And yet again there were other times, perhaps for Henry the worst times of all. He'd have to pull himself together and go and knock on the boss's door, and once inside he'd have to ask the boss to sign a cheque for wages. Because if he didn't, they had found out, neither of them would have ever got paid.

Still, there were days on end, besides odd days now and then, when the boss never turned up at all, though sometimes you could tell he'd been there after they'd gone home, because the mail would have been opened. And going into his room in the morning, seeing the signs of his having been there, frowning over them, Henry would think of the boss as something you just had to put up with – a worry, a bad spot on something that was sort of perfect, though you only thought how sort of perfect it was when you realized you were getting to that corner, and were turning it, and more than half-expecting to run into the boss. And even though the boss never turned up there were always those five o'clock whistles waiting to blow, and then the girl couldn't put on her hat and get down the stairs fast enough. He would try to stop her from going too fast if he could, he'd make jokes, or stand in the doorway with his arms spread out so that she couldn't pass, and she'd giggle and say please, or hit him on the arms until he gave in – then he'd go down the stairs behind her, waiting a moment at the top, to go down with a rush and a clatter, just to make her think he was falling down on top of her. Then near the bottom he'd pass her and hurry on ahead to get to her bicycle first. He'd feel the tyres, say they wanted or didn't want pumping, ask her how long it was since she'd put any oil on the chain – until he couldn't keep her there any longer, and wheeled the bicycle out of the passageway into the street, where he'd have to let her take it, and could only stand and watch while she got on and rode away, perhaps turning into the wind if there was a wind, and having to ride one hand, so that she could hold on to her skirt with the other –

no

– And after that, until the next morning, the only thing was just somehow to make do with being alive.

Then there were those times, usually somewhere about mid-morning, when they'd settled down for another day together, and Henry was feeling wonderfully contented, when the girl would make him feel suddenly cold all over. She'd say that she was sick of having nothing to do, it wasn't right to get money for doing nothing anyhow, and she was going to try for the next job she saw advertised in the paper. And he'd argue against her. Where would she get such an easy job? Yes, the girl said, but with nothing to do she was forgetting her shorthand. And how would she ever learn enough to get a better job with more pay? And she didn't like loafing the whole time anyhow. And Henry said well, wasn't it the same for him?

But the girl said it was different.

Because *you* don't have to earn your living, she said.

And Henry laughed, and said didn't he!

Go on, the girl said, you can't tell me. With all that money your father's got.

And Henry asked what made her think that?

Well, the girl said, look at all his property.

And Henry said what property, and who'd told her?

Everybody knows those religious people own property, she said. That's what my dad always says, people that have got money make religion a cloak.

And Henry laughed again (after all it was best just to laugh at such nonsense, and it made you laugh, anyhow), yet it made him wonder how people could be so ignorant and get such wrong ideas into their heads. At the same time it pleased him to think that he knew better, and could explain things to this girl so that she wouldn't be so ignorant.

Listen, he would say, listen . . .

And the girl would listen. There was hardly any way of getting out of it, and after all, there was nothing else to do.

Yes, she said, it's all very well to talk, but my dad always says one half of the world doesn't know how the other half lives.

And pleased, feeling how clever he was, he came out with it, Yes I know, but haven't I just been trying to tell you?

And she had to think that over, but at last she said, You think you're smart don't you? Anyhow, you can't tell me your father doesn't own that big house you live in. You can't tell me he has to pay any rent.

No, he said, but he has to pay the rates.

And she couldn't say anything to that, so he went on, and said you had to have people with money. Because they gave people work, didn't they?

And the girl said she didn't know, she supposed they did, but if she asked her dad she knew what he'd say – something different.

And full of confidence, Henry could have said, What? But on occasions like these it was sometimes just as well to let the girl think it was *his* turn to be squashed. After all, it didn't always do to make yourself out too smart. And besides, there was the fun of laughing to yourself, thinking how this girl, who'd never been to high school, made mistakes like sending letters to the Commissioner of Taxis, and had pointed to *Honi soit qui mal y pense*, and said that Latin was the language of the dead. She had said her father had told her that, so there you were, and what could such a man know about people who owned property, and had money and education? Why, all his life he'd done nothing except milk his cows out on that little rented place away beyond the edge of the town.

During the talks they'd had Henry had got to know quite a lot about the little farm where the girl lived. And because it was all so closely connected with her he was always ready and eager to listen, and hear all about it. There were mum and dad, and two older brothers, and three younger sisters. Dad and the boys got up before daylight to start milking the cows, but the boys soon had to be off on the milk-round, so mum went across to the shed to help dad finish the cows, while the boys went back to the house to eat the breakfast she'd left ready for them. Then they had to harness the horse into the float and be off on the round. And when the milking was finished mum left dad to clean up while she went back to the house, and while she was getting the rest of the breakfast ready she had to be calling to the rest of the family to get up. As for the girl, she had to see that the three younger ones washed their faces and dressed themselves properly, and got ready for school. And after breakfast she had to help her mother wash up and do things about the house before she left for work.

Well, Henry could picture all this life quite clearly. Because the girl was part of it. And because the girl now seemed to be part of his own life, there were times when he had the feeling that he was in the picture himself. He knew where the place was – out beyond the showgrounds. He remembered one time, years ago, when his teacher had taken the class for an afternoon in the fair-sized bit of bush that was over in the far corner of the showgrounds. The children had gathered ferns and learned their names, and the names of the trees, and looked for wetas and huhus, and listened to birds – afterwards they'd had to write compositions on What I Saw In the Bush. Anyhow, they went right through the bush and came to a fence on the far side, and beyond there was a swamp, with tussocks, and frogs croaking, and a paddock with cows, and further off a house and a cowshed. Near the house you could see some young children running about, and a man was chopping wood, chopping a log by the sound of it. You could see him lift the axe up over his head, and bring it down fast, but it wasn't until he'd got the axe up above his head again that you heard the sound it made. A sort of hollow, plonk! And the whole class saw it and watched, saying, See, Hear – until a boy asked why you had to wait for the sound, and the teacher explained. Well, now it turned out that the man chopping the log must have been the girl's father, and Henry had never seen him close-to that he knew of, but he'd always remembered, because that was the time he'd learned about having to wait for sound to travel to you. Also, although the girl couldn't be certain about it, one of the children running about might have been her. And now, after so many years, it was all somehow quite pleasing to think of, to recall and talk about.

Though it somehow didn't please Henry at all to discover that his mother was a customer of the girl's people, that it was one of the girl's brothers who was calling with the milk. Henry had seen him often enough, a big boy in dungaree trousers, well-patched and much too tight and short for him, making him look all feet in his heavy working boots. And his face, covered with freckles, with blue eyes, and straight clipped-off hair showing underneath his hat, never seemed to change its expression. It made him look sort of half-silly, Henry had thought, and he had noticed because sometimes he'd been about when his mother had been saying, Now you'll have to do better than this, because I'm not at all satisfied with the milk you're bringing me, or, You've-had-your-cows-on-those-turnips-again, or perhaps just, Now don't you dare spill any milk on my nice clean step. And to Henry it somehow wasn't at all pleasing to think of that brother of the girl coming round to the back door, particularly if he should just happen to be about at the time. It somehow made him feel that he himself wasn't anywhere in the picture after all.

Of course it hadn't been long before he'd begun to tease the girl about whether or not she had a boy. But when at last she told him all right, if he wanted to know she had more than one, it was hardly the sort of answer he'd expected or wanted to hear. And it didn't make it any better when she went on and told him about the trainer's place that was next door to their farm. There would usually be a few jockeys about there, especially as there were other trainers not far away, and they all brought their horses to exercise at the showgrounds. Well, she liked jockeys, they were always good fun, and if they took you out they'd always have plenty of money to spend. She wouldn't mind if she got married to a jockey, because you'd always be reading your name in the paper, and you'd never have to worry about not having enough money to spend, although it would be a worry always wondering if he was going to fall off and get hurt, or even killed. And another thing, she'd hate to marry any man that was smaller than herself.

And of course giving tit for tat she said anyhow, what about *his* girl?

Anyhow, she said, if your father doesn't give you any you don't get enough money to take her out.

And Henry said well, he wouldn't have much chance anyhow, because every night he had to do his swot.

So the girl wanted to know how long he'd have to wait until he was a lawyer, and how much a week he'd get then.

Well, she said, I'm glad I don't have you for a boy.

And it wasn't so much that he felt hurt – it was more a feeling of disappointment.

Why don't you go into your father's office? the girl said. Because you don't have to study for a land agent, and look at the thousands *they* make.

And Henry said did they? And money wasn't everything. And anyhow he wanted to be something better than a land agent – but then he remembered, that wasn't the right thing to say. No, not at all, because it didn't matter what you did so long as you had ideals for serving your fellow men. Why, during part of his life the apostle Paul had been only a tent-maker. But at the same time you had to remember the story of the man who was given the talents, yet . . .

And so this was their life together, just about every day of the week that they went to work. And it was no time before the summer days belonged to the past, and even the autumn ones were beginning to change into winter. Some days the girl would turn up dripping wet after her ride into town through the rain. All day the wind would be rattling the windows, and looking out they'd see the squalls coming up over the wet roofs and swaying trees, the wind driving the rain until it slanted nearly level with the roofs it pelted on. Henry would say it was a good sort of day to be indoors, and the girl would say yes, just think of her dad and her brothers having their jobs to do on a day like this. Though on other days it would be beautifully cloudless and sunny, but nippy after an early morning frost. Henry took shillings out of the petty cash box to put in the meter, and they'd sit in front of the gas fire to warm their hands and feet. Though on days when the sun stayed out the best place to be was the window of the boss's room, you got the sun there; and it wasn't long before the girl was spending nearly all her time there, no matter what the weather was. Nor was it hard to tell the reason why. Because the building next door was being added to at the back, and you could look out and see the men working down below. And as the building went up the men would be working closer and closer to the window, until the levels were the same, and you could talk to them from only a few yards away. Though Henry never knew what to say to them, so it was the girl who did nearly all the talking. Nor could he stay there by the hour as the girl did, he felt it wouldn't do at all to let the men know he had nothing to do. So he'd sit just out of sight at the boss's table with one of his swot books open in front of him, wishing the girl would go with him into the front room so they could be on their own, and feeling sour because she preferred talking to the men instead. And sitting there, pretending to swot, yet all the time listening, he'd get himself worked up into a state over the things he heard. Because it was bad enough having the feeling that you somehow didn't fit in with what was going on, yet listening to yourself being talked about was even worse.

At first the men had thought he was the girl's boss. And she'd thought that a good joke.

Him! He's just like me. He only works here.

Well, where was the boss?

I don't know, the girl said. In the pub I suppose, drinking beer.

Gee, that would be the life! Some people had all the luck.

Some people might have, the girl said. *I* don't.

Well, what about the boyfriend she'd got tucked away somewhere inside there?

Him! the girl said. *He's* not my boyfriend.

Go on, bet she'd sat on his knee.

Oh, I never have, the girl said. You ask *him*.

Why should he tell? Anyway, bet she'd sat on plenty.

That's different, the girl said. Why shouldn't I?

No reason, wouldn't mind if she'd sit on his, though.

Well, I wouldn't, the girl said. I wouldn't not if you was the last man on God's earth.

Go on, bet she didn't know her own mind.

And it went on day after day, with Henry not wanting to listen, yet not being able to stop himself, and feeling more and more choked up with his sourness. Also some of the men began saying things to the girl that were very suggestive – awful things, Henry thought. At first he hoped she didn't know what they meant (because if she had known, she wouldn't have stayed at the window – would she have?). But then he'd hear the girl saying things back to the men that showed she knew all right, and sometimes what she'd say would sound just as bad, or even worse – until Henry would be wanting to get up and pull her away from the window, to stop her from saying such things, or listening to them either.

Then there came a morning when it rained so hard that Henry wasn't very surprised at the girl's not turning up to work. Later on the weather cleared, but still there was no sign of her. He worried, then. And not knowing what to do with himself he could only wander about the office – until he looked out the window of the boss's room, and from quite close one of the men looked back at him. He'd been having a drink of water from the end of a hose, and now he wiped his hand across his mouth, and squatted on his heels while he rolled a cigarette.

Don't go away, he said. How's things? he asked.

He looked a rough specimen, Henry thought, with his thick untidy hair full of dirt, and dirt in the creases on his face.

Where's that Molly? he wanted to know. And he went on and talked about the girl. He said he'd bet he could get her out with him some night. She was a hard affair, he was ready to bet on that. She'd make a tasty little armful, too right she would. And anyhow, you could tell by the look in her eye. He'd bet Henry knew that too. That was the type, that short type with plenty up above the waist.

But of course Henry couldn't stay there and listen to such talk, so he interrupted and said he was sorry, but he'd have to get on with some work.

Wait a minute, the man said. How old do you reckon she is?

And Henry said well, he couldn't say for certain.

Because, the man said, I don't go looking for trouble with brushes that are under age.

But Henry said sorry, he'd have to be getting busy.

And even though he had to spend the whole day just filling in time, he didn't go near the window again, but he was all the time thinking about what the man had said, and wondering how anybody could have such a filthy mind. And even though the weather turned out soaking wet again, he was all day wishing the girl would turn up, and feeling annoyed with her because she didn't, because he had to give her a serious warning about having anything to do with that man.

And next morning he was all on edge, but the girl turned up all right. And it somehow surprised him that she looked just the same as usual, and he wondered how she could, when she was going round in such serious danger from the man he'd been talking to. But of course the poor girl didn't know, so naturally she looked innocent. And he couldn't help thinking how different she'd look once he'd told her.

Well, he had to bring the subject up sooner or later, so the sooner the better. He'd been talking to one of the men, he said, and he told her which one.

He was talking about you, he said.

Well, I like that, the girl said. Anyhow, she said, he doesn't know anything about me.

No, Henry said, but he reckons he's going to. Though said that way it sounded suggestive, and he felt his face getting hot.

Then he'd better go and have another reckon, the girl said.

And Henry had a wonderful feeling of relief, then. But he couldn't just leave it at that.

He reckons he's going to get you to go out with him some night.

And after she'd waited a moment the girl said, Well, I wouldn't mind going.

And Henry felt all upset again, and he didn't know what to say.

But he's a bad man, he said.

How do you mean, bad? the girl said. How do you know?

I know, Henry said.

You! the girl said. If you ask me, I reckon you've got a filthy mind.

And it was too much.

Accusing *him* of having a filthy mind!

I know who's got a filthy mind, he said.

The girl wouldn't answer him, though. She sat and stared at him, then she went across to the boss's room, and Henry heard her start talking out the window. And for a time he stayed where he was, not knowing at all clearly what he thought or how he felt, only knowing he was so terribly worked up, and feeling worse (or so it seemed at the time), than he'd ever felt before.

But it was impossible to stay just sitting there. He went across to the boss's room and sat in his usual place, bending over one of his swot books, and the girl, leaning out the window, must have heard him come in, but she took no notice. And he sat there, listening to the usual talk, until at last he was in a state of knowing only one thing – that he couldn't stand it any longer. So he got up and went back to the other room and waited a few moments, then he called, Miss Grigg! But the girl didn't answer. He called again, louder and trying to put a sound of authority into his voice. And then again. And he heard the girl interrupt herself and say, Hark to him! Well, she said, and what do *you* want?

I want you to come here, he said. Please, he added.

She said, Oh, all right, and out the window, Just wait a minute.

She came, and he said, Miss Grigg we have to check over the deeds in the strongroom.

Who said? she wanted to know.

The boss, Henry said. He said yesterday, and to get you to help.

She started to argue, but he said the boss wanted it done right away, so she'd better go inside the strongroom, and he'd sit at the table with the deeds book and call out the numbers.

And the girl said well, they didn't need to start just then, but Henry said yes, they did. And he swung open the big heavy door and switched on the light. But the girl had hardly gone inside when he swung the door shut again, and turned the key.

*   *   *

VIII

The weather hadn't been any too good for weeks on end, but now it looked as though it was going to be all right for the opening day of the tennis club. It had all been well organized too. The gents' committee had had working bees going just about every night after work for several weeks, so the courts were in apple-pie order. And the ladies' committee had made all arrangements for the usual refreshments.

All that Saturday morning Henry was going and looking out his window, but no, the day was going to hold out all right. The wind was blowing a bit too hard, but it was coming from the right direction, and the clouds coming over were all the time getting fewer and thinner. Yet Henry kept on having a look out, and when he went into the typists' room he leaned over their big table and looked out of that window.

What do you think girls? he asked. Is it going to keep fine?

They said they hoped so. One of them was hoping to play tennis also, but the other would be spending the afternoon just sewing.

Henry went along to the conveyancing clerk's room and said, What do you reckon Sid? How's it going to be?

And Sid, with his mind on his work as usual, but knowing what Henry meant all the same, took a quick look up through the window and said, Be bloody hot this afternoon.

Yet later on the boss came into Henry's room and caught him standing at the window, with his hands in his pockets too. And grinning, looking young, fresh, clean, well-fed-and-clothed, full of bounce and go and good-nature, he said, How are things in the common law department this morning? And he grinned wider and said, Nobody wasting time, I hope.

Henry said no, not at all, he was just taking a look at the weather.

And the boss wiped the grin off his face and put his head out the window.

No need to worry, he said. Be a bonser afternoon.

He was playing tennis too, at the big club's opening day. He asked Henry if his club was connected with the church, and what sort of a game he played. He said they must have a game before the season was over. But now, how was the work going that Henry had in hand? And Henry was ready for him. Everything was in pretty good order, and right up to date, so the boss hadn't any complaints. He said only a few things like, Get a summons out there rightaway, and, No, don't summons there without referring to me.

And it was past time to knock off before they were through. The rest had left, so Henry went down the stairs with the boss, who said he'd better hop in the car and have a lift along to the corner. And crossing the street Henry was mainly looking at the weather, and didn't see the girl coming on her bicycle, until the boss grabbed him by the arm and held him back. The girl wobbled and nearly fell off, but recovered herself and went past holding on to her skirt, and smiling at Henry under the brim of her hat.

Ah ha, the boss said, and grinned. You young bucks, he said. What's she like anyway?

And Henry could only mumble something –

oh oh oh it was over three nearly four months now, he'd counted the days, nearly half the time gone now oh thank you God. But

– And the boss, leaning back easily, with only one hand on the steering-wheel, and grinning until his eyes nearly disappeared into his face, kept on with his teasing.

You young bucks, he said. My God I wouldn't mind having my time all over again. Anyhow, he said, you go right ahead while the going's good – that's my advice. A man's only young once.

And passing the courts he slowed down, looking and saying they seemed to be in good nick, then he stopped to let Henry out just beyond, outside the church on the corner. And Henry wished he'd drive off, but instead he sat looking out past Henry at the church, still grinning, taking it all in – the notice that said, YE SAD AND WEARY, COME IN AND REST AWHILE AND PRAY, and the other one, ONLY JESUS SAVES, and the biggest one of all, DRINK AND BE DAMNED.

No, the boss said, speaking out of his grin. No, I can't agree with that. My old man was a pub-keeper. Well, so long.

And Henry went home the length of the street without once taking any notice of the weather. Because, let it rain if it was going to –

and God dear God was on his side, because he HAD to tell the boss that afternoon, and they heard him coming up the stairs, the terrible crash when he was nearly to the top, then not a sound. And SHE made him go out and see, the boss trying to get up, the blood from his cut lip oh such a lot of blood on the stairs and over his face and clothes. He helped him, the boss holding on to him tight until he was in his chair, and saying little accident, nothing at all, get money from petty cash and buy me six handkerchiefs, oh and stiff collar size fourteen. And after SHE had gone home he had to do it, he had to, the boss sitting in his chair, his lip swollen up with the blood drying and gone all colours, putting down the letter he'd been reading, saying isn't this just a bit sudden? But Mr S— I've been waiting a week to tell you, and Mr Graham wants me to start tomorrow. I see, so you're not satisfied here? And how oh how could he answer, how could he? He said Mr S— I'd like to say I won't ever talk about anything I've seen in this office. No? And what exactly do you mean when you say that? Oh oh please. I, I. Come now Griffiths what have you seen? I well about you being away from the office Mr S—. And the boss looked down at the table, putting a handkerchief up to his face, dabbing at his lip and blowing his nose, yet still smiling when he looked up again. All right Griffiths, we'll leave it at that. And good luck for your future, and gripping his hand and letting him go oh thank you God

– Dinner was on the table and father was just saying grace, and mother called out for him to come along at once. But when she saw him she said he'd first better go and brush his hair, and she wished he'd learn to be a bit more tidy and take more pride in his personal appearance. And when he came back Auntie Clara said he was a positive disgrace, the way he flung things about in his room, did he think she had nothing better to do than go round and tidy up after him?

All right, all right, he said.

All right, Auntie Clara said, all wrong! And she called him a great slovenly lout. Of course it was nothing to do with her, but if *she* was his mother –

All right, all right, he said. You're not anyhow.

No, Auntie Clara said, and thank heaven I'm not.

Ditto to that, he said.

And Auntie Clara jerked her head back, the light catching her glasses, and those big wide nostrils of hers widening out even further.

Don't dare to talk to me like that, she said.

But father banged the flat of his hand down on the table.

Stop it, he said, stop it the pair of you.

And Auntie Clara was nearly screaming at him, trying to get her words out.

Who started it? You let him talk his impudence –

But mother interrupted.

Clara!

Almost like a gun going off.

And Arnold said could he have his pudding straightaway, because he still had a lot of work to do on the bike? Henry said he couldn't eat any more dinner, and he didn't want any pudding. He got up and went and lay on the sofa, but father made him come back to the table again. It's manners to sit at the table until others are finished, he said.

And mother said *why* couldn't he eat his dinner?

Because, he said. And mother told him not to talk like a baby. Well, because he didn't feel hungry.

Well, *why* didn't he feel hungry?

He didn't know. No, he didn't feel sick. Well, if they wanted to know he felt just tired.

And that made them all laugh.

Tired!

He *must* think he worked hard.

Auntie Clara said if he had her work to do he'd know what it was to feel tired. Even Arnold, who usually just left him alone, had something to say. And father said well, if he was too tired to play tennis he could do an easy job weeding mother's flower garden, but first they'd have to wait and see if he had any strength left after he'd dried the dishes for Auntie Clara.

And mother laughed again.

She said she didn't think there was much wrong with him, though he could certainly do with a bit more flesh on his bones. So he should be sensible and eat up his dinner. After all, she and Auntie Clara had gone to a lot of trouble getting it ready for him.

But he couldn't eat any more, and for the sake of peace while he was drying the dishes he managed to hold his tongue, and never once contradicted Auntie Clara while she was rambling on.

Then he had to go and change into his creams, but alone in his room he just flopped on the bed, lying quite still, closing his eyes and trying not to think, trying to forget, thinking everything would be all right, wondering why he was feeling so tired, trying to forget, trying not to think, with his eyes closed – but you saw everything clearer than ever if you closed your eyes. So he opened them and looked at his writing-table, with his swot books lying open there –

oh oh property contracts torts CRIMINAL LAW oh no. It was printed there, a girl under sixteen, imprisonment with hard labour, they could LOCK YOU UP for years. Oh oh think of that NO. No please. And he hadn't done anything, he hadn't. But say SHE said he had. Say yes say she went out with that man or jockeys and blamed him instead. Say she was going to have yes say she was. Oh no NO. And he hadn't done anything, he hadn't. Only he'd been up there with her so many days, up there so many days all on their own. Say she said he came into the strongroom while she was in there and shut the door and oh no no. Say shè just said he LOCKED HER UP, what would he say?

– Oh, oh, he said.

But he hadn't intended to say anything out loud.

Henry! mother's voice said.

Yes mother?

Is there anything wrong with you?

No, I'm all right.

Then what are you moaning about?

And he heard her come along the veranda to his room, and she pushed open the door without asking if she could come in.

Aren't you going to tennis? she asked, and she looked down at him lying on the bed. She was dressed for croquet, hat on and everything, father would be taking her along in the car as he went to bowls. She had her gloves on, but she took one off and put her hand on his forehead.

I don't think you've got any temperature, she said. So if you're not sick you'd just better buck up –

you felt sick and wanted to throw up, but mother would always come and hold your forehead, and then you didn't mind being sick

– It's all wrong mother, he said. And he gave a sort of shiver and went on, No, I mean it's all right mother. I was just feeling like having a bit of a rest.

And going along to tennis later, not feeling so tired, feeling glad because it was going to stay fine for sure now, feeling smart wearing his cream flannels and his Old Boys' blazer, with his racket under his arm –

say he told father and mother. NOW. Told them he'd never done anything so they'd know. THEN. But of course nothing was going to happen so why tell? And what about locking her up? He needn't tell that. If SHE told it was just another one of her lies. Anyhow, didn't she deserve it? Wasn't he only trying to do his best for her, trying to keep her out of harm's way, LOCKING HER UP oh

– And he felt the sweat start to pour off him –

And now he might be going to get LOCKED UP HIMSELF. Five years. Oh no no. He'd better tell mother and father. But say they didn't believe him, say they thought he HAD done something, and because he was feeling guilty and frightened he was telling lies? Say father went and spoke to the girl's father oh no no. And say the girl was asked and she said oh no. Because if mother and father thought he had done something what would they do? He'd get the worst hiding he'd ever had in his life. Yes, of course. But what else? That time he'd looked through the keyhole yes, and mother had said if he was a few years older he'd have deserved to be LOCKED UP FOR THE REST OF HIS LIFE oh no please God no you mustn't let. But nobody was going to tell and nothing was going to happen of course

– And turning in behind the church he could see there was a crowd along at the end of the drive. He was late too, and old Mr Burnett, the oldest member, with Mrs Burnett standing beside him, was just finishing off the opening-day speech he always made. And so on Saturday afternoons, he was saying, and in the evenings when our daily work is done, we meet together in the shadow of the building that is the home of our spiritual life. But on one day of the week we do not do this. No, we meet elsewhere, and our courts are empty on that day – but I say shame on us all that as much cannot be said for some tennis clubs that are associated with other Christian bodies of our town.

And the dear old man (as everybody said), with his pink cheeks and long white beard, and his trousers held up by braces as well as a belt, took his wife by the hand and led her on to the first court. She served him an underhand serve and he sent the ball back again all right, but an easy one that she sent over to him again, and he missed it on purpose you could easily tell, and everybody said Oh! and began to clap.

And thank heaven *that* was over, and proper games could begin.

Henry was with the crowd round the notice board, everybody talking, and looking at the lists to see who they were down to play with. The ladder was on the board too, and there was Henry's name, second from the top. He'd already put in a challenge to Peter Burnett, the old man's grandson, but there wasn't a hope of playing it off this afternoon with such a crowd – there'd be room for only mixed ladies' and gents' doubles. Henry was down for two games anyhow, and somebody (it was Peter), was calling his name out. And where was Marge Hayes? Oh, right you are, Marge. Well, Henry and Marge played him and Mrs Forster on number three. Yes, rightaway. Right-oh, come on then. And they were going out to number three, but why, look! Another set had just begun there. So there's been a mix-up, but oh well, never mind, and they'd be next.

And sitting there waiting Henry talked to Marge, who'd gone away to study for her B.A. and was only home now, back in the old town, on holiday. She was wearing a blue dress that went well with her blue eyes, her beautiful fair skin, and her goldy hair (goldilocks was the nickname they'd given her at school), and she wanted to know how Henry liked going to work.

Oh, Henry said, I quite like it.

Do you, Marge said, do you really?

Well, he said, how do you like going for your B.A.?

Oh, it's all right, she said, it's a stepping-stone.

Well, she meant it was going to be a means of getting away from a place like this – all these old stick in the muds. Oh yes, mum and dad were all right, they were different, but some of the peoplé! Anyhow, she wasn't going to let herself get caught and have to stay. She was going to live in Sydney first, then she'd get to America if she died. Because there was simply nothing here at all.

Well, Henry said, it would be a joke if she went and got married instead.

But what nonsense! Because of course she wouldn't. Why should any girl get married these days? There was simply no need to at all.

And when Henry asked her what church she went to up in the city she said sorry, but she just had to laugh. Well, of course she didn't go to any at all, though she'd gone once to the Roman Catholic cathedral – just to hear the music. And she wouldn't mind going again sometime, now she had read James Joyce. No, it would take too long to explain about James Joyce, but Henry ought to get a job in the city and go for his law exams there, because if you stayed at home you never got your eye teeth cut at all, and had hardly any idea you were even alive.

And Henry said well, he didn't altogether agree, but he could have gone on listening all the same, and was sorry when Peter called their names out and said there was a court ready. Because it all sounded so very strange, almost as though somebody was speaking out loud the thoughts that came into your mind sometimes. Yet to have the feeling of hearing your own thoughts being spoken out loud by a girl like Marge! He could never have imagined such a thing.

But they had to go and play, and it was a good game and a close go. They were even at five all, and the eleventh game went to deuce.

And then the first big slow drops of rain came.

Well, of all things!

Henry and Peter were keen to play it out, but their partners weren't having any. Wet spots nearly the size of pennies were all the time showing up on their frocks.

Of all things!

They ran, and everybody was running and crowding up the steps into the Sunday school, while the raindrops, coming thicker and heavier, rattled on the roof almost as though they were hailstones.

What awfully bad luck!

And there was hardly a soul that had noticed the dark cloud that had slowly come up against the wind, come up out of the east, while the sun went on shining in a beautifully clear western sky.

Oh well, you couldn't ever be sure.

No, not at this time of the year.

But listen to that, now!

And yet, the sun was shining still. Fancy, over in that direction people would still be having fine weather.

Well, that's cooked it anyhow.

And it was hoped that nobody had left any rackets or balls out, or anything else.

There was the afternoon tea anyhow, and the ladies in charge were rattling crockery, beginning to fill the cups from the urn, burning their fingers as they turned the tap on and off, and calling for volunteers to carry the trays round. And handing cups of tea and plates of sandwiches and cakes, Henry wished he could be talking to Marge instead. But then, where on earth was she? He took tea round everywhere yet didn't see a sign of her – unless she was playing 'Pack Up Your Troubles' on the piano up on the platform. He couldn't see who it was, because so many had crowded round the piano to sing. He went up to look but no, it wasn't Marge. And while he was standing on the edge of the platform, looking out over all the heads, he heard some sort of a commotion back in the room where the tea things were, and he was going back in there to see what it was all about, when Marge nearly bumped into him in the doorway. By the look of her face she certainly seemed to be in a temper, nor would she stop shouting out things like Scum! and Low-down louts!

Well, the ladies all crowded round Marge, trying to calm her down, while everybody said for goodness' sake, what on earth was it all about? And it turned out to be something really very silly, besides terribly vulgar.

You see, Marge had gone out the back to the ladies' place, you know, and while she was in there somebody had fastened the catch on the door and she couldn't get out again. So the poor girl must have been locked up in there for quite half an hour.

Now, whoever would do a childish thing like that?

Somebody was asking for it anyhow.

But who do you reckon it could have been?

And old Mr Burnett was talking to Peter, and they came over to Henry, wanting him to go round with them and ask everyone personally to be a man and own up if they had it on their conscience.

But Henry got out of that, because Marge had quietened down at last, and almost laughing now she came over and took hold of his arm – making him feel he must be looking all sorts of things. Well, she wanted him to walk home with her. But then, what about the rain? Well, let them get away from all this crowd anyhow.

And out in the porch, standing at the top of the steps, Marge said it just showed you. That was the sort of thing you had to put up with if you stayed in a town like this. And she said that just quietly she had a pretty good idea who it was. No, she wasn't letting on, but she'd got a look at a pair of feet, and they were wearing that cheap kind of tennis shoes with black soles – and she thought she'd seen black socks underneath trousers that didn't have any cuffs. So it was one of those no-class kids who were going to work when they still ought to be going to school, and who oughtn't to be allowed on the courts at all (not on a Saturday afternoon, anyhow), even though they did belong to the church. Though of course you couldn't blame them, they didn't know any better, and didn't Henry think the same as she did? – that things would be different under socialism.

Well, he didn't know.

Wasn't he a socialist?

Well, he couldn't really say. He was afraid he didn't know much about it.

Don't you, Marge said, don't you really? But no, she supposed of course he wouldn't know anything about it – how could anyone know what they were, or hardly anything at all, when they were stuck in such a hole of a place?

But then the Burnetts' car came suddenly round from the back of the Sunday school, with the old couple in the back seat and Peter driving. And Marge said yes, thank you very much, she'd be quite glad of a lift.

And while she was getting in Mrs Burnett said, Fancy it turning out so wet, it usually did give you some sort of a warning didn't it? Marge said yes, it was too bad wasn't it? And to Henry she said that of course she would be seeing him again.

And left there on his own, through the sound of the singing and the banging on the piano, he could hear them calling for volunteers to help with the washing up. But it wasn't raining so much now, and he buttoned his blazer over his racket, and turned up the collar, and started off down the drive. Besides, he was feeling that tired again – he felt he could hardly drag one foot after the other the short distance home, let alone stay and carry buckets of hot water –

but she'd promised, he had her promise, oh God oh God he'd had to work hard to get her to make that promise. But she HAD promised. He hadn't always kept his own promises, no, not nearly always, but sometimes he had. Cherry. No, he'd never told on her, he'd never even told a single soul. Ever. So perhaps. If she told NOW he could say if it was true why hadn't she told THEN? Why, because oh because he'd made her promise. Sobbing, sobbing, he'd expected she might rush out and smack his face and say she was going to tell the boss, but he hadn't expected oh. After all, he hadn't left her in long. Walking about the office, whistling, with his hands in his pockets, feeling pleased, going to the boss's window and looking out, staring back at those men, thinking they couldn't do her any harm NOW with their filth, and wanting to shout it out at them. And then all of a sudden thinking, thinking differently, shaking all over, thinking she might have suffocated oh no, feeling sick, but knowing, knowing he had to oh God. And no rushing out no getting his face smacked oh no. Down on the floor, shaking and crying and sobbing. He couldn't get her to move, to come out. It was hours before she could stop that sobbing, and hours and hours he was saying please. Please. Oh please do. And promise please you will promise won't you. Kneeling beside the chair and taking her hand and stroking it, and reaching up to stroke her hair, and saying won't you. Dear

– Oh no please, he said, and the sound of his voice made him jump. But he was lucky, because there weren't any people about in the street –

oh oh when she smiled, and when he told her she had such a lovely smile, and when she said look at my handkerchief, and he looked at his own and it was clean enough. And he said promise, holding her hand, promise, please promise, you WILL promise won't you? And she squeezed his hand back and she promised. And smiled, and smiled oh the rest of that day was so wonderful no, he was so happy NO. And that night doing his swot he'd come to it in his criminal law. A girl under oh no NO

– And there was nobody home, even Auntie Clara must have gone out somewhere. And he was feeling shivery in his wet blazer, and so tired he had to go and lie down. And after tea he'd have to do his swot, because the exams were getting close now. And –

staring at the page, starting from the top again, staring, starting again and turning over, but turning back again because he hadn't understood, starting at the top again, staring. But she'd promised. But then he'd left. He HAD to leave. He hadn't told her he was leaving. What did she think? And she might. Going out with jockeys or that man. But she'd.

*　　*　　*

IX

and before God he was innocent of any sin. Yes, before God. So why was he doing all this worrying? Because even if, there was Jesus and His Sacrifice. Lover of my soul. Safe in the arms. All tears from all eyes. Washed in the Blood. Though your sins be as scarlet. Only against the Holy Ghost oh no. NO. He could ask the reverend, but no no it couldn't be? IF? Never forgiven, never NEVER. Because he HAD. Yes, OFTEN. Not for a long time, oh not for. But he HAD. And IF? Just once oh only just ONCE, and never NEVER. But it mightn't be, no it mightn't be, and all others. Washed in the Blood. And before God he was innocent. So why? But what would people think? And father and mother? And the reverend? And if he said yes, he did lock her in. Why? For her own good. Would they? And if he said no. Making her out a liar, lying himself, sinning, oh perhaps sinning against the oh NO

– It was a shame it couldn't have stayed fine on Saturday afternoon, specially as it had been beautiful all day Sunday, when nobody could have minded very much if it had rained all day. And now you couldn't have asked for a better spring morning, it was almost enough to take away the awful Monday-morning feeling.

And turning the corner into the main street Henry found himself walking along just behind Mr K. P. McDermott. He was the biggest lawyer in the town, and you heard it said that he could have easily been a judge by now if he'd wanted to be. But Sid had told Henry that was the trouble – it didn't pay a man with a good big practice to go on the Bench, because the money he'd get wouldn't make it worth his while. No, not anything like. And although it would have been a feather in the town's cap to have somebody made a judge who'd been born and brought up there – still, the people were very fortunate in being able to keep him. He'd several times been mayor, and for years and years he'd been a lay reader in the Anglican church (what is called a local preacher in *our* church, as mother always used to explain).

Anyhow, there was Mr K. P. McDermott, the town's biggest lawyer, and president of the law society as Henry knew, carrying a walking stick and wearing what looked like a brand-new pinstripe suit, yet walking along as if he might be just nobody at all if you didn't happen to know. And Henry thought well, just wait a bit, and the day might come. Or rather he should say, the day certainly *would* come. Then it would be his turn to be walking along like Mr K. P. McDermott, and he'd be swinging a walking stick too. And yes of course, some young law clerk would be looking at him, and feeling respectful and envious all at one and the same time. Though, Henry told himself, he'd be a bit different from Mr K. P. McDermott, he'd always be on the lookout for that young law clerk. And he'd talk to him kindly, knowing just how shy he was feeling (yet at the same time wanting to be taken notice of), knowing all about the hard row a young man had to hoe before he was qualified in his profession, and only too willing to say an encouraging word or two.

And he followed along behind, enjoying his fancies – until not far ahead of them, the local magistrate came into the main street off the pathway to the footbridge over the river. He saw Mr K. P. McDermott coming, and waited a moment for him to catch up, and still following along behind Henry could hear something of what they talked about (yes, they had called a meeting and discussed the matter: pity that such an excellent fellow should ruin himself in that way), it somehow giving him a wonderful feeling of importance that he could. But he didn't hear much, because it was only a short way on he had to go – and there was Sid coming across from the other side of the street, and Henry waited for him and they went up the stairs together.

And the girls had already opened up, and were standing talking, combing at their hair before they took the covers off their typewriters. And Sid as usual got busy right away, bustling about, and putting his head out of his doorway to say he had some dictation for whoever was ready. So one of the girls gave a few last pokes at her hair, and picked up her notebook and pencil and went. And Henry opened the window for the other one, and she said, What a lovely day! Why, she didn't believe there was a soul living who could help feeling happy on such a day. And Henry looked at her, feeling there was something about her words, and she looked back at him in such a way that he had to look somewhere else. Because her look seemed to be saying yes, she knew she had told him something about herself, but what did she care if she had? And he was wondering –

oh no

– when there was a knock at the door, and he looked out and there was somebody wanting to see Mr Graham – a small man in working clothes, with only a waistcoat on over his shirtsleeves, and a bag for money fastened on to his belt.

Well, Henry was afraid Mr Graham hadn't come down to the office yet.

So the man felt in his pocket and pulled out a blue paper, and Henry knew what it was and asked could he see?

And it was a summons that he had issued: Hunter Bros. Emporium Ltd, plaintiff: James Watkins, labourer, defendant: the amount being £9 15s. 9d., plus costs.

Do you want to pay up? he said.

And the man swore.

And his swearing was loud enough to be heard all through the office. Sid's voice, dictating (gentleman of the first part), seemed suddenly to come to a full stop. And because all three of them were certainly listening, Henry's uncomfortable feeling over such bad language was made even worse.

You'd better come in here, he said, and they went into his room and he closed the door.

Then the man went ahead and told his story, though Henry had to keep on telling him not to use those words *please* – it just wouldn't do at all for the girls in the next room to hear.

He'd been doing his best, the man said, he'd been paying off a few bob every time he had a few to spare. Jesus Christ, what more could a man do? And then he gets a blister!

Well you know, Henry said, in these matters we simply have to carry out the instructions of our clients. And wait a minute, he said, and he looked through his papers for the ones he wanted. Yes, he said, you apparently disregarded my letter warning you that a summons would be issued.

Christ mate, the man said, you talk a bit hard, don't you?

And Henry said he was sorry if he did. But let him go ahead and explain his position, and reference could be made to Hunters for fresh instructions.

Well, he'd been right up against it, the man said. He had a wife and half a dozen kids to keep, and the wife had been two months in hospital. But then, seeing the look on Henry's face, he said, I suppose you blokes get told a lot of yarns about a crook missis and a swag of kids. All right mate, I'll tell you the trouble fair dinkum, only it's just between you and me – see?

About a year ago he'd got into trouble, the man said, and that had knocked him back a lot. He'd been working on a milk-round then, and he'd been a bit short in his cash. Well, he didn't know how it happened – he was always allowed to keep a few bob back for change, and sometimes when he was having a lie-down in the afternoon, one of the kids might get hold of his bag and start playing around with it. Anyhow he'd been sacked and put up for it, and he'd only got six months probation, but there'd been a bit in the newspaper. And that made it hard for him to get another job. And it was while he was out of a job that the missis had run up the bill. She'd had to of course, or else the kids might have gone a lot hungrier than they did go. Anyhow now he had a job on a baker's cart, but it would make things tough for him all over again if there was going to be any more court cases. It was fair dinkum about the missis too, and if it hadn't been for that he'd have just about got it paid off by now.

And Henry, balancing his chair back on two legs said, I see. And snapping the front legs of the chair down on the floor he said, How much could you pay off each week *regularly*?

Well, he couldn't pay much. But hadn't he said he'd been doing his best? Well, so he had been. He'd got the use of a bit of empty land next door, and all winter he'd been slaving his guts out during his spare time getting in a crop of early spuds. He'd been doing it so as to get a bit of money and pay up all he owed in one hit.

And Henry said that sounded promising, and when would he have the money?

Jesus boy! he said, and he used his swear words all over again. You birds that are sitting pretty want to pull your fingers out a few times now and then, he said. It hasn't half rained lately mate, has it now? Or is it just a bad dream I've been having? And a bloody wet one.

And he said he'd hoped the spuds wouldn't come up until the frosts were over, and that had panned out all right, but since they *had* come up there'd hardly been a dry day. So the bloody disease had got started, and that downpour Saturday afternoon, with a hot day following, might turn out to have cooked things properly. And if you asked him there'd be a lot of regular growers that would be finding themselves in the cart this season. And he'd like to ask Henry how did *he* work it out? – birds that sat on their backsides all the year round could always manage to get themselves kept in plenty of good tucker, but them that worked to grow the tucker were liable to go short. And didn't Henry think it could be the other way round sometimes, just for a change? As for him, he wouldn't mind sitting back while the blokes that sat on their backsides all day had a go at keeping him.

But of course all this had nothing to do with the summons that Henry had issued, it was simply wasting his time. And besides, the man should surely have realized that this was no way to talk when he was hoping to be allowed time to pay up his debt. So he said he really didn't see any point in discussing such a question, and anyhow he was afraid he hadn't got any more time to spare. But he'd get in touch with Hunters, and if the man would call in again he'd let him know whether they were prepared to make an arrangement to meet him in some way. That was all he could say in the meantime, but by tomorrow he'd certainly be in a position to say something further.

Well, the man said he hadn't any more time to spare either, because he'd left his horse standing outside, and he had a lot of customers waiting for their bread.

Thanks mate anyhow, he said, and he got Henry to shake hands, saying
that he reckoned he was a real sport – and he'd say that, even though he
wasn't any too shook on paying compliments to no lawyer-blokes.

And when he'd got rid of him Henry thought well, he'd better see what
Hunters had to say. So he twisted round in his chair to reach the phone.
And while he was waiting to be put through to the accountant he heard
the boss come up the stairs, heard him talking just outside the door. But
just as the door opened, and he heard the boss say, He's phoning, but go
on in, he also heard the accountant saying hullo. And until he had finished
speaking into the phone, with his face to the wall, he didn't see the two
men who had come in and sat down across the other side of his table. One
of them he didn't know, but along at the court he'd often enough seen that
detective.

But then it went all of a sudden too dark for him to see, and he heard
a long drawn-out sound, like the sound of the fire-engine siren.

*   *   *

X

*trying to count the colours but they wouldn't stop moving, and you couldn't
tell where one ended and the next one began. Count them one by one, count them
name them. Blue and green and yellow and red yes, but a lot more in between
and you didn't know their names. And they wouldn't stop moving and mixing.
That big red blot was getting bigger and spreading over all the rest. Look out
now, it was coming at you. And it was only red round the edge now, a red rim
and all lemon colour inside. But look out now, there was a black spot in the
middle and it was getting bigger, blowing up and coming at you. And the little
green worms wriggled, they wriggled and disappeared. You tried to look at just
one of them, but it wriggled and disappeared. Look now, that one there, but it
wriggled and disappeared.*

– And he heard mother's voice saying Henry, Henry.

Well, if she was wanting Henry.

Yes mother.

I want you to drink this.

Yes mother.

And he felt the glass against his mouth, and the taste a nasty taste. He
tried to swallow, but instead he was spitting out.

And mother was saying, Oh *Henry* –

*sinking, struggling to stay on the surface, water swishing and boiling, sizzling
over your ears. Sinking, with the water plugging your nose oh no. Beating with*

your arms, clawing, plunging and kicking, you had to hold on, struggling, holding your breath, hearing only the roar, and no light only the thick and heavy blackness. Weight, and stillness even though there is still the roar, weight and suffocation, the plug in your nose and fire and flames in your chest, yet clawing and kicking, not giving up even though oh no. Yet sinking, gripped and held by the weight, and bursting, and dissolving, and dying oh NO. And then floating and crying, wet tears running, crying because you could lie so easily, and breathe, and float, water lapping, light shining, floating

– And he could hear voices talking, and mother said, Yes doctor. Very well, I'll remember to do that doctor. But he didn't trouble to open his eyes and look. After all, mother was there all right. Yes, and she must be all right too, if she was there talking to the doctor. So there was no need to worry –

oh crybaby, crybaby, running home from school, crybaby, boys that were tied to their mothers' apron strings wet their pants in school. Crybaby. Mother had to wear her glasses and didn't see oh oh, oh my finger and Knocky had his tongue cut and the blood dripped and ran down, and you ran home safe to mother. You didn't tell, you didn't oh no, but you ran home safe to mother and nothing could hurt you then. And mother was safe too, after all the blood, blood dripping and running, the muck all red round the cow with that leg sticking out behind oh no. Because, because just because. Because what? Because I couldn't help it. But you MUST help it, a big boy like you, you're not a baby any more, you're getting a big boy now. To think after all these years, after all I've done for you, I couldn't bring you up CLEAN. And Cherry oh no. But you didn't tell, you didn't oh no. You poor little boy, and Cherry in her little red hat, it was red because, because, and because oh no. And Cherry sitting in the back seat and the bell rang, and rang again, and once more, and it was wonderful oh no. Because, because Cherry oh no. But there was always mother, inside the ball and seeing Deerfoot, but mother said it's your bedtime oh no. She made you oh no please no. But when you were sick mother would always come and hold your forehead while you

– And mother's voice said, Are you awake Henry?

Yes mother.

Then he had to have his temperature taken.

Now under your tongue, mother said, and see you don't bite it.

Yes mother.

Are you feeling any better?

Yes mother.

And mother said, You *are* a duffer to go and get sick.

And he swallowed and tried to speak, and he bit but oh he didn't mean to. And there was a taste in his mouth, and he was trying to spit out. And mother was saying, oh *Henry* –

Uncle Bob was hidden in the roses, but the grin on his face with petals stuck on all over it looked out, and a hand came out from lower down holding a glass of beer with the froth running over. And you held on to mother's hand and hid behind her skirt so that Uncle Bob couldn't see you. Nothing could hurt you when you could run to mother or father. But Uncle Bob was sitting in the back seat with Cherry on his knee, and he had Cherry's little red hat on instead of her, and the motor car was going down into the hole, and Uncle Bob had his two arms round Cherry and the two of them were laughing and bouncing up and down, and you were saying isn't he naughty mother? Good riddance to bad rubbish. And the bell was ringing, and mother was kissing you goodbye, and you had to go, you had to, and all the time you were wanting to stay at home and look after her. But you had to sit in the motor car with Cherry and Uncle Bob, and they were laughing but you were crying. Down, down, getting darker and darker, you were being shut in, covered over. And before you died you got the dirt in your eyes and you couldn't breathe. And in the dark you could hear Cherry and Uncle Bob laughing and the sound of them kissing. Oh no no. And all you wanted was to stay with mother and look after her, and she'd look after you, snug as a bug in a rug, even if she had to get father to give you a hiding sometimes. Oh oh. Naughty, naughty. But you MUST help it. Bad wicked people. What would happen to the world if you didn't have good people like father and mother. Who loves you. And our father which art

– And he woke up in the afternoon and the blinds were pulled nearly down, but mother was sitting there sewing, sitting near the window so that she could get the light. And the sun was shining, he could tell, and there was no wind blowing; and he heard the birds. There must be a thrush sitting in the peach tree outside his window. Be good, be good, be good, it was saying, very sharp and loud. And then softer, and sort of loving, We *knew* you would, we *knew* you would. And he lay there and watched, not speaking to let mother know he was awake, watching her needle going in and coming through, and being lifted right up with the thread hanging on. And every now and then he could hear the tips of her fingers grate on the silky kind of stuff she was sewing. And while he was watching mother said, Botheration take it, and she looked up from her sewing, and saw him with his eyes open, watching.

Well, mother said, are you feeling any better now?

Yes mother.

That's good, mother said. But just wait a moment, and I'll attend to you presently.

Yes all right mother.

And mother went on sewing but faster, and talked while she sewed.

Mr Graham had rung up every day to inquire about him, she said. It was really very good of him, and he wanted Henry to understand that it didn't matter how long he was sick, his job would still be there waiting for him when he was better again. All the same he must buck up and hurry up and get better, so as not to keep Mr Graham waiting too long.

He thinks very highly of your work, she said, and your father and I were very pleased to hear that.

And while she was about it she might as well tell him about that Mr S—. Such a disgrace! Just fancy, he'd been taking what didn't belong to him. They'd been looking into his affairs and he'd been found out, and he'd be lucky if he didn't get put in gaol. And after all, it was only what people deserved if they couldn't keep their hands off other people's money.

My word, mother said, you did well for yourself when you bustled round and got yourself another job.

Be good, be good, be good, the thrush was saying.

And he turned his face sideways on the pillow and closed his eyes tight, but the tears *would* get through. And mother heard him sniff, and looked up from her sewing and said well now, it was time for his medicine again –

good, oh yes yes, it was best to be good, there were good people like father and mother, and all those other bad wicked people. Goodness always pays, mother said. And honesty is the best policy. Yes, and he prayed and God had answered his prayer. For Christ's sake. Oh yes oh thank you, God. All tears from all eyes. Like as a father pitieth his children. Ye must be born again. And Mr Graham had said oh thank you God. And he'd get better in time to sit his exams, and he'd carry a walking stick like Mr K. P. McDermott, and he'd give all his money to mother, because as she always said, father didn't make nearly as much money as some people seemed to think he did. Oh no. And he was floating, floating

– And after work Arnold came in and talked to him, saying, How are you feeling now, son? And father and Auntie Clara came too, and father called him a duffer, but even though she stayed and rambled on for quite a long time, Auntie Clara never said one single word against him –

oh thank you God

– And mother came and asked him if he was feeling hungry, and what did he fancy?

Well no, there wasn't any smoked fish, and besides, he couldn't have any of that for yet awhile. But a poached egg on toast wouldn't do him any harm, and he could have a little rice pudding afterwards.

His mouth began to water when mother brought in the tray, and he said he was so hungry, and mother said she was glad to hear that, but he was to be sure to eat *slowly*. But he was too hungry, and it was no time before the plates were empty, and he was calling out to ask if he could have another helping of pudding.

Mother sang out for him to wait a bit and she'd see, and she hoped he hadn't bolted what he'd eaten already.

But when she came he said he didn't want any more to eat.

You said you did, mother said.

And when he said he felt as if he might be going to be sick, she said well, if he'd bolted his food it probably served him right.

But it was no good her just standing there to say any more because he was retching.

And he was expecting –

you felt sick but mother

– But he was being terribly sick, and mother was just holding the basin, and clicking her tongue and saying dear oh dear, now perhaps *this* would teach him a lesson.

*   *   *

XI

It was a thousand pities he hadn't got well in time to sit for his exams. But mother was always saying never mind, cheer up, better luck next time. And she got him to count the years, and tell her whether he could still be a qualified solicitor by the time he was twenty-one.

Well yes, it was possible if he studied hard, and only had a bit better luck when exam time came round.

So there now, what had he to worry about?

He'd find he'd pick up a lot quicker if he'd stop worrying.

And he said he wasn't worrying at all.

Then he'd better buck up and be a bit more cheerful, try to look on the bright side.

Why, who could stay down in the dumps for long when they were having such beautiful weather so early in the summer?

And besides, it was getting high time for him to go back to work again. He really must try to pull himself together. He should go and see Mr Graham, tell him he wasn't feeling quite up to the mark yet, but say he'd like to begin by doing only half-time work for the first week or two.

Yes, he ought to do that, and mother was quite sure if he did he'd find himself heaps better off than spending his time just moping about the house. And getting himself in Auntie Clara's way.

Now, didn't he think it was a good idea?

And he said, No, I don't.

Henry!

Surely there was no need for him to be rude about it.

Well, he didn't feel energetic enough to do any work yet.

All right. If he didn't feel well enough he could have a week longer. After a week though, if he didn't pull himself together, she'd have to speak to his father.

And mother said she remembered what he'd always been like. If he'd had to stay away from school he'd never wanted to go back again. And she couldn't make him out, because she'd never had the same trouble with Arnold. No, nor anything like.

No, she wasn't criticizing or making comparisons, but there you were. She'd hate to think that any boy of hers was going to turn out a lazy good for nothing, and she wasn't saying he was, and he always *had* done a lot better in his schoolwork than Arnold had. But schooldays didn't last for ever, and when they were over everybody had to begin making their own way in the world – growing boys had to get out and start bringing home grist to the mill. They certainly couldn't expect their fathers to go on doing it for them.

And that was all she had to say on the subject. He might find out that his father would have something further to say though, if he didn't buck up. And she only hoped that he wouldn't have to say it along with a stick – it would certainly be a terrible disgrace if the father of such a big boy was driven into using the stick.

All right mother, he said. I won't be feeling so washed out after another week.

And he asked if she'd mind him going to play tennis even though he didn't feel like going to work.

Well, she thought that if he was fit enough to play tennis he was fit enough to go to work. Still, she'd given him one more week, so he could please himself, and anyway *she'd* be more than pleased if he'd do anything at all except just mope about round the house. Though he'd better be careful not to let Mr Graham see him playing tennis, because she wouldn't be at all surprised if his ideas on the subject weren't just exactly the same as hers.

*

And he spent quite a lot of time on the phone, but of course it was no good because nobody could have a game with him until after work. But Peter Burnett said he'd tell him what, how about their meeting along at the courts early next morning before breakfast? There'd be nobody there then, they'd have the pick of the courts, and they could get in some good practice for the ladder match they'd have to be playing off as soon as Henry had got his form back again.

And Henry said yes, all right, he'd be there.

Though what would mother have to say about him staying away from work, yet getting up before breakfast to go and play tennis?

Still, there was no need to say anything. He'd be out of bed and well away before father got up and they wouldn't know. And he might even be able to get back without anybody seeing, and afterwards pretend that he'd only just got up out of bed.

As usual mother made him go to bed early, and to make sure he'd wake up early in the morning he left the blind up, just so the sun would shine in on him. But for a long time he couldn't get to sleep, and then when he did he kept on waking up long before it was daylight. And all the time he was dreaming, and each time he went off to sleep again he'd be back in the same dream. And it was only the same old dream he was always having, but he was sick and tired of having it so often. It was an awfully long dream, and it always sort of made him feel tired out. Yet there was nothing in it, because all he ever did was try to walk through miles and miles of dry sand carrying a heavy sort of swag on his back. And the swag weighed him down so much that he could hardly get his legs to move. And it seemed to go on for hours and hours, with him being dragged down by the weight of the swag, and every minute feeling he'd have to drop, yet somehow managing to keep his legs moving. Though after all those hours it never seemed as if he'd travelled any distance at all. But still he'd go on, trying and trying to lift up each foot out of the thick heavy sand, and place it down in front of the other one – until it seemed as if the sweat was soaking him, and his bones and muscles were cracking and trembling, and his body was feeling as if it was on fire.

And when he woke up the sun was shining in on his face.

And it was getting a bit late he knew, because he could hear the sounds of father lighting the fire in the kitchen. So he'd have to wait until he had gone out into the garden. And he wished he'd never told Peter he'd play tennis, because he was feeling too tired to get up out of bed, let alone go and chase around the tennis court.

Father had raked out the stove, and gone outside for kindling wood, and now he must have lit the fire because you could hear the wood crackling. He had gone outside to fill the coal bucket, and when he'd put some coal on the fire he would go and feed the fowls.

So he ought to get up and be all ready to slip out.

But he turned his face away from the sun, and closed his eyes.

And it was the sound of Auntie Clara's blind going up that woke him up again.

And he had to sit up because now there was nowhere on the pillow where his head was out of the sun, and he couldn't stand the heat any longer. And sitting up he could see into the garden, and see father out there. And father was sitting on his heels but he wasn't doing anything. No, he was sitting there nearly hidden behind a gooseberry bush, and he was sitting quite still, while from behind the gooseberry bush he looked over towards the house.

And Henry could hear Auntie Clara moving about her room in her bare feet while she was getting dressed. And then her door banged and he heard her in the kitchen.

And all of a sudden father stood up and went away farther down the garden.

And Henry slid down into the bed again, and pulled the clothes up over his head.

Later on, when mother called out for him to hurry and get up, he said he didn't want any breakfast, and he was feeling too tired to get up.

*   *   *

XII

Naked on the grass, face down against the slope of the bank, he was lying in the sun.

Father and mother always got in a temper if they saw him without his shirt on. Father always said nobody should be allowed to go in swimming without a bathing suit that covered them from neck to knee. And mother said of course they shouldn't. And why people couldn't be decent she didn't know.

He turned over, propping himself on his elbow and shading his eyes with his hand. Beyond and below the length of his body, not ten yards from his feet, the bank ended and the river began. Far out it was green, opaque, and solid even though the surface was all the time sliding away. Near in it lost its colour and was clear, the current idling, with baby whirlpools wandering about uncertainly on the surface. To the left and to the right the tips of the willow branches dipped in the water, were carried on and suddenly released, jerking back only to be carried on all over again. Behind him, up above where the bank got steep, there was a tangle of blackberry, the long runners reaching out into space, and almost overhanging the place where he was lying.

When mother asked him how he was feeling now, he always said he wasn't feeling any better. It was just as well to be on the safe side. That new doctor had said try getting some sun on his body, and feed him up, and let him take it easy for at least six months. And in all other ways just leave him alone. So as long as he wasn't feeling any better they couldn't do anything.

A grin came on his face and he said, Poor mother. But as usual he hadn't intended to say anything out loud, even though there was nobody to hear.

Nobody would get down through the blackberries, and he reckoned he'd hear anybody coming along the bank, underneath the willows, long before they could get close to him. Across on the opposite bank there wasn't any house in sight, and he reckoned there wasn't much chance of anybody seeing him from over there.

The sun was getting too hot and he sat up, brushing off grass and twigs from his back before he got on his feet. All down the front he was a good shade of sunbrown, and he knew from standing and twisting round to see in his bedroom mirror that he was a rather darker colour all down the back. He did arms upward stretch, knees bend, hips firm, counting one two, one two. He bent over, slapping his thighs, making his muscles taut and then relaxing them again.

At the winter show Auntie Clara had taken him into a sideshow to see the tattooed woman. She had on a skirt that had slits in it, and she put her big fat legs out the slits to show people the pictures. Then she turned round, and you could see all the pictures on her back because there was hardly any dress there to cover them. She said she would make a good wife for some gentleman to have, because when he couldn't sleep at night he could sit up and look at the pictures. But Auntie Clara said it was disgusting and wouldn't look. And when she said any gentleman who liked could rub her back, just to prove the pictures wouldn't rub off, Auntie Clara pulled him out of the tent by the hand. But he looked round and saw a man lick his finger before he tried to rub off one of the pictures.

Poor Auntie Clara, he said.

He marched this way and that, raising his knees up high and counting left right, left right. Then he went in a circle, faster and faster, until he was running.

One Saturday afternoon when he was very very young, father had taken him to see a lady who was to go up in a balloon. There was a fire going in the middle of a paddock, and the balloon was jigging about in the air up above the fire. And all round the fire men were pulling on the ends of ropes that were fastened on to the balloon. And they were pulling as hard as they could, and shouting and saying they couldn't hold on much longer. And everybody was saying where was the lady, and was she going to turn up too late, when a Ford car came along the road with the driver sounding the horn. And the lady, all dressed in tights like men in the circus, and wearing a hat with an ostrich feather in it, got out at the gate into the paddock and came running across to where the balloon was. And the men pulling on the ropes pulled harder and shouted, but just as the lady nearly got there they couldn't hold on any longer and had to let go, and the balloon jumped away up into the air. And the lady pushed her hat on to the back of her head, so that the big feather hung down over her shoulder, and she put one foot forward and put her hands on her hips, and shouted out swear words at the men. And father pulled him away by the hand, and they started to go home, and father said the lady was a fraud.

Poor father, he said.

After all, he mightn't have been looking, he said.

And he stopped running, dropping on his knees at the edge of the bank, breathing hard, and looking in the water. Down at the bottom some little freshwater crayfish were crawling over the sand. Two of the bigger ones were trying to circle each other, holding their claws raised up in front of them.

That was the best holiday he had ever had in his life. The whole family went in the train and he sat next to an old lady who was talking to a man sitting next to her. I only went to the races once in my life, the old lady said, and I won ten pounds. All my friends said, go home now, your purse is full. But I wouldn't go, no, I stayed, and I lost all my money, and the rain came on and spoilt my beautiful ostrich feather. And when they got to the station they had to go to the farm in a buggy. And Arnold made a bow and some arrows, and they went and shot at fantails down the gully. And Mr Jones gave him a ride on a horse bareback, his arms were very brown and hairy, and he wore stiff boots that had silver nails driven into the soles. And in the creek they saw the crayfish and Mr Jones said he called them crawlers, but the Maoris called them koura. And father took them all for a row up the creek in the punt, but he went under the branch of a tree and mother sat in the water.

Poor mother, he said.

But if father wasn't looking, why did I think he was? he said.

I don't know, he said.

And he sat on the bank and let his legs hang in the water, rippling the surface and making it impossible to see the crayfish. And when the water was still again they had gone.

He slid down until his feet touched the bottom, and first he waded out, then he swam in a circle back to the bank again. And then, hanging on to the grass on the bank, he thrashed the water with his feet.

He got out and stood on the edge of the bank, wiping the water off himself with the palms of his hands. He stood in the sun, turning back and front until he was dry.

I don't know a thing, he said.

He went over to his clothes for his handkerchief, and getting it out of his pocket he got out as well the letter from Marge to read all over again. Her lawyer uncle would give him a job in his office, she said, and he'd like him to start after the Easter holidays.

ALLEN CURNOW

Landfall in Unknown Seas

*(The 300th Anniversary of the Discovery of New Zealand
by Abel Tasman, December 13th, 1642)*

I

Simply by sailing in a new direction
You could enlarge the world.
                                                You picked your captain,
Keen on discoveries, tough enough to make them,
Whatever vessels could be spared from other
More urgent service for a year's adventure;
Took stock of the more probable conjectures
About the Unknown to be traversed, all
Guesses at golden coasts and tales of monsters
To be digested into plain instructions.
For likely and unlikely situations.

All this resolved and done, you launched the whole
On a fine morning, the best time of year,
Skies widening and the oceanic furies
Subdued by summer illumination; time
To go and to be gazed at going
On a fine morning, in the Name of God
Into the nameless waters of the world.

O you had estimated all the chances
Of business in those waters, the world's waters
Yet unexploited.
                                But more than the sea-empire's
Cannon, the dogs of bronze and iron barking
From Timor to the Straits, backed up by the challenge.
Between you and the South an older enmity
Lodged in the searching mind, that would not tolerate
So huge a hegemony of ignorance.

There, where your Indies had already sprinkled
Their tribes like ocean rains, you aimed your voyage;
Like them invoked your God, gave seas to history
And islands to new hazardous tomorrows.

II

Suddenly exhilaration
Went off like a gun, and the whole
Horizon, the long chase done,
Hove to. There was the seascape
Crammed with coast, surprising
As new lands will, the sailor
Moving on the face of the waters,
Watching the earth take shape
Round the unearthly summits, brighter
Than its emerging colour.

Yet this, no far fool's errand,
Was less than the heart desired,
In its old Indian dream
The glittering gulfs ascending
Past palaces and mountains
Making one architecture.
Here the uplifted structure,
Peak and pillar of cloud –
O splendour of desolation – reared
Tall from the pit of the swell,
With a shadow, a finger of wind, forbade
Hopes of a lucky landing.

Always to islanders danger
Is what comes over the sea;
Over the yellow sands and the clear
Shallows, the dull filament
Flickers, the blood of strangers:
Death discovered the Sailor
O in a flash, in a flat calm,
A clash of boats in the bay

And the day marred with murder.
The dead required no further
Warning to keep their distance;
The rest, noting the failure,
Pushed on with a reconnaissance
To the north; and sailed away.

III

Well, home is the Sailor, and that is a chapter
In a schoolbook, a relevant yesterday
We thought we knew all about, being much apter
    To profit, sure of our ground,
No murderers mooring in our Golden Bay.

But now there are no more islands to be found
And the eye scans risky horizons of its own
In unsettled weather, and murmurs of the drowned
    Haunt their familiar beaches –
Who navigates us towards what unknown

But not improbable provinces? Who reaches
A future down for us from the high shelf
Of spiritual daring? Not those speeches
    Pinning on the Past like a decoration
For merit that congratulates itself.

O not the self-important celebration
Or most painstaking history, can release
The current of a discoverer's elation
    And silence the voices saying,
'Here is the world's end where wonders cease.'

Only by a more faithful memory, laying
On him the half-light of a diffident glory,
The Sailor lives, and stands beside us paying
    Out into our time's wave
The stain of blood that writes an island story.

ANNA KAVAN
The Red Dogs

Exactly a year ago today the first red dogs made their appearance in this country. How short people's memories are! A year doesn't seem long to remember such a momentous happening: yet no one so much as acknowledges the anniversary. Of course I don't suppose everyone has really forgotten the significance of the date; most likely they've decided to keep it quiet. And that sort of supineness makes one inclined to despair. What a rare thing human integrity is – how few and far between are the individuals who possess it! Humans on the whole aren't much more stable than weathercocks, changing with every fresh wind.

If one recalls the passionate outcry that went up when the presence of the red dogs in our homeland was confirmed for the first time, it seems incredible that the violent storm could have subsided in twelve brief months into mute acquiescence. To begin with, twelve years would not have been deemed long enough to bring about such a volte-face. This time last year, I doubt whether a soul could have been found who wouldn't have felt outraged by the idea of relaxing before the last red dog was hunted out of existence. To hint that so-and-so tolerated the invaders would have been construed then as a mortal affront. Yet here are the protagonists of last year's burning protest tamely resigning themselves to the visitation, out of prudent respect for their material welfare. At this rate it won't be long before the coming of the red dogs will be not merely accepted but positively acclaimed – we may well be celebrating the anniversary next year, instead of keeping it dark!

Should the human race ever achieve sanity, how future generations will puzzle over the fluctuations symptomatic of our sick, crazy epoch! What a legacy of confusion we are handing down to any rational being who later on tries to discover a coherent design in the scrawled pages of our aberrant conduct!

'But how is it possible,' one imagines such a researcher crying out in despair, 'for a fundamental mass change in public opinion to take place so inexplicably, so unobtrusively, and in such a short space of time? First there's intense resistance to the red dogs, linked with horror, disgust; then an abrupt silence, full-stop to the struggle; and immediately afterwards comes assent, with approbation upon its heels, and the once-execrated state of affairs stands magically established, as if a conjuring trick had been performed – consolidated, as though by the backing of centuries of tradition.'

Well, I can't supply any learned theories as to how or why these things happened. I don't propose to criticize or to attempt an analysis of matters I don't properly comprehend. All I can do with my observer's training is to note down some of my own impressions, quite simply and briefly, as I've been accustomed to do in keeping the records, and as I'm doing now. Perhaps an inquiring mind, unshaped as yet, may be stimulated by curiosity to read what I've written. I like to think so, at any rate. It pleases me to think that a descendant of mine (living in those better days we're always told lie just round the corner), will be helped by my notes to understand the chaotic maze through which his ancestors had to grope, and to judge us more leniently in consequence.

How shall I begin my observations on the red dogs, after this preamble? It's hard to know where to start for, strangely enough, I can't recollect exactly how or when I first got to hear that there were any such creatures. Others have told me that they too feel a similar vagueness about the preliminary stages of the invasion. Knowledge of the red dogs seemed to steal into our minds in the same stealthy way that the beasts themselves penetrated and possessed the territories of the globe.

When I think of the beginning I think of voices. There was a day I woke to an atmosphere of whispering – that's one point which I do recall. Not that it happened abruptly like that, as I've written it. The whispers must have been there, growing louder and stronger for a long while before they forced themselves on my notice; and long afterwards they continued to grow without arousing any special reaction.

Long before their actual coming – for well over a year, I should say – rumours about the red dogs filled the air: rumours which spread mysteriously from one country to another; jumped from island to island; ran from village to town. Why we weren't warned – why we didn't pay more attention – these are the sort of questions I cannot answer. The whispers seemed innocuous at first. We, in our distant province, are outside the general current of gossip that's going about, and rumours coming to us from far off never seem very real. We listen to the tall stories that strangers tell us; we marvel; and then forget them. Such travellers' tales as eventually reach our shores make scarcely more impression than spray from the waves which have been thundering there since time began.

The rumours, then, in the first place, not only seemed unconvincing, but trivial too. To me, there was something downright silly about them.

I'm as fond of animals as anyone else, and of dogs in particular; but my interest doesn't extend to listening to gossip about some new foreign breed. Haven't we got enough queer-looking dogs in the world already? Breeders are for ever experimenting with the poor brutes, trying to produce some monstrosity with a sky-blue tail, or with feathers instead of hair.

That's how unimportant the whispers seemed to begin with: believe me or not, they seemed as foolish as that. The one peculiarity of the rumour – or, I ought to say, the thing which struck me as odd – was its persistence. Again and again it seemed to be fading out; for weeks on end there was silence, as if it had died a natural death in the usual way. Then, just as the whole rigmarole was almost forgotten, sure as fate it would turn up again somewhere, in a slightly different form.

The animal concerned wasn't always a dog, though it generally did belong to the canine breed. Sometimes the story centred around a wolf, or a jackal, or a coyote. The creature was described in many extravagant ways, rumour-mongers supplying the details to suit themselves or their hearers. But a rather surprising consistency was preserved on two points: the beast was always a queer colour, and it was always ferocious.

My own opinion (when it became impossible to ignore the tale any longer) was an epidemic must have broken out among the dog population; perhaps an especially virulent form of distemper, which turned its victims into those moody killers we hear of from time to time. This, by the way, was later adopted as the official theory; compulsory inoculation of all dogs being enforced – with the net result that a lot of money went into the pockets of the chemists who made the serum, and of the vets whose job it was to give the injections. But the step wasn't taken till it was too late to do any good; even supposing that immunization could ever have been in the least effective.

Anyone looking back from a distance, surely must be staggered by the procrastination and lack of initiative the authorities here displayed. They had ample notice of danger; plenty of time to discover an antidote to the plague by which less isolated places were surprised and poisoned before realizing the deadly nature of the infection that threatened them. We were forewarned; why were we not forearmed? Were our officials blind, negligent, incapable, misinformed? Or were they corrupt, and guilty of a positive breach of trust?

But I have no right to set myself up in judgement, nor do I wish to do so. Standing too near the event, perspective becomes falsified, and much information still remains inaccessible. Only the future can give an impartial verdict, when all the facts have been made fully known. Who am I to blame others for being slow in the uptake when I, with my special qualifications, took so long to see what was coming? One has to be extra sensitive for my type of work – to turn oneself into a negative for recording impressions – so that I'm generally one of the first to feel whatever is in the air. Yet I was as dense as everyone else where the red dogs are concerned.

Thinking things over, I've come to the conclusion that we must have been subjected to a distorting alien influence at that time. It was as if we were all slightly light-headed; as if, with each breath, we drew into ourselves some sort of gas which interfered with our perceptions and caused us to act in an abnormal way. Not only human beings behaved strangely; corresponding irregularities appeared throughout the natural kingdom; animals, clouds, even roads and stones, deviating erratically from their habitual forms. I originally used the word 'influence' to express the idea that we were affected by some unknown cosmic force completely outside our sphere of control. But after all, what's more likely than that man himself, in his reckless experiments with the universe, may have accidentally loosed the principle of disorder? It certainly looks as if an anarchic tendency, no matter what its source may have been, was working towards a general disorganization: disturbing the unity which gave shapes their meaning, so that warped patterns ceased to adhere to their centres, and fell apart. Such widespread derangement can't occur without reason. Just as a certain morbid state has to exist before the proliferation of body cells forms a cancer, so a disruptive impulse must have been present in nature, stimulating the growth of those freaks and deformities of which the red dogs are the extreme example.

I happened to be at work on meteorological records when whispered news of the creatures was coming through. The weather turned as crazy as everything else at that time, and I couldn't have helped observing its vagaries, even if it hadn't been a part of my job to do so. Our climate is never exactly genial; winters are apt to be hard and long, and warm spells shorter than they are sweet. A late spring astonishes nobody here, although we shiver and grumble. But last year's spring never arrived at all.

Stark trees, looking as if they'd forgotten how to put forth a leaf, still lined the bus route by which I travelled to my work when midsummer was in sight. The bus ran through the suburbs for a part of the trip, and one of my outstanding recollections is the pleasant shock of seeing some lilacs in a sheltered suburban garden at last beginning to flower. When I looked out for the blossom next day it had gone. Naturally, I guessed the flower-sprays had been cut for a decoration: not for some seconds did I identify the sad shrubs, already moribund and shrouded in limp drooping leaves, plumed by a weird soot-black inflorescence which the frost had charred as effectively as a bomb.

On the whole, it was a relief when this bogus summer gave place to a month better suited (by association, at least) to the prevailing atmospheric conditions. The red dog rumour in all its infinite variety was now in full swing. Yet I remember a queer liveliness in the air as autumn came on: a feeling I can only compare with the undertone of excitement in a school near the end of term. People hung up their heavy coats – they'd never dared to discard them since the previous winter – in more prominent places – I was about to write 'in the place of honour'. The gesture was defiant, as if they were betting against the weather; and the weather forthwith accepted the challenge, determined to prove how wrong anyone was who thought its repertoire of tricks was exhausted.

At the time when days shorten and leaves are supposed to fall, the sun began to shine with unseemly ardour. The overcoat-owners smiled, telling each other that the heat was a flash in the pan which couldn't possibly last. But day followed day without any sign of change; temperatures became stabilized at a high level; the unnatural heatwave went on.

Once they'd got over their first surprise, most people, characteristically thoughtless, took the unseasonable sunshine for granted. In a better-late-than-never spirit they banished their heavy clothes and switched to a summer programme. Everyone with any spare time dashed for the open air. Overnight we became a town of sun-worshippers. Every garden and park was crammed from an early hour with crowds who seemed to have nothing to do but loaf and chatter and stare at the passers-by.

When I'd begun to suspect we were moving towards a disaster, I used almost to envy the idlers I saw on my way to work, sunning themselves any- and everywhere; in churchyards, on the roofs and the steps of buildings, wherever they could find a scrap of room to sit down. There they lounged, in unconventional attire, girls wearing next to nothing, even minor officials stripped to their shirtsleeves, oblivious of all but the immediate present. Eye-shades and dark glasses can only have symbolized holiday time to those who sported them. I don't know how many wearers realized that their dazzled eyes were caused by the low winter arcs the sun was describing; at any rate, they all appeared totally unconcerned.

There were days when I could have found it in my heart to emulate those irresponsible holiday-makers; when I'd have gladly exchanged my duties and preoccupations for the carefree outlook enabling them to behave as if nothing in the whole world mattered more than their gossip.

Important their gossip may have been with a vengeance, in the sense that rumour couldn't have found a better nursery in which to breed. And who knows that the aura of collective credulity, rising from the town as mists smoke up from the marshes, may not in an obscure way have helped to prepare the ground from which the red dogs themselves were soon to emerge? I refer, of course, to the psychological, not to the concrete, ground: but the dual application of the word is significant. Does that sound superstitious? At the risk of being thought something worse, I must ask anyone who has the patience to read these pages to set down the word 'dog' in mirror-writing, and then to remember how those whom the gods wish to destroy are proverbially first driven mad. The gods by whom we were maddened were, so to speak, in reverse; but they no less competently achieved our downfall. As I've said, we were already well on the road to disintegration; and the untimely heat of the sun streaming down day after day was exactly what was required to complete our ruin. Unfortunately for us, early pathological signs were limited to the restless excitement I've called liveliness. Had the course of our deterioration been more spectacular, we might have been moved to take prophylactic measures. But I must try to keep to the point and describe things in some kind of order.

Throughout the heatwave, the morning sky dawned quite clear: but tall upright clouds, of a type never seen before in our latitudes, used to collect about noon, stationing themselves in the zenith well above the sun's orbit, where they remained, motionless, erect and portentous, till darkness hid them from sight.

It was gratifying, of course, that the task of observing this important celestial phenomenon had been given to me. But perhaps I appreciated the appointment less than I should have done, because the extraordinary interest I felt in the clouds seemed almost to entitle me to it. It was really something much stronger than interest that I felt in them from the first; fascination would be a more appropriate word. Long before midday I used to find myself glancing up at the sky to see if they'd begun to materialize – though, as a matter of fact, they always seemed to mould themselves instantaneously out of the empty air, so that I was never able to watch the process of their formation. My feeling bordered upon the obsessional, I suppose: but I didn't realize it as being noticed by other people till a certain day when I was a little late in starting for work, and the bus ride to the observatory seemed unusually long.

I distinctly recall the impatience I felt on the journey, how I couldn't sit still, but kept twisting and turning to look out of the windows, eventually leaving my seat to stand on the platform outside where there was a wider range of vision. The clouds had not appeared. But all at once I became aware of the conductress staring at me with such fixed intentness that I felt obliged to explain what I was looking for, as she evidently expected me to say something. All she did was to order me off the platform. (I'd forgotten the by-law forbidding people to stand there.) But the queer phrases she used impressed themselves on my mind. Was it solicitude or disapproval which made her expression so oddly set and her voice so earnest, as she motioned me back to my seat, at the same time urging me to take care? 'You can't be too careful with clouds,' was the way she put it. 'You never know where you are with clouds. They sometimes lead people on.'

Certainly I'd always found these particular clouds somewhat eerie. It was disquieting to observe their serene majestic aloofness, as they looked down on the sun, which, being tied to its lowly course, could neither approach them nor dissipate them with its beams. On this special day I noticed as soon as I entered the glass observation room that the cloud shapes had something unusually awe-inspiring about them; a solemn symbolic quality I can express no better than I can describe the feelings which they aroused. Apart from vague general terms like metaphysical, super-normal and so on, there don't seem to be any words for the sensation by which I was wholly possessed as I gazed up through the dome. When I try to find a comparison, I recall automatically the look of dread I once saw on the face of a man struck down by a heart attack in my presence. When he had recovered the sufferer told me that, far worse than the pain of the seizure, was the sense of imminent dissolution accompanying it. I believe there was a similar element in what I experienced that afternoon; though mine was not so much the fear of death (which is normal, insofar as nature has implanted it in each one of us), as terror inspired by an extra-normal concept of being changed into a different life form. Try to imagine how much more ghastly than loss of life in the accepted sense would be transmutation to a type of existence absolutely unknown. Such a change is almost too appalling to con-template, involving the loss of contact, communication, memory, hope, trust, dreams; everything, in fact, which supports the individual in the enormous void – all that mitigates the frightful solitude which is being.

Suddenly this unthinkable loss became possible; and no sooner possible than unavoidable – save by an alternative hardly to be preferred. It was as if the universe itself had suddenly lost its reason. As if the glass dome overhead opened on boundless nothing, where dead stones without end hurtled and howled in ceaseless, senseless flight. Of this idiot nothingness, divorced from my known self, I must become a part; or else set out, isolated and lost, upon a search of which I could not see the end.

This was the choice presented to me by the revelation I saw in the clouds: though, indeed, the question of choice never really arose, so clear was the issue from the beginning. Even at the original moment of shock, I knew that I was conclusively implicated, dedicated once and for all to the tremendous task, as if King's Messengers had arrived with orders addressed to me personally. But these cloud envoys were kings in their own right.

I've gone into all this in some detail, hoping to make myself understood; without, I'm afraid, being very successful. How is one to convey an impression of something which can't be objectified satisfactorily, and is hardly comprehensible to the subject? I'd better pass on, just saying that all sense of time and reality disappeared while I was in the observatory that afternoon. It always got very hot in there with the sun beating down on the glass, and possibly I was partly dazed for a while.

Anyhow, there's a blank; and the next thing I remember is feeling the sweat turn cold on my flesh as I stepped into the open air.

For a moment I couldn't think which door I had just closed behind me, or where I was. Everything looked unfamiliar until I realized it was only dusk making the grass slope outside the observatory seem strangely large, and brightening the white stones at the edge as with phosphorescence.

There was hardly enough light left to see my watch; but I managed to make out that I'd still be able to catch the last bus with a few minutes to spare. The observatory, I must explain, is in the hills at the back of the town where the air is supposed to be clearer. It isn't very far out; but the road is rough and steep, and I didn't feel like walking so late in the evening. However, I decided to start off and let the bus overtake me. It was chilly standing about, for autumn asserted its rights these days by producing a rapid fall in the temperature as soon as the sun went down.

Fifty yards or so from the gates, the road made a hairpin bend and then dropped sharply, so that the observatory was soon out of sight. I might have been miles from anywhere then. It was hard to believe that suburban streets began just over the hill; they were hidden from where I was so completely that not a solitary light appeared anywhere as dusk deepened to darkness.

When I got to the foot of the hill I stopped, wondering why the bus hadn't caught up with me. During the last few minutes I'd been listening half-consciously for the engine. But the sound of my footsteps died away into unbroken silence, the stillness they had disturbed settled down again with the finality of a last curtain. Now it was much too dark for me to see the time: but I had the idea I'd been on the move considerably longer than I should have been if the bus had kept to its schedule. Why was it running late? The last bus on this route – mainly used by workers from the observatory and the inhabitants of the hilltop village beyond – is invariably punctual. The bad road makes the journey unpopular after dark, and drivers are always in a great hurry to get back to the town. Could there have been a breakdown this evening? Was my watch slow? Or did I mistake the position of the hands when I looked at it? I told myself there was no sense in worrying: either the bus would come (and there'd be nothing to worry about), or it wouldn't – in which case I'd have to make the best of a bad job and walk all the way home. But somehow I couldn't get rid of a vague anxiety as I walked on up the next slope.

The night seemed exceptionally dark: but it wouldn't have been a pleasant walk even by day. The road was a mass of potholes and loose stones, into and over which I was bound to trip: and though I began by thinking it was lucky there were no roadside ditches which might have caused a bad fall, the lack of them made it hard to tell the road from the open country. Soon I wished there was some sort of boundary in spite of the risk of falling; I was afraid of wandering onto the hillside and getting completely lost. The road surface must have been rough indeed: for I didn't realize I had actually gone astray until I found myself blundering among boulders and briars and rank weeds.

Finding I really and truly had lost my way on the hills gave me a nasty jar; it made me realize too how easily one might lose one's head in a predicament of this kind. All sorts of forgotten tales recurred to me from the past, about travellers roaming in circles for days on end, and lost children starving to death in the woods. I had to remind myself, as I groped and stumbled about, that I was between the town and the observatory and no great distance from either. But even so there was a point where I felt as utterly, hopelessly, lost as I could have done in the remotest desert – when I almost despaired of emerging from the sightless nightmare of rocks which bruised me and barked my shins, and brambles which tugged painfully at my hair and did their utmost to scratch my eyes out.

When the feeling of more level ground told me that I'd at last got my feet on the beaten track, I was so exhausted and shaky that the first thing I did was to sit down on a tree stump with which I'd collided the previous instant. I was too tired even to think; but as soon as I'd got my breath and recovered a little, I began wondering how much time I'd wasted in my wanderings, and what my chances were of getting home before dawn. Dreamlike adventures, as I knew very well, often seemed deceptively long: and though I felt that the night had already lasted an age, I was quite prepared to believe it might still be early.

Now, when I started off again, I hardly dared put one foot in front of the other for fear of getting lost for a second time. I was wishing the night were warmer – thinking it would be better to sleep under a bush than to keep on at this snail's pace – when I noticed the sky getting brighter, and realized that the moon must have risen behind the clouds. There was not enough light to illuminate things distinctly or in any detail. Only the black hills showed their outline, with blacker shadows of rocks and bushes upon them like crouching forms.

Anyone with any imagination who has walked alone, at night, on a lonely road, must be acquainted with the chill I felt then, touching my skin like a snake. Every child, every dreamer, has known at some time that cold breath which comes quite suddenly out of nowhere – blown back from ancient chaos perhaps; the wind of the unmade worlds. Whatever nameless prototype of alarm haunts the edges of consciousness came very close to me there on the hills while the moon was climbing into the covered sky. Gradually the diffused light was becoming stronger; but instead of clarifying my situation its effect was just the reverse. Much more than the contour of the land was visible now – I could actually see where I was walking. But never in my whole life have I felt more confused, more astounded, than I did then as I stopped dead and stood staring round – I daresay rather wildly.

Was I really asleep and dreaming the scene before me? I shut my eyes hard and waited: but when I looked again it was still at the same strange landscape. Instead of the easy rolling hills which form the town's background, I now saw a vast chaotic mountainous vista, tumbling away to infinity like a turbulent sea. It was as if in a fit of maniac excitement the land had turned spendthrift, madly piling range upon range: while by the same token the road had become parsimonious, shrinking itself to the insignificance of a mule track. Not so much as one familiar rock appeared anywhere in the unruly perspective of crags and gorges, which my eyes went on searching of their own accord for some recognizable landmark.

The measured increasing of light quickened; and I saw that I wasn't far from a towering crest above which the moon at this moment moved ahead of the clouds, standing in front of the wedge-shaped cloud trail in the attitude of a figurehead or a leader, precise and hard. And suddenly there was a woman running along the hilltop; I saw her loose hair wild as cloud and as long as a river, streaming back in the clouds over the hill; so that she became the small chiselled shape shearing the wind, and all the wake of cloud streamed back from her as she ran.

She seemed to be calling out; or perhaps just screaming, for I failed to catch any articulate words. I shouted in what was intended for reassurance, leaving the loops of the graded path, as I started clambering up directly to where she was. For a second I saw her poised there above, on the verge of stillness, balanced with bent head, looking down for me: and the word 'dogs' was in the sharp rain of sound that came cascading about my ears like a shower of stones. Then she raised her head, and ran on, and vanished behind the great standing stones of the tor.

I went on climbing the rocky bluff, with the general idea that I might be able to help, but with no notion what form of help was likely to be required. I hadn't much time to consider the question either; for, even with the moon lighting up pitfalls and obstacles, the ascent was a stiff one, and I knew that I had little chance of catching up with the woman unless she stopped running. She'd probably be out of sight by the time I got to the summit: and supposing I could still see her, how was I going to overtake her in this wild, rough country where I was completely astray? It suddenly occurred to me that to slip among these rocks and ravines would be the easiest thing in the world; to continue the chase was simply asking for a broken arm, leg or ankle: and yet I never thought of giving it up.

I just kept blindly on, trying not to reflect on the serious consequences which might result from an accident in such a lonely region. I had to concentrate on each step, I hardly so much as looked where I was going, and it took me quite by surprise to find that I'd reached the grouped rocks which had suggested a primitive monolith from below, but which seemed at close quarters a great deal more impressive and regal than any symbol constructed by human hands that I'd ever seen. It was impossible not to feel awed by these mighty columns which the Creator himself might well have set in place to uphold the sky. I almost forgot, as I looked at them, what had brought me to the spot: and when I did turn to the vista beyond, no long-haired wraith was in flight there. Far more disconcerting than anything I expected to see in that abominable wasteland, was what I took to be the apparition of a lighted vessel, frozen among cataleptic breakers of stone. I stared at it dumbfounded; not recognizing – till the moon struck a glacial sparkle from its superstructure – the very dome beneath which I'd recently been at work.

No wonder I thought for a second that I was suffering from an optical delusion of some sort! No wonder I felt confused! How could I be looking *down* on the observatory, I asked myself, when I'd left the place behind long ago, far above me? I was too tired and preoccupied to grasp for a moment that I'd been walking away from my destination instead of towards it, ever since losing my way out on the hillside.

From the height where I stood now, I should have been able to see the lighted streets of the town, though I don't recall actually doing so. My eyes had first been attracted and held by the lights in the middle distance; and from there they naturally followed the road that wound its patient, thread-like way through the wilderness, to be hidden at length by an escarpment which dropped almost vertical, a stone's throw from my feet.

Nothing stronger than the normal impulse one has to look over the edge of a cliff made me go to the edge of this precipice and look down. I had no premonition of any kind; no warning instinct whatever. Perhaps because I was so totally unprepared, the significance of what I saw didn't strike me at once. The huge disorder of the whole landscape in itself suggested that some cataclysmic convulsion had taken place. And in this setting, neither the bus, lying on its side like a matchbox splintered and broken open, nor the scattered smudge shapes surrounding it, seemed anything but appropriate.

The scene of the smash – a curve which the driver must have tried to take far too sharply – lay some distance below, just at the foot of the cliff over which I was peering. I remember wondering in a futile way how the woman I'd seen had managed to climb that nearly perpendicular slope, and why she hadn't kept to the road where one would think she'd have had better chances of finding assistance. Was she the sole survivor? If there were others, they must have got away; for no one seemed to be moving down there as I began (not very enthusiastically, I admit) to make the awkward descent.

The difficult scramble was all I could manage, tired out as I was, and I suppose I was halfway down before I looked again. The nearer I got to the wreckage, the more the distortion due to the queer crosshatching of black and moonlight seemed to increase, so that I wasn't sure now if I saw movements or imagined them. But the possibility that injured people might, after all, be lying there needing my aid made me hurry, I didn't waste time on another look until I'd finished the climb.

This time there was no doubt that movements in and around the debris were going on – no doubt at all. And I was too near to put them down to those tricks of light and shadow I spoke of. The idea flashed through my mind that several children had been involved in the accident, buried by some freak of impact in earth and stones, and that it was their limbs I saw fitfully stirring. But this I can't have believed for more than a split second, because I neither moved nor called out, as I certainly would have done if I'd thought I was looking at anything human.

There was really something essentially non-human about the movements, as I recall them. At the first glance they gave an impression of feebleness; of weak, blind persistence, like stirrings within a chrysalis or an egg. And they somehow revived in my mind a long-buried association, concerning (of all absurdities!) the ratcatcher of bygone days. As a child, I'd been shown pictures of this official, who used to go round the town, collecting live rats from the traps and drowning them in the river. How the rats writhed and wriggled and fought and struggled inside the sack on his shoulder, as he humped them along the streets to their doom! Now it was no longer in my imagination, but there under the ground in front of me, that these frantic undulations were taking place.

With the old ratcatcher story at the back of mind, I first thought a horde of monster rodents was being spawned, their wormlike appendages already extruded from the heaving earth. After all, there isn't such an enormous difference – except as regards size – between the rat family and the red dog breed, with their sniffing sharp-pointed muzzles and slender long hairless tails. Anybody unlucky enough to witness the prehensile-looking, tremulous, questing snouts of the red dogs nosing out food, will notice the similarity to the rodent mammals. By day of course, colouring makes the comparison seem less apt; and even now, when I first saw the beasts, and in spite of the bleaching moon and the queer cross-shadows, their blackness seemed unduly intense. I remembered suddenly that at night red and black look the same: and then it dawned on me that red dogs were coming forth in front of my eyes.

In a profession like mine one learns to take startling sights in one's stride; but I doubt if I'd have been able to face the scene coolly except for my rigid training. It was as if a violent rape had resulted in the forced unnatural labour to which the earth was reluctantly given up. With my own eyes I was seeing the apotheosis of that force of disintegration I mentioned. It was that same force which within myself had produced the sense of everything being changed. And what a hideous change deprived our mother earth of her true self and integrity, compelling her to give birth to this monstrously foreign brood. What a perverse alchemy caused the components of the soil thus to extend their scope. For I soon observed that the red dogs were not only coming out of the ground but were actually composed of it; at first fused with the dust and at one with stones, gradually scaling themselves off like the scabby crusts of a hateful murrain on the flesh of our land.

Doubtless the proximity of the accident explained their prolific and rapid growth; but I knew nothing then of the sensitizing device by which the red dogs develop and attain independent life at high speed whenever environmental factors are specially favourable.

As I haven't judged others, I hope those who come after me won't judge me too harshly because I didn't try to strangle one or two of the beasts with my bare hands, or kick and stamp them to death, before my own blood, tissue and bone gave nourishment to more of their tribe. Such an act could have had no practical value. Long before I reached the scene of the crash the bus passengers were beyond human aid. What could I or any other weak creature have hoped to achieve, when the frenzied throes in which earth herself repudiated the monstrosities bred from her substance, failed to consume them or to throw them off?

But I won't excuse myself. Let other people decide whether I am more or less to blame than those contemporaries of mine who made their peace with the invaders at the price of our liberty. The truth is, we are a slave race now, no matter how we try to ignore the fact by our silence, or to disguise it behind a mask of free will. A traveller returning from abroad might not perhaps become immediately aware of the extent of our sub-jection. Convenient compromises have been arranged. We have found ingenious ways of living side by side with our masters. Everything is managed discreetly, and as unobtrusively as may be. Vacant lots, disused markets, and obscure dead ends, have been chosen, where the minimum of notice is drawn to the truckloads of carcases upon which the red dogs heap themselves as high as the rooftops. No one is obliged to frequent these places, except the specially picked gangs whose powerful hoses sluice them down after nightfall. By methods like these we have so far contrived to maintain the pretence that life continues as usual. But such a semblance of normality, based upon falsehood, is neither durable nor convincing. Even today it starts to show symptoms of breaking down.

One keeps asking oneself how and when the situation will end. Have the red dogs come to stay? Or will they eventually disappear from our planet, as inexplicably as they came? If they are to remain, it's clear that nothing which by the old standards makes life worth living is going to survive. In that case, human life, as we understand it, is doomed. If our kind does persist at all, it can only be in some form which doesn't bear thinking about – degenerate and diseased – debased to the service of carrion-feeders. But I can't afford to let myself dream for an instant that this is intended. Would the clouds have signalled me to begin my search if we were no more than an unsuccessful experiment to be swept aside?

How could I go on searching if I believed that our way of life was to give way ultimately to the savagery of the red dogs? How could I go on living if I lost faith in my goal? Even if the mass of humanity falls so low as to become identified with the red dog regime, some individuals there must be somewhere who look upon such a fate with as much horror as I do. These are the unknown brothers I have to find. And though I don't know their names or their faces or where they live, I'm confident that we shall meet and recognize one another at the appointed time. One of my secret friends may be close to me as I am writing: at this very moment he may be walking along the street or sheltering in my doorway from a sudden shower. But on the other hand it's just as likely that the people I'm looking for inhabit a distant country, on the underside of the world. One hasn't even the slightest clue. Sometimes, I confess, I feel unequal to the tremendous search I have undertaken: the magnitude of the task seems overwhelming.

Some days I can't help feeling discouraged and lonely. And on those days I have to struggle against the wish that I could hand on my charge to some indefatigable person, more assured than myself. But this doesn't mean I am pessimistic about the outcome. I must not doubt the final success – I do not doubt it. In spite of everything, I'm convinced that a part of the earth still exists, uncontaminated by the red dogs, where I and my brother strangers will find a home. I'm sure that in the end we shall live again, as we once lived, in freedom, in peace, in our own right; without shame or subterfuge or alarm. That is my faith, by which I intend to stand. If a cynical voice were to whisper into my ear the words 'wishful thinking', I should refuse to listen. One must believe in something to keep oneself going.